Everything but the Truth

Everything but the Truth

GILLIAN McALLISTER

PENGUIN BOOKS

PENGUIN BOOKS

UK | USA | Canada | Ireland | Australia
India | New Zealand | South Africa

Penguin Books is part of the Penguin Random House group of companies
whose addresses can be found at global.penguinrandomhouse.com.

First published 2017
002

Text copyright © Gillian McAllister, 2017

The moral right of the author has been asserted

Set in 12.5/14.75 pt Garamond MT Std
Typeset by Jouve (UK), Milton Keynes
Printed in Great Britain by Clays Ltd, Elcograf S.p.A.

A CIP catalogue record for this book is available from the British Library

ISBN: 978–1–405–94031–3

www.greenpenguin.co.uk

MIX
Paper from
responsible sources
FSC® C018179

Penguin Random House is committed to a
sustainable future for our business, our readers
and our planet. This book is made from Forest
Stewardship Council® certified paper.

To Dad.
We said we would never leave each other.
And now our ideas are forever in print together.

Our character is what we do when we think no one is looking.

H. Jackson Brown, Jr

It ended with an accusation I never thought I'd make, thrown across the room at him like a grenade. And after the ending, there was the rest: the door slamming, waking alone with the knowledge of what I'd done, unable to stop replaying the look he gave me.

But it began with love. That part was easy.

I loved the way he was forever appearing in photographs on Facebook, caught self-consciously in the background at parties, like a grumpy meerkat looking towards the camera. I loved his hypochondria. How often he rang the doctor and said, 'It's me,' in his embarrassed, Scottish way.

I loved the person he was trying to be: a tidy, early person who occasionally threw out all of his clothes in the name of minimalism and then had to go and sheepishly buy more socks. I loved, too, the person he tried not to be: the man who was always late, tucking his T-shirt into his jeans as he waited at the train station, trying to flatten his hair that spiked up at the back when he didn't have time to gel it. I loved the things he did without thinking: putting a hand out to stop his younger brother from crossing the road; using the last of the milk for my tea and not his. I loved the way he came home from the gym, intimidated by the 'big men'.

And I loved his body, of course. His small ears. The

1

curved edges of his smile like pencil etchings on his face. How nice his forearms looked in a shirt with the sleeves rolled up.

And the rest. The tiny, insignificant things. That he couldn't whistle.

I loved his politics and his religious views – 'I don't believe in God, but I'm terrified of him' – and the way he couldn't sit still. I loved the way he was the only person still buying Wagon Wheels and I loved the way he dipped them in tea and called it breakfast.

And I loved the way he looked at me. Heavy lidded. A special, dimpled smile. Just for me. I loved that more than anything. That look came before everything.

Before the baby.

And before the lies.

PART I
Who?

I

Present day

We were almost asleep. We were like one being then; our bodies as close as could be. But the flash lit up the room so brightly, grey turning to a blueish white, that I could see it even with my eyes closed.

I sat up, the duvet falling away from my skin and leaving goosebumps in its wake. Jack's house was always so cold. I tried to locate the source of the light. It was coming from the iPad resting on the bedside table.

I don't know why I looked. Perhaps I was actually already asleep, because I was unfurling from the covers, stretching out to pick it up, my naked torso ghoulishly reflected in the large windows, before I even really considered what I was doing.

ITEM 1

From: Charlie Masters
To: Jack Ross
Subject: Fwd: Douglas's Atrocity Rears Its Head Again

Hi, sorry to dredge up your history, but I thought you should see this . . . that you'd want to know.

Charlie Masters. Charlie – I didn't know him. I'd met only Jack's family; not a single one of his friends.

I paused, my finger poised over the email. One swipe and I could see it. I must have waited a second too long, because the iPad dimmed, and I replaced it on the table, the email and my mad moment almost forgotten.

The Newcastle night outside was completely black. I knew the countryside was just beyond it, but I couldn't see it.

'Rachel. What you doing?' Jack yawned. I loved that Scottish *what*; the soft rush of the pronounced 'h'. *Whotyadee'n?* It was so deep, his voice. Strangers commented on it.

He rolled over and switched the lamp on. His dark hair was all over the place, and as he sat upright and revealed his beard, and then his chest hair, I thought he looked a bit like a caveman.

'Something lit up,' I said.

'Probably the cat doing stuff,' he mumbled.

'Maybe. He was in here,' I lied. I looked at the room. He hadn't decorated – not really; not in the way I wanted him to – but there was one thing on the wall. The only thing, against the exposed brickwork and the lack of curtains and lack of *anything*, was a grainy pregnancy scan, curling slightly at the edges.

He saw me looking. 'What's Wally up to?' he said.

We called the baby Wally, because neither of us could see it on the scan. It had stuck.

'Sleeping,' I said with a smile.

I drew the covers self-consciously up to my neck,

imagining the lamplight showing the fat blue veins that had appeared almost overnight on my breasts, running across my skin like plant roots; covering up my pink and wilted nipples.

Jack smiled back at me, then stood up and left the room. I watched his long body retreat down the hallway, his olive-toned skin catching the moonlight that filtered in through his windows. He walked duck-footed, which made my heart sing. My groin churned as his bum flexed, ready again even though we'd had sex just hours previously: the insatiable appetite of new lovers. He returned a few seconds later with a hot-water bottle in one hand and with Howard, his ginger cat, in the other.

He'd started doing that recently. Making hot-water bottles. He'd seen me do it the other week and had wordlessly taken it on as his task. Every night, no matter whether we slept at my place or his, he brought a hot-water bottle up to me, handed it over with a smile.

'Told you he was around,' I said, gesturing to the cat.

Howard turned and looked at me, his head upside down, his eyes surprised.

'He's a pain,' Jack said, as Howard squirmed and jumped on to the bed.

Jack was working temporarily in Newcastle for *City Lights* magazine. He'd moved down from Scotland, for a while. The first time I went to his house, I had asked him why he had bought a cat. 'A man living alone with just a cat for company?' I had teased.

'Every house needs a cat,' he said. 'Every single one. Anyone who disagrees is *wrong*.'

Jack sat down next to Howard now, and looked at me, a half-smile curving his lips.

I wondered when I'd stop feeling giddy when he looked at me like that. I was punch-drunk, could often be found smiling happily, deliriously, at myself in his bathroom mirror while I scrubbed my make-up off with his Nivea soap.

'When will you get curtains?' I said, instead of saying all that; feeling stupid with only my head poking out of the duvet.

Jack considered my request seriously, though he no doubt didn't care about curtains himself. 'When we move. The neighbours have seen it all, anyway,' he said with a raised eyebrow. It was one of our inside jokes, that. How much sex we had. How good at it we were. So good we made a baby. 'What would you like?'

'Nice ones. Thick ones,' I said. 'The light wakes me up.'

'Consider it done.' He pointed behind me. 'Pass me that?'

I blinked, then looked and pretended to notice his iPad for the first time; that I hadn't just been holding it, my finger paused to open his email with a swipe. It felt hot in my hands as I passed it to him. He held it for a few moments, the screen blank.

'Rugby season started Saturday,' he said.

I turned over and lay on my side, propped up on one elbow. Howard settled between my feet, not pleasingly warm and silky, like most cats, but fat and weighty, like a doorstop. 'I've never known a rugby player,' I said with a grin.

'Not at school?'

I gave a derisive snort. 'Seriously?'

'Oh, I forgot you went to school in *the Bronx*,' Jack said with a laugh, his hand disappearing underneath the duvet and resting on my hip. My whole left side immediately stood to attention, prickling; a Catherine wheel of fire spinning in my belly. I tried to concentrate, but it was almost impossible.

'Just Newcastle's finest,' I said. 'Not all of us can go to schools that have their own hymns and live-in staff. Tell me again what you used to have for lunch?'

This was one of our favourite games, and I made Jack tell my friends and family about it all the time. He always managed to come up with another pretentious dish. He hung his head in mock shame. 'Tiger prawns with pak choi?' he said with a meek laugh. It was deep and low; more of an amused exhale. Like music.

He covered his face with his hands. 'For the record, I am sorry.'

'Pak choi,' I said with a hoot of laughter. '*Pak choi.*'

'One simply cannot play lacrosse without being fuelled by a hearty lunch of pak choi,' he said.

'Our teachers had bullet-proof vests,' I said.

'They did *not.*'

'Only for a term, after Jonny Steele brought a rifle in.'

'Wow,' he mouthed. He moved his hand to my thigh, fingers dancing lightly, as if he was playing the piano. His hand felt relaxed against my body, but the expression on his face was troubled, momentarily. 'Anyway, you should come. One Saturday. Not to the match. That's boring. But after. There's drinks.'

9

'Okay,' I said, a fresh zing of happiness working its way up my spine. From our brilliant beginning, spent gazing at each other in cafes, kissing outside restaurants, ignoring waiters because our heads were full of each other, to our shaky period, that shocking afternoon in front of the positive pregnancy test when we both barely knew what to say to each other, and now here we were on the cusp of autumn and I was going to his rugby club, like a proper girlfriend.

'You mean I'll actually be meeting people you know?' I said.

I was teasing, but Jack's hand stopped moving across my skin, and he withdrew it.

'If you want,' he said. He was still looking at me. His eyes were crinkled at the corners.

It had been nearly seven months, and I still hadn't met his friends. I was three months pregnant, and Wally had grown from two cells, to four, to eight, to a tangerine-sized foetus. Now here we finally were. Better late than never.

'There's a clubhouse where everyone drinks, after. It is a bit raucous, though.'

'Too much pak choi?' I said.

Jack laughed softly. 'Mostly just misogyny. Ignore them.'

'Oh good.'

He smiled at me. It was only quick, brief, but genuine. I smiled back and we held each other's gaze for a moment too long.

He looked away first, and I watched the tip of his

index finger blanch white as he pressed the 'home' button on his iPad. Something closed down in his expression. No, not closed down, exactly. Opened, then closed, like somebody intruding on two strangers in a back bedroom at a party, then closing the door again. His stubble-covered cheeks hollowed, then filled, as he swiped across the screen. And then he dismissed the notification. It was gone, deliberately unread, and he was opening his Kindle app and reading Austen again – he only ever seemed to read books by women, a fact which made me love him even more – his skin swarthy and tanned against the white pillows, his expression entirely neutral. I looked at his full, dark red lips for a second before turning over myself.

I stared, eye level with the curtainless window, wondering about the look that had crossed Jack's face. I could still see it in my mind; something came before that forced neutral expression. Didn't it?

'You get an email?' I said. 'I thought it lit up.' I was still facing the window.

'No, no,' Jack said.

And that was what did it, I suppose. That was the moment that everything sprang from.

I said nothing in reply. What could I say? I was mistaken. It was spam. He'd forgotten, already. Or it was a work email. Just work. And he didn't want to discuss work.

'Look at that,' Jack said to me a few seconds later.

I turned back to face him. One of his pectoral muscles was twitching.

'Palpitations,' he said, his eyes sliding left and locking on to mine. His breath smelt of toothpaste and the coffee he'd finished ten minutes before bed. It was his evening routine. Coffee and chocolate, then bed; his way of eking out the last and best part of the night.

'No – muscle fasciculation,' I said sleepily. 'Twitches. Too much caffeine. Or maybe you're run-down.' I laughed gently at this; another of our in-jokes.

He'd been a political correspondent and court reporter, in Scotland, and then branched out into travel writing, which he much preferred. He would admit he could never be run-down. He got up at ten and did things only the self-employed could do in the morning: put washing on, made proper filter coffee, opened post. He finished work at four in the afternoon and watched *Pointless* with tea and biscuits.

Where Ben, my ex-boyfriend and a teacher, would cagily refer to *marking* and *long hours* and *parents' evenings*, Jack embraced his status as a slacker. 'Yeah, I can take Wednesday afternoons off, if I like,' he would say over dinner. 'Best job in the world.'

He wasn't a slacker, though, not really. He'd spend weeks working until midnight, his beard gradually growing longer and longer and his sleep patterns more nocturnal. And then he'd produce a handful of beautiful articles, lovely prose, and revert back to his old routine.

'Take a muscle relaxant, if you like,' I said. 'Buscopan.'

'Will that work?' he asked, sounding delighted.

It was a classic anxious-type response. Textbook. He

wanted a fix, a solution, and some reassurance from a doctor. But he was *my* classic anxious type.

'Well, muscle twitches aren't serious,' I said. 'But yes.'

'I'm not about to shuffle off this mortal coil, then?' he said, an arm snaking its way around my shoulders before lightly ruffling my hair.

'No,' I said. 'You are a massive hypochondriac, though.'

'I know. But it's handy knowing a doc.'

'Hmm,' I said quietly, and he sighed.

We resumed our positions spooning in the bed, Howard settled between us like a small barge. Jack fell asleep immediately, but I didn't; I never do.

It happened again, like it always did, when I eventually slept. I dreamt of the boy in front of me, sitting on the floor, a nasal cannula tracking underneath his nose like a transparent worm. He reached towards me, but I waved my hands through his. He disappeared, as he always did, when I woke.

2

I kept idly thinking about the email. No, not the email. The look. And the lie; that little white lie. The first time I'd caught him lying to me about something, however small.

I was at work, amongst the dusty law books, when I looked it up. I was supposed to be typing attendance notes. Audrey, my closest friend, had helped me to get a job typing for one of the partners at her firm. I hated it, of course, but he was a medical negligence lawyer, and I enjoyed reading the notes, was the only person who could decipher the doctors' handwriting.

I got out an English dictionary and searched for the definition.

ITEM 2

> **atrocity** > *noun* (pl. **atrocities**) an extremely wicked and cruel act, typically one involving physical violence or injury.
> — SYNONYMS: act of barbarity, act of brutality, act of savagery, act of wickedness.

I nodded, then closed the dictionary. It was just out of interest. Curiosity.

3

I awoke to a gentle shaking of my shoulder. It was a Saturday morning, the room a greyish blue. 'Rach, Rach,' Jack was saying.

That deep voice, his hands on my skin, reminded me of the early days. Before the pregnancy. How he called me five minutes after our first date officially ended, said he wanted to cook a meal for me. When was I free? The next day, I replied. We played no games. I went over straight from the office, in my work clothes, my make-up fading; he was cooking chicken fajitas, barefoot in his kitchen. He introduced me to his cat. 'I think you'll get on,' he said. After that, he kissed me, straight away, a full, deep kiss, standing in his hallway. Then he said, 'I want to carry on, but Howard will eat the chicken.'

I opened my eyes in his bedroom. 'What?' I said, the memories of months ago fading.

'We have to go.'

'Where?'

'That breakfast meeting. The interview. With the music guy – about his festival.'

It wasn't Jack's words that forced me to open my eyes, but his tone. It was urgent. Perhaps the most urgent I'd ever heard him. I checked the digital clock, glowing green across the dimly lit room. 'At seven in the morning?'

'His idea . . .' He paused, his gaze still on me. 'I love you,' he said.

He told me often; he wasn't shy about it. It was refreshing, how demonstrative he was.

I sat up against the pillows, conscious of my snarled hair, and looked at him. I was unable to wake up, really, in those early-pregnancy days. Everything was hazy until about noon. I opened my mouth to ask if I could stay, then closed it again. Were we there yet? I didn't know. It wasn't my house. His parents had bought it for him, his temporary Newcastle house. We didn't yet live together. Maybe it was strange to suggest such a thing – lazy and entitled.

Then I shook my head. We were having a baby. We'd live together soon, anyway. We had to be there, whether we liked it or not. 'You go,' I said. 'I'll look after Howard and make you a bacon sandwich.' I smiled up at him.

He paused; he wasn't smiling back. He said nothing.

My eyes gradually adjusted to the dim light, and I saw an unmistakable look of panic cross his features. I could see the whites of his eyes, all around his black irises, like a dog hearing noises at a front door in the middle of the night.

'No, no,' he said. 'You can't do that.'

'It's fine,' I said.

'Please get up,' he said. His tone was bizarre; wheedling, almost.

I frowned at him.

'I need a lift, you see,' he said.

And it was less his words and more his body language that made me swing my legs out of bed: he was standing over me, making hurrying gestures. Huffing. Bouncing slightly on his toes, like somebody very late for something.

'Jack, you need to drive again. You can't pass your test and then not drive – for no reason.' I don't know why I said it. It wasn't the time.

'I know how. But it's been too long since I've done it, I'd need lessons,' he muttered. 'Come on,' he urged.

'Alright.'

'Your stuff,' he said. He was bundling up my clothes, my dirty socks strewn across his floor, stuffing them into my hands. My arms overflowed with them. My bra dropped to the floor and he sighed.

'Just leave them,' I said.

'No.' He found my bag and started cramming it full, taking the clothes back off me. His face was impassive. But his hands were shaking. With panic, it seemed to me.

'What's wrong?' I said, my eyes on those hands.

'I'm just late. I'm always late,' he said.

I backed off, then. It was true.

I got dressed. All the while he stood, waiting, at the door to the bedroom. It was just a rushed Saturday morning, I told myself. 'What's up?' I said to him. 'You're being weird.'

'No, I'm not. I'm just late,' he insisted.

What could I say? Where I might have challenged him, I didn't, because of Wally. To keep the peace, but also because I was responsible, I felt, for that pregnancy. I didn't want to add to the things I'd done to make things hard for us.

17

He put his shoes on and washed his hands in the sink, in that way that he always did. 'They're dirty,' he said to me, with a smile, as he saw me looking. 'Shoes are dirty.'

'I might start doing it myself,' I said.

'It's actually perfectly logical. Try it.'

He stood against the counter, his back to the sink. He beckoned to me, palm up, his index finger slightly extended. I went to him. He was warm and his chest muscles were firm against my fingertips. He hugged me for a moment, burying his head playfully in my neck and breathing me in. I put my shoes on, and he turned the tap on for me.

I didn't even notice I was doing it. I rolled my sleeves to my elbows, squirted the soap on to my hands, and did a full, scrubbing-up wash. Between my fingers. The tops of my hands. My palms. Up my forearms, to my elbows, my hands held up vertically.

'You do it just like in *Grey's Anatomy*,' Jack said.

'Ah,' I said, laughing self-consciously. 'Once you've been taught how to wash your hands, you never go back.' I grabbed a tea towel and dried them, trying to ignore the look Jack was giving me.

And so, less than five minutes after being woken, I was in my cold car, make-up-less and wearing jeans that felt too stiff against my skin for a Saturday morning. They should have been pyjamas. It should have been a sofa, Jack's bed. Not this.

'Where am I going?' I said.

'I'll tell you – keep going on this road,' he said.

I drove for less than half a mile before he asked me

to turn left and pull into a car park. It was a well-known cafe, one we'd considered going to for brunch but had never got around to. We were in the car for three minutes. It was less than a ten-minute walk.

He leant back against the passenger seat, visibly relaxed. 'Sorry,' he said.

'Are you late?'

He smiled quickly at me, as he was getting out. 'Always,' he said.

I looked at the clock. It was quarter past seven.

'Thanks.' He poked his head back through the open window of the car. 'I'll come over later?' he said. He was holding his house key, close to his chest.

'Okay,' I said.

He paused, momentarily, his elbows resting on the window frame. His eyebrows were raised. He was biting his bottom lip. His teeth were white and straight. He looked like he wanted to kiss me, but he was late and it was awkward for him to reach into the car. Instead, he extended his hand towards me, his fingertips just brushing my shoulder.

I watched him go. At the door, he turned to me and blew me a kiss.

I flushed with pleasure, but my mind was spinning as the car idled. There was something strange about his behaviour, I thought, but then dismissed my nosiness. He was probably just late. Scatty.

Jack pushed open the door to the cafe and took a seat on his own. Nobody was waiting for him.

*

He let himself into my flat later that evening. The building was always busy, so he often managed to get in without buzzing me. I didn't mind. I left my front door on the latch for him.

I looked up when he arrived. He didn't seem sheepish, or contrite. His expression was open, his smile wide. He was holding a fruit pie from Waitrose.

'I bring pudding,' he declared triumphantly, balancing it on the palm of his hand like a waiter.

I didn't say anything. I was pulling washing out of the machine but had stopped when he arrived, a wet towel wound around my hand.

He saw my expression and his smile faded.

'Earlier,' I began. The events had steeped all day in my mind and had become a stewed and bitter tea by then. 'You woke me up.' I started ticking the items off on my fingers. 'You made me pack up my clothes. You made me drive you a totally walkable distance.'

He was waiting for me to finish, the pie still in the air.

'And you were – well, you were mean to me. Like you were angry,' I said, hating how small my voice sounded. 'And then there wasn't even anybody there. I saw the cafe. It was empty.'

'Oh,' he said, turning momentarily away from me and putting the pie on the counter. 'I'm sorry.' His gaze when he turned back was direct and unwavering.

'And?' I said.

'I prefer unreserved apologies. Otherwise they're meaningless.'

'But why did you . . . ?'

'I just panicked. I'm sorry. I'm always late and I'm such a shambles. Sorry. I shouldn't have used you for a lift. I'll start driving again soon.'

'It's not about driving. It's about being treated – like that.'

'I'm sorry,' he said again.

I shrugged, picking up the washing again. He'd apologized. We couldn't turn back time.

He came over to help, grabbing the pile and taking it over to the airer. 'This'll be Wally's tiny clothes soon,' he said. 'A little row of tiny baby socks.'

Baby socks. He'd said that to me once before. On the day we took the pregnancy test. That strange, shocking, bitter-sweet afternoon.

We'd bought a digital test from the Spar. Jack said digital was best, said he could easily imagine a pink line where there was none; that we needed certainty.

I knew, but was ignoring it. The hot nausea. The late period. The strange dizzy spells. The memories of that night we didn't use a condom. I knew, but was postponing my knowledge.

We took it back to mine and sat on the side of the bath together while it rested on the window sill, like a ticking bomb. We checked it after two minutes; both peeping over at it, as though looking slowly could change anything.

Pregnant 1-2.

That's all it said.

He spoke first: 'Ah.'

'Ah, indeed,' I said. I had darted a glance at him then. In that moment where everything changed.

Later, I might have said the reason I never considered an abortion was because of my medical training. That I knew what went on, had seen it happen. The suction device. The remains; the hospital cremates them.

But no. It wasn't that. And it certainly wasn't because I felt sure I would be a good mother. I didn't. Not after Mum, and not after the boy. I still lost sleep over that. Wondering whether I could be trusted. Whether I would ever be good enough.

So, no. It wasn't those things. It was Jack's face. He was staring down at the test with an unmistakable expression of joy. He had his fist to his mouth, like an excited child, and when he looked at me his eyes were shining.

'I know . . . it's not ideal,' he said. 'I know we're so new. But . . .' He pointed down at the stick, still saying *Pregnant 1-2*. 'That's you and me.'

'It is,' I said, unable to stop smiling myself.

'And we're pretty ace,' he continued.

'We are.'

'Also – baby socks. The biggest argument for babies, ever.'

'Baby socks?'

'Tiny baby socks,' he said. 'Is there anything cuter?'

The memory of that afternoon fading, I went over to him and wordlessly hung up a sheet.

'I can leave if you'd like,' he said. 'If you're pissed off? I know it was unfair – waking you up was rubbish. I am sorry.'

I thought about it for a second. But it was too hard. The lure of him, here, helping me with the washing, sharing a pie later on and laughing. His warm body next to mine that night in my bed. It was too hard to resist.

Besides, he was always good at apologies.

4

One year ago

The boy and I got on well immediately. He was sixteen when he initially came into my hospital clinic. It was my first clinic as a newly promoted registrar; the buck stopped with me, for the first time. My palms were sweating.

He liked collecting Topps football cards; he had hundreds of them. They fell out of his pockets when he shifted on the chair. They cascaded down on to the floor and he hastily picked them up, carefully putting them back in an order only he knew. He was young for sixteen, still childlike in that way. Collecting things. Obsessing.

'That's Ralph Callachan,' he muttered to himself, his dark fringe falling in his eyes.

His mum looked at me. 'Sorry,' she said. 'He lives in the bloody seventies.' She pointed to one of the cards in the boy's lap. It was of a blond player sporting a mullet. 'Collects these old footballer cards.'

'Very retro,' I said, nodding to the cards. 'Very hip.'

The boy smiled. He had pale skin and dark hair, dark lashes. Red cheeks. He could sell that blush, if he could bottle it.

He'd been having trouble running, he said. The school yard felt uneven; his knee ached during playtime. He'd had a slight limp when he came on to our ward, and I'd sadly diagnosed him in my head right away. Sixteen, just. No previous injuries. Near-constant knee pain. Bad enough to be presenting at a paediatric outpatients' appointment. Osteosarcoma. Bone cancer. He took his jeans off and put a gown on. One knee was bigger than the other, by far, and that's the moment I truly knew.

I sent him for a scan and watched him go, the limp more pronounced as he transferred from the pinkish grey carpet of our clinic to the vinyl of the hospital corridor. That's where the journey continued for him – from *it's nothing; it's bound to go soon; give it three weeks*, to *it's something*.

I didn't see him for the rest of the day. Audrey's husband, Amrit, and I had a Coke together in the afternoon. I told him about the boy. His eyes were sympathetic. And then I forgot about him. I had to; I always had too many patients, too much to do. But he reappeared, later, at seven o'clock in the evening. A cleaner was polishing the linoleum outside the CT room. The corridor smelt of wax and lemon.

'Oh, hi,' the boy's mum said to me. She was putting a letter in her handbag. Her face was drawn. Her hair was messy at the scalp, as if she had been raking it back. She was wearing large hoop earrings, and her pale eyeshadow contrasted starkly with her black eyeliner.

'I thought you'd be home by now,' I said.

'We got called in, after the scan . . .' She frowned, confused at my lack of knowledge.

And that's when I saw the confirmation. It was

written somewhere on her frown lines, on the red-raw skin she'd peeled off around the nail of her right index finger, on the letter in her hand. You didn't get letters if you were discharged. And I knew that she knew.

'Your colleague. The junior doctor. He managed to see us. After the scan,' she said. 'It wasn't good news.'

I nodded once.

The boy wasn't looking at us. He was shuffling his cards.

'I'm sorry,' I said. I reached for her. I wanted to tell her everything I knew: that bone cancer was one of the better ones, that this might be a minor past event which he would reference casually in twenty years' time to a shocked girlfriend, that *now* wouldn't always feel this chaotic and shocking and out of control. Instead, I scribbled my mobile number on a blank prescription I had with me and handed it to her. 'Any question. Any time,' I said.

She didn't look grateful. She wasn't there yet. She wasn't ready.

The boy looked up at me. His blue eyes were shining. 'The doctor – the man doctor,' he said. 'He's got Alan Gowling at home.'

'Alan Gowling?' I said, looking curiously at him.

The boy waved his stack of cards at me. 'Newcastle centre forward. He's going to bring it to my next appointment.' He stopped and looked at me. 'Is this serious?' he said, less teenagerish, less sullen.

I looked at his mum.

'We'll see,' she said.

5

Present day

We met in Newcastle. By the Monument. It was a chilly March. One month after my break-up with Ben, and only a few months after the worst winter of my life. I, a native Geordie, and Jack, a Scotsman on secondment. It was funny: how many times had I passed the Monument? It must have been thousands. I passed it to buy *Smash Hits* magazine and sweets when I was eleven and allowed into town for the first time. I passed it on nights out to The Boat nightclub. I stopped passing it when I moved to Manchester for university, but started again when I moved back. It was less like a landmark and more like a person.

And then I met Jack right next to it – the best person I ever met, the father of my child. In hindsight, I would never have imagined anywhere different to meet the man I wanted to end up with. Ben and I had met at high school and our relationship mirrored its backdrop: we were provincial, small and self-conscious. But Jack and I were flamboyant, always kissing in Sainsbury's and giggling. We were like the Monument: lit-up, standing proud and tall against the sky.

Jack was over here researching the best things to do

for *City Lights* Newcastle. 'Sorry,' he said to me, a hand moving nervously by his side.

And in that moment my life took a new direction, though I didn't realize it then. I was alone, without Ben, and worried about my future, and then my future was right there in front of me, suddenly certain.

'This *is* the Monument, right?' He waved his phone in front of me. An image of the Monument was showing on Google Images. He held it up. It looked different on his phone: resplendent, illuminated against the night sky. In reality it seemed shorter and shabbier, somehow.

'Oh yes,' I said. I patted its sides, like it was a dog I knew well. 'It is.'

'I thought I'd check. It doesn't look quite the same.'

'No,' I said. 'That's the one.'

Looking back, it was a very Jack thing to say. He liked to check, even when he was sure. He would check all sorts: symptoms on Google, that the hobs really were switched off, that the bathroom window was definitely locked. I often wondered about it.

'Don't worry,' I said with a smile. 'You're not local?' I had recognized his accent. I knew it was Scottish, not Geordie, but couldn't place it beyond that. I don't know what made me take the conversation from its natural end and on to a new track. It wasn't his brown eyes, so deep they were almost black, the irises lost in the darkness. It wasn't his broad shoulders or stubble, though I liked them. I think perhaps it was his self-awareness that drew me to him initially. Where Ben had blustered – would have pretended to know what the Monument was, even when he didn't – Jack was self-conscious, self-effacing. Interesting.

'No, well, yes,' he said. 'I'm here for three months. For *City Lights*.'

And that's where it began.

From that moment, time became classified into Jack-time and non-Jack-time; the latter was to be wasted, passed, so that I could be with him again. My heart would thud in my chest as I drove over to his house after work. And those first few minutes would be the best. Not because he would greet me with a kiss, pressing the length of his body against mine, but because the hours would feel full, stretching ahead of me, like doses of medicine.

Five hours of Jack. There could be no better prescription.

We were in Oban, Jack's tiny Scottish hometown, late on Friday night, ready for the rugby on the Saturday. Our visits had become less like visits and more like slices of living there: gone were the meals out and the country walks, replaced slowly by more mundane tasks – Jack sorting through his old school books in the loft, me leaving a toothbrush behind.

It was almost always misty in Oban. The boats in the harbour looked half formed; only their hulls were visible, their masts disappearing up into the white air. Pieces of cloud seemed to hang, suspended, above Jack's parents' house, as if they had been ripped off from the main clouds and planted there instead.

His old rugby team was having a commemorative match, for a friend of theirs whose neck was too damaged for him to play any more. I didn't watch the match. Jack had told me not to bother. 'Come after 7 p.m.,' he'd said, 'when the match will have ended and the festivities have begun.'

I went shopping alone, instead, fingering the Babygros and the tiny socks in Mothercare, and turned up at the club after it had finished. Jack had sent me a long text about how to get in, which had made me smile. He was a writer, and text was his medium.

> When you get to the club park at the front, to the left of the row of oak trees, then come around and go into the white side door – not the navy-blue one. That will take you past the changing rooms and into the excitement of the makeshift bar area. Look for me; I am tall, dark and incredibly handsome xx

I stood outside for a good ten minutes. I should have gone straight in, but I was too nervous. I was having a baby with Jack, but somehow meeting his friends felt scarier. And that was partly due to how long it had taken. Literally months. Not a single friend met. Countless visits to Oban but the friends were always busy.

And so I had stopped asking, not out of fear, but because it had become embarrassing. Yet there I was, about to meet them.

The rugby club consisted of a floodlit pitch and a run-down white wooden clubhouse. Autumn mists swirled in front of the floodlights and steam puffed out from the heaters on the veranda. There were at least fifty people there, I realized, as my eyes adjusted to the darkness. They were standing, drinking, smoking, looking out over the grass.

'Hello?' Jack's voice called out into the gloom as I was hovering outside the white door, one gloved hand on the handle.

'Hi,' I said to him.

He emerged, smelling freshly showered, his hair damp, his lips on mine suddenly hot in the cold air. A cheer broke out on the veranda and he smiled at me, an arm firmly around my shoulders. His hand was moving. It always was, the fingers rubbing gently across my coat, the other hand stroking up and down my lower back. I loved that.

'Come and meet everyone,' he said. He led me up four rickety steps and on to the balcony. It smelt like the end of summer: mown lawns and grass drying out in the heat. Spilt cider and cigarettes. It reminded me of summers before; when Kate, my sister, and I were free to roam on our bikes.

'JD,' a stocky, blond man said. 'We finally meet the lady.'

I felt Jack stiffen next to me. 'Rach, this is Pricey,' he said. He gestured towards both of us, and Pricey shook my hand. 'Pricey: *this* is Rachel.'

My name was imbued with pride and significance. Pricey's eyes crinkled at the corners.

'I've heard a lot about you,' he said.

31

And maybe that was a thing everybody said, but I didn't think so. Jack slung his arm over my shoulders. I liked the warm weight of it, and I smiled to myself. That meaningful introduction. *This* is Rachel.

'Come to the bar?' Jack said.

I looked out at the rugby pitch, at the mild, early October evening that would soon be replaced with the endless cold and rain and snow of winter. 'I'll have a lemonade,' I said. 'Wild.'

I'd enjoyed a glass of wine, before Jack, and before Wally. But Jack didn't drink and I *couldn't* drink, so we found ourselves doing other things: where previously my summer would have been spent in beer gardens, this one had been spent bowling, playing minigolf, on evening walks. It had been heady, that summer.

'Come,' Jack said.

It was only really then that I registered what Pricey had called Jack. I paused, then said, 'JD?' to Pricey. I couldn't work it out. He was called Jack Ross – no middle name. 'Why not JR?'

'It was my drink of choice,' Jack explained.

Pricey looked at him, then got clapped on the back by somebody else, and turned away from us. Jack pointed to the bar, and I walked over to it. And all the way there, he was right behind me, his hips against my back. Somebody spilt a drop of cold beer on my hand on the way.

When we got to the bar, I turned to Jack. 'But you don't drink,' I said, 'JD.'

'I said *was*,' he replied. 'I used to drink. Quite a bit.'

He looked at me. 'I was a liability. A total bloody light-weight idiot.'

I stepped closer to him. Getting to know somebody in those early days was like looking around a beautiful English garden: I wanted to find the next bit, the next pathway leading to the next surprise. I could never get enough. I didn't say that, though.

'Did you? Drink lots?' I said. 'I can't imagine that.'

'Yep. I've got a cat now, though,' he said, pulling me towards him. 'Got to think of him.'

My mouth twisted into a smile. We were fond of pretending the cat was Jack's offspring. We'd praise him for sleeping through. We'd pretend we were rushing to drop him at nursery. It was another one of our things: our many, many things we joked about.

'Think of the habits he'd pick up if he saw his daddy drinking,' I said.

'Exactly. He'd be hitting the bottle before he's a teen.' He grinned at me, leaning back against the bar. His hands were pink, cold-looking, even though it was warm. He kissed me, until two other men joined us.

They spoke with plummy accents, like so many of the doctors I had worked with over the years. I always found their body language to be different, these people. It seemed to say *I belong here*, wherever they were.

'I'm Roger,' one of the men waiting beside us said to me. He was tall and had an enormous neck. The other, Ian, introduced himself, and then there was an awkward pause.

'Roger's a classic alpha male,' Jack said to me.

'Surely not,' I said. Jack was tall, and broader than the others.

'You're a beta male, at heart, aren't you?' Roger said.

Jack nodded, smiling sheepishly, and I loved him more than I had a moment before.

'I'd be the shy, scared gorilla,' Jack said. 'The one all the others bully.' He ducked his head, and they all laughed.

'How long've you known JD?' Ian said.

'Oh, not long,' I said. 'We met in March.'

'How long've we known him?' Ian said to Roger. 'Twenty years? Twenty-five? Saw him every week till he pissed off to Newcastle.'

'It was the under nines, where we met,' Roger said. 'So twenty years. Jesus. I still think I'm twenty-one.'

'Under nines. Sounds serious,' I said.

'What was your thing?' Jack said to me. He was often asking about me. He seemed – totally unselfconsciously – to want to know every aspect of my history.

'St John's Ambulance,' I said to him with a grin. 'Though they were too disorganized, and it annoyed me.'

'You wanted to be running it?' Jack said.

'Absolutely.'

'I did footie as well as rugby,' Roger said.

But Jack ignored him. He always followed my thread of conversation, so I felt like it was just us, alone together. I fizzed under his interested gaze.

'So you went from that to medicine?' he asked.

'Yeah – with a bit of doctors and nurses, too, with dolls,' I said.

He flashed me a quick smile, and nodded.

'Come on, get the lady a drink,' Roger interjected.

'I'll have a lemonade,' Jack said. He tilted his head back, a half-nod to the bar behind him.

'Chivalry's dead, eh?' Roger said.

Jack reluctantly turned away from us. And even though he was facing the bar, his elbows in his worn grey jumper resting on it, a ten-pound note between his fingers, he kept turning around and looking at us.

'So when were the JD years?' I said.

Jack's head whipped around, halfway through his order. 'Lemonade,' he said to us instead of the bartender, nonsensically.

'The what?' Roger said to me.

'The JD years. The drinking.'

Roger and his companion exchanged a glance, evidently confused, then looked back at me. Jack took a step away from the bar and appeared by my arm. He didn't have our drinks. I glanced at him, confused, but he ignored me.

The moment passed. But I didn't miss the look he gave them, the look that wasn't meant for me. It was part warning, part question. Eyebrows raised, eyes widened.

I don't know what made me do it, but I deliberately turned my body away, as if admiring the view of the clubhouse, but slid my eyes back to Jack. He made a gesture. I couldn't see it fully, but I got the gist. He drew his hand across his throat: not a finger slitting motion, his whole hand. The meaning was clear: *cut it*. I turned back to look at him and frowned, letting him know I had seen, but his expression was blank, his eyes as warm and affectionate as ever.

'Where are the drinks?' I said.

'Coming up,' Jack said easily. That laid-back tone didn't fit with his facial expression, like a curdled cake mixture beginning to separate.

I excused myself for a minute, feigning my phone ringing, and escaped to stand behind my car.

What was that? I was suddenly desperate to be on my own; or rather, I wanted to speak to someone who knew me.

The grass was spongy underfoot. Mushrooms were sprouting up out of the undergrowth. I could see the floodlights, the mist, and a crowd of silhouettes on the balcony, the occasional orange glowing orb arcing in the night to smokers' mouths and back again, the funnels of smoke they blew out afterwards.

My hand went to my belly again. It wasn't a calm, maternal touch. It was grasping. This baby. This man I hardly knew.

I needed to speak to Audrey, my best friend. We had grown up together, gone to the same university, *like losers*, we said. And then she met my friend Amrit, who was studying midwifery. I hardly saw him now.

I dialled her number. 'I'm being weird,' I said when she answered. I heard her mute *The X Factor* and tell Amrit it was me.

'Hi, big boy,' she said; a long-standing nickname we used. The day she got a mortgage with Amrit, she told me she was a grown-up and we, at exactly the same time, said, 'We're big boys now.' It was one of those serendipitous moments that come to define a friendship.

'I'm being weird,' I said again. I took a step forward. My hips ached. It was just the ligaments stretching, adjusting to the pregnancy, but I couldn't take ibuprofen. There seemed to be so much I couldn't do.

'What do you mean?'

'I'm outside the rugby club. In Oban.' I tilted my head back, trying to calm down. I tried to look at the Scottish sky, still pale blue at this hour in October – the beautiful white nights – but it stung my eyes and I closed them. Mum's face flashed through my mind in the momentary darkness, as it often did. I wondered where she was.

'Oh yeah, of course. How's it going?'

'Really weird.'

'Him or you?'

'Him. His friends. They call him something else here. JD.'

'JD? Why?'

'He said it used to be his drink of choice.'

'So? Are you alright?'

'Yeah, I'm just . . . I don't know.'

Audrey hesitated. I could hear it, like seeing a *typing* sign on my iPhone that disappeared and reappeared as its sender drafted and redrafted. 'Maybe this is . . . pregnancy stuff,' she suggested. 'You said yourself you're not sleeping well. Crying at Andrex adverts. I don't want to be a horrible sexist, but . . .'

I kicked a conker across the grass. A couple got into

their car nearby and their headlights swept across me as they left. 'I dunno,' I said after a few seconds. 'When he was at the bar, I asked them about when he used to drink it and it was . . . there was a weird atmosphere. They looked odd.' I perched on the bonnet of my car, still warm from when I'd driven over here so full of hope fifteen minutes ago.

'What did they say?' Audrey's voice sounded distracted, quieter.

'Nothing. They just didn't get it,' I said.

My voice sounded strangled. That got her attention. I wasn't making a chatty call, having popped outside just to catch up.

'Rachel. Tell me. What's up?'

'I just feel like one day my baby might ask me something about its father and I'll have no idea. None –' My voice caught on the last word.

I didn't even tell her the rest: the things I mourned late at night. The excitement of trying for a baby on honeymoon; the approval an engagement after a few years of dating would've brought. Not this stuff. The raised eyebrows. The knowing it was an accident; that people might think *not planned* would mean *not wanted*.

'Oh, no, don't think that,' Audrey said. 'Babies take nine months to cook, to give you time to prepare. You'll know Jack really well soon. Especially by the time Wally can talk.'

'It was just . . . he made this signal.' I found myself making it there, in the car park, my hand drifting up to my neck and lingering on it. I rearranged my hair and shivered, a branch cracking under my feet as I took a step towards the club. 'Like he was telling them to shut up.'

'Really?'

I closed my eyes against the night air. I opened them again and looked at the sky. I was only a couple of hundred miles from home, but it felt like a million. 'I think so.'

'Are you sure?' I could hear the scepticism in her voice.

We'd been here before. Right after Mum. With Ben.

I thought back to the gesture Jack had made. I was so certain ... and yet. Could I really *see* him doing it? Maybe he was adjusting his jumper. He thought it didn't fit him; had lamented he looked like a dickhead when he appeared in a photo on Facebook wearing it. Maybe he didn't hear. Maybe he wasn't bothered. Perhaps I was ... perhaps it was grief. Perhaps I was going mad.

'I bet he wasn't. As if he'd do that in front of you. He's such a ... gent,' Audrey said. 'Maybe it's just like the stuff with Ben.'

'Maybe,' I murmured.

She had known my ex-boyfriend, Ben, so well. She was the only person who knew what really happened; who understood the nuances. That, eventually, my accusations had driven him away, but that there was more to it than that. That perhaps it had been for the best, anyway; that we hadn't been crazily in love, not really. That he was more of a security blanket to me than a boyfriend. She didn't know Jack at all.

'The paranoia,' I said.

'That old chestnut.' I could hear her relaxing again. 'It's exactly the same. Fear that someone's not who they say they are. But it's not real.'

'Maybe you're right,' I said.

'I'm sure he wouldn't make a gesture like that right in front of you. Want to speak to Am?' she added. Her tone was hopeful.

He missed me, too, I thought. 'I've got to go,' I said. 'Sorry.'

After we said goodbye I went back and stood next to Jack, his warm arm around my waist, his leg touching mine all the way down. The atmosphere was still tense. It was nothing concrete. Nothing tangible. Or rather, it was lots of small things, added together: the silence as I arrived back, not comfortable and conversational but abrupt and sudden, like someone had pressed 'mute' in the middle of a story. An exchanged glance between two of Jack's friends. Pricey clearing his throat.

'Something I said?' I joked, but my voice sounded tinny and flat.

'No, no,' Jack said, smiling at me.

Conversation resumed. Or actually, it seemed to me, it started over – one of Jack's friends talking about his girl-friend's new dog – and the air soon felt different again; sociable and loving and warm. Though that only reminded me of how it had felt a few minutes before: not hostile, exactly. But as if something had been hiding behind a curtain, hoping it wouldn't be revealed.

I turned to Pricey, wanting to start our own conversation.

'What was that . . . what was that JD stuff all about?'
I said.

I saw his reaction before he could hide it. A flash of
the whites of his eyes, his brows shooting up. Shock.

'All what stuff?' he said.

'You know – he went all weird . . . when you called
him JD. And then when I asked.'

I could feel Jack's gaze on me, but I avoided looking
up. I probably only had a few seconds before he might
interrupt, I thought.

'No, we didn't,' Pricey said. He didn't break eye contact. And then he looked away, raising his eyebrows. He
thought me weird. Jack's paranoid girlfriend.

I'd imagined it all. I glanced up. Jack wasn't looking
at us, wasn't paying any attention to us at all. I'd imagined that, too.

We left at just gone half ten. Jack led me out the back
way – amid many tongue-in-cheek comments – and
past the changing rooms where he grabbed his bag, his
arm flexing as he lifted it.

'Alright,' a tall man with an afro said from the corner
of the changing room. He was standing with his kit bag
over his shoulder, a lit-up phone in his hand.

'Oh, we didn't get a chance to see you,' Jack said,
releasing my hand from his. 'This is Rachel. Rachel,
this is Charlie.'

'Yes,' Charlie said, reaching for me. 'Masters. Nice to
meet you.'

It was one of those moments where I didn't hear

what he said until a few minutes later, and even then I didn't register it until I was flicking the indicator to turn right out of the car park.

'How are you and Wally feeling?' Jack said, his hand on my thigh, his fingers moving. He'd taken to referring to us in this way. 'We could go for a curry in the bay. It's not that late?'

Jack was always suggesting things like this. They still felt decadent, naughty, to me, after an upbringing of Dad brewing his own beer to save money. Dad was fussy and frugal. He was forever using coupons. He liked to check his tyre pressures every single week, even though they were always the same, for no real reason at all – other than a relic from the seventies. Mum had been tolerant, for a while, and then frustrated. At her first hospital appointment, the first thing she said was that Dad would resent all the car parking fees during her treatment. He hadn't, of course. But she was like that. Funny, but barbed, always aimed at Dad.

The lifestyle Jack and his family led; it was different. They would all still be up when we got back. Eating cheese and biscuits. Drinking wine. Ordering a film on Sky Box Office like it was Christmas all year round. They'd be jolly and happy. No acerbic remarks.

'Okay,' I said.

I turned the steering wheel, and my brain landed on Charlie's name, like it had been rifling through the filing system of my mind ever since I shook the man's hand in the changing room.

Charlie Masters. That man's name was Charlie Masters. My curiosity piqued, I spoke up.

'Do you work with him?' I said, pointing back at the rugby club with my thumb.

Jack leant back against the passenger seat, looking at me childishly. 'Imagine if we lived here,' he said, looking out as the harbour lights whizzed by.

'Ah,' I said.

'We're like dual citizens.'

'You, me and Wally?'

'Yeah,' he said. 'Will he be Scottish or English?' He smiled at me, his eyes dark in the dim light of the car.

Jack brought this up often. He'd extended and extended his job with *City Lights*, but we had to decide. We skirted around the issue, brought it up in moments like this: in cars or as we were walking into parties or right before sleep. Never at the right time.

'Oban's quiet. Plus, Scotland has free prescriptions,' Jack said.

I couldn't help but laugh at that: Jack was forever on antibiotics he didn't need, having scans that weren't warranted, getting referred to specialists he was frightened of.

'True,' I said lightly, my mind elsewhere. I left a beat, waiting for him to answer, but he didn't. 'So, Charlie?' I said again, just as a car came up behind me, its headlights flashing brightly in my rear-view mirror before it overtook.

'No, I just play rugby with him.'

I stayed silent, thinking. So what, Rachel? So his

43

friend from the rugby club emailed him? I shook my head, trying to concentrate. I couldn't ask about the email I'd accidentally read some of, so instead I asked about the nickname.

'It seemed like you weren't happy when I mentioned your nickname?' I said.

'Did it? Why?' Jack said.

I liked that *why?* I settled back, comfortable against the seat. My curiosity was sated again.

'Just – you had this look on your face . . .'

'I was an idiot. A drunk young man. Riding in shopping trolleys. That sort of thing.'

'Mmm,' I said. It made sense. Would I really want him to know about the things I'd done as a teenager? How Audrey and I, in our halls of residence at nineteen years old, had performed an actual Wiccan spell when everyone else was out drinking? 'I guess I'm with you there. I wasn't a drinker, really. But I was a goon.'

'I can't imagine *that*,' Jack said, flashing me a smile.

'No?'

'No, most definitely not. Coolest girl in town, you,' he said, but his tone didn't match his jovial words. It was tense. Frightened.

We didn't speak for the rest of the journey after that.

6

One year ago

I was at home, the morning after a night shift, eating a risotto dinner, when the boy popped into my head and it occurred to me that I could look him up.

I had never looked up a patient before, but there was something about this case and this patient that felt different. I needed to know more about him.

He was easy to find on Twitter. The first hit.

'#Lovinglyf,' he had recently tweeted, with a photograph of his hospital tag. It had sixteen retweets; he had quite the following.

Ben appeared in the doorway. It was his morning and my night, like we were in different hemispheres. He sat down heavily next to me on the sofa, his stomach rounded where his T-shirt had ridden up. He smelt sour, of sleep.

'What are you doing?' he asked. I must have looked shifty. I tried to close the laptop without him seeing, but he picked it up and slid it on to his legs. We shared a computer, and he liked to read a gaming forum every morning. 'What's this?' he said, scrolling down the screen. The boy had checked into my hospital on Foursquare, just a few posts before, and Ben raised his blond eyebrows. 'Oh,' he said. He turned to me in surprise. 'Is this a patient?'

'Yeah.'

'Isn't that . . . isn't that not allowed?'

'It's public,' I said with a defensive shrug, trying to finish my dinner.

'You shouldn't be looking at this,' he continued, gesturing to a topless selfie the boy had posted, showing his hairless body. *I used to have body hair, I swear*, it was captioned. 'Why are you looking?' There was a note of derision in his voice.

'I don't know,' I muttered. I didn't try to explain. Mum had been diagnosed a few years ago. Perhaps it was that. Perhaps I wanted a window into the suffering, so I could try to understand it. Cure it.

'I really don't think you should be doing this,' he said again, closing the laptop with a soft click.

I said nothing in response.

7

Present day

I decided to ask Jack about the email. It was more of a tidying-up exercise than anything. I just wanted to know it was nothing. Like doing a repeat blood test to clarify the problem had gone away when I knew that it had.

I didn't ask him that evening in bed. The rooms were cold and echoey and we could even hear the clock ticking in his parents' room, magnified by the stone and the emptiness.

And I didn't ask him the next day, when we were walking his parents' enormous dogs, Mozart and Sebastien, and we got left behind in the rain by everybody and were finally alone in a way we hadn't been before in Oban.

I was constantly on the verge of asking, that weekend; annoying myself with opportunity spotting, and the way my stomach churned constantly, but I didn't ask. I used to do the same with Ben, when I had been convinced he was cheating on me. I was always looking for openings. Rifling through his gym bag, wondering if I'd see a half-open packet of condoms. Peering over his phone at his text messages. *Madness*, he called it, and it was. *Trust issues*, Audrey had said sympathetically. *Maybe it's to do with your mum?* she had added, and I had looked away, not able to meet her eyes. Because the thing was, Mum had died. And she hadn't been who she said she was. All at once. All at the same time.

The Rosses' house was vast, set right into the Scottish hills. From the outside, I expected Agas and throws on cosy sofas, real fires and wild gardens, but inside the house was different. It wasn't cosy but neither was it modern. It was cold and shabby and dated, with a 1980s pink bathroom suite and a brown sofa that sagged at the back. There was a fine layer of dust almost everywhere, and it wouldn't be uncommon to find dirty glasses back on the shelves. It wasn't for lack of money. It was something else. A sort of snobbery. They wanted it to be unkempt, I thought. So it would feel properly old.

So in the end I did it while a toastie cooked in Jack's parents' enormous kitchen, late at night. It took three minutes.

His mum was passing in and out, carrying washing and banging the outside doors and organizing the shoe cupboard. They were all night owls.

'I actually missed you,' Jack said to me as I arrived in the kitchen.

I'd just been in the shower, psyching myself up.

He was wearing jeans, no socks and a soft grey T-shirt. His bare feet made little slapping noises on the floor as he moved around the kitchen. 'How ridiculous is that?' He turned and looked at me. 'Don't come any closer,' he said.

'Oh, charming.' I opened my mouth to ask him about the email. But then I stopped. I heard footsteps upstairs.

48

It was Davey. He was Jack's younger brother. He had learning difficulties. He kept funny hours, emerged often in the afternoons. He liked space missions and playing World of Warcraft. He liked me, too, though I hardly ever saw him. He sometimes asked about my day, even though it seemed to make him nervous. He couldn't communicate much about his own. When he did speak, it was in bursts: meandering, illogical, random.

'Seriously, stay there,' Jack said.

And that's when I saw them, in a neat line across the orange-tiled kitchen floor. Little wooden boards with springs attached. Bright red Vs branded on them, a rat's face in the centre of it. *Victor*, they said across them.

Traps.

'Er . . .' I didn't know what to do. Dad had a spider catcher he used to rescue trapped house spiders and occasional bumblebees, freeing them outside, delicately.

'We have a problem.'

'With what?' I said, though I already knew the answer.

'Rats. Huge country rats.' He grinned at me wolfishly. 'Sorry. Gross, I know.'

'Oh,' I said. Audrey had a boyfriend once in our first year at university who kept two rats in a cage in his halls of residence. After she broke up with him, we called him Roland, after Roland Rat, and we laughed every time he walked by. Those were happy times, when we'd eat spaghetti hoops and moan about our workloads and paint our nails together. They seemed like a different lifetime.

'It started with the flies.'

'Flies?'

'Yeah. There were about twenty flies in here the other day. Then they found a dead one – a rat – behind the fridge. So now we've got the traps down from the loft again. It happens at the end of every summer. Autumn time. Can't stop them. Too many nooks and crannies. You block up one and they find another.'

I had never lived in the country, had spent my teenage years listening to the Metro and the city-centre buses rattle past. It was eerie, the misty Oban countryside. The thought of the dead rat languishing behind their fridge. The traps. That strange stone house.

'Mum and Dad wait for me to come and lay them because they're scared.'

'You're afraid of pectoral twitches but not of rats,' I said.

'Correct.'

Jack pulled out a fifth trap, opening and spreading it like a book, cracking its spine. He set it on the floor at my feet. 'They're nocturnal,' he said.

'What do they . . . ?' I pointed down at the traps.

'They crush their skulls.'

He was standing, his weight back on his hips, surveying the traps. He nudged one with his foot. They all had blobs of something on them.

'Peanut butter,' Jack said, catching me looking. 'They like it.'

'Oh my God,' I said, looking at the traps and imagining the scene in the morning. 'Can't you just . . . ?'

Jack didn't finish my sentence, or reach out to me, or console me. Instead, he was looking curiously at me.

'I mean – you're going to kill them.' I wished I hadn't been sidetracked in that way, diverted from my question about the email, but I was. I couldn't help it.

'Rach. We have no choice. There'll be an infestation otherwise.'

'Hmm.' I couldn't stop looking down at the traps, imagining the rats' necks, cracked and broken by the morning. Would they die quickly or slowly? Would they see the other rats die first? Would they consider what the traps were; that they had been hunted and murdered?

'It must be – it must be pregnancy hormones,' I said. My voice caught in my throat. I was often feeling bewildered by my own emotions. It was a strange thing.

'Oh no, no, don't cry,' Jack said. And he did reach for me then. One hand enveloped my waist, and the other crept up into my hair. His fingers were moving and I leant against his chest, my breathing immediately slowing. 'Country life, eh?' he said to me, softly, in my ear.

'Brutal,' I said. 'For somebody awash with maternal hormones.' I wondered briefly if my mother had felt like this. She had never seemed to. Never wanted to touch me, to hold me. She was always upright and stiff. I'll never forget the moment when she died, and she reached for my hand. Hers was cool and bony, but I liked the feel of it. Her grip in mine.

'Mmm,' Jack said, a long-drawn-out sympathetic noise in my ear.

We stood there, in the dim kitchen light, surrounded by the rat traps, for ages.

'Do you want me to stop? I'll stop, if you like,' he said.

He would have done anything for me.

'No,' I said.

'The last time I was doing this, last autumn, I was single,' he murmured.

'And now you're about to have a family.'

'Yep,' he said easily, a wide grin spreading across his face. 'Can't believe my bloody luck.' He put the bread and the cheese in the toastie maker.

'You're such a goon,' I said, though inside I was delighted. 'Ever heard of playing it cool?'

'I can't. Not with you.'

And then Jack's mum, Cynthia, shouted through that he needed to feed the dogs, and I asked right then, as his back was to me. He was holding a bag of dog food, and the dogs were padding impatiently. They seemed to know to avoid the traps. He kept up a steady stream of dialogue with them. 'This evening, sirs, we are having a consommé of reconstituted beef with a side of cardboard biscuits,' he said. 'Will sirs be having wine?' The dogs looked at him, and he turned to me and smiled, but I couldn't concentrate enough to banter.

'I saw something on your iPad,' I said. 'When we were in bed, the other weekend. There was an email . . . from Charlie Masters.' I couldn't bring myself to say *atrocity*.

The dogs' eyes shifted to me as I spoke. They were silent. Watchful.

Jack was looking at them, too. 'I wanted cats,' he said, gesturing to them. 'Dogs are just so . . .'

I didn't say anything.

' . . . so simple. Look at them,' he said with a grin, as

their eyes followed his hands. 'All they care about is food. Cats care about philosophy.'

I couldn't help but laugh at him. He laughed too, ignoring my question.

I tried again. 'So – that email?'

I was watching Jack closely, but there was nothing to see. He didn't blush or stammer. His hand didn't still. He didn't drop the dog food or turn away from me.

'Yeah?' He bent down and started filling the bowls.

Mozart licked Jack's hand, leaving a tiny damp stain on his fingertip. Jack tutted, then ran a hand down Sebastien's spine. Mozart pushed his face into the bag, and Jack laughed.

And then his black eyes were on me.

'I – I haven't been able to stop thinking about it,' I said. The thoughts emerged in a rush, tumbling over each other like lemmings falling off a cliff. 'I just wondered . . . it said something about Douglas having done something?'

'Matt Douglas is our old friend,' Jack said. 'He assaulted someone. Punched them. Outside a bar.'

'Oh. Really?' I said, but already I could feel the tension ebbing out of my shoulders and neck.

'Yeah. It was weird.' He stood up straight, putting the dog food away.

I caught a waft of Olbas Oil – he had an autumn cold – and the sweet smell made me momentarily pause, remembering dotting it on to my pillow when I was a child. It always made my eyes water. Kate hated the scent of it in our shared bedroom.

'It mentioned an atrocity,' I said. 'In that email. Strong word.' And Charlie apologized, I thought to myself, for dredging up your history.

'It was pretty violent,' Jack said, turning the sides of his mouth down and giving a little shrug. 'It escalated. This lad glassed Matt, so Matt punched him. Too hard. Fractured his skull.'

'Why did Charlie email it to you?'

'I don't know,' Jack said. 'We keep an eye on the articles, I guess.'

'It said sorry. About bringing it up. History.'

'Yeah. It was – not very nice. That time. For any of us.'

The apology didn't mean it had been about him, I reasoned. And yet: the email had said *your* history.

I tried not to watch him too closely, but it was fascinating. He didn't seem to care. It seemed mundane, to him. Either that or he was an absolutely excellent liar. His face was entirely neutral, impassive. And yet I couldn't stop remembering how his expression had closed down when he first read it. Perhaps I had imagined that?

He stroked Mozart's head, looked at me quickly, then smiled. And then the toastie was ready – the smell of the melted cheese made me feel sick; a relic of the first trimester – and in a moment the conversation would move on. I could feel it, like a boat slowly pulling away from the shore. The ropes were running through my fingers the further away we moved, and soon we'd be too far out for me to bring it back up again. So that's what made me say it. I threw the anchor overboard, stalling us.

'But it was nothing to do with you, then?' I said with a forced laugh. 'You weren't involved?' I couldn't help but ask.

As I spoke, Jack turned slowly to me. The bread burned his fingers and he dropped it abruptly on to the waiting plate. I was showing him my hand, with that sentence, but he ignored it.

'Bed?' he replied.

He wasn't going to answer. Not a word. It didn't need an answer, did it? My rhetorical question, my poor joke.

The pause yawned and yawned. He might have told me it wasn't awkward, but it was. I knew it in the same way I knew what sort of time it was when I woke up. And when a patient was about to arrest. I knew it. Deep inside me. Jack was busying himself, not looking at me again.

I tried to fill the silence. 'I don't know, I . . .'

'Jack – when you move back up,' his mum said, coming into the room, holding a stack of books, 'can you take these? They're just sitting here.'

She was wearing an actual twinset. I'd never seen anybody wear those outside of American 1950s sitcoms.

I stopped speaking when she entered, as I always did. She ignored me, as she always did. She had accepted a scan photo, but nothing more. She didn't know whether I had brothers and sisters, where I'd gone to university. Nothing. She always wore the exact same shade of pink lipstick. Once, I'd seen her in the morning without it, and she'd looked almost ghostly.

'Well, we don't know what our plans are,' Jack said.

'We both live in Newcastle,' I said, unable to help myself. I watched his mother wince at my pronunciation: they all said *New*-castle. Everybody native knew it was New-*castle*.

'Well, we'll see,' she said.

I looked at Jack again. He was placidly cutting the toastie, his gaze trained down towards the counter, but I knew – from what little I knew about him – that his mind would be whirring with what his mother had just said.

Three days after we met, I was Facebook stalking him. Who wasn't partial to a bit of Internet stalking? We all did it. I dived into Facebook – and then Google, though the only things that came up were his articles, and charity stuff he'd done – ready to explore the likes and photos of a man whose lips had kissed mine for the first time on the Tyne Bridge two days previously.

Jack's Facebook page was almost completely locked down, and it was too early for a friend request, but I could click on his friends. And so it was Jack's mum's profile I ended up scrutinizing, fascinated in the aftermath of my own mum's death. I had made my mind up about her, there and then.

Jack looked up at her now. 'I don't think Rach really wants to move up here,' he said.

'But don't *you*?' she asked.

'Not if she doesn't,' he replied, glancing quickly over

at me. He didn't mention my mum, and I was glad of that.

As she left, I turned to Jack, keeping my expression expectant. He wasn't looking at me, and eventually, I said, 'Are we finished? About Douglas?'

'What do you want to know? Ask me anything.'

The combination of his expression and his willingness to talk extinguished my anxiety, as if I'd blown out a candle. The email was about his friend. It was such a non-event, he hadn't even answered me when I probed. It was nothing. Nothing.

But, as was always the way, another anxiety had been lit in its place: Oban.

'Yeah,' I said. 'So what about your mum? Why does she think . . . ? I can't move. My dad. It's all so recent.'

'I know.' He leant over and opened the window.

The misty countryside air floated in. It looked spooky outside, a spider's web across the window lit up by the security lights, strung with raindrops from the evening shower. A proper autumn.

I remembered the first time I'd told him about my mum. I'd told him things in parts. Piecemeal. About Ben first, and then about Mum. I didn't want him to run a mile, thinking I had issues. Unresolved, recent things. He'd listened intently, his eyes on mine.

The second time we'd spoken about her, I'd cried as I told him the kernel of truth at the heart of all of it: that I hadn't always liked her. That, once, she'd shouted at Kate for not winning a tennis match, when Kate was trying to turn professional. That she'd told me not to do paediatrics because it wasn't prestigious enough. That she constantly belittled Dad and we found it embarrassing. That, after she died, he'd uncovered an affair, with their mutual friend. That it had changed everything. Their past. Our future. One truth, and everything fractured around it.

'It's complicated,' Jack had said. 'She was your mum and you loved her and she died. And she'd been unfaithful and she wasn't always nice to you.' He'd held his hands out like weighing scales.

I could see it, then, for the first time. Both sides could be correct. The truth was complicated. I could love her and miss her and not miss her, all at the same time.

Now, in his Oban kitchen, Jack gave me a small smile. 'Let's let Wally choose. It bloody stinks of burnt toast in here.' He took a huge bite of the toastie, then proffered it to me. I took a mouthful, ravenous for it even though it had smelt so horrible just a few minutes ago. He held the toastie carefully, scooped a string of cheese from my chin, licking his finger.

And then he said, as cool as anything, 'Why were you looking at my emails?'

I stuttered, couldn't answer him, and he dropped the subject.

Later, in bed, the email about Matt Douglas forgotten, my bump was itching. It was still tiny, but starting to feel tight, the skin stretched strangely. I wasn't sleeping well.

I was thinking about Oban. I knew nothing about being Scottish. I didn't understand what the SNP stood for and I'd never been to the Edinburgh Fringe and I liked the bluebird spring days in Newcastle and the sunset over the Tyne Bridge and the lilt of the local accent.

But then, I thought, as I listened to the Oban night, I could learn to love it in my own way. The perpetual autumnal feeling. The cosiness. The tartan gift shops and the funny blue five-pound notes. The quiet of Oban. I listened out for it. No cars. No aeroplanes. An occasional owl hooting.

And that's when I heard it. A snap. Like a loud staple gun going off. Like a knife being sharpened. I sat up in alarm, and Jack's hand reached for mine, in his sleep, unconsciously.

And, as I sat there listening intently, the duvet falling around my waist, I heard another.

It was the traps.

Downstairs, the rats were dying.

8

On Monday evening we arrived back at Jack's temporary house in Newcastle. His parents had bought it for him when he got the contract with *City Lights* and needed somewhere near the city centre to live for a few months. It was only temporary, but they would let it out, they said, when he was finished. They had so much money, it wouldn't matter if nobody wanted to rent it. They'd buy one for us in Oban, too, they said. They'd provide the capital, if only we'd move up. That part was tempting; a real house, and not a flat whose walls rattled when lorries drove past.

We were standing in his kitchen. Audrey was coming to collect me in five minutes for our cinema ritual, put in place after Mum died. To give me something to do other than miss her phone calls. We saw anything; whatever was on. And each film we saw – and each ice-cream pot consumed – added another in-joke to our repertoire. We had jokes about the *Toy Story* films and *Mad Max* and about a random, indie film we'd seen about aliens. Everything.

'I sleep so much better in Oban,' Jack said. He was mentioning it more and more, at that time. Almost every day. Oban. Moving.

'Apart from the rats,' I replied.

Jack had disposed of them wordlessly that morning. I hadn't seen any bodies.

'It's Howard that wakes you, not Newcastle,' I added.

Howard was obsessed with Jack. He waited for him to wake up at 8 a.m. every day, eventually meowing loudly if he didn't get up.

'Were you staring at the automatic cat feeder all weekend?' Jack called through to the living room, where Howard was asleep on the sofa. Jack smiled, then got a glass out of the cupboard and filled it from the tap.

'You missed him,' I said. I placed a hand on Jack's arm.

'I either miss him or you. Unless you're both with me. In my bed.'

'Howard. Your other lover.'

'We could live anywhere round here. Together.'

'Maybe . . . just . . .' I couldn't explain my hesitation. It was everything I wanted. I'd met his friends, his family. He was letting me in. I should have been happy.

Jack's home line rang. He glanced at the number on the black handset standing on the kitchen counter, then looked back at me.

'Leave it, I think,' Jack said, more to himself than to me.

The answer machine clicked on. I'd never had an answer machine. Coming in and checking for messages always felt so *Sex and the City* to me: 'Jack here. I'm not around. Please leave me and Howard a message.'

I smiled at that, but then we heard the message. A deep breath. Jack's mum's voice.

'Hi. I just –'

Jack sprang to life. He was pressing buttons on the handset, but his mother was still speaking.

'– wanted you to . . .'

Finally, he pressed 'answer', even though the speaker-phone was still on. 'Hi, I'm just with Rachel,' he said. His words were rushed. 'Hanging out,' he added, though we weren't. I was about to leave. We were standing in the kitchen, drinking water. Hardly hanging out.

I frowned, looking at him. Was it my imagination, or . . . no. It was normal to say who you were with. Or, at least, not abnormal. Wasn't it? Stop it, Rachel, you awful person, I said to myself. Ben had never cheated on me. Jack hadn't done anything. It was all in my head. Kate would agree. She told Dad she was *concerned* about me after Ben and I broke up. He passed it on, in his diplomatic way. I'd ignored it, but I hadn't forgotten. Concerned. Such a strange, loaded choice of word.

'Great, Jack. Glad you're home okay,' she said.

'Yep,' he said. He finally got the phone off speaker and ended the call.

'Just checking we got home alright,' he said over his shoulder to me as he walked into the living room and sat down next to Howard.

I stared after him. There was a wide archway between the kitchen and living room and he was in full view.

It was things like this that made me not want to live with him. Silly things. But things that stood to attention in my gut and said *look at this*. A feeling that opened emails in the night and analysed looks exchanged in rugby clubs.

I used to get that gut feeling all the time; I based an entire career on it. I would include it as evidence in my working day. The test results. The scans. And my gut feeling. They would tessellate together comfortably. I thought back to baby Grace.

'Her bloods are good,' the FI junior doctor Natalie said to me a year ago. She had a grease stain on the left leg of her blue scrubs. We'd been eating toast, before we were called to look at a baby girl's test results, and a drip of butter had pooled there. She wasn't supposed to be assisting with neonates, but we were short-staffed. It was August and she was fresh out of med school. Her skin was grey with stress, her lips cracked. I caught her eye and smiled.

'You won't always feel like this,' I said to her as I inserted the needle into Grace's heel, found a vein and drew the blood out. 'I'm repeating the bloods,' I said. 'She's not alright.'

'Isn't she?' Natalie said. 'And thanks. It's not what I imagined. Being a doctor.' A strand of her long red hair fell out of her bun as she looked back down at the blood results, scanning for an anomaly, something she'd missed.

She'd have breezed through med school. No resits, I was sure. And then she was there, with me. And it wasn't easy any more. That she had a job where she might push a door open and come across a patient being intubated before she'd had her morning coffee would surely have shocked her. How could she ever go home and eat dinner, drink a glass of wine, relax, after seeing all this? Like returning from war. I knew, because I'd felt the same too, once. Time and experience had anaesthetized me to it all. But then the numbness wore off, for me.

'Look,' I said.

Natalie scanned the papers furiously.

'No,' I said. I placed my fingertips on her arm. She was still freckled from her summer holiday. 'Look at her.'

And she did. The baby was grey, tiny specks of sweat on her upper lip. Her skin was the colour of a winter's sky. Babies shouldn't sweat. And they shouldn't be that colour.

'She's sick,' I said.

It was the kind of sticky August day outside where everything felt reversed: inside was cold and outside was warm, even at night, and my upper lip was sweating, too. Those hazy days and nights were so surreal. I had breakfast when I got home and went straight to sleep, then dinner when I woke up. The other way round felt wrong, too: dinner when I got in and breakfast in the evening. I never slept enough. Ben's dogs would keep me up.

Grace's second bloods came back: she was in the early stages of sepsis. I had been right. And that was the feeling, the feeling I had trusted for years and years. That month, Mum got sick, and died in the October. I didn't spot it. No doctor would have: pancreatic cancer is almost asymptomatic. And yet. Shouldn't I have seen it? Shouldn't some instinct have told me about my own mother? I laid a hand across my stomach now and vowed to be in tune with Wally; to notice things. To act on them.

I looked at Jack in the living room, as I stood on my own in his kitchen.

'It's a bit unreal, isn't it?' Jack called out, his voice low and sexy.

I tried not to let that sway me. Not to let it mask the feeling of unease I held with me in his house.

Howard was kneading the soft material of Jack's jumper. Jack was holding his phone and I saw how it lit up his face.

'Unreal?' I prompted him.

'How happy we are.'

We talked often about our happiness, how lucky we were, how weird it was that we both loved to eat glacé cherries out of the pot and hated *The One Show*.

'Yes,' I said, unable to stop a small smile. I could feel myself being swayed, persuaded away from the darkness of that feeling and into the light.

He patted the sofa next to him and I went to him. He was looking at his phone – I saw Facebook Messenger open – and he quickly exited it. And that was it, I suppose. The gut feeling, so nebulous, became a concrete action. I only waited a few seconds before asking.

'What's in there?' I said.

'In where?' Jack turned to me.

'In those messages.'

'What messages?'

'Facebook Messenger. You had it open. And then, when I came within reading distance you – you shut it.'

'No, I didn't,' Jack said.

I was still sitting next to him, so close I could smell his deodorant, his washing powder. He smelt amazing, but it felt strange to be so close when the conversation had turned this way, like sitting stubbornly on a sun lounger even though it had started raining.

'You shut your messages,' I said. And then, like somebody in a soap opera, I held my palm out.

'What are you doing?' Jack said, his eyes darting from my hand to my face and back again.

'I want to see those messages.'

'I don't want you to,' he said. He shifted then, his body moving just slightly away from mine.

'Do you have something to hide?' I questioned, the things I'd been curious about adding up to more than the sum of their parts: the atrocity email, the JD nickname.

'No,' he said, looking straight at me. 'But I don't want my girlfriend to check my messages.'

'I need to see those messages,' I said, my tone urgent.

The past few weeks' worries had erupted like a volcano. It was then or never.

Jack picked his phone up where it lay, face down, on the sofa. He opened Facebook Messenger and angled it towards me. Seven messages were showing on the screen. I scanned them. A rugby season round robin. His mum saying thanks for coming. A mate sending a gif of a writer at a typewriter. It went on and on. Nothing. Nothing sinister. Nothing worrying. No women sending him a row of kisses. Nobody sending ominous articles they thought he should see. Nothing.

The relief was huge. Like an injection of happiness. It was nothing. He had shown me.

'God,' I said, closing my eyes. 'I'm so sorry. I . . .'

He shifted again, looking at me. His expression was

66

attentive. He was nicer than Ben – a nicer person. He wasn't defensive or unkind, merely interested. His eyes were running all over my face, a hand to his chin.

'You remember Ben,' I started. 'Right after I quit my job, I . . . I don't know. I started accusing him of things. Cheating. He never did. It was awful, the things I accused him of. Once, he took some spare boxers to the gym and I said it was because he was shagging someone there. It was . . .' I glanced at Jack, to check he was still listening. 'It was just . . . mad. I was certifiable.' I gave a tiny laugh.

'I see.' Jack's voice was quiet. 'Do you think it was about your mum?'

'Probably,' I said. 'I don't know. Yeah. It must have been. Or not doing medicine. The perfect storm. Feeling like I couldn't trust people . . . and not having anything to investigate.' I paused, feeling my eyes starting to prickle. 'So, I'm sorry. I love you more than I ever loved him and . . .'

Jack put his hand on my knee. He did it casually, like it was his own knee. 'Shh,' he said. His eyes met mine again. 'I will never, ever cheat on you,' he said. And then he lifted three fingers up. 'A Brownie salute,' he added.

I giggled. 'Were you a Brownie?'

'*No.* I was a manly Cub Scout.'

'Of course,' I said.

'Thank you – for telling me of your madness,' he said. 'I thought I was the only one.'

I especially loved that about him; that he understood

and tolerated neuroticism. I shifted closer to him. Instinctively, he lifted an arm to let me in, close to his chest.

'Can I tell you another thing?' I said. I was trying to cross the bridge, to get to know him. I didn't know how to get to know somebody faster. It felt urgent, my need to know him well, before Wally came. So I wanted to tell him one of my earliest memories.

'You are *more than* welcome to tell me another thing,' he said.

He was always happy to hear about me. He never nodded quickly, like Ben, urging me to get to the end of the story. He never said *yes, you've told me* or *I think you're overanalysing it*.

'When I was about five I used to think everyone with a big stomach was having a baby.' I could feel his body shaking slightly with laughter, Howard jiggling up and down.

'You are seriously cute,' he said, and he had the decency to look serious, even though his eyes were crinkled at their corners. 'So mums and dads were . . . ?'

'One of them had the baby. They got to choose.'

'How very equal. When did you realize?'

'At med school,' I joked, and he grinned.

'I like learning new Rachel-things,' he said.

That's what he called them. He had made a list, after we'd known each other for two months, and published it instead of a weekly column. It was called *50 Things I Love About My Girlfriend* and it began with: '1. The way she tilts her head back when she really laughs.' I had read it with tears in my eyes. Nobody had ever done such a thing for me.

'Let's do it,' Jack said softly, and I knew what he meant. 'This. Us.'

It was something to do with his open body language and his clear love for me that made me agree.

'I'll put my flat on the market.'

'You'll come and live with us?' His face cracked into a broad smile, his eyes crinkled. His body suddenly relaxed, as though he'd been tense for months.

And that was the thing that sealed it: the *us*. With him and Howard.

'Yes,' I said.

'But we'll have to move somewhere else,' he added. 'Somewhere new.'

Later, I kept thinking of Matt Douglas. I took my iPhone into the bath with me and googled him. There wasn't a single relevant result. Matt Douglas didn't seem to have done anything at all. No assault. No atrocity. But how could I tell Jack that?

I typed the full headline of the email into Google. I couldn't help myself. *No results found*, said Google.

Satisfied, I locked my phone and dropped it on to the floor beside the bath with a thud.

9

One year ago

'We can wait again,' I was saying to the boy. His leg was in a brace, his skin mottled and bruised, like it was covered in black mould. 'We can leave the brace on longer.'

'It weighs nine pounds,' he said. 'It's a pain in the arse. With no guarantee the bone will even knit.'

'Yes,' I said. 'But the alternative is . . .'

'I want it gone,' he said. 'Let's just get it over with. Not prolong the agony.'

'We'll speak to your mum. I shouldn't be discussing it with you alone.'

'Because I'm a child.'

I spread my hands wide. 'Yes,' I said honestly.

'You've taken almost all my bone out. Just get it over with,' he said, turning away from me.

'We'll see,' I said. I fussed with his bedding, even though it wasn't my job.

He turned to me. 'This is all pointless,' he said. 'And it's distracting.'

'Distracting?'

'All this faff trying to save my leg. All this time. All these resources. All these drugs. I don't need my leg saving. I see the prostheses. They're realistic enough. Let's get on with the main event.'

'Trust me. You're in good hands. No one's distracted.'

'I'm so scared, Rach.'

'I know.'

'Are you?'

'Scared?' I said.

He had a vase of sunflowers on his window sill. He wasn't supposed to have them in his room – too much risk of germs for the immunocompromised – but he'd picked them himself; he'd been so pleased with them that I had bent the rules for him.

'For me. Honestly.'

His eyes met mine. They were a navy blue, almost violet.

I answered honestly. 'Yes. I wish you didn't have it. I wish we could guarantee a cure. I wish your bones were knitting better.'

'Cut the leg off. At least that'll be over.'

'It'll feel differently when you're the other side of the operation,' I said. 'You can't take it back.'

'He who has a why to live can bear almost any how.'

'Who's that?'

'Nietzsche.'

'You're a nihilist now, are you?'

His face gave way to a smile. He'd discovered philosophy, during his treatment. He was forever spouting off about it. I enjoyed it, learning those brief nuggets whenever I spoke to him. It was like speaking to a prodigy or a prophet, sometimes.

'No. I just like that quote. Once the chemo's back underway, I'll feel better.'

He was right. We amputated two weeks later. The surgeon said he was a *surprisingly clear-sighted boy*. He seemed to know more than any of us.

I told Ben about the boy's amputation the day it happened. He didn't always listen to work stories; he used to say the same stock phrases to either commiserate or celebrate with me.

'Yeah, the one you looked up,' Ben said curtly. He often spoke like this. As though his aim was always to curb how much we chatted.

'Yeah. I don't know. With Mum and everything,' I said, 'it's like they're running in parallel.'

Mum had been diagnosed right before I had seen the boy for the first time. They were linked, in my mind. Her cancer and his. The boy's overprotective mum. My hands-off mum.

'You know what, Rach,' Ben said, his expression forthright but kind. 'You care too much.'

He switched on his PlayStation after that.

I said nothing further: he was right.

10

Present day

It was Jack's father's birthday the following weekend. We were on the motorway again. It felt as if Jack and I were stretched thin, like cheap cling film, pocked and wrinkled; trying to get to know each other, our families, all our friends, all at once, all before the baby came. We were in a relationship moving at speed, as if we had jumped on to a freight train.

I wish he'd told me the previous weekend that we'd be going again, or that I had known. But how could I know? I had to think twice about when Jack's birthday was, after all.

It was a five-hour drive, and it all fell to me. It was also, of course, five hours, regularly, of watching the windscreen wipers go back and forth – ruminating, which didn't help.

'The M74 again,' I said conversationally.

'Oh. God, I don't even know.'

'How can you not know that?' I said, looking across at him. He was grinning sheepishly. He was a typical non-driver. He didn't know anything. He didn't know which roads were which or how to get anywhere. Audrey and I used to have a thing about adults who

73

didn't drive. We called them kidults. We had a whole host of kidult criteria: people who didn't do their own washing or who couldn't use an iron. *Kidult*, Audrey would sometimes whisper to me when we were in the cinema watching a film featuring a man-child.

I privately wondered what she thought about Jack.

'You *did* pass your test, right?' I said to him.

'Yeah.'

'What happened? Did you never drive again?'

I frowned as I said it. Oban wasn't exactly London. He would have driven. He would've had to. It was so spread out.

'Was always pissed,' Jack said. He stretched his legs in front of him and put his arm around the back of my shoulders.

'Ah,' I said with a smile. 'I see.'

'I did drive, till I was in my twenties. A bit. But then I stopped. A few years ago. Now I'd have no idea.'

'Why did you stop?'

'Just got out of the habit.'

'Hmm. Well – we were on the M74 last weekend, is all,' I said.

'Okay, Mr Grumpy,' he smiled.

'Me?'

'Yeah.' He stretched lazily. His hand was still resting on my shoulder, his forearm on my back. It was nice; warm, even though a new layer of fat sat around the back of my waist. I had naively thought I would grow only a bump.

'It's just a long way. It would be nice to stay in.

Saturday mornings. Netflix and chill,' I said, looking sideways at him and laughing.

'Did you just say Netflix and chill?'

'Yes. I did.'

'You're almost thirty,' Jack said, but he was laughing, too; a soft, knowing laugh.

'Do you even know what it means?'

'Oh, I know what it means,' he said to me.

And I felt a rush of pleasure move up my body, and down my arms as they gripped the wheel in the driving rain. He could always do that to me.

'Why don't we Netflix and chill in Oban?' he suggested.

'Mmm.'

'It's home,' he said simply, the teasing flirtatious atmosphere evaporating.

And I understood that. He'd only lived in Newcastle since he'd met me. Seven months. Barely any time at all. He didn't even know where the Tyne was, not properly, not in the way locals always knew whether it was on their left or their right. He wasn't brought up by a native Geordie father who used to sit up and drink Newcastle Brown Ale. And he wasn't interested, either. He'd had a temporary placement here, and then he'd met me, and everything had changed. But he didn't love Newcastle; not the way I did, anyway. He thought it grubby, thought the locals strange. He never said, but I could see it in the way he looked at the city's underbelly: the hen and stag dos that flooded in every Saturday night. The Primark with the graffiti written on its side – *hope*, it said – which I quite liked. The virulent Thatcher-hating. The social housing. Oban was remote and rich and empty; the opposite of Newcastle, really.

'I'm an ex-pat. A nomad,' he said. 'A foreigner.'

'You're hardly a foreigner,' I said.

But maybe he was.

We lapsed into silence then. It was raining, as it always was on that motorway. He produced two Wagon Wheels.

'Are you willing to share?' I asked, changing the subject.

'Yes,' he said, slowly proffering one. 'You are very, very special.'

'Thank you,' I said seriously, taking it out of his hand.

'They're jam ones,' he told me. 'The best. Not so easy to find.'

'How many do you have?' I was giggling; he was forever producing Wagon Wheels.

'Approximately one hundred,' he said, yawning. 'There's a man on the checkouts in Tesco who thinks I have a lot of parties.'

We stopped at the services. He went in for coffees and came out with a doughnut cushion to relieve pregnancy piles, which he handed to me, unable to stop laughing. 'Saw this and thought of you,' he said, one hand covering an impish smile.

'Oh, thanks.' I took it from him. 'Why would you need one of these urgently in the services?'

'Who knows when piles can strike,' he laughed. And then he handed me a decaf coffee – my favourite

Starbucks Caramel Macchiato – and as I took it he turned the cup around. *Rachel is so cool* was written on its side in black marker pen.

'You told them to write that on there?' I said with a laugh.

'I told them that was my name. Very seriously,' he replied.

We were in Oban by 10 p.m.

Netflix and chill by eleven.

Jack's father, Tony, wanted to go on a walk for his birthday. His mum, Cynthia, was frantically finishing making three different batches of cupcakes. She was one of those people who were always *busy* doing non-essential things. The kind of person Kate and I secretly laughed at when we were run off our feet in our mid-twenties, me with medicine, she with tennis. Our successes had come so easily to us then; they had made us arrogant. Our mum had been a civil servant. Always working. We'd grown up with it. Once, soon after Mum's death, Kate had asked me if I wished it had been different; that we'd had a cuddly mother who picnicked with us in the garden, making dens. I'd said no. Not because it was true, but because I didn't want to talk about it, and Kate had stopped asking.

'We'd need to go quite soon, if we definitely are walking,' Tony said.

'Why didn't you say so earlier?' Cynthia hissed at him. '*Davey*,' she added.

They walked off huffily. I looked at Jack questioningly.

'He doesn't like new places,' Jack said. 'Or wearing his coat.'

'No?' I said, wanting to talk about him. I didn't even know his diagnosis. I had a few guesses in mind, but nothing seemed to fit.

'He just . . . he likes things the way they are,' Jack explained. 'No changes.'

'Was he always like this?'

'Yeah.' Jack leant his elbows against the kitchen counter. 'It was weird, growing up. To have such a . . . particular brother.'

'With my patients I always asked how the siblings were,' I said. 'They suffered too.'

'Bet you were a good doctor. I didn't really suffer,' Jack said. 'He is so lovely. So uninhibited. When he was fifteen he grabbed Mum's hand in the Post Office and asked why a woman had a moustache.' His cheeks dimpled. The same smile he reserved for me; reserved for people he loved. He reached over and covered the cakes up.

'What is his . . . ?'

'Autism, but other things too. He's childlike.'

Davey appeared then, thundering down the stairs with his heavy steps. He was lanky, with long, thin hands and feet. He had pale skin, dark red lips and bright blue eyes.

'Alright,' Jack said, gently, to him. 'Fancy a walk?'

'No.'

'We're going on a mission. A World of Warcraft mission.'

Davey looked at him warily. 'Really?' he said, his voice flat.

'Yeah, mate. Will you appoint me at your mission table?'

I turned to look at Jack, but he wasn't looking at me. For once he didn't care what I thought. He didn't care that World of Warcraft wasn't cool.

'Okay,' Davey said. 'Okay. If . . . is it a Garrison mission? Outside?'

'Of course,' Jack said. He smiled at Davey, and Davey looked at his feet.

'Okay,' Davey agreed, after a few moments.

'And then tonight – you know what it is?' Jack said.

'What?'

'It's bin night,' Jack said.

Davey loved taking the bins out. He pretended they were horses.

'Yes!' Davey exclaimed, raising his hands in the air.

I walked into the living room and surveyed the weather out of the mullioned front windows. They made the mist look even more oppressive, distorted it; made it look thicker or thinner, depending on the angle. Cynthia came into the living room where her walking boots were standing in the corner.

'Where is he?' she said to me. 'Not gazing at that bloody mole again? I've stopped him twice.'

'Jack?' I said.

'Yes, Jack. Bloody hypochondriac. What would doctors say it is – hysteria?'

'Health anxiety. OCD,' I replied.

I used to tell Audrey stories of the occasional hypochondriacs I saw while I was on a general medicine rotation. We used to laugh while telling each other we were being unprofessional. Audrey would tell me about her juiciest cases and I told her about the time a patient thought they had a 'widespread unexplained painful sensation' on their skin but they had actually just got sunburnt.

'Right, well. That.'

'Has he always been that way?' I said, trying to get closer to her, trying to understand Jack better.

Anxiety usually came from somewhere, especially obsessive checking. Some event. Mine had. It didn't take a psychiatrist to work it out. Mum's affair had taken root, somewhere in the recesses of my mind, like a persistent weed; a poisonous plant. It made me think things that weren't true. I had to resist them. I hoped one day Jack would tell me what his was. I thought about it sometimes when I watched him triple-check the gas was off.

'Jack? Oh, absolutely not. Most relaxed child you could meet,' she said.

The weather was drizzly, misty. But rather than detracting from the atmosphere of the place, it added to it. Oban was better in the mist. I felt safer shrouded in it.

We went to Loch Melfort. It was bright blue, even in the drizzle, with wisps of cloud that looked like pieces of torn-off candy floss floating above it. The Scottish heather purpled the grass; a two-tone shade of green-pink which seemed to shimmer in technicolour as we moved.

I had thought we were going to walk around the entire loch, until we arrived, and I realized it was more like a small sea. I could see some Scottish hills in the distance, but only just, and the water lapped and had a shoreline made of stone and shingle. It smelt like the sea, too: tangy.

A mansion stood casually at the edge of the loch. There was no division. No front garden. No fence. The land just sort of stumbled down to the shore, becoming thinner and lower, until it became water. I liked the informality of Scotland. I turned around, looking west of the house and back up the hill we'd just driven over and down. The evergreen trees rose up behind us. They looked bent, buckled, rising out of the hill in the mist; taller than they really were. The clouds were moving quickly, like a stop-motion film, and my face was getting wet as I watched them.

'Bonnie Scotland, hey?' Jack said to me, watching me looking.

I nodded.

It was just us: Jack, his parents, Davey and the dogs. They bounded off. Nobody else was around. I'd borrowed a mac from Jack's mum, given wordlessly to me in the car as we drove over.

Davey wandered off. He liked to be alone, muttering to himself. He kept turning around and miming at Jack; holding up imaginary World of Warcraft weapons and ducking behind trees.

Jack was laughing, shouting, 'Look out for the dragon spawn,' and, 'Bang!'

'Do you play?' I said. 'With Davey?'

'God, no. He's a control freak. But I educated myself about it. To – to reach him, I suppose. Speak his language.'

'So if Wally turns out to be a geek . . .'

'I'll be set.'

We lagged behind the others. Jack held my hand. It was warm, but clammy with rain. 'Look,' he said, pulling me over to a patch of undergrowth. It was a plant so red its shiny fruits looked like pomegranate seeds, bright in the grey weather.

'Mountain bearberry,' he said. He plucked a leaf and passed it to me. 'It's rare. And *very* Scottish.' He stood up straight and grinned.

'Nice,' I said. I reached inside the mac and put it in my own coat pocket, safe. The leaf's surface was rough against my fingers, like calloused skin.

We walked for a while in silence, Jack's hand in mine. He always reached for me when we were walking. No matter where we were. In the cheese aisle in Tesco. Walking fewer than ten steps from our car to a restaurant. He always held my hand.

Another couple was circling the loch, the opposite direction from us. An elderly couple.

We passed them. The woman – in a purple fleece – stared at Jack, her vivid blue eyes looking bright and fixated. There was a strange expression on her face. Disbelief, maybe? But then I blinked and soon they were behind us.

But then something happened. A few moments later, somebody shouted.

The elderly woman had turned around and was yelling, but the breeze was carrying her words away from us. She was motioning in the direction of me and Jack. Instinctively, I started back towards her, but Jack put an arm out to stop me. His grip on my wrist was too firm. But it wasn't only his grasp. It was other things. His body language, hunched over, as if bracing himself for a blow. His parents' body language, too. They'd stopped, stock-still. Only Davey looked as I felt: confused, wanting to find out what was happening. He looked at me, very briefly. He didn't often make eye contact. Cynthia reached out to stop him, just as Jack had done with me.

Jack's father, Tony, strode over to us. He'd been upbeat, pleased with his birthday presents, excited about the walk, but his entire demeanour had changed. His eyes were wide, his hands reaching towards us. 'Why is she here?' he said in a low voice to Jack.

The couple were still standing about twenty feet away, still watching us. The woman had stopped yelling, but she was pushing her hair behind her ears, looking anguished.

'I don't know. I don't know,' Jack said. 'I don't know where they live now. I didn't know. There's nobody here,' he said, his eyes darting around the loch. 'I thought it would be deserted.'

I'd never seen Jack like that. He was desperate, that's the only word I can think of to describe it. His hands were wringing and he kept looking at the woman.

Her jacket blended with the heather. Her hair was stringing across her face, sticking, wet with rain.

And then she seemed to decide something, and started back towards us. Almost running. Her long grey hair fanned out behind her as she stumbled across the grass and the heather. She kept losing her footing. I had been, too; it was spongy and unpredictable underfoot.

Jack's dad turned to him. He'd been in business his entire life – a whisky distillery – and I could see he was good in a crisis.

'How did they know?' he said.

Jack's eyes narrowed. He looked across at the woman still striding towards us. 'I don't think they did,' he said. 'Bad luck.'

'Let's get off the main bit,' Tony said to Jack, indicating a section of the loch path that was slightly more worn than the rest.

We walked unsteadily up the hill, turning away from the woman. I complied because I didn't know what else to do. Someone would explain it soon. Surely?

The woman stopped at the bottom of the slope we were climbing. Her husband was shouting at her, imploring her to leave us alone.

I don't think it was our moving up the hill that had put her off. No, she looked defeated in other ways, turning away from us, bringing the cuff of her fleece up to her mouth and sobbing into it.

And then, before striding off, she turned and yelled just one sentence, sounding tinny and reedy in the wind and the rain. 'How can you sleep at night?' she said, her accent thick and Scottish.

I couldn't tell who it was directed at. It was hurled at all of us, standing in a group against the wind.

She turned and walked away, and we made our way around the loch at a higher level, dodging wild animal droppings and feral plants whose firm stems tangled around our ankles.

'What was that?' I said to Jack in a low voice when she'd gone. I could still see her, in the distance, raking her hair back, shaking her head, bent against the wind.

His parents both turned around and stared at me. There was a strange expression on their features, unless I was imagining it. Realization, I think it was.

'Don't worry about it,' Jack said tightly.

'Who was she?'

Jack looked up at his parents. 'Just somebody who has a grudge against Dad.'

I blinked. I couldn't imagine belonging to such a family. Nobody would ever bear a grudge against my dad, with his penchant for unplugging every single electrical item before bed and tapping his weather barometer every morning.

I caught a look that passed between Jack and his father. I didn't know what it meant, but it seemed important.

'I bought some land near her house. Paid a developer. Then put a factory on it,' Tony said with an easy shrug. 'Factory fumes. Unspoilt Scottish countryside. Protecting the greenbelt. That sort of thing. It went to court. It got ugly. Didn't expect we'd ever see them again,' he said. He waved a hand over to where she'd come from. The tone of it was condescending, as though he felt she was a crazy hippy or something. I didn't think that at all, though. I couldn't get the image of her out of my mind. Her anguish. The way she'd raked her hair back off her face. It looked like grief, to me. I'd seen enough of it.

Cynthia was nodding vigorously. They all turned away from me then, and the wind and the rain were so fierce that it was impossible for me to ask any further questions. Only Davey continued to turn around and look at me. He was craning his neck, the vivid blue of his eyes catching the pale sunlight.

It was much later when I realized Jack had left marks on my wrist. I only spotted them in the shower.

'Did you know her, too?' I said to Jack later, when we were alone.

We were standing on the patio. The sun was setting beyond the pond. *The moat*, I teased, the first time I visited Jack, and he'd smiled sheepishly.

'Who?' Jack said, turning to me. He was drinking squash. His fingers left marks on the glass. He looked down. 'God, this is amazing,' he said. 'Strawberry squash.'

'The woman at the lake.'

'Ah. Yes.'

I waited.

He ran a hand through his hair. 'We were all involved in the legal stuff. It was really horrible. Dad basically carved up her land. For his factory. It was – she was very emotional.'

'With good reason,' I said.

'Yeah. But we created loads of jobs. In a recession,' Jack went on. 'It was really awful, though. I felt bad for her.'

'She recognized you.'

'Yeah. During the whole case, she really appealed to me. She thought I was sympathetic. Which I was. It was traumatic, for everyone.'

'It sounds it,' I said.

We lapsed into silence.

'Is it just Ben?' Jack said, looking sideways at me as he raised his glass to his lips.

'Just Ben?'

'Exes.' His tone was conversational. I must have looked wary, though, because he added, 'I just realized I'd never asked.'

'Yeah,' I said. 'Basically. I didn't have any real, proper boyfriends before him. We were young. You?'

'Hardly anyone serious. Nothing like this.'

'Like what?' I said, even though I knew I was fishing for compliments. I expected him to trot out the baby line; to say that was what made us more serious than any previous relationship.

But he didn't. 'Being in love,' he said, his eyes on me.

'You've never been in love before me?' I asked, unable to stop smiling.

'Not like this.' He looked at the ground, scuffed his socked foot on the concrete slab. 'You're awesome.'

The dogs padded outside into the chilled autumn sun.

'Are you a dog person?' I said, still smiling.

'Not really, no. We always had cats. I wanted more cats. They caught the rats for us, too.'

'Why the change?' I said, fingering Mozart's silky ear between my finger and thumb. I wondered idly if Wally would like doing that, when he was one, maybe. Or two.

'We . . . I don't know. We just got the dogs. A few years ago. For no reason.' He spoke quickly.

It was as though, for once, rather than keeping information back, he had told me too much.

We all stayed up too late. It was no issue for me; I'd given up trying to sleep entirely. My body felt squashed in bed, and I woke up almost every hour.

Even Davey stayed downstairs with us. He abandoned his mission for the night, though he was mostly silent. Nobody mentioned the elderly woman from the loch.

I came last at Trivial Pursuit. I wished Kate was there to laugh at me, rather than look aghast when I didn't know when the last Spanish election was. We had such poor general knowledge, Kate and I. I once confessed I couldn't point to Iraq on a map and she told me she didn't actually know how the sun came to rise.

Jack was amused, but I think embarrassed, too, because he shoehorned in the fact that I'd been a doctor.

'What kind?' Tony said. He was wearing reading glasses, and he looked over them at me.

He was hard-looking, in some ways. I wouldn't have

been surprised to find out he'd been a diplomat or a politician. He looked so serious and powerful. Greying hair and grooves in his forehead where he frowned. No laughter lines. He looked nothing like Jack.

'Paediatrics,' I said.

'And what are you now?'

I paused. Cynthia had lit candles and they were flickering around us, the light changing as they moved.

What was I? A woman, a girlfriend, a daughter, a sister, a friend. 'Nothing medical,' I settled for.

'Fair enough,' he said. 'Fair enough.' It was repeated more slowly that time, as he fished around in the clear plastic bag for the winning piece of pie. Audrey and I had nicknamed Jack's dad *the silverback*, though she'd never met him. He had to be in control, to be moving the conversation forward. 'NHS too troubled?' he said to me.

This was my party line. The long hours. The ever-increasing litigation. The antisocial shift patterns. The constant pressure. But, actually, not one of those things had ever bothered me.

'Yes,' I said. 'It wasn't enjoyable any more.'

I wanted to add everything else that had gone into me quitting. The events of that strange, chilly winter. The perfect storm. But I didn't. I couldn't possibly talk about my mother's death during a casual games night. To explain how I felt when I saw two parents, sharing the load, making tea.

The pangs of nostalgia. Let alone the rest.

*

Later, everyone had gone upstairs. I was getting my phone out of my handbag in the hallway. I liked to take it up to bed, to use the Wi-Fi and look at Facebook, to WhatsApp Kate back – she'd messaged, saying: *how are the bonnie Highlands?* – and Instagram my cosy feet in the bed with Jack. It was what made me happy, late at night, with him.

Davey was still in the living room at the end of the hallway. He liked to blow the candles out. It was one of his things.

The living room was still lit, amber, as he moved around, and I could see his shadow projected against the far wall. His hair was moving as he leant down to blow another flame out. He had huge, unruly hair. He raked his fingers through it so much that it was almost always standing on end. I could only really see his outline in the darkness, black against the orange backdrop, but I saw him raise his arm, then a shadow of movement.

I kept looking, and he did it again. He was beckoning to me.

I walked along the hallway and down the three steps into the living room. Only two candles remained lit. One tall church candle sitting on the mantelpiece, and a tea light in a lantern on the window sill. The room was almost in complete darkness. Davey was standing in the centre. He was tall, like Jack, but lanky, not broad.

He was still beckoning to me to come closer. I inched slowly towards him in the darkness.

'You don't know, do you?' he said. His eyes were downcast, looking at the dusty red rug.

I was clutching my phone, and I pressed the 'home' button so it lit up the living room and I could look at him carefully. It changed his face from a burnished, candlelit orange to a spooky, light blue-green. A portrait hung on the wall behind him, above the mantelpiece. An ancestor. A past Ross. They came from old money. A whisky distillery started in Victorian times, passed down and grown through the generations.

'Know what?' I said to Davey, trying not to look at the creepy portrait behind him, its face so like Jack's. The heavy brow. The serious eyes. The broad shoulders.

Davey's eyes were downcast. He rarely looked at anybody, but especially not at that moment.

'What happened,' he said. 'To upset that woman.'

'The woman at the loch?'

I was looking at him, imploring him to look up at me. It was the most coherent I had ever known him be.

He ignored me. He strode suddenly across the room and blew out the candle on the mantelpiece. My phone's light went out, and the darkness rushed in, the only illumination coming from the tea light on the sill, reflected in the window so that there were two tiny flames, darting unpredictably in the night.

'What happened?' I said.

Davey ignored me. He blew out the final candle. Everything went black.

'About the death,' he said. 'About what . . . Jack planned.'

He left the room as soon as he'd said it. I called after him softly, but he didn't stop. I heard his feet on the stairs and the squeak of his door handle, and I was alone.

I raced up to Jack's bedroom as if I was being chased. Davey's door was closed; the sound of explosions came from within. Jack was in bed, sitting up, with *How to Be a Woman* by Caitlin Moran in his hands.

'Davey just said something.'

Jack folded a page down, but didn't look concerned. 'Yeah?' he said, starting to close the book.

'About that woman.'

'What woman?' Jack said, though he was blushing, the tips of his ears turning pink.

'He said that woman was shouting because of what happened. Because somebody died. And then he said . . .' I paused. 'That you had a plan.' I paraphrased it deliberately.

Jack's hands stilled. The book stayed half open in them. He was staring at me. 'God,' he said. 'Sorry. He used to scare guests sometimes. My friends.'

'What did he . . . what did he mean?'

'He meant nothing, Rach. He doesn't know . . . he doesn't know what he's saying. He doesn't make any sense.'

'Really?' I said. I thought back. It was true that Davey had looked vague. Besides, how often was he lucid? Hardly ever.

I got undressed and slipped into bed. Jack spooned

me into him, as he always did, and I reached my hand out into the cold to turn off the light.

I closed my eyes, pretending to sleep. After a few minutes, Jack's breathing became even and heavy. Beyond us there was no noise at all. Nothing. No distant road sounds. No neighbours. The silence seemed heavy against my ears.

And then I heard something. A scream. A fox. It sounded like a child's cry in the night.

I knew I'd have to visit Davey in his room to ask him what he had meant. I couldn't resist probing, and it was the only way to see him. He only came out when something was arranged.

So the next morning, I went upstairs on the pretence of pregnancy sickness, but stopped just outside Davey's bedroom.

I could hear explosions from within. Spaceship sounds. His guffaws. I knocked on the door and pushed it open slowly. It was dark. The curtains were closed.

He didn't look up at all. Didn't move. Didn't acknowledge me.

'Davey,' I said, looking over my shoulder quickly. 'Davey.'

He ignored me. I winced, standing a few feet away from him, my arms across my body self-consciously. His room was huge, and full of things. His different obsessions. Space. Computer games. There were photographs, magazine clippings, all over the walls.

He must have finished something, because his games

console went quiet and he moved his gaze. He wasn't quite looking at me, but he was no longer looking at the screen, either. He was wearing tracksuit bottoms, a T-shirt and no socks. I'd not seen him so casual before.

'I wanted to know . . . when you and I were downstairs last night . . . what did you mean?' I stammered on my words.

He didn't say anything, and I advanced slightly further into the room. 'Sorry, Davey – but when you said about what Jack planned? What did you mean?' I kept my voice low, tried to speak quickly. I'd just find out, then I'd leave again.

As soon as I said Jack's name, Davey's head turned quickly towards me. His eyes locked on to mine for the briefest of seconds. And then he whispered, 'I'm in trouble.'

'No, Davey, no. You're not in trouble.'

'Trouble,' he whispered again. And then he stood up, his hands over his ears, and shouted, 'I can't play if I get in trouble any more.'

'No, I just wanted –'

'Trouble,' Davey yelled. He strode across his room and covered his games console with his hands.

And then I heard an icy cold voice behind me. 'What are you doing?'

I turned. It was Jack.

'Oh, I just – I was just paying a visit,' I gabbled.

Jack was holding an orange drink. He gestured to it. 'For your morning sickness. Vitamins.' His face was furious. 'Why are you in here?'

He walked over to Davey and knelt down, trying to catch his eye. 'You're not in trouble, mate,' he said softly. 'No trouble at all. None whatsoever.'

Davey nodded quickly, seeming appeased, and sat back down on his bed. I backed out of the room slowly, walking down the hall to Jack's room, my cheeks burning.

Jack arrived after a few minutes. He didn't say anything, just opened the door and held his hands out, palms up, as if to say: *so?*

'I'm really sorry,' I said. 'I was just –'

'You can't do that,' he cut me off. 'You can't go and just chat to him. Go into his space. He can't . . . it's not cool with him.'

'I'm sorry,' I said again. 'I know.'

He placed the drink on the chest of drawers and said nothing more. I looked up at him from my position on the bed. He hadn't heard. I exhaled slowly through my nose. He didn't know what I'd been asking him. That I'd been snooping. I lay down on the bed, saying nothing more.

I mustn't do that again.

11

I listened to the tick of the clock on the wall, the soft whir of my computer as it started up. I finished the letter I'd begun late in the afternoon yesterday and put it on my managing partner's chair. He hated that, but he forgot things otherwise, and they became buried in the books and court papers and correspondence that constantly littered his desk. It wouldn't have been tolerated in hospital, that kind of disorganization.

'Rachel,' he said, striding in.

His name was Paul, but he liked me to call him Mr Grint. I jumped. I'd been listening to a medical podcast through my headphones and felt guilty, even though it was still before nine. He glanced dismissively at me before picking up the letter and reading through it.

'No, no,' he said, holding it up and coming over to me. 'I dictated *hyperglycaemic*.'

'Yes,' I said.

'You've written *hypo* – please sort it.'

I scanned the letter: *The Claimant suffers from ongoing episodes of hypoglycaemia and has to keep a chocolate bar on her at all times.*

I looked across at Paul. He was scrolling through his phone, sighing impatiently as his ancient computer sprang to life. He never switched it off, because he said it took too long to start up. He wiggled the mouse and exhaled loudly again.

I stared back down at the letter. It was definitely correct. I stood up, my feet feeling uncomfortable in my heels, then sat down again. No, Paul was wrong – I stood up again – and I should tell him.

'It's *hypo*,' I said, walking over to him and trying to find a spot for the letter on his desk. '*Hypo* means below.'

'No. That's *hyper*.'

I stared at him.

'A hypochondriac,' he said to me, 'is somebody who's concerned about their health – overly concerned. *Hypo*. Too much.'

'*Hypo* means below and *chondria* means the stomach. Hypochondria refers to the anxious feeling you get in the pit of your stomach. *Hypo* blood pressure is too low and *hyper* – as in hyperactive – is too high. I promise it's *hypo*,' I said. I tried to make an apologetic face. I was out of line, of course I was, but at least he wouldn't look like an idiot to anybody but me.

'Right, right,' he said, blinking. His eyebrows were black, with fine white lines threaded through them. 'You've got a medical background, right?'

'Right,' I said, as if *medical background* could sum up all those years: the mornings feeling the stomach acid slosh around my belly on the way to the hardest exams I'd ever sat; nightshifts in Preston because it was apparently in the Manchester deanery; the births and the deaths, and the laughs over toast in the kitchen.

'Nursing, was it?' he said.

I chose not to answer. The less said, the better.

He passed the letter back to me. He hadn't signed it. I frowned.

'My reference is incorrect,' he said. 'It's PG1. There's another PG here.'

I resisted rolling my eyes. Did it really matter?

'Redo it, please,' he said crisply, then typed something into his timesheet.

We went to the Hoppings that evening. It was a fairground on the Town Moor. It came late that year, mid-October, but the sun was hot and shining; an eerie displaced summer's day in the autumn.

Kate and I had been to the fair every autumn as children. I could remember Mum, one year, proffering me some pink candy floss on a stick. Kate had been obsessed with the toffee apples – one of her early obsessions – and had tried to make them, disastrously, when she was fourteen.

We arrived late, as the sun was setting, orange slanting beams travelling across the grass. We had spent the early evening after work in the bath together; one of our favourite places to be. Jack was reading a police procedural. He read them voraciously. I could smell that old-book smell as the steam heated it. I read a magazine to him, and we laughed at the advice columns and the incorrect medical recommendations.

'This book is irritating,' he had said. 'The interviewing officer can't be the investigating officer.' He huffed and put the book down by the side of the bath, its spine creaking as he did so.

It wasn't that sentence that made me start and look at him; it was the one which followed.

'I know because of all the court reporting,' he said quickly. 'Outside Oban. Petty thefts.' It was the pace of it. It seemed, somehow, that the sentence had been preceded by a bundle of rushed, panicked thoughts.

I was still thinking about what he'd said when, at the Hoppings, he turned to me and said, 'That doesn't look safe,' pointing upwards.

A fairground ride loomed above us. Chairs were suspended on the end of metal sticks, whirling around a central pole. As the ride slowed to a stop they drifted back to the centre, then out again as it sped up, like an umbrella being opened and closed.

'I'm sure it's been tested,' I said.

'Hmm.' Jack's brow creased as he studied it. The chairs began their descent again, and he flinched.

'I never saw anybody admitted to A&E due to fairground rides,' I said.

'No?'

'Never,' I smiled.

His eyes met mine. We stared at each other for too long, standing there in the sun. We were always doing that. Our mouths had stopped speaking but our eyes hadn't.

A stall owner held a ball out to us. His skin was burnished brown from the long, dry summer we'd had. He was ageless; somewhere between twenty-five and fifty.

Jack sidestepped him, waving a dismissive hand, but grabbed my wrist lightly with the other. He glanced back, over his shoulder, twice.

'So you don't want to go on rides or throw balls at coconuts?' I said.

It was common, though, this retiring behaviour. He was shy, would leave a shop if somebody spoke to him.

Jack looked across the fields, the grass vibrant after all the rain. 'Let's just walk,' he murmured. 'It's my favourite thing to do. Just wander around with you.' He reached for my hand.

I took a selfie of us. Jack pulled a horrendous face, poking his bottom lip out.

'You wonder why you always turn up on Facebook tags looking like an idiot,' I said, zooming in on the photograph and holding it up.

'I can't help it. It's like my face transforms into an ogre's. Look,' he said, pulling his phone out and opening Facebook. He used it a lot. He liked to post wordy updates. He shared feminist articles occasionally, which I loved. He was often tagging me in articles about couples; the secrets of long-lasting marriages, the hidden psychology behind sleeping positions. He was so very public, so open, about us. So proud.

He passed me his phone and pointed to a photograph of him. I'd already seen it, earlier that day, but didn't say. I liked checking his social media, reading all of his most interesting thoughts. He was with two other *City Lights* writers. They were both smiling normally. Jack looked hunched, and he was grimacing. He took his phone back as soon as I'd looked, plucking it from my hands.

'What a catch. Look at me, though. A balloon,' I said. Even my hands were fatter, I was sure of it. My boobs definitely were; they were climbing up cup sizes at an alarming rate.

'You're gorgeous. *Blooming*. Can you send me on a smiling course? Before Wally comes?'

'I love your smile,' I said to him. 'You are lovely.'

Two women were sitting cross-legged in front of us, playing with a giant Jenga tower on the grass. They were sitting on their jumpers. The sky was a lavender colour as the sun set, and I shivered as a warm breeze moved across the exposed skin on my shoulders. This could be the last warm day of the year, I thought, as I watched a teenager stride past us in tiny denim shorts. And then, the autumn and winter. I used to be obsessed with the seasons, when I was in school, always knowing what time it would get dark and when the days would start lengthening again. But then med school happened and then junior doctoring, when my days and nights seemed always inverted. And now here I was, barely even half aware what month it was.

'Miss – bet you've got a right good aim,' somebody called out to us as we passed their stall. His accent was somewhere between Irish and Geordie; the 'r's harsh but the vowels lilting.

Jack jumped. Well, not jumped exactly. Started.

'Oh, I really haven't,' I said with a laugh, remembering

netball games in school where teammates tried to stop me getting hold of the ball.

'You can't even get your socks in the washing basket,' Jack said with a sly smile towards me.

'It's shooting, though,' I said, 'not throwing. Look.'

'Ah,' Jack said, stopping and glancing at the stall. 'No way.'

He appraised the stand. He looked outdoorsy, posh, in his khaki top, his sunglasses pushed back into his hair.

'I want a go,' I said to him.

'No way,' he echoed, a hard edge to his voice.

I looked at him then. His face was pale. Grey pallor, we called it at work. A very specific shade.

'Are you alright?' I asked him, my eyes running over the beads of sweat on his upper lip that he self-consciously wiped away.

'Yeah, I just don't like guns,' he said.

'A person with anxiety who doesn't like guns: you're hardly the first,' I said with a little laugh.

'Maybe not.'

'Why don't you like them?'

He paused then. It was infinitesimal. I only noticed his hesitation because I was watching closely.

'Because they're dangerous,' he said, after a few moments.

'Not those little pellet guns,' I said, to which he said nothing. 'Have you ever used one?'

'Yeah – clay pigeons. I'm posh, aren't I?' He gave a self-deprecating shrug.

'Oh yes, of course. I forgot you people go shooting with Mallory and the dogs.'

'*Mallory?* Who's Mallory?' he asked. His mouth was open but the edges were turned up, a tableau of a laugh.

'Somebody generically posh.'

'Of course. I had a target practice tree. I could hit it from anywhere in the garden by the end of uni.'

'But now you're afraid.'

'Yeah. Well. Practising on that tree was a mistake.' His tone was dark, as bitter and black as tar.

'What? Why?'

'It used to scare Davey,' he said curtly.

'But why was it a *mistake*?'

Jack didn't answer. He was still eyeing the stall, though he had more colour in his cheeks. I frowned. He wasn't making any sense.

'What changed?' I prodded again. 'To make you anxious?'

His arm came around my shoulders, his fingers rubbing my bare skin. Immediately, goosebumps appeared all over my body, and I hoped he wouldn't notice.

'I don't know. Life. Anyway. Choose another stall. What shall we try to win? You want a big cuddly toy and a fish in a bag?' he said, turning his head to look at me.

'No, I just want you,' I said, feeling bold.

It should have been romantic, but he pulled his Facebook photograph face. Stooped over, a sneer across his features.

'You want this?' he said, still grimacing.

'Yes,' I said.

We left the fairground later, without looking back.

That night, I was reaching for a tea bag, the sound of the kettle drowning out the television in the living room, when the noise of Howard coming through his cat flap startled me. I glanced up and caught the expression on my face in the blackened kitchen window.

It was the same look, I realized, seeing my pale complexion, my round, scared eyes.

The same expression Jack had worn when he saw the guns.

Fear.

12

We were at my sister's, just outside the city centre. Kate had been all over the world playing tennis, until recently. Her rank had been 608 at its best, but it had stopped climbing. She just couldn't win the matches, once she'd reached that high. She came back over the summer; thirty and ready to give up.

'Those who can't . . . coach,' she said drily, the first night she was back. She'd been fierce when she was striving. She played a match the day after Mum's funeral, and won. I had often wondered if she felt bad for being away so much during Mum's illness, but I could never ask.

The kitchen television was on, set to an obscure sports channel. The Valencia Open was playing.

There was a strange expression on Kate's face as she was following the television. She used to watch hours and hours of her own matches back. Dad would record them for her.

She and her husband, Mez, had opened a mushroom farm when she came home; a business venture my dad found endlessly amusing. Mez was convinced it would make them a fortune. They were growing the mushrooms in their garage. Mum would've hated it, Kate and I privately agreed. She didn't like mess.

We were sitting around Kate's kitchen table.

'I've got hold of a film. The new James Bond. The one that's showing in the cinema,' Dad said. He looked slyly across at me and winked.

He was forever trying to cut corners. He loved frugality, said he felt like he was beating *the system*. He once posted a McDonald's coupon through my door before his holiday because he wouldn't be able to use it in time. He'd got worse, since Mum died last year.

Sometimes, I still expected her to be there when I went over to their central Newcastle house with the little red front door, where the rooms were full of her stuff that Dad hadn't yet thrown away. Sometimes, I felt dread that Mum would have baulked at my secretarial job, at my unplanned pregnancy. But then, at other moments, I felt hopeful as I remembered how much we had both loved watching *One Born Every Minute* together, and I'd feel a wave of loss – like I'd been picked up and transported somewhere alien and desolate.

'Great,' Jack said. I caught his eye. He hated James Bond. Said it was misogynistic. 'The women end up dead or silenced,' he would say to me. 'What a load of crap.'

Jack's body language – a jiggling leg, wild eyes – betrayed his anxiety: he was, after all, the quite new boyfriend who had got me pregnant. Dad kept looking at him, bemused. Jack was still on his best behaviour at these gatherings. Or so I thought, anyway.

'I've downloaded it. It's not *legitimate*. It's a screener copy,' Dad said, leaning in dramatically. 'It's still in the cinema.'

He was delighted with his thrift and I was momentarily embarrassed. At Jack's, we had posh cheeses, dessert wines, home-made chutneys. When we were with my family, we watched illegally downloaded movies and sat around the kitchen table underneath a fluorescent strip light. Ambient it was not. I wondered what Jack thought. I wondered how we'd raise Wally; whether he might end up at a boarding school far away, keeping company with landed Scottish gentry.

'I was hoping to make it another tradition,' Dad declared.

Dad, Kate and I had a Tuesday tradition of going out for pudding. One night, after Mum died and everything felt hard, we sat down and decided that Tuesdays were the most rubbish day of all, and we decided to try to do something about it. We went out for dessert, that first Tuesday, and we'd been trying to do it weekly ever since.

But he was a creature of habit, our dad, so he was always looking for more. Let's start Friday Films, he would say, or Saturday Salad, and we'd roll our eyes at him.

'Let's not watch Bond,' Kate said to Dad. 'We never speak to each other. And I've seen every recent movie.'

'She really has,' Mez said.

Mez was one of my favourite people. The only person who'd never pushed me about all the changes that had happened after Mum died: leaving medicine, breaking up with Ben, moving into my own flat. There was no judgement from him, and I loved him for it. He was pale, with dark eyes that always looked slightly moody.

'Trivial Pursuit?' Kate said. 'We got a new one.'

I barely suppressed a smile. Kate was an obsessive. She had been fixated with tennis, of course, but also computer science and knitting for a while. Whittling wood, for a time after that. Yoga three times a week for two straight months, then never again. Now, this autumn, it was Words with Friends and Trivial Pursuit. Soon they would rotate, and it would be badminton, pontoon and boules. Or flower arranging, or cycling.

'You sure you're ready to embarrass yourself in front of Jack Ross?' I said, looking sideways at him.

'I am totally ready,' she said.

She always addressed Jack in that way: *Jack Ross, Journalist*. She'd said it the first time I told her about him.

She was wearing loads of gold bangles that slid down her arm as she retrieved the game board. She was often wearing such things now. Things she couldn't wear before.

'Are we still on for meeting your parents next weekend?' Dad said. Ice cubes clinked in his glass as he lifted it. Behind him sat a set of weighing scales. He still weighed his pasta portions. Kate once called him *anal personified*.

I cringed. I hadn't forgotten Dad's insistence he meet Jack's family once he'd got over the shock of me being pregnant, but I had tried to deflect it – did our families really need to meet? – although, it seemed, both sides wanted to. A polite 'Oh yes, you should come up to Oban and stay', proffered through Jack, had, somehow, become firm plans. Dad was needier now than he had been previously. Mum had been his social life, however much they had annoyed each other. And so now, cursory gestures loomed large and Dad always took people up on them.

Jack gave me a sidelong glance. 'Yes,' he said. 'I'll double-check, but yes. They mentioned it last weekend.' His voice was overly keen. He sounded false.

He had said to me, the day before meeting my dad for the first time, 'What if I totally mess this up?'

'What's the worst that can happen?' I had said.

'He hates me and we cause a *family rift* and everyone needs therapy,' Jack had said immediately. He'd then looked at me, sheepish. 'Sorry. I'm too good at worst-case scenarios.'

'You are,' I had agreed.

'I mean – you are *it*,' he'd said. 'And the pressure . . .'

'What do you mean "I am *it*"?' I'd said, though a smile was beginning to slide over my features.

He had looked at me directly. 'I am so . . . I have never . . .'

'What?'

'I'm so in love with you. It's insane,' he'd said, bringing his hands up in front of him. 'I know I sound like a complete prat, but there it is.'

I smiled now at the memory, watching him nod earnestly at my dad.

'They've got all sorts of plans,' Jack said. 'Oban tours. The lot.' He was drumming his fingers nervously on the table.

'Best take your walking trousers,' Kate said with a smile.

It was our favourite family story – that once, Dad bought walking trousers that zipped off at the knee, and only bought three-quarters of them. He had to go back to Matalan for the last shin, much to our amusement. *They didn't make me pay for it, but I did have to present my Matalan card*, he'd said proudly.

'Want to come?' I said to Kate. I threw her a meaningful look.

We were trying to ensure Dad didn't feel like a single parent; that he wasn't alone too much.

'Hell, yes,' she said, lining up the counters and getting the dice out. 'I want to watch this weird parental blind date play out,' she added, which made me laugh.

One of Kate's long-standing obsessions was people. She loved to people watch. The tennis world was brilliant for pop psychology, she'd once said.

'You're like the disgraced sister,' she said.

'Disgraced?'

'Yeah, you know. Illegitimate, accidental child and all of that.' Her gaze travelled to my stomach.

I knew she was only joking.

The thing was, we told everyone it was an accident, but it wasn't. I was a doctor. It was 2.5 per cent. That was the percentage chance of pregnancy on a one-off: too high if you didn't want to get pregnant. But nevertheless, we weren't stupid, or reckless. We *decided*.

Jack's tongue was on my thigh back in June; the longest day of the year. The sky was still a pale pink outside, even though it was past ten thirty. The night was warm, Jack's breath hot and ticklish. We should've stopped. He murmured about condoms but we were all out.

And so I said the thing I'll always remember. The thing that made Wally: 'A baby with you wouldn't be the worst thing.' I had loved him so much, it had felt like it was overflowing inside me.

Jack had moved up my body, met my eyes. 'I entirely agree,' he had said.

That was that.

No, we weren't stupid. Or maybe we were, but not in the way people thought.

'Illegitimate. I'll have to marry her, then,' Jack said, reaching over and taking my hand.

Kate grinned at me across the table. I could see the happiness on her face, in the raise of her eyebrows, in the way her broad smile showed her bottom and top rows of teeth excitedly.

Jack loved me. That much was obvious. It was so simple; he was so simple in his love for me.

'Mum would've liked you,' Dad said, raising his glass to Jack, and I felt happiness bloom across my chest.

'Right,' Kate said, smiling. She pulled a question out, and fired it at Jack. 'Mr Ross . . .'

'We haven't even started yet,' I said, trying to snatch the card from her hand.

'Mr Ross,' she said, dodging me. 'History, geography . . .'

'The yellow ones,' he said. 'I like the yellow ones.'

'Which country suffered a major earthquake in January 2010?'

'God . . . er.' He paused.

I turned to Jack in surprise. I didn't read the news enough. I didn't watch it at all. I watched reruns of *Friends* after work. But even I knew that. And Jack was a *travel journalist*. Surely he knew? How could he not?

Kate was looking at Jack too. 'I'll give you a clue . . . it begins with "h" and ends with "i" . . .'

Jack was staring down at his hands. I looked back at Kate. I mouthed *Haiti?* at her, and she nodded quickly.

'Are you having a brain fade?' I said kindly to Jack. I'd had them all the time in early pregnancy. I'd had a cheque returned because I had dated it 1995. I was taking a note of a meeting with my manager and had forgotten completely what it was about and had to ask. It was like losing my mind. I had sympathy for those on-the-spot moments in a way I never had before.

Jack looked across at me. I expected his expression to be grateful, maybe embarrassed. But there was anger in those eyes. It disappeared as soon as mine locked on to his, though I was sure I had seen it.

'I was –' he said, then stopped himself.

'You were?'

'I don't know the answer,' he said stiffly. 'Sorry.'

'It was Haiti,' Kate said.

'I was . . .' he said again.

'What?' I said, turning to Jack.

He laid his hand on the table. No. He didn't lay it. He banged it. Slapped it. It disturbed Dad's gin and tonic,

112

which jumped very slightly across the coaster with a chink.

'I . . .' I began, but I couldn't think of anything to say.

'You what?' Mez said to Jack. His eyes were narrowed. He had shadows underneath them, as if he was always wearing smudged eyeliner. He looked more like an ageing rock star than the mushroom farmer he was. He was principled, but in a highly strung way. He was always sharing political articles on Facebook. He stood up to bigots when watching Newcastle United. Almost got himself in fights a lot. That kind of thing.

So, of course, it was Mez who pushed it. And there was no one worse to do so. Dad and Kate were staring down into their laps, embarrassed. Dad ran a finger over the rim of his gin and tonic until it made a high-pitched humming sound.

'Nothing,' Jack said. 'Nothing.'

'Right. Well – no need for rudeness.'

'Yeah.'

'Haiti. Biggest disaster of the year,' Mez said, spurred on by Jack's sullen response. 'Best look that up.'

'You don't know,' Jack said to Mez, 'why someone might not know something.'

'Seriously, mate, there's no need for attitude.'

'No attitude here,' Jack said, slapping both of his hands down on the table again.

Nobody spoke for a few seconds after that. It was excruciating.

My phone beeped, dispelling the atmosphere. It was Amrit: could I chat to him soon, he missed me? I ignored it. It wasn't his fault, but every time I saw his name, I remembered. The expression on my consultant's face. The frost that crunched underfoot as I thought, over and over again, *what have I done?* Driving away from the hospital for the last time.

Jack ignored us, necking his lemonade and helping himself to another. Dad's eyes tracked him as he moved across the kitchen. I tried to catch Dad's gaze. To apologize. For everything. For Mum dying. For leaving medicine. For Ben. For getting pregnant. He'd been my confidant, all that year, but I'd leant on him too much; put him through too many traumas. He didn't meet my eyes, though, didn't seem to want to.

We played for real after that. The atmosphere dissipated, but it didn't go completely, like the ever-present mists in Oban.

Mez watered the mushrooms after the game. I went with him. I had always liked him. Maybe more than I liked Kate.

They were still flirtatious, Mez and Kate; still laughed at each other's jokes, never jibed at each other in company. A few weeks before Ben and I broke up, we went for Chinese with them both. While we were trying to choose between prawn toast and crispy duck, Mez leant over and planted a kiss on the side of Kate's shoulder. I was transfixed, staring at the damp shining mark on her skin, embarrassed to be privy to such a gesture. That was one of the things that attracted me to Jack: I wanted, shamelessly, what they had.

'God,' I said. 'I haven't seen them since they were planted.' They were spectacular. They were growing in his garage, which he was in the process of extending. The light was dim and the mushrooms were in six rows, on top of each other like bunk beds. Their white tops loomed out of the soil like bright eyeballs, the darker stems almost invisible in the gloom. They were growing them in old coffee grounds. Upcycling, Mez called it. Then selling them as 'grow your own' gifts.

'I know – my babies. Shame they bloody need watering all the time. It's quite hard work,' he murmured. 'Kate said you had a syringe trick.'

'Me? Yeah,' I said.

He handed me a syringe I had given to her years ago, for getting the lemon into lemon drizzle cake. The needle had been removed, but the rest was just how I remembered. A blue end. The mls in black.

I filled it with water at the sink, then pointed it in the air, tapped it, and pressed the end to dispel the air that had floated to the top.

'Jesus, this is like *Trainspotting*,' Mez said.

'Just getting the air out,' I murmured. Then I took it to the mushroom bed and injected it, in four sites around the mushroom. 'Easy,' I said. 'It'll get into the soil more deeply.'

Mez was looking at me in that way people sometimes did when I did something medical; when I sewed a hole in a coat using a perfect interrupted stitching pattern, because the previous day I had used the same method on somebody's arm. When I asked if Kate's shoulder pain was radiating and accompanied by nausea. When I inspected people's moles at parties, close up, looking for the irregular edges. When I had known Mum's exact drug doses off the top of my head.

'You're a regular hipster,' I said, reaching out and fingering a particularly long mushroom whose top was protruding out into the aisle. It was silken, warm. The room smelt of peat and dank.

'I know. Planning on starting to brew craft beer next,' Mez said, turning to me and flashing me a white smile.

'Beehive on your rooftop garden?'

'Maybe,' he said. He turned a red lamp on. 'You alright, anyway? Just come for the watering fun?' He grabbed a metal can and started trickling water in. It sounded soft and pleasant, like a nearby stream.

'I . . .' I said, and then I stopped. I looked at Mez. He'd stopped pouring, was looking at me. I could only see the white of his eyeballs. 'Things with Jack are . . .'

And that's as far as I got. Any further would have made it real. I couldn't go on. But I didn't need to.

'I know,' he said. 'I can tell.'

'I don't know him,' I said. 'And his baby is . . . already here, really.'

Mez nodded. He was still looking at me with that direct gaze. 'I'm glad you said something,' he said. 'Do you trust him?'

I frowned. Why did he go there so quickly?

'I don't know,' I said. 'Why?'

'I only ask because I don't.'

'Oh.' I couldn't say anything else.

Tears and fear and sadness were budding in my throat, growing and blooming like the mushrooms that surrounded us. Multiplying exponentially. Filling the gaps. Audrey thought I was fragile. Mad, even. Imagining things. But Mez agreed with my doubts. Who was right? I thought about it, there in the gloom of the garage. Audrey was more sensible. Less hot-headed. I trusted her more.

'Because of . . .' I trailed off.

Mez said nothing, but he heaved a small, sad sigh. He came and stood closer to me, his cold hand on my shoulder.

'What?' I said.

The private feeling of foreboding I held in my stomach, next to Wally, reared up again. Change was thundering along towards me. Everything that happened that autumn seemed to happen so fast. The relationship. The pregnancy. Like my life was a black-and-white silent film on double speed.

'I would never have said something if you hadn't, but I saw him,' Mez said. 'He was . . . he was yelling at someone.'

'What? When?'

'Last week. I was on Millennium Bridge. He was in that Starbucks nearby. He stormed off.'

'Who was he yelling at?'

'A man.'

'Why didn't you ask him?'

'He was pretty far away,' Mez said. 'I saw him through two windows.' He shaped his hands into a square. 'As I was walking. I couldn't see him properly. I don't know. It was really weird, Rach. I wish you could've seen it.'

'What date? I'll ask him.'

'I don't bloody know the date,' he said with a laugh, and that lightened the tone, and I was thankful for it. 'Last week. He should know, shouldn't he? How often does he yell at people?'

The door at the back of the garage creaked open and I saw Kate's blonde hair shining in the hallway lamplight.

She eased the door open further. 'You alright?' she said. 'You've been ages.'

'Filling her in on Jack,' Mez said, turning away and watering another trough.

'Oh – what was all that earlier?' Kate said, gesturing with her thumb behind her. She was wearing a hammered silver ring.

The door closed softly and we were in darkness again.

'I don't know,' I said tightly.

'I was telling her what I saw on the bridge,' Mez said.

'I thought of something else,' Kate said, and she moved towards him, putting her hand on his arm.

I raised my eyebrows. 'Something else?'

'We're a bit obsessed,' Kate said with a smile. 'There's something. I don't know.'

'Obsessed?' I said. 'God. Don't turn the tractor-beam Kate obsession on Jack, please. He's not Brody from *Homeland*. He's not up for deconstruction.'

'Tractor beam?' she said, frowning. I'd offended her.

'You're just . . . you know. When you get obsessed with stuff.'

She ignored me. 'Look at his phone,' she said.

'What do you mean?'

'Look what he does with it.'

'Whatever,' I said. My stomach was clenching at the thought of confronting him. Because of Wally. Because it was so crucial that we all just *got along*.

I thought of the time I'd demanded to see his phone. It had been face down on the sofa. And he'd passed it to me; I'd been relieved. But hadn't he opened the Facebook Messenger app *for* me, shown me just that? I'd never had access to everything in his phone, not really.

'Just tread carefully,' Mez said. 'In the meantime. You hardly know him, after all.'

I couldn't argue with that.

We did watch the film, in the end. I sat next to Jack. He scooted closer to me, so that our legs were touching, his arm around me. He always sat like this with me.

He was jiggling his knee the entire time. The nervous energy seemed to be rolling off him, less like waves and more like a fine coastal mist that infiltrated everything. He kept sighing, too, at the sexist moments.

An hour in, his phone buzzed. It was lying, face down, on the arm of Kate's rust-coloured sofa. He picked it up and tapped something out. The room was lit up only by the television and his phone, and it disturbed everybody. I turned my head, just a few degrees, towards him, and he immediately tilted the phone into his body. Away from me. It was only marginal, but it was obvious.

I frowned, and he put it down.

After the film was over, he was stretching while Kate flicked the big light on.

'We'd better go,' I said, checking my watch.

'Need a wee,' he said quietly to me. 'Too many lemonades. I am *off the rails*.'

I couldn't help but laugh at that. 'Wild,' I said.

He took two steps away from me. Then stopped, as if he'd met a threshold, a wall, an unexpected force field across his path. 'Ah,' he said, turning around. His tone was faux casual. I could hear the nuance in it. If I wasn't looking for it, I wouldn't have noticed.

His left hand was already extending as he turned, reaching out towards the arm of the sofa, like he'd left something precious there. And hadn't he? He snatched his phone up and disappeared out of the room. He dropped it into the back pocket of his jeans as he walked. I saw the rectangular shape of it. How I wished I could pickpocket him, I found myself thinking.

When I looked up, Mez was staring at me from across the room, his eyebrows raised. I couldn't see his eyes. Kate was still standing by the light switch, watching us both thoughtfully. They didn't look at each other. They were both looking at me.

To be honest, it wasn't thinking about his phone that made me decide to google him again. It was the other stuff; peripheral things. His weird cafe meeting. Him yelling at somebody. If there was anything really awful, I reasoned, Google would tell me. If that temper had ever got him into serious trouble.

I'd done it before, of course. Early on. When I was intrigued, not paranoid. Nothing. But had I read every hit? Had I been paying close enough attention?

I went straight to the bathroom as soon as we got in, determined to do it. I didn't even take my coat off. And there, leaning against his spotless sink, I typed in his name.

Jack Ross.

The first few hits were familiar. A sponsorship page showing he'd donated to Parkinson's UK, last year. He'd done a run for it. I smiled at the thought of him running; he hated it. *What was the point?* he'd say. *You end where you started.* But he'd done a charity run.

I looked at the photograph. It was blurred and small. But it didn't look like Jack. I took a screenshot of it, then zoomed in on the photograph. There was something off about it. It didn't look like his stance. I might have been googling him, discussing him with my family, digging into his history, but I knew his body better than anyone. The arms were wrong. He always stood with the tops of his hands facing ever so slightly forwards. This man had them by his side.

I shook my head. I must be wrong.

I looked at the rest. Articles upon articles. Most for small travel sites, one for the *Guardian*. More for *City Lights*. A romantic article about how he'd met me, in Newcastle, that he'd already emailed to me.

There was nothing else.

13

I had to get that phone.

Jools Oliver had been in the *Telegraph* last weekend, claiming to occasionally check Jamie's text messages. I found myself thinking: if that posh, wholesome, Boden-wearing woman sometimes lowered herself to checking her husband's phone, why couldn't I?

Maybe I thought it was okay because it was just a phone, a slice of electronics, and not a diary, or an underwear drawer, or looking through a keyhole at somebody.

Or maybe it was the scientific side of me, the doctor who enjoyed digging, investigating blood results, biopsies, going deeper and deeper until she got to the right answer.

Or maybe, actually, it was just the way he handled his phone. I tried to ignore my instincts these days, but they were hard to discount entirely.

I'd watched him enter the passcode, looking side-ways at him as he did so, moving only my eyes and not my head. It took three days. I got it one number at a time. 6865. I memorized it the way I used to memorize dosages and interactions: with ease.

Night-time was the only time I could do it. He was attached to his phone at all other times. It was in his jeans pocket, or in his hand, or – face down, always face down – on the arm of his sofa, right next to him. It was in his hand when he opened Howard's cat-food tins, and in the bathroom, on the window sill, while he showered, and dropped into his coat pocket as he was locking the doors. He placed it on the kitchen work surface while he cooked, even though fat from the frying pan would sometimes sprinkle over it.

But at night-time, it was alone. It was charging next to him, but it was alone.

That night, he fell asleep quickly. He always did; a fact I would come to wonder about later on.

It was easy. We had the same iPhone, so my finger was poised to press the 'sleep' button as I unplugged it, to prevent it lighting up the room. I decided, even though it was a risk if he woke up to discover it gone, to take it away with me, creeping along the cold corridor, past the curtainless hall window and into the bath-room. I'd say I was feeling sick. I'd blame Wally, I thought, with a guilty wince.

It was in my hands and I was standing, leaning against the sink. The door was locked. I swiped right, entered the passcode, and started reading.

ITEM 3

Marsha: Hey J, just to let you know the cheque is (finally!) in the post to you. SO sorry for the delay! X

Jack: No problem. Thanks so much. Did you send the VAT invoice too?

Marsha: No, sorry. Will do right away. X

Mum: Davey's got a fever.

Jack: Oh no!

Mum: Yeah. Seems okay though in himself.

Jack: Good.

White Cross Vets: Howard Ross is due for his vaccinations.

Mike: Ruggers on Sat or are you busy, JD?

Jack: Up for that. Am I starting? Or passed over due to age and infirm status?

Mike: Need to review your performance. A committee will meet. I'll let you know the outcome.

Jack: Ha! Thanks.

Gavin Kelly: Hi, can you come to my offices next week?

Jack: Yes. Why?

Gavin: Things to discuss. Need to protect your position.

Jack: You still at Lorn?

Gavin: Yes same place. Can do Saturday pm?

Jack: Think I can get away in the day. 5?

Gavin: See you then. Regards.

Jack: Just running slightly late.

I exited the text messages and opened Safari. I googled Lorn. It was near Oban. I googled Gavin.

He was a lawyer.

Those messages pre-dated our weekend there a couple of weeks ago. Had he . . . had he met him? I thought back to that day. I'd been in Mothercare. Why? *Come after 7 p.m.* That's what Jack had said. That's why I wasn't invited to the rugby match. And maybe that's why we were up there then in the first place.

He hadn't ever played rugby. He'd pretended to.

He'd met the lawyer. Before the drinks. It seemed obvious. And then – I swallowed, feeling sick at the duplicity as I remembered his damp hair, his minty smell – he'd showered. He'd showered to make it look like he had played when he hadn't.

And, of course, Jools bloody Oliver didn't point out the main problem with looking at somebody's text messages: unless you found something which incriminated them beyond all reasonable doubt, you had nothing. You couldn't confront. Your hands were unclean.

14

Audrey pushed a mug towards me in Starbucks. The milky liquid slopped over the side. 'The barista said *fall*,' she said, rolling her eyes. We were drinking Pumpkin Spice Lattes and sitting in the draught of the automatic doors, which were opening and closing like self-aware beings as pedestrians unknowingly activated them. It was raining outside. It had been on the news, how much it had rained that autumn. Record-breaking amounts.

'How was the silverback's birthday in Oban?' she said to me.

'Excruciating,' I said, and she grimaced. 'Lots of displays of dominance.'

'Oh dear,' she said. She looked at me then, in the way best friends do; inviting me to talk.

I told her everything. She listened, her eyes watchful – she had lawyer's eyes; calculating, sometimes thoughtful – as I stacked up the incidents like a house of cards. A tower of my suspicions.

'Well, I'm sure most of it's just circumstantial,' she said with a self-aware smile. 'The phone behaviour. Seeing a lawyer – probably about his tax return. Having a bit of a pop at someone in the city. They probably just barged into him or something. These add up to nothing. Don't they?' She fiddled with a ring that was sitting just above the knuckle of her thumb. She was always far more fashionable than me.

'I don't know, I . . .' I couldn't articulate it.

The science – the evidence – said one thing: he was innocent. It was nothing. Circumstantial. And I had to rely on that. I had to ignore my spurious gut instinct. It had got me into trouble before. Besides, it was nonsensical, my gut instinct. It looked past the lack of hard evidence and at the other things. Not at the email itself, but his facial expression, the air puffing out his cheeks. It wasn't the strange nickname at the rugby club, but his reaction to it.

It was illogical, but hard to ignore. It had been important to me, once. It had saved lives for me, backed up by the test results. They hadn't ever contradicted each other, the science and the instinct. Until they did. With Ben, and with work. My instincts went awry. I couldn't rely on them any more, just like an alcoholic who knew – no matter what their thoughts said – that they couldn't even have one drink. Now I was to ignore my thoughts as best I could.

I went for the most concrete example. 'This email I saw. It mentioned *Douglas's atrocity*, but that doesn't exist. There's no evidence of this assault. And the message, the way it was worded. It sounded like it was about him. It said *sorry*. It said *your history*.'

'Well, it is his history. His friend's history. And they're not all reported. Assaults.'

'But atrocities are.'

Audrey shrugged, stirring her drink with a wooden stick. 'Papers call anything an atrocity.'

I sat back. 'True,' I said. I couldn't ignore that. She was right. There were headlines like that every single day. I was being ridiculous; naive.

'And wasn't he a court reporter? Maybe he didn't report his mate?'

'Yes. Maybe . . .' I paused. Perhaps I was mad. It was all unfounded. 'He woke me up the other morning and made me drive him a mile. Half a mile,' I added. There was more evidence. There was. 'He made it seem so urgent. To get me out of his house. He acted like he was late. But he wasn't, I don't think.'

'Right. So you were both at his?'

'Yes.'

'And you're thinking he didn't want you to be alone there?' she said immediately.

I pushed my chair back. I hadn't realized. I was clueless. Literally *clueless*. 'Do you think?' I said.

He'd had a meeting. But he wasn't late for it. He said he was, to get me out of the house. To ensure I couldn't stay there, wait for him.

'Maybe. But what I mean is, that's normal. Isn't it? Amrit and I didn't spend any time alone in each other's houses for ages. Maybe a year,' she said. 'I still wee with the door closed.'

I smiled. 'I hope I always do,' I said.

And then she knocked over my house of cards.

'All of this – it's just nothing, isn't it?' she said. 'Being afraid of a gun. A mad woman yelling at them in Oban.

Taking his phone to the toilet, probably to play Candy Crush. An email about his mate. What's really wrong? Is there something else going on?'

'What?' I said.

But, of course, she couldn't see the strange anger that rolled across his facial expressions like a vicious summer storm. She couldn't see the panic in his eyes as he played Trivial Pursuit against my family and did not seem – inexplicably – to know about a global catastrophe from only a few years ago. She didn't know his lips like I did, and so couldn't see them blanch when he read an email apologizing for bringing something up. Something they'd all tried to forget.

She nodded. 'You've had a bit of a year.'

'What do you mean?' I said, though I knew exactly what she meant.

'With your mum and then Ben and losing your job . . . a new boyfriend. A baby.'

I nodded quickly, my eyes damp, trying not to be offended. Audrey had been there through all of it, quietly shocked about Mum and mostly supportive of me leaving Ben. She knew it all. She knew that Mum had made me feel minuscule sometimes, when she told me that relatives were wondering why I wasn't yet married. She knew I only used to call her out of duty, that I went over to see Dad when I knew she'd be out. And yet Audrey had held my hand at Mum's funeral, tighter than Ben had. Because she understood that, too. Loss.

She'd been the second person I'd discussed the pregnancy with. We'd met for a walk along the Tyne. I'd told her and she hadn't looked surprised or worried or anything bad. I'd loved her for that reaction. The summer sun had been warm on our faces as we walked along amongst families and people with '99' ice creams. She'd told me not to eat one, because they were rife with bugs for food poisoning, and I'd laughed.

'I'll be a bad mum,' I had blurted, out of nowhere. 'I've hardly had a role model.'

She had shrugged and licked her ice cream, and I'd loved her for that shrug, too. The casualness with which she treated my worst fears, as though they were nothing at all, insubstantial wisps. 'It's scarier not to do things, too,' she had said.

I considered that, thinking about the women I'd met on my obs and gynae rotation. Nobody told me they regretted having their children. But plenty regretted not trying. Leaving it too late. It was a sad fact of being a woman.

'You could keep waiting for everything to be perfect,' she'd gone on, 'or you could just – do it. Like, it's pretty close to the right time. You're not sixteen. You love Jack. The rest you'll figure out.'

'Yes,' I said. 'That's true.'

I didn't want to risk it. That was the truth. I had seen the women in the clinics when I was a house officer. Their empty arms. Bodies were strange, and baby-making even stranger; the most mystic area of medicine by far. This was my chance, and I was going to take it.

But . . . the boy. We hadn't talked about that, though I'd wanted to. To ask Audrey what she thought. To find out whether what had happened meant that I couldn't really be trusted to be good any more. But something stopped me and I couldn't. I just couldn't say the words.

'After everything that's happened,' she continued now, 'maybe you've just, I don't know. Lost your confidence.'

'Lost my confidence?' I winced, but I knew what she meant.

She, Amrit, Ben and I had gone everywhere together, before; to a caravan in Wales one Easter where we stayed up late playing Cards Against Humanity. And then I left medicine and then I became suspicious and horrible, and Audrey always tried to stop me confronting Ben, but it never worked. And then Ben left me and I met Jack too soon, and everything – *everything* – changed.

'You think I'm being mad again,' I said flatly.

'No. Maybe. Do you feel – rational?'

'*Yes.*'

'Look, it's normal. When I'm on annual leave, like when we went to Bali, I went fully mad,' she said.

'Did you?'

'Yeah, because I wasn't . . . I don't know. I wasn't investigating any cases, I suppose. It was like my mind had all these pathways formed but it wasn't kept busy, so I started to make up worries instead. Stupid stuff. That I would come home and our house would've burnt down.'

'Hmm.'

'And then we came home and I went back to work and I was fine. Maybe you're just . . .'

'Under-stimulated?'

'Yeah. Maybe you need medicine in your life. To be *you*. Because you find satisfaction in investigating things. Solving them. And maybe realizing your mum wasn't . . . who she said she was – maybe that's made that urge greater. The need to *solve* things.'

'What – so I'm crazy without medicine?'

'No! I just mean, maybe your brain isn't very good at being more idle. You've had a hard year. Just enjoy Jack.' She reached over and touched my hand briefly.

It was nice, that sentiment, and the touch that went with it.

Maybe Audrey was right. Leaving medicine, and my reaction to it, had driven one boyfriend away. Maybe it was happening again, and I was too messed up to see it. Maybe it was grief. My mum dying. It had seemed so enormous, and only one year ago. Maybe I needed to see somebody.

'Do you think it *is* about Mum?' I said.

She shrugged. 'Maybe. It's huge.'

'It doesn't feel huge. I don't know. I don't – I don't miss her as much as I should,' I said, admitting something I could only admit to Audrey.

'That's okay, Rach. Really. It was – it was tough with her sometimes. She used to make you feel – tiny. But don't take it out on Jack.'

'So I shouldn't ask him?'

'*Ask* him?'

'Like lay it all out. That's what I'd like to do. All the facts,' I said, imagining it like a medical case. There

132

were no concrete test results, no positive scans, no cancerous biopsies, but everything else was there: the evidence. The lump. The grey pallor. The anaemia. The death rattle. No, Rachel, no, I said to myself. None of this is real.

'Definitely *do not* do that,' Audrey said, adopting her best, directive lawyer voice. 'That would be insane.'

'Would it? This gut feeling, I . . .' My hand drifted down to my stomach and clutched at the layer of fat sitting there. I was embarrassed to find myself close to tears.

'Oh, no,' Audrey murmured, seeing my expression.

I glanced up, and she looked concerned, then thoughtful, then she lapsed into silence.

'Look, Rach. There is something you can do,' she said after a few moments.

'Hmm?'

The doors opened, and the temperature dropped.

Audrey drew her coat around her. 'If he's not legit. There are ways to find out. Ways that wouldn't mean anything. Nobody would ever know.'

'What ways?'

'If he's got any form at all,' she said. 'There are ways to find out. It's just been rolled out.' Her tone was tentative. 'Clare's Law.'

I frowned. I'd seen something somewhere about this. A murder. The victim's parents campaigning. Killing, domestic violence, the underworld. Not my middle-class world in Starbucks.

'It's just googling him,' she continued. 'Getting the police to google him. Using their database. You just ring up and make a request. And it'll just tell you if he's done something. Nobody would ever know.' She shrugged. 'It's up to you.'

'What would you do?' I said. I'd lost my nerve. There was no evidence – nothing. But this was serious. Audrey's suggestion made it serious. 'It seems . . . I don't know, extreme.'

She raised her hands to me. Her wedding ring caught the light. I'd given a speech as her 'best man'. It was full of all our in-jokes – nobody else understood it – and she'd cried, laughing at their bafflement.

'In twenty years, everyone will do this. Why not?' she said.

I looked at her. She probably didn't want to be spending her Thursday night giving me legal advice in Starbucks because of my spurious gut feelings. But her slightly irritated, hassled expression reminded me of Jack's, at Kate's house. Only her irritation was a tenth of his; a thousandth.

I stirred my Pumpkin Spice Latte with the stick, watching the foamy liquid creep up the wood, sinking in, making it darker. I might never know. I might never know if all of these tiny things added up to anything. And I should know. I looked up at her again.

'I'll do it,' I said.

I googled Clare's Law and submitted the form as soon as I got home.

And I cleared my Internet history immediately afterwards.

15

It was the weekend our families were meeting each other. We set off on the Friday. Dad and Kate were coming the next day, staying till Tuesday to make the most of the trip north.

I had hardly said a word for the first part of the journey. Jack looked cold and his arms were folded across his body. He hardly ever sat like that. The car journeys to Oban were too long. Too enclosed. Time became stretched out, sluggish and slow-moving, and thoughts would drip slowly through my mind like percolating coffee.

After a couple of hours of silence, I'd thought a hundred times about how Mez had described seeing Jack shouting at somebody, and I was ready to ask.

'Mez said something about you,' I began.

'Did he?'

'Yep. When we were watering the mushrooms.'

'What?' Jack was fiddling with the radio, trying to find a different station as we lost signal. 'We'll end up with the shipping forecast,' he mumbled.

'He said he saw you yelling at someone.'

Jack looked up at me. His expression was almost amused. 'Yelling?'

'Yeah. He said he saw you in the town centre. Yelling.'

'Me?' The amused expression gave way to a full-on grin. 'I'm not sure I've ever yelled at anybody.'

'No?'

'You worried I'm terrorizing the locals? Maybe it was when Twitter went down and I went insane.'

'Don't joke, though – he really did see you.'

'When was this?'

'A few weeks back.'

'I really don't . . . what was I even doing the week before last?' He paused, thinking. 'I had that deadline. I wasn't even in town.'

I thought back. He'd been subsisting on toast and coffee and typing a lot, I remembered that much. 'No,' I agreed.

'Yelling,' Jack said softly to himself.

I thought back to Ben, after I had started accusing him. Right after Mum. Right after leaving medicine. He had snorted, at first. Been derisive. Not like Jack. He hadn't taken me as seriously as Jack did.

But that didn't mean Jack wasn't lying, I thought, while looking at him. He was considering me, looking sideways at me in the car.

I thought of my Clare's Law application, made the previous day. It was too early to hope that somebody would have looked at it by now.

It was pouring with October rain. The windscreen had been covered in leaves when we set off, and a lone one remained, being wiped mercilessly back and forth, back and forth, almost escaping and then getting trapped against the screen again. Eventually, it was ripped in two, one half fluttering away on the motorway.

It was Saturday morning. It was a sunny, cut-glass autumn day, and it was strange.

We were in bed and Clare's Law was forgotten.

'Guess what my first thought of the morning always is?' he said.

'What?' I said. I was thinking: *is Saturday morning not the absolute best time of the entire week?*

'It's "what am I worrying about?"' Jack said.

'That's your first thought?'

'Yep. And once I've found something, I feel happy again.'

'That's crazy. And kind of sad,' I said, but my heart was singing. 'I wish you weren't always anxious. Though I like learning Jack-things.'

He looked at the clock on the wall. 'Oh, everyone will arrive soon. They'll think we're slobs.'

'We are slobs.'

'It's a thing in our family. That I'm always late.'

'You are,' I said. I had lost count of the number of times I had threatened Jack, saying I would leave without him, sitting with the engine running on the drive while he faffed.

'I read something about it. Late people forget to factor in the time it takes between tasks. So we think it takes no time to leave the house. Or to walk from the train station to a cafe two minutes away.'

'I saw that. On your Twitter.'

'Creeping on my Twitter, are you?' he said. He tried to raise an eyebrow, then collapsed into laughter. 'I just can't flirt,' he said. 'I'm a goon.'

Of course my suspicions felt a thousand miles away as we lay in bed.

Jack's parents were out. Supplies, they'd said. Cheese and Quality Street and wine. Kate was texting me every junction along the way. We could have come together, but Jack wanted to come up earlier than they did. He always wanted as much time in Oban as possible.

Eventually, Jack got up and showered. I lay there for a few minutes in the warm bed, listening to him. He showered silently. He would never sing. He would be too embarrassed, too self-conscious.

I got out of bed, moving through the cold air to go and make a cup of coffee. Tiredness shrouded me like a fog. I hadn't slept much, again. Maybe pregnancy was preparing me for babyhood. I felt a rush of pleasure as I thought about holding a sleepy, milky newborn who was *ours*. 'Got your dressing gown, sorry,' I said through the bathroom door, the mint-scented vapour smelling fresh and sweet, like a steam room in a spa.

'I bet you wear it better than me,' he called through the door. 'When're they due?'

'An hour,' I said. 'Maybe less.'

And even though I'd been content, I'd been ignoring the impending meeting, and Jack reminding me made me shiver with nerves. It felt as though there was a pit of snakes in my stomach. At best, they weighed me down. At worst, they awoke, twisting over each other and making me nauseous. It was hard for me to tell quite what caused them. Maybe it was the anticipation of a familial clash; the awkward strain of keeping the conversation going, with everybody being on their best behaviour and not being able to escape up the road to a hotel for some banter, alone. Maybe it was concern at how different our families were; perhaps I was worried Dad would speak loudly of the Aldi daily deal as Jack's father was decanting fine whisky. It was hard to say.

I went into the bathroom and looked at Jack as he lathered shower gel into his forearms.

'Mozart woke me up, in the night. Came and put his head on my chest. Thought I was having a heart attack,' he said.

I laughed. I closed the door to the bathroom behind me and walked down the stairs.

It was perfect timing, I suppose. I heard the thud of the letter box as my foot was on the last stair. Davey was safely in his room. I was alone.

It was a split-second decision to stride over to the front door, the mat prickling the soles of my feet, and pick up the small stack of post. My hand stopped on something before my brain realized what it was.

'J. Douglas,' it said in bold type in the address window.

My entire body fizzed with shock. Douglas. Douglas. Douglas.

16

One year ago

'I have a seven-letter word to start with,' the boy said.

My shift had officially ended over an hour ago.

'Seriously?' I said. 'I have four As.'

He began picking his Scrabble tiles up. It was a slow process. The rack was balanced across his chest, tilting up slightly on one end where it crossed with a wire. 'CARPETS,' he put across the star in the middle. He coughed.

He was in for his latest round of chemo. We thought it had been going well.

I placed my tiles –'AGA'– coming down to the S of 'CARPETS'.

'Very posh,' he said with a grin. 'Ovens or army generals?'

'Army generals.'

He looked better when he smiled. He had those distinctive red wine-coloured stains underneath his eyes. They disappeared when he smiled, and he looked more like himself: the boy who was good at long division and loved Topps football cards and liked it when his mum brought him a Nando's on a Friday night, much to the nurses' disapproval. Not this boy with a life or death battle on his hands. He had changed, already, even though it was early days in his treatment. He was self-aware. Ironic, sometimes. Was starting to explore what music he was into, which cool books he could read. He grinned again, his steroid-bloated cheeks dimpling strangely, then turned my 'AGAS' into 'AGASTACHE'. He let his arms flop by his sides, clearly exhausted by the effort of picking the tiles up and placing them on the board balanced on his stomach. 'It's not many points, but I'm pleased,' he said.

'Erm, for God's sake,' I said. 'I'm going to resign. If this is part of my doctor duties, I'm failing.'

'I'm just very, very bright,' the boy said. He was joking, but he was confident like that. Pretty matter-of-fact about his skills: I'm good at maths and bad at cancer, he would say.

'What is *agastache*? It had better not be a medical term.'

'It's pronounced *agastacky*. And no. It's a flower.'

'You know too much,' I said. 'Science, maths, Latin names for flowers.'

'It's Greek.'

'Technically you're not allowed foreign words.'

'Don't penalize me for being smart.'

I laughed, and so did he, but then his laugh turned into a hacking coughing fit.

'How long have you had that cough?' I said.

'Few days. Nothing serious. Mum had a cold.'

'Right.'

'Where do you live?' he said, looking at me curiously.

141

I knew that curiosity well. I had often wondered about my university lecturers and the consultants who managed me. Who *were* they? I'd think as I watched them check mobile phones on the way out and get into cars with kooky air fresheners hanging from the rear-view mirror.

'Just up the road. A ten-minute drive,' I said. 'Not far.'

'Did you always want to be a doctor?'

I met his eyes. 'Why – do you?'

'No. It's a bit . . . I don't know.'

'What?'

'Rudimentary? That surgeon who cut my leg off had a Black and Decker.'

I thought it was a fair assessment. Medicine was often more of a bodged job than a precise science. Sometimes, drugs worked where we thought they wouldn't, and we simply shrugged our shoulders.

I looked down at the bed. The blanket fell away at the boy's stump like a cliff face unexpectedly crumbling into the sea. There should be flesh there, and instead there was nothing. I hoped it would always be strange to me; that I would always find it upsetting, even after he – my first difficult cure as the registrar in charge – had been discharged.

'Yes,' I said to him. 'It's an art, not a science, really.'

'Are your parents doctors?'

'No. God, no,' I said with a laugh, imagining how anal my father would be in a hospital setting. 'Dad's an IT technician. Mum's . . .' I spoke before thinking, and wished I hadn't. The car park lights were coming in through the window, getting in my eyes, and I reached to close the blind. The boy shifted in his bed, still looking at me.

'Your mum?'

'She died. Of cancer,' I said quickly. 'Not that long ago.' I was embarrassed by how recently it had been, just the previous month. He might wonder why I was working, but life went on, even with that heavy weight on my chest, even when I was visiting Dad every night.

'Bloody cancer,' he muttered, sounding like an adult. 'It's everywhere.'

'I know,' I said softly. 'I know.'

He lifted an arm, then, to scratch his bald head, and he looked so like Mum had, as she had died – too thin, and bald – that I had to look away from him.

'Is it hard, then? Treating people with cancer?'

I blinked.

Hardly anybody asked me that. Perhaps they had too many inhibitions that he didn't have.

'Yeah,' I said quietly. 'But it's doing good, too.' I shrugged then, embarrassed in the small, dim room.

He gave a little smile, before changing the subject. 'So, Rach – want to see something cool?' He shifted again, and lifted his black T-shirt up. It revealed a Topps football card, tattooed on his ribs. A Newcastle United one.

'Up the Toon,' he laughed.

I stood up, leaning closer, surprised. 'When did you get that?' I said.

'Last week. To celebrate the halfway point, coming

up.' His chemo schedule was long. The longest of any patient I had treated.

'Your mum didn't let you?' I was aghast; tattoos have all sorts of implications for people who are immuno-compromised. 'You won't be able to give blood for ages. To give back.'

I was admonishing him, and I had to stop myself. I wasn't his parent.

'She doesn't know, obviously.' He grinned and let his T-shirt go, so the tattoo was covered again. I couldn't help but think clichéd thoughts: how would it look when he was sixty, and no longer interested in Topps football cards? What if he wanted to forget he ever had cancer?

'Don't tell her,' he said quickly. 'Please.'

I ran a quick checklist in my mind. Did it affect his care? Probably not. 'Okay,' I said. I'd keep his secret.

I leant over again. He drew the shirt up. It didn't look infected. I rolled my eyes at him instead. Something in my gesture made him laugh, and it escalated to a giggling fit, and then to a coughing fit.

There was something about the tone of that cough. It sounded too productive; like there was more phlegm than there should be.

'Hang on,' I said, pulling my stethoscope from behind my neck and putting it to his chest. 'Breathe,' I said.

He was still coughing, trying to slow his breathing.

I didn't like the sound of that cough.

*

'What's this?' I asked Ben as soon as he arrived home. An old Nokia phone sat in front of me on the table.

Ben was wearing a shirt and jeans. He'd been to the pub. He went every Thursday without fail, with his IT friends. He glanced at the phone, confused.

'My old phone,' he said, like it was some kind of trick.

'I found it down the back of the sofa,' I said.

'Yes . . . ?'

'Why? What was it doing there? Is it a second phone?'

His expression was perplexed, and then angry, a line appearing between his eyebrows. 'No – no way,' he said. 'What?'

'You have a second phone.'

'I got my old phone out to find my passwords. I'd put them all on a memo thing.'

I stared at him, scrutinizing him. The phone had been stuffed down between the cushions of the sofa. As if hidden. I'd turned it on, but it was password protected.

'Can you show me?' I said.

'Why?' Ben said, his expression changing from angry to wounded, like I had physically hurt him.

I felt a flip then. From suspicion to nothing. I could see, immediately, that he wasn't lying. Why had I asked?

'Sorry,' I said. 'I . . . sorry.'

'You think I'd cheat on you?' he said, still standing in the doorway.

'Sorry.'

'Is this about . . . ?' He looked over his shoulder, as if indicating something.

I knew immediately what he meant. Mum. Dad had found the emails just a few weeks ago. Not just the emails; texts, too. The sordid messages my mother had sent to their mutual friend. Those smutty texts that had betrayed us all.

'No,' I said. 'I just saw the phone and I thought – something.'

But I could see he had a point. It wasn't like me. Jumping to conclusions. Usually I considered everything. What was happening?

'Rach, maybe you should speak to someone. About your mum? It's all been so sudden.'

'Don't psychoanalyse me,' I said. 'Please.'

17

Present day

I looked behind me at the stairs and listened for a second. I heard the squeak as the shower switched off. He'd get dressed: I had a minute. I needed to look at that letter. That inexplicable letter to Douglas. I just had to find out more, to keep moving forward like a marathon runner.

I ripped the envelope and slipped the letter out. It was as easy as buying a pint of milk, that act, that illegal act.

ITEM 4

www.scottishreview.co.uk

J. Douglas
The Pine Needles
Gallanach Road
Oban
PA34 4PG

Dear Mr Douglas,

Novel Competition

We wanted to tell you about our novel competition launching in January of next year. As a past contributor to *The Scottish Review* we wanted you to be the first to know. It's being judged by a top literary agent and has a prize of £500. The length can be anything between 50,000 and 100,000 words and the deadline closes on 31 March.

We look forward to receiving your entry! Please see our website above for more information.

The Scottish Review

I ran my finger over the letter. Over his name. Maybe it wasn't for him. Maybe it was old post, for an old occupant. But . . . Douglas. Writing.

I kept reading and rereading it, thinking I'd missed something. Of course I knew my boyfriend's name; of course I knew what Wally's surname was to be. Didn't I?

His Facebook was Jack Ross. His Twitter handle was @jrosswriter. He even joked he'd got mistaken for Jonathan Ross once on there and got loads of abuse. His parents' surname was Ross: the other post still clutched in my hand was addressed to Mr and Mrs Ross. Davey was Davey Ross. What was I on about? Get a grip.

Those irrelevant, petty thoughts about my boyfriend's name were circling like vultures, but at the centre was the other thought: the carcass they were circling over, swooping down on, pecking at. Jack received bizarre emails about a Douglas; and he was, it seemed, sometimes called Douglas himself.

I put the letter back in the envelope. There was some

Sellotape in the drawer in the kitchen and I taped it up. I put the pile of post back on the doormat. And then I paused, waiting in the hallway, listening for Jack's feet on the stairs.

As soon as I heard him, I acted. I remembered that adrenaline rush, how useful it was, the hypothalamus telling the adrenal glands to do their thing. I wasn't dwelling on what I'd found or worrying about it. I was going to fix it, like a doctor rushing with a crash cart to a patient in need.

I headed with purpose for the hallway. 'You've got mail,' I said to him over my shoulder as he began descending the stairs. I managed to say it with a smile that felt stiff.

Jack hesitated, and that bolstered me. He slowed, both feet on one stair, then reached his right hand out towards me, as if to stop me crossing a busy road.

I stood with the post, flicking through it, as if just seeing it for the first time. 'Oh, wait,' I said, faux casually. 'Two for your parents, one for Davey and – what's this? It's not for you?' I held the offending envelope up.

'Oh no, it is,' Jack said, but didn't explain. Instead, he walked into the kitchen and filled the kettle, his back to me. 'You want caffeine? Or are you over your limit?' he said.

He was solicitous like that; he knew I preferred proper coffee, proper tea, but worried about Wally.

'I think there's some posh herbal stuff somewhere,' he said, opening cupboards and rummaging.

'But it says J. Douglas?' I said, trying to keep my tone light as I followed him into the kitchen.

Should I be asking this sort of thing? I could no longer remember what it was like to be in a normal relationship. Was this an interrogation or was it acceptable? I held my breath, waiting for this miniature mystery to be solved. Waiting to see what it led to. If the birds took flight or stayed.

At that moment my phone rang. It was Dad. He always called me, had not quite entered the twenty-first century of sending updates by text message. I answered because I had to.

'We're on Argyle soil,' he said.

'Okay,' I said woodenly.

'Do we need directions from here? The roads are so windy,' Dad said.

'Call if you need me.'

'I've got Kate, too.'

'I know.' I started making wrapping-it-up gestures, though he couldn't see me.

'Oh, and we didn't know whether to bring wine or what. I mean they're bloody whisky connoisseurs, aren't they? But then if we brought whisky that wasn't theirs –'

'See you soon,' I said, jabbing the red button on my phone and turning back to Jack.

I was still holding the letter but, sadly, he capitalized on – or allowed himself to be distracted by – the interruption, and turned away from me.

'Did he say they're nearly here?' Jack said. 'I could hear him booming.' He darted a quick smile at me.

I looked at the phone, as if it might hold answers for me, and then up at him. He was looking at me expectantly. His eyes were friendly, not guarded. Safe and warm.

'Yeah, I think so,' I said.

'Don't know where Mum and Dad are,' he said. 'You should probably put something else on, though.' He turned to me. He indicated the dressing gown I was wearing, palm up, his index finger outstretched. There was something intimate about it. Something proprietary. And then he turned away from me and opened the dishwasher and began loading it, even though only a plate and a knife lay on the counter. The dogs came running, as they always did when anybody made noises with crockery, and Jack addressed them, saying, 'Lads, lads, lads. You're ten hours from dinner time. Yes, you are. Yes, you *are*.' He looked up at me and grinned self-consciously. 'Aren't they greedy?' he said.

Wally kicked then, one of his earliest kicks. Not the first, but nearly. It was less a kick and more like somebody was stroking my insides with a feather, but it was nice nonetheless. Only I ignored it, at first, and later recognized it as a source of inner knowledge, as though Wally were saying: *no, you're right, I think that's strange, too.*

'I don't really think we've finished,' I said, pushing the letter towards him, like he was a difficult patient evading treatment.

He glanced quickly at it and took it off me. He peeled the Sellotape back – his fingers stilled over it, momentarily, and I thought he knew – and pulled the letter out. He crossed one leg over the other as he stood at the counter; a pose so casual I wondered if he thought we were having a completely different conversation to the one we were actually having. He sighed, his eyes looking down at the tiled kitchen floor. But it was his hand I was looking at. It was moving. The tips of his fingers fluttering, like they did when he was thinking quickly.

'I used two surnames for my writing, for ages,' he said eventually, but the pause that had come before it had gone on and on. 'Douglas for the news and politics reporting and Ross for the travel. So I could happily get pigeonholed with each name. But I gave up the politics. Prefer the travel. It's just old – marketing.' He held it up between his index and third finger. His words were casual but his tone wasn't. Could I ask about Matt Douglas? He looked at me as he scrunched up the letter, then lifted the lid of the kitchen recycling bin and pushed it inside.

He flicked the kettle on and it roared to life. The dogs jumped, then left the room.

'Decaf coffee, then? Can't find the herbal stuff.' He waved a mug at me.

I nodded because I didn't know what else to do. My brain was whirring, landing on different facts like a fly, then taking off again. 'Why Douglas?' I said.

'Mother's maiden name. Oh no, now you can answer all my security questions,' he said. He didn't do anything I thought he might do: look at me quickly or nervously. Address the Douglas issue. Tell me to mind my own business. Maybe I was wrong, I remember thinking. Maybe I was totally mad, down a dead-end cul-de-sac of my own imagination.

'But Douglas's . . . Matt Douglas,' I said. I couldn't resist.

'Oh, yeah?' he said easily. 'Matt Douglas had the assault. The big punch-up.' He turned to me and smiled.

It was a friendly smile, sinister only because of its context. If it had been anybody else, I would have said it was a threat, that smile.

He provided explanations for everything. The email was about Matt. They were both called Douglas.

I stared at him, watching for any sign he was lying. My curiosity had turned to suspicion, like a clay pot slowly hardening.

I couldn't press it. They would ruin things, my accusations. They always did. I remembered the look Ben had thrown me, after the final accusation when he came home late. 'I won't do this any more,' he had said. Not angry. Not upset. Just sad.

Accusations did things to healthy relationships. Like a pickaxe to an ice block.

I looked at Jack's body language. It was open. Trusting. Happy. A normal Saturday morning during which I was just getting to know my boyfriend and his writing aliases. Surely?

Jack poured the coffee. He asked me to get the milk and I did so and handed it to him, all the while thinking: *what is your name?*

'Where exactly *are* they?' he said. He looked at the place where his watch would be, even though his arm was bare, still damp and glistening from his shower.

'I don't know,' I said, about as capable of conducting

a meeting between our parents as I was of flying a plane or performing in *Swan Lake*.

'Douglas is the most common surname in Scotland. And Ross is the second,' Jack said with another smile. 'I'm common.' He nudged me then, referencing an in-joke which already felt ancient.

'Working class, you,' I said automatically.

I made my excuses after that. I left my coffee, growing cold on the counter.

18

I had less than five minutes. And, depending on what I found, I had to call it off. Tell my father to turn the car around.

My phone was discarded on the bed. I went upstairs to get it and took it into the living room with me, sitting by the window so I could look out on to the drive. I opened my phone's cover like it was a treasure chest, intent on asking Google instead of Jack.

He was still faffing in the kitchen. I should have excused myself. Gone home. But I couldn't, not without alarming him, embarrassing myself, annoying everyone. And I couldn't risk that. Not if it was for nothing. I'd look it all up right now, in those five minutes, and then I'd know.

I was nearly there. The loose thread was dangling, lengthening; it just needed to be pulled. I typed *Jack Douglas* into Google.

'You left your coffee, madam. The finest decaf for the finest pregnant lady,' Jack said. He brought it to me and thankfully disappeared again.

I considered telling him I was looking for things to do in Oban, but stopped myself. Good liars didn't over-explain.

I looked down at the screen again as he walked back into the kitchen.

I typed: *Jack Douglas Atrocity*.

No results.

I removed the quotes and got a million results. The most common surname. Douglas. I had no hope of finding out who this man was; what he had done.

I began working my way through them, regardless. I kept looking at the door in case Jack emerged.

Jack Douglas (record producer) – Wikipedia, the free . . .

Jack Douglas | LinkedIn

Jack Douglas – Microphone Lab

I sighed in frustration, clicking the last link only, which took me to a website about Jack Douglas the record producer, holding a pair of microphones up with a smile.

'How near are they?' Jack said, emerging again. He looked at me, still in his dressing gown. 'Stay in that, if you like,' he said. His eyes lingered over my phone in my hands, slightly closer to my chest than I would usually hold it, but he didn't say anything.

'Will you call Dad?' I said. And then the lie escaped; I was unable to stop it. 'I'm doing emergency research on Oban.'

'Oh yeah?' he said with a grin. 'Not satisfied with visiting Londis and the only Thai restaurant?'

'No,' I said.

He got his phone out, dialled a number, and wandered back out of the living room.

'It's Jack,' he said, and I heard my dad boom back.

I looked at my search again and typed '*Douglas's Atrocity Rears Its Head Again*' into the search box.

No results found.

This time, Google suggested something, though it wasn't helpful.

Did you mean <u>Religion</u> Rears Its Ugly Head Again?

I looked at the search, frowning. Then searched for *Jack Douglas's Atrocity*.

One result. I opened the *Herald Scotland* article eagerly. A sign-in prompt popped up and I tried to read around it.

9 JANUARY 2001

THE JURY found . . . 41-year-old **Jack Douglas's atrocity**, said Judge Benson, was . . .

Forty-one? The article was from 2001, which would make Mr Douglas now in his mid-fifties.

I rolled my eyes. What did I expect to find, anyway? A damning crime? So he used his mother's maiden name sometimes: so what? So his friend assaulted someone: so bloody what? Douglas was the most common name in Scotland; Jack said it himself.

Jack appeared in the doorway again. 'What colour should the skin under your eyelids be?' he said to me. He looked worried.

'What?'

'What colour should it be if you pull down your lids?'

'Erm, pink,' I said, still looking down at my phone. 'Where are they?'

'Very close. I've had loads of iron lately and mine's white.'

'White? Really?' I said.

Jack's body physically moved backwards, the way it always did when he panicked, rearing up like a stallion.

'Yes. Why? What does that mean?'

It was as though there were two Jacks: the Jack in my mind and the gentle, vulnerable, anxious, funny man in front of me.

'Are you telling me you think you have no iron in your body? When you feel perfectly healthy?'

'*Maybe.*'

'Are they white? Or a pale pink?'

'Well . . .'

'White: yes or no.'

'No.'

'You're fine, then.'

'Yes. Yes.' Jack didn't move, though. 'Thank you,' he said, looking at me. 'You're totes the best.'

I would usually have smiled. He was often using language like this. New slang. But this time I ignored him.

He went back upstairs. The dogs followed him. They went everywhere with him.

Jack called down: *your dad will be five minutes.* My hands were clammy and cold, and my stomach was churning.

I typed the search query again, this time putting the *'Jack Douglas'* and the *'atrocity'* in separate quotation marks. I added an asterisk. It was a way to tell Google that you weren't sure of one of the words. I'd learnt it when googling rare conditions I couldn't spell at work, as a clueless junior doctor.

Did you mean John Douglas?

I stared at the words on the screen. John? John? Of course. *John* and *Jack* were often the same name, after all. Especially in Scotland.

The doorbell rang.

'They're here,' Jack called, then thumped down the stairs and opened it with a hearty *hello*.

The dogs padded after him, and I was dimly aware of a commotion: the dogs running out the front, Dad expressing mild surprise.

'Rach, you're not even dressed,' Kate said, walking into the living room.

I looked up at her. 'I'm pregnant,' I said with a faint smile. 'Leave me alone.'

'You don't look pregnant. You look unemployed,' she said. 'This place is insane. Like a National Trust property. Get dressed, anyway. I'm doing you a favour being here. Dad-sitting.'

Usually I would have nodded, and thanked her, but I didn't. Instead, I angled the phone away from her and clicked on Google's suggestion.

I watched the searches populate. John Douglas. Bingo.

19

'Seriously, why aren't you dressed?' Kate said. 'Where are Jack's parents?'

'At the shop. You're early.'

'Yeah – Dad told you he left later than he did. He was adjusting it. He thought it would take ages. You need to get dressed. He's been so excited all the way up.'

'Hang on. I'm just . . .' I said. I was scrolling frantically through Google's pages.

I clicked a link which had the words 'John Douglas' and 'crime' in it. Google must have substituted the word 'atrocity' for similar words, too. It was a tabloid. It was slowly loading.

ITEM 5

HTTP 404: File not found.

The page cannot be found.

The page you are looking for might have been removed, had its name changed or is temporarily unavailable.

Please try the following:

If you typed the page address into the Address Bar, make sure that it is spelt correctly . . .

I wordlessly stood up and walked upstairs, sitting back down on the end of Jack's bed, my iPhone in my lap.

Next, I googled *John Douglas Scotland*.

The results were different. Articles about charity events. Articles written by *John* about politics – acerbic, intelligent commentary about quantitative easing, the SNP, Labour, the Tories. Court reports, from outside Oban Court. More charity events. It was him. I recognized his turn of phrase. I knew it.

There was a photograph of Jack, captioned *up-and-coming writer J. Douglas*. It was grainy and blurred, but it was definitely him. He was holding – what was it? A writer's prize. For J. Douglas. My Jack.

I raced through the results. At the bottom of the fifth page there was an article about 'Douglas's court appearance'. *Article not found*, it said. The same for the next one.

I clicked on to page six. Another article was nestled in amongst the charitable work and the politics, right at the bottom. I clicked it thirstily, but received yet another 404 error. There were four more, in total, on the first ten pages of Google. I'd pillaged it, like a burglar ransacking a room. And wasn't I doing just that, in a virtual kind of way?

None of them loaded. All 404 errors. I scrutinized the snippets, anyway.

ITEM 6

The Scottish Star – News on Twitter – Douglas: Friend or Foe?

The Disaster in Oban – what really happened? – cached Guardian article on Stumble Upon

It began as a normal night for Mr **Douglas**, one that ended in the witness stand of a . . .

John Douglas: Profile of a Man Who . . .

Guest blog: **John Douglas** is a university-educated political correspondent and legal reporter. A lefty. But he's also, now . . .

Enemy in the Mist – news archives

John Douglas committed a crime nobody thinks they ever will. But how . . .

Blogger's commentary on Douglas Day 2: What is self-defence?

John Douglas has invoked the defence of reasonable force in the Glasgow High Justiciary Court . . .

'What are you doing?' Jack said. 'You look stressed.' He'd appeared from nowhere. 'You're not dressed,' he added.

I looked at him. Who was this man?

'Rach?'

'Nothing.'

I locked my phone. I had to see an article. There were too many Douglases. What if I was wrong? What

163

if there was some other *John Douglas*? I didn't know it was him. I'd not *seen* the articles or a damning photograph of him in the dock. It could be a horrible coincidence, his second name; his common name.

'Ready?' he said.

I got dressed woodenly, like a mannequin in a shop, feeding my arms into the sleeves of my cardigan without really thinking.

'Are you coming?' Dad called up the stairs.

'Yep,' I said. I didn't know what else to do. I suppose I could have stalled more, continued searching, but I didn't. I was feeble. I just kept the peace.

His parents arrived as I was scraping my hair back into a ponytail. I heard everyone introduce themselves to each other.

I arrived at the bottom of the stairs, and Jack was staring up at me, a frown across his features. It disappeared as soon as my eyes met his.

'Finally, you're being the late one,' Jack said. 'Is this a secret Rachel-thing?' His eyes crinkled at the corners as he looked at me.

'No,' I said.

I'd have to speak to him, to ask him. But there was something else, underneath that; something I'm ashamed to admit. That I wanted to spend time with him, to pretend I hadn't just discovered something. To be in love a little while longer. That's why I stayed, I suppose. Because I loved him; the way he stood at the bottom of the stairs in his scruffy Converse trainers. That his hands were wet, no doubt having just been washed to get rid of the *shoe germs*.

'When you're torn between two choices,' Kate's tennis coach once said to her, 'don't ever try to do something in the middle of both of them. Commit to one of them.'

But I didn't do that. I could have ignored it or I could have confronted him, but instead I met myself in the middle. I'd stay, and get him alone, and then mention it, and hope he told me. And then I'd decide what next after that.

I practised confronting him in my head. I'd be effortlessly insouciant. I would skirt around the details of how the atrocious email had loomed in my mind: so large that I had committed its entire headline to memory. So large that I was merely waiting to see the word *Douglas* again sitting innocently on his parents' hallway floor. The details blurred in my mind like the rain smudging the Oban windows as I played out the ideal, movie version of our conversation. He'd tell me everything. And it would be nothing. Nothing at all. Only, I couldn't imagine how.

20

Jack's parents were unloading wine in the kitchen. Dad and Kate were sitting awkwardly at the table. Sebastien was resting his head in Dad's lap.

'I feel like Mr Darcy,' said Jack.

'*Mr Darcy?*' Kate said.

'You know, we're introducing our families,' he said. He was smiling, leaning casually against the wall. He seemed to unfurl in Oban; become more himself. 'Like in the nineteenth century.'

His parents had shown us around. We all walked down the stone steps that fronted their house. I saw the moment Dad really realized the Rosses were rich. His eyes trailed upwards, like watching a balloon drift from a child's hand towards the heavens. Up at the drive, the steps, the frontage of the house, and then to everything else beyond it. The woodland behind the house – theirs. The casual riches – brand-new cars on the drive. A stone statue of a woman in the fourth window from the left on the second floor, looking out at us. A ride-on lawn mower, abandoned on the grass in front of the house.

'Well, usually we'd meet at the wedding,' Jack's mum said now. She laughed, but there was an edge to it. A horrible edge. Not only disapproval, but a faint look down at my stomach.

Jack's dad followed her gaze, and the atmosphere worsened. I suppose it was the fact that these people, these uptight parents of his, now knew about our less-than-careful sex life, because I was an emblem of it.

'Ideally,' Jack's father said.

'I think we're doing pretty well, actually,' Jack said, smiling at me. 'Me and my girlfriend,' he murmured, catching my eye.

His parents had finished unpacking the shopping and stood proud, like lions, looking Dad in the eye. Dad was still looking up at them, skittish, like an antelope about to run.

It wasn't until much later that Jack and I were finally alone. It was close to midnight. It was completely dark outside. If we'd been in the garden, we wouldn't have been able to see our hands in front of us. But we were in the living room. The fire was glowing softly, the embers red but no longer flaming.

I'd tried to reload the articles, every time I was alone for a moment; every time I was in the toilet or left the family gathering on the pretext of making cups of tea. And every time, none of the articles were there. I could ask him, I thought. But it would change everything forever. For me, and for Wally, if I accused his father of something. We'd split up. Surely. And I was probably wrong. Catastrophically wrong. It had happened before.

Kate walked into the living room. Jack flinched. He was by the window. I was in the armchair.

'You alright?' I said to her, no longer so absorbed by what I'd found that I couldn't speak.

'Do you know, I was going to bail. Couldn't be bothered to come. Sorry. It is interesting to meet them, but it's a long way. But then I had a row with Mez. So I've escaped.'

I turned to her in surprise, jolted out of my self-involved problems. 'What?' I said. I'd never known Mez and Kate fight. Not once. There had never been an atmosphere, no sniping remarks, nothing. No more, I thought. No more drama in our family. At least not for a while.

'He's so bloody high and mighty, sometimes,' she said.

I had to concede that, much as I liked him. He wasn't the type of man I would choose. He was serious, intense – not self-effacing or funny, like Jack. He had no perspective.

'He hasn't texted,' she said, waving her phone in the darkness.

'Text him,' I said, sinking back into my own mind. I stared at the mullioned windows. I could see the embers reflected in them. Kate disappeared, her socked feet making padding noises on the stone floor, and Jack and I were alone again.

'How are my Wallies?' he said softly.

I couldn't help but smile, and as I did so, my eyes filled with tears.

'I feel weird,' I said instead, wiping a tear away.

He immediately walked away from the window and came and sat in the chair with me. There wasn't enough room for both of us, and his hips squeezed against mine uncomfortably.

'Are you being a mad pregnant lady?' he said softly.

'I sometimes feel like I don't know who you are,' I said, and then the tears overcame me completely, juddering sobs like a boat that couldn't quite get started.

'What? What?' Jack was saying softly, those Scottish 'h's, his arms around me. They weren't on my stomach, on my bump; they were around my shoulders, just for me, and I appreciated that. It wasn't about Wally. It was about us.

'I just . . . it's all so fast.'

'It is fast,' he murmured in my ear. 'Really fast.'

'We were a bit stupid,' I said, turning to him.

His eyes weren't on me. They were on the windows. He was squinting at something out there.

'I just feel like – who are you?' I said.

'Me?' he said. His eyes swivelled to me. They were so dark and direct. As dark as the coals in the fire. As dark as the Oban night outside.

'The Douglas stuff. I didn't even know that was a name you used. Is your first name even Jack?'

He paused, looking at me. 'It's John,' he said, eventually. 'I use John Douglas.'

It was bitter-sweet. He was telling me the truth. But he was John Douglas.

'You see, I didn't even know that,' I lied.

He wiped a tear away from my cheek. His thumbs were rough. His eyes were locked on to mine. He was blinking slowly. His thighs were flush against mine. His hand was resting, lightly cupping my jaw. My hands were on his firm, warm chest. We were one being, in that chair in the dark. It was so authentic, sitting there with him. His body was warm and his breath was softly tickling my face.

'I promise, there's nothing you need to know,' he said. His eyes were still locked on to mine. His dark eyelashes were long, but not curly. They were straight.

I almost told him then. About the boy. Maybe he should know, I thought, with a twinge of guilt. Maybe he should know, because he was having a child with me. Maybe he ought to know that I can't be trusted. *In loco parentis*.

But I didn't.

He kissed me, lightly at first, and then more deeply. A bonfire collapsed in my stomach.

I pulled away from him and he looked back at me. He was hiding nothing.

I had an email in the morning.

ITEM 7

Private and Confidential
By email only: rachelanderson1@gmail.com
Your ref: AK/46248/JR197

Dear Ms Anderson
Confidential: Request under The Domestic Violence Disclosure Scheme

Further to your request dated **29** October under the above-named scheme, we have reviewed the relevant documentation and can confirm the following:

Jack Ross: Aberdeen, **UK**: no convictions

Jack Ross: Birmingham, **UK**: no convictions

Jack Ross: Cornwall, **UK**: no convictions

Jack Ross: Cardiff, **UK**: no convictions

Jack Ross: Edinburgh, **UK**: no convictions

Jack Ross: Enfield, **UK**: no convictions

Jack Ross: London, **UK**: no convictions

Jack Ross: Orkney, **UK**: no convictions

Jack Ross: Preston, **UK**: no convictions

Jack Ross: Somerset, **UK**: no convictions

Jack Ross: Suffolk, **UK**: no convictions

If you have any queries you should contact us on the telephone number below and quote the above reference. Alternatively you can refer to our website below. In the absence of any further communication from you your enquiry will be closed in **28** days.

Kind regards
Nicola Smith

Information Governance Officer

I deleted the email once I'd read it. It was the wrong name, anyway.

21

We were walking along the high part of the coast and into Oban on the Sunday, for a roast. I was trying to pretend my legs weren't cramping up from very mild exercise.

Kate and I broke off from everybody.

'Pregnancy's rubbish,' I puffed.

'Your hair looks amazing, though,' she said.

'Does it?'

'Yeah. So thick and shiny.'

I smiled at that. 'The way to any girl's heart is a hair compliment,' I said, and she grinned too.

We walked past McCaig's Tower, a coliseum-type structure overlooking the harbour that had large ovals for windows. We were so far ahead of everybody that we sat down in one. The windows were large enough to seat both of us, side by side, our legs swinging down to the stone below us.

'Got to hand it to you, Oban's pretty,' Kate said.

It wasn't raining, but there was a very fine mist in the air. It might have been sea spray. It was hard to tell, sometimes, if it was weather or atmosphere on the west coast. The sky was a blank, flat white, and the sea reflected that; a pale grey as far as we could see.

'Mum would have liked it,' I said.

'Yeah,' Kate said softly. 'She liked castles and stuff, didn't she?' She patted the stone.

'She did. Dad hated being dragged around them.'

Kate said nothing for a few moments. Grief was strange. It seemed so large from afar. But, up close, it was just one day after another.

'You seem really weird this weekend,' Kate said.

'I feel better now,' I said. And I did. My talk with Jack had helped.

Somehow, articulating the anxiety to him had almost eradicated it, as though I might have been a person with a guilty secret that needed to escape, or a blood disease of the Victorian times which needed letting. I hardly cared about those articles, those half-articles, that afternoon sitting on the stone monument with Kate.

Jack had been straight with me. He wouldn't lie.

'I wonder if I could hit a ball through these gaps,' Kate said in a musing tone. It was nice, her way. So non-confrontational.

'If anyone could, it'd be you,' I said. I looked at her. She was wearing mittens with owl faces on. 'I bet you haven't worn mittens for years.'

'Nope . . .' she said with a nod.

It was warm where the tennis tournaments were. She'd lived in shorts year-round, inexplicably turning up at Newcastle airport in neon in the winter.

'. . . no way I could. My aim was pretty poor.'

'For a tennis player,' I said. 'Which is better than most.'

Kate shrugged. It was her story – that she'd failed. Anybody else would regard her as a success. We both regarded ourselves as failures; people who'd tried but couldn't hack it. Dad was always saying we were successful, just at things that weren't in our original plan, but we didn't agree.

'What's Mez done, then?' I said.

'He was being self-righteous.'

'How?'

'He was being a dick.'

'Don't say that. You're *married*,' I said, like that really made a moral difference.

Kate swivelled her gaze towards me. 'So?'

'Well.'

'Mez is quite often a complete prick,' she said. 'You don't know. You don't know what he's like sometimes. Belligerent. He totally doesn't get the tennis thing. I'm home and everything is totally different and – it turns out, despite what everybody thought – I'm *not* going to be a tennis star. And he doesn't get it. Thinks I should just move on and be positive.'

'Don't say that. You and Mez are like . . .' I was denying it. I thought their marriage was perfect, didn't want to hear if it wasn't.

'What?'

'My Patronus,' I said with a grin.

Kate and I loved *Harry Potter*. She once declared, 'It's a very important part of my life, okay?' to a fellow tennis player, who told her she was immature.

But then I thought back to the times I'd seen Mez

baiting people with different political opinions to him on Facebook. I loved him for those principles. He knew himself. He'd always do the right thing. He had conviction. I liked that. But he wouldn't leave it; would harangue people. I nearly always agreed with him, but maybe that wasn't the point. I bet it wasn't even Jack he saw in the street. It seemed ridiculous now I thought about it. Why would Jack be yelling at anybody? Had I ever heard him even raise his voice?

'We are *not*,' she said.

And, after that, after knowing that they were unhappy sometimes, less than perfect – well. Everything was a little bit worse.

'We fell out over schooling a hypothetical child,' Kate said.

She picked at some moss on the wall, then ran her finger over and over a rough divot in the stone. I wondered what had formed it.

'Who wants what?' I said.

Kate waved a hand. 'Doesn't matter,' she said. 'The only thing that matters is that he – he came at me.'

'Came at you?'

'Just shouting.' She looked at me quickly. 'Nothing more. I know you love Mez. But he was just like a stupid boy spoiling for a fight. Following me. Yelling at me about his own bloody *opinions*.'

The word was imbued with distaste. I guessed it was a common word used in their household, to explain and defend his behaviour. Mez was almost defined by his opinions. Maybe that's why I liked him so much;

I could relate. I used to spend every working day having to have an opinion on something: what to do next? Was the patient in Bed C septic? Should we try targeted or whole-brain radiotherapy?

But it seemed that even my favourite, Mez himself, was flawed. *He came at me.*

'Right,' I said. 'That's horrible.'

I drew my knees up to my chest, sat curled up like a snail on the cold stone wall next to Kate. My bum was getting wet, but I didn't care. Jack would never do that to me, I was thinking. He would never follow me around like that, be aggressive.

'What're you going to do?'

'Nothing. I don't know. I love him,' she said. 'I really, really like him, too. He's my favourite person.'

We sat in silence for a while. What could any of us do? We all compromised for love.

'I hate those bloody mushrooms,' she said after a moment.

'Oh,' I said with a laugh.

She looked at me and smiled, her eyes crinkling. 'I don't even *like* mushrooms.'

'It's definitely too late to admit that,' I said. 'Definitely. Anyway, I get it. I do get that. Loving someone. Them being your favourite.'

With Ben I had thought love meant getting on really well. I liked the way he looked. I liked his manner. I enjoyed the things he said. So we progressed to living together, building a life, as if it was merely a dance whose steps we needed to follow.

But then, later, Jack came into my life and everything changed. I was love sick, those first few weeks. It was exhilarating, but intense, like watching a birth or a curative operation. Nothing was better, in those early days, than rereading Jack's messages to me, or turning out my light at bedtime and not sleeping, instead imagining and re-imagining all the times we'd kissed. They were so sweet, those fantasies; that time of my life. Despite everything that had preceded it. I would remember it forever.

'I do know,' I said. 'Look at me, up-duffed.'

Kate sighed. 'I put up with his shit. Because I love him. It's as simple as that. Sadly.'

I remembered when she met Mez.

'I've met a boy,' she'd said, the day after a wedding.

She'd looked tanned, happy, a bit smug. He'd come over the next day, and he'd gone to every single tournament with her after that.

'I know,' I said now. I did know it well.

And we'd do anything for that feeling. Both of us. All of us.

I tilted my head and looked at the sky. If you had asked me a few weeks ago, I would have said their relationship was what I aspired to; that it was complete perfection. It was funny how things changed as you looked at them from different angles, like an optical illusion. Everybody's take on their own story was different.

'How do you feel about becoming a mum?' she said quietly.

I considered the question as the Oban wind whipped my hair around my face. It smelt of Jack's shampoo which I'd used to wash it. Cheap stuff. Apple-scented. I liked it.

'I do feel worried.'

'We didn't have the best role model,' she said.

I nodded. 'Yeah. Not the most maternal. I feel bad saying it now,' I confided, bringing my hand to my face and pushing my tangled hair back.

'It's complicated,' she said. 'She wasn't perfect.'

'I think I'll either be too remote, like her. Or I'll be smothering. I feel like – like I need to work through it. Somehow. I don't know. I feel a bit mad.'

'Mad?'

'Yeah. Like I've been suspicious of things. I was suspicious of Ben.'

'I know,' she said, though I could barely hear her as the wind carried her voice away. 'Must be from Mum.'

'Probably. It's all tangled up. I think I'm imagining things.'

'About Jack?'

'Yes . . .'

I filled her in briefly on his name, told her that there were some dodgy articles and I didn't know if they were connected with him. But they had disappeared off the Internet, anyway.

'Oh, but you should try the Wayback Machine,' she said. It was offhand. She was like this. Obsessed with something one minute, but had forgotten about it the next time you spoke to her. She and Mez were fighting, so her attention was on that, instead of on me.

'What?'

'The Wayback Machine. God, I used that so much. Oh – or the dark web.'

'The dark web?'

'Yeah. Tennis players used that. For drugs tips, I think. You need this browser, called Tor. Then you can search things that aren't on search engines. The deep illegal web. Apparently only five per cent of the Internet we see on Google is the real web. The rest is the dark web. The underworld.'

'Bloody hell.'

'I didn't use it. Anyway, try the Wayback Machine. That's legal,' she said with a laugh.

'What did you use it for?' I said.

'Looking at all the old training blogs of my opponents,' she admitted sheepishly. 'Their deleted tweets.'

'So what exactly is it?'

'The articles have been deleted, right?'

'Yes.'

'It's like the Internet's recycling bin. A snapshot of the Internet before things were removed.' She typed it into her phone and handed it to me.

ITEM 8

Wayback Machine: Tips on Usage

The Wayback Machine is an Internet tool which will allow you to access the sordid underbelly of the Internet. Most websites have been sporadically archived over the years. Simply go to the Wayback Machine's home page and type the URL of the page that's missing. You can then choose the date on which you would like to see the page, as it was then.

<u>That website you created aged 14? Available. Your old LiveJournal entries that you deleted? Also available. Anything that was deleted off the Internet</u> – gone forever – isn't really. It's recorded right there for you to look at – and it's completely free.

'So just type in the URL of one of the articles, or whatever,' she said. 'One of them will be cached.' She didn't seem concerned.

She didn't know the whole story. But her indifference rubbed off on to me. In the open Oban skies, with Jack having promised me and met my eyes the previous night, the text of the articles felt irrelevant, somehow.

'Anyway. Don't be paranoid,' she continued. 'I bet it's just about Mum and stuff. I've found it hard. Missing tennis. Missing her.'

'Yeah,' I said, a fat feeling in my throat as I thought of the way she would always – without fail – call me every Monday. Even though she had nothing to say.

'You'll be a great mum. Trust me. You're pretty conscientious. You practised *medicine*. That's hard.'

I nodded. I didn't tell her what I was thinking, though. That I hadn't practised medicine well enough. That I sometimes thought of the baby inside me as the boy. That maybe I had to pay for what I did. Penance. That I could atone with this child. My child.

My heart sped up as I thought about it. Here I was, confused about Jack, wanting to know more about him, and there was a huge secret that sat in the middle of our relationship that he had no idea about.

He didn't even know there *was* a secret. He was clueless.

22

I realized slowly that I was going to keep searching. It was as though Jack's late-night promise was a painkilling injection that gradually wore off.

Kate and I carried on walking, in silence, and I kept thinking about Jack's locked-gaze look, the reassurance I got from it. But, like all reassurances, it became less potent over time.

I could just take a little look, I thought. He'd never know. It would ease my worries. And then we could all move on. I didn't stop to think what would happen if the articles said something I didn't want to see. I'd already made up my mind.

But I could not get away after the walk. We had dinner. Then Jack's father insisted on going to a whisky bar near the water. Davey didn't want to go, was shouting in the restaurant car park about getting home, but Jack talked him down.

And all the while I had my phone with me. I could have snuck off to the toilet, copied the URL of one of the articles, pasted it into the tiny Wayback Machine in my miniaturized browser, but something stopped me.

The pub Tony chose was beautiful. It was strung with fairy lights running like webbing across its ceiling. It was in the bay, but high up, so the sea mists drifted across the cliff tops and over towards us. On any other day I could have sat and watched those drifts for hours, but not that day. I couldn't wait to be alone.

We sat inside, though some brave people sat outside, rubbing their hands together and holding them over the candles that flickered in the sea gusts. There were floor-to-ceiling windows with a view of the roiling, churning ocean. The sunset in the west had reflected back over the sea, and everything was tinted a strange, heather purplish-blue.

I was next to Jack, nervous. He put his arm around me. His jumper was cold from outside. The ocean was drawing in, slowly, and I saw the wet sand marks getting higher and higher up the beach the longer we watched.

'Nice to meet your ken,' Tony said to me, raising his glass. 'Whit's fur ye'll no go past ye.'

I smiled at him, but was frowning inside. *What?*

Cynthia toasted too, laughing. They were always doing things like this. Little Scottish in-jokes.

Jack's parents and Dad started chatting and Kate was at the bar, so Jack, Davey and I sat in a row. Davey was scrolling aimlessly down his phone. He was often doing that. He didn't seem to be reading. He would take his phone out, scroll, and put it away again. Over and over. He received texts, but never responded to them. He didn't write, Jack said. He could – but he didn't.

Davey's head snapped up after a minute. 'I want to blow that candle out,' he said. His eyes focused across the room.

'Uh oh,' Jack said in a low voice. 'Not now.'

I followed Davey's gaze. Only one of the tables inside had a candle on it, a taper candle dripping wax in an old wine bottle. Davey's body language had changed. He was sitting up, rigid, like a dog waiting for a ball to be thrown.

'That's their candle. They like it lit,' Jack said gently.

'I'm going to get it,' Davey said. He began to push himself off his seat.

Jack looked at him, then at me, and then at the couple across the room. 'Hold on,' he said. He strode over to them.

I couldn't help but look at his small waist, the inverted triangular shape of his back, at the way his large hands faced forwards. I loved his walk, I found myself thinking. I loved his walk and his clothes and the way he was reaching out an arm to the couple, who were looking up at him. I couldn't hear what he was saying, but he gestured over to us, and they smiled, then nodded, looking understanding.

Jack arrived back with the candle. 'It was theirs,' he said to Davey. 'So enjoy it.'

Davey grinned at Jack – a rare, wide, genuine smile – took a deep breath, and blew it out. He inhaled slowly, looking at the softly curling smoke. That smell would forever remind me of Christingle services at church when I was young; a candle pressed into an orange, hundreds of them blown out at once. Davey was dabbing his fingers in the cooling wax, rolling it into balls, and Jack turned to me.

'In a year,' he said, in a low voice, 'where will we be?'

I calculated it in my mind, as I always did. Time wasn't time any more. Time was *how long until Wally*, or *how old will Wally be?*

'Wally will be seven and a half months,' I said.

'Quick maths.' Jack flashed me a smile. 'What do babies do at seven and a half months, then?'

He was drawling; a special voice he reserved only for me. It was deep, quiet; private.

'They smile, they sit, they eat some solid food.'

'Wonder what he'll like?'

'Isn't it weird? All the possibilities. From their hair colour to their build to what food they like, what job they do, if they're funny or sensitive or both.'

'I know. And he'll be *me and you*. Combined. Wonder when he'll have his first Wagon Wheel?'

'He might be a girl,' I said, though I felt like Wally would be a boy. 'Besides, they'll have discontinued them by then.'

Jack lived in fear of Wagon Wheels not being made any more.

Jack pulled a mock-horrified face. 'Don't say that ever again.'

'I hope he's more like you,' I said. And in that moment I meant it.

Jack's straight, dark lashes. His almost black irises. His self-effacing humour. His anxiety. His swagger. The way he took a cup of coffee into the shower with him to drink. There was so very much I liked about Jack.

'No way. You're excellent,' he said. He started ticking

off items on his fingers. 'Smarter than me. More attractive than me. Cooler than me.'

'I'm not cool.'

'You so are,' he said. He reached over and brushed a strand of hair out of my eyes. 'Super cool.'

It was such an intimate moment that I couldn't help but ask, one last time, before I went back to his parents' house and read those articles.

'Does everything we said last night still stand?' I said. 'About you and me?'

'Of course,' Jack said, without missing a beat. He covered my hand with his. It was cold and slightly wet from holding his Coke. He met my eyes and smiled.

It was the death knell, that smile. It started ringing out that night, and it didn't stop until morning.

23

One year ago

'I'm very, very sorry to say that the cancer has spread,' I said. A sentence no doctor ever wants to say, and no patient ever wants to hear.

The boy's eyes widened, and he turned instinctively to his mum, just as I had turned to my own mum in a similar appointment room not that long ago.

'What does that mean?' she said.

'I'm afraid it means that while it can be treated, it can no longer be cured,' I said. 'There are mets in his lungs – hence his cough.'

He'd become a six-feet-something music aficionado; a sixteen-year-old man who described himself as a socialist, who could pick up a guitar and play virtually any tune, and who could beat you at chess in less than fifteen minutes. But he was also terminally ill. He wouldn't see seventeen, I was sure of it. His cancer had defied the chemotherapy, metastasizing even during his treatment. He'd had his primary diagnosis less than three months ago.

I looked at them. They looked utterly bewildered. Bedraggled, almost, as if the news was a huge gust of wind that had knocked them over and they'd only just picked themselves up again. They could never un-know that news. Once you know something, you can't fool your brain any more. Never again.

'But you literally took my leg off,' he said, nodding at his grey-and-black prosthesis, even though it was only just detectable underneath his jeans. 'I've been having chemo. How can it have spread?'

'It blooms out,' I said, looking straight at him.

It did. It was like blowing a dandelion. His was vicious, aggressive, and he'd harboured it for a long time before we could cut it out and find a drug that worked. In hindsight, it's amazing when it works, when it doesn't spread. All it takes is one determined seed, blown around in the winds of the body.

'What . . .' he began. 'What about my GCSEs? And seeing Foals?'

I looked down at my lap. Foals were a band. I was only twenty-eight, still half-aware which bands were touring.

I didn't answer him then. I couldn't. All of that was to be shut out like a light. Life would go from looking to the future – to university – and slowly diminish. Soon he wouldn't book a gig more than a month in advance. And then, a week. And it wouldn't be a gig, it would be a trip to see a friend for half an hour. And then nothing. Nothing, nothing, nothing. Forever.

'We'll try to keep it at bay for as long as possible,' I prattled, moving stealthily back into doctor mode, the words running out of my mouth.

'But aren't there . . . ? There are different therapies to

try, aren't there? Radiotherapy, more chemotherapy? Can't you just – why can't you just cut it out of him?' his mum said.

'We can definitely manage this,' I said, and I saw the boy brighten. 'All those are options. But what I need you to understand is that this will never go away.'

I tried to be as clear as possible. It was kinder, in the long run, though not every doctor agreed.

'So this is terminal,' she said.

'We prefer to say incurable. Who knows how long anybody has?' I said.

And the boy looked straight at me, navy-blue eyes looking bright in the slice of sun he was sitting in.

'What now?' he said, directly to me.

I thought of all those nights I'd kept him company when he was neutropenic, playing Scrabble, chatting, and I felt an ice cube of sadness settle in my stomach. He leant forward, his head between his knees, for a second, and let out a kind of animalistic noise. And then he reached across to my desk, snatched up a heavy glass paperweight and threw it into the corner of the room. It marked the wall, then settled next to the skirting board. His mum stared at him in shock. He was still looking at me, as though it had never happened.

'Some people live for years with incurable cancer,' his mum said. 'Don't they?'

And so the balancing act began, between medicine and compassion, between quality and quantity of life. There was no point having two years if you were sick from chemo every single day of them. I knew that, and yet part of me wanted to buy him as much time as possible, like doing a deal with the Devil.

'Yes, they do,' I said, my voice barely a croak. But not with cancer like this. Like Mum's. Aggressive. Determined.

I could cite many platitudes: that it could be considered more a chronic illness, these days. That people often defied the odds. But it wouldn't be right to offer them to him, because, in his case, I didn't believe them.

I saw them both, much later, when I was locking the door to my office for the evening. They were limping along, the boy coughing, too. They didn't notice me.

The boy's nurse walked over to him. 'Get that down you,' she said, providing him with his prescription for oral chemo. 'That'll do you the world of good.'

'The doctors can manage this, can't they?' his mum said.

'Oh yes,' the nurse said, folding her arms across her ample chest. 'Absolutely. I knew someone who had bone mets for fifteen years. It's not as it was.' She reached an arm out to touch the boy's shoulder.

I saw the relief flash across his face. His eyes closed in a slow blink, and when he opened them again he was smiling. I wanted to interject. To tell them how voracious Ewing's sarcoma was. To tell them how high his tumour markers already were. But I didn't. I stayed silent, watching. Thinking.

24

Present day

It was midnight, and I was finally alone in one of the Rosses' bathrooms. I had my phone with me, hadn't got changed, so it was ensconced in my jeans pocket. Jack was in bed. I hoped he'd fall asleep, as he often did, before me. Everybody else was in bed. I'd waited. I had a fully charged phone and I knew the Wi-Fi password. I was ready.

One of the bath taps – they were brass, maybe copper – was dripping. The cold one. A tree branch was beating against the side of the house. I could hear unidentified snoring and smell the whisky that seemed to have seeped into the walls of Jack's house.

I looked down at the phone and steeled myself.

ITEM 9

Now I don't need to tell you how rubbish the police are at responding to calls about repeated break-ins. Just look at the case of John Douglas. (Edited to add – *link broken* – basically, he was a man who was burgled repeatedly. The police ignored his and his family's repeated cries for help, until one night, when the burglars arrived again, John Douglas shot one of them in the head.)

I sat on the side of the bath for a long time after reading the blog post. Okay, Rachel, think, I kept saying to myself. Only I couldn't. I couldn't think. Why had I looked at midnight? Why had I looked in Oban? Why had I looked the weekend Dad and Kate were sleeping soundly in the spare rooms?

He'd shot someone. I'd found out in parentheses on some blogger's site. That was the only mention in the whole post.

I carried on reading the comments. I couldn't stop. One of them was from the writer of the main post: 'I managed to find a screenshot of the Douglas article,' he had commented. The article had been pasted by him into the comments below, buried deep in the bowels of the internet. I clicked it to enlarge it, and read every word.

JOURNALIST WALKS FREE AFTER KILLING CHILD

The Flying Scotsman

10 April 2010

A SCOTTISH journalist has walked free following a murder trial in Glasgow High Justiciary Court. The verdict of not . . .

[To read this article and all our articles, subscribe for full access here. If you already have a subscription, please log in here.]

Murder.

Jack had killed someone.

Could it be true? It didn't feel like it could. The world felt changed. I couldn't believe everything was still standing. That the bath was still over there, taps still dripping. That my phone was still lit up. That everybody was still sleeping.

The window was misted up, and I wiped it to look out. The pond behind the house was a greenish-black, like an onyx stone. I wondered if it had happened here. The shooting. The killing. The death.

And then, right there in the bathroom, I had my first ever panic attack. I'd read about them in medical school. I understood them: the sudden release of adrenaline, like turning on a fast-running tap. The amygdala activated into fight or flight mode. But I'd never experienced it, until then.

My boyfriend. He'd killed someone. My baby. Me. What would we do?

I couldn't breathe. Oh God. I couldn't breathe.

I waited out the night. I don't know how I did it.

The only time I'd ever stayed up all night was when I was paid to do it, the splintered on-call hours rushing by, distorted and confusing.

This was totally different. The hours moved like honey dripping from a spoon. It was two o'clock for ages, and then three. Jack snored next to me, and all the while, I looked at him. And the worst of it was that I lay there, next to him, and my only thought, at the end of the night, was: so you are an excellent liar, after all.

All those hopes I'd had.

All those times I'd rationalized his behaviour.

Every inconsistency I'd spotted and dismissed as paranoia.

I'd been totally wrong.

Blind.

The next day I couldn't get him alone, not for long enough. My knees trembled every time we sat down with everyone. I didn't eat. My stomach felt acidic and queasy. Jack reached for my hand while walking back from lunch, and I jumped. Time drifted by, like the Oban mists, so slowly it felt sometimes like it had stopped entirely.

'We're stealing off,' I said eventually to Dad.

He was drinking tea with Jack's parents, around the kitchen table. There were two horns on the table. Long and slim. They cost a fortune, no doubt. Their house was like that. No papers or handfuls of coins or biscuit packets. Just strange ornaments, huge statues, artefacts.

'Are we?' Jack turned to me in surprise.

He didn't look like somebody who wanted to go out. His hair was messy and his feet were bare in his soft grey tracksuit bottoms. It was already late afternoon – he often didn't get dressed unless he had to. He called it *the freelance way.*

'Yes. To those boats in the bay,' I said.

There were rowing boats down in the harbour, which was walking distance from his parents' house. We'd been meaning to go out in them, but it was never usually dry enough.

'Okay,' he said. He was always happy to do whatever I wanted; to please me.

194

I should leave, I thought. Anyone else surely would have; the shot from that night in Oban ringing out behind them, chased by the fizz of the lies. But I didn't. I stayed. I needed him to tell me what had happened. To let him have his say, and to make it real. So I could believe it. My eyes felt heavy from lack of sleep. My hips ached.

Jack's father came out with us. The Rosses were always maintaining their house. It needed it, I was sure, but somebody seemed to be doing something every day: painting the window frames, picking apples from the orchard, jet-washing the drive. He began raking the leaves that lined the grass verge of the long, sweeping driveway.

'That's sociable,' Jack said sarcastically.

He agreed that his father raking the leaves was rude when my dad was sitting just inside, feeling out of place at their table. He was *like me*. He read the *Guardian* and liked Netflix and checked his iPhone too much. He was tidy enough but not a neat freak. He did a great line in his cat's interior monologue. He agreed that buying Starbucks was unethical and financially stupid but we both did it, anyway. He frequently didn't get dressed at the weekends but wasn't lazy. Did his past really matter?

But no. That wasn't true at all, although I wanted it to be. It did matter. Of course it did. It mattered more than anything.

'Let's get out of here,' Jack said to me, raising an eyebrow.

It was a warm day, a pleasant start to the week, and I reached for him. His hands were always cold, but I liked that; I liked the sharpness of it. I'd talk to him in a minute, in a minute. When the time was right. We were still in love with each other, and I wanted to enjoy our relationship's dying moments like an Indian summer in a final autumn.

For a while, I was still being the Rachel I was when I was part of Rachel and Jack, and I didn't know how to stop cracking jokes with him, moving close to the spot between his neck and shoulder, catching his lingering gazes.

'So, will you row?' Jack said. 'These limp arms don't maintain themselves.'

He was always doing that, putting himself down, even though he was quite broad, and looked pretty muscular to me.

'What happened to chivalry?' I said, but I was smiling.

'I have no upper body strength, that's what happened.' He pulled his Facebook photo face again, and I laughed quietly.

We walked through the woodland, our feet thumping on exposed tree roots, and I looked back at the house. Did it happen there? 'When did you move there?' I said.

'Few years ago.'

'Oh,' I said. Maybe they moved afterwards. Because of the memories.

The harbour was horseshoe-shaped, ringed by pubs and restaurants which were pumping steam out into the crisp autumn air. The beach was pebbled, and a lone fisherman stood, taking five-pound notes in exchange for a push out to sea in a tiny, rickety wooden boat. I thought of how I could approach the question when we were in the queue.

The autumn afternoon light was slanted and amber, casting rays across the dock. I could taste the tang of salt on my lips, inside my mouth. My hair took on a coarse quality immediately; holiday hair.

I didn't go for subtext: the kind I would use on parents whose children weren't responding to treatment. I could have. I could have used caveats like *to rule it out* when I was, in fact, testing specifically for it, because I suspected it. I could have said that he could talk to me about anything; that I wanted to get to know him better; that I, too, had a past. That would have been the best.

But instead I said, 'I wanted to read your Douglas articles.'

We were in the boat. The seats were wet, the cold water seeping through the bottom of my jeans.

'My politics?' he said with a raise of his eyebrows.

He was correct in presuming I wasn't interested in politics; that I would never normally feel the need to google him or read his articles. I had barely read his Jack Ross travel articles. They weren't him; they weren't memoirs or funny columns. They weren't living and breathing in front of me. They were summaries of bars, restaurants, with the occasional flash of Jack's wry humour, like seeing an incredible likeness in a portrait only for it to disappear again a few seconds later. They were facsimiles of him. I thought that it was plausible enough that I would one day read his columns, but that eyebrow raise said it wasn't.

'Yeah, just a bit of cyber stalking,' I said; a sentence that was much closer to the truth.

The fisherman pushed us, and we became weightless.

Jack reached for an oar, not looking at me. The rowlocks that the oars rested in had started rusting at the edges.

'Did you like what you saw?' he said, but his voice was strained.

'I saw some other things, actually —' I began.

And that was all it took. I never even finished the sentence.

His entire body language changed, sitting bolt upright like a rabbit that had heard gunshots.

25

'I told you I use two writing aliases,' he said, ignoring my murmuring and talking over me.

His tone was apologetic; sheepish. He knew he'd been found out. He was game-playing.

'I've seen an article about you on the internet.'

'Charity events?' he asked. 'I said, for my writing about politics –'

'No. About something else.'

'Oh, yes, wait – maybe . . .'

It wasn't his tone this time; that he was pretending to remember when he knew. I didn't like that, but no. It was the backtracking that did it. He didn't look me straight in the eye and say, 'You've read about the shooting, haven't you?' He drip-fed it. And that made it much worse.

'Oh?' I said, sounding like an idiot.

A particularly fierce wave broke, and the boat lurched unpleasantly. Spray arced over us.

'That's Balliemore,' Jack said, pointing to a mound across the sea.

'Right,' I said. *That's Balliemore.* 'What is your actual full name?' I continued. 'On your birth certificate.'

He avoided my eyes. 'John Ross,' he said.

'And Douglas is your mum's maiden name?'

He looked straight at me. 'Yes.'

'I think your name's John Douglas.'

A pause.

'You got me,' he said. 'It is. Mum's maiden name is Ross. Does it matter?'

'Yes,' I said quietly.

He said nothing. His name wasn't Jack Ross. He had lied to me right from when we met. I tried to look past it.

'The thing I saw. It was a trial. It was about a trial,' I said. I was embarrassed by my lack of anger, by my tentativeness. Why did I care what he thought, at this stage? But, oh, I did.

There was a metallic taste in my mouth. This was it. The conversation was unfolding in front of us and there was nothing I could do to stop it.

'What?' he said.

I frowned and wrinkled my nose, trying to look like I was comically confused, not desperate – absolutely desperate – for him to tell me.

He took his eyes off mine. He was looking all around us. Behind me, at the shops and pubs, flitting up to the sky, down to the oars. He pulled a loose thread on his gloves, but it wouldn't come.

'It said . . . it said you were . . . that you shot someone.'

The water was lapping all around us, steel grey with slices of reflected blue sky marbled throughout it like sudden shards of glass. I could smell the scents of the restaurants pumping out into the ocean from the shore: fresh, fried fish, vinegar, the kiss of butter in a pan. I could smell the tang of the salt on the shells that lined the beach and the cut of Jack's deodorant and the mildew, the rotting wood, of the boat.

'Was that you?' I continued.

He was looking straight at me.

I thought I could feel his fear like it had been taken out of his chest and placed right in front of us.

No. I couldn't. I was imagining that, too. I was wrong. Please let me be wrong.

It was another John Douglas, maybe.

It was something he'd reported on, and that's why his name was on it.

It was made up.

The theories piled up, none of them seeming plausible. But, like a patient about to get a biopsy result, I was praying.

'Rach,' he said. 'What've you seen?'

Maybe I had got it all wrong; had taken small pieces of information and added them all up together incorrectly, like a conspiracy theorist convinced we didn't land on the moon or that aliens lived in Area 51. There would be a logical explanation, like the time I treated a patient for repeated bruises and we were sure her family was abusing her but she actually had Ehlers-Danlos syndrome, which was causing the skin marks.

I couldn't see an obvious, easy solution that explained everything, but that didn't mean it wasn't there. I looked at him, waiting. But I also couldn't stop the tears collecting behind my eyes, the hot wetness, the tightness in my throat.

'Did you – did you kill somebody?' I said.

And, standing in the wings, against the backdrop to it all, was another me, the past me, who had never met Jack and certainly had not got pregnant by him. She was standing at the shore and screaming: *how has this happened to you? How are you having to ask this question?* And then she was gesturing frantically. *Stop*, she was crying. *You'll ruin things again with your paranoia. You can never take this question back.*

I opened my mouth, ready to speak, to retract it. So he had two names. So someone – maybe – with a similar name had killed someone, ages ago. It wasn't the same person. It *wasn't*. I knew he was good.

But, as I went to speak, Jack looked at me. His eyes were red-rimmed.

'Yes,' he said.

PART 2
What?

26

'It was December,' he said, the Oban afternoon light blanching his features.

A mist had descended and had bleached the orange light to white; less like the sun and more like a blinding floodlight, the full-beam headlight of an oncoming car.

'We'd been burgled three times before. They'd taken Mum's laptop. She lost all her photos. And Davey's stuff, too. His toys . . .' Jack paused, then added, 'gadgets,' with a self-aware laugh. It was very *him*. He knew that most teenagers didn't have toys worth stealing.

'We weren't . . . where we are now. We moved, afterwards. It was up on the hills, out in the countryside. You probably know,' he said. 'The press made a really big deal out of the fact it was a mansion. We should let ourselves be burgled because we're rich.' His mouth twisted, one side up, one side down, into an annoyed smile.

'I've hardly read anything,' I said. I didn't say that I'd tried to, that I'd trawled the Internet, tried to excavate it.

'How did you find it?'

'The Internet.'

He frowned and, to my disappointment, pursued it. 'There shouldn't be any,' he said tightly.

'There is. One. Some. Bits and pieces.'

'Right.' He paused, looking out at the water, then spoke again. 'Well, it was our house, called Thornfield. I was in with Davey. I was twenty-five. And I was ... I don't know, Rach. I was nervy. You ever been burgled?'

'No.'

'Well, it's like – they're right, what they say. It does feel like a violation. It feels worse than it actually is. I'd happily hand over my goods. But it's the other stuff. The second time, Mum's underwear drawers were open. Nothing taken. Just looked through. Stuff had moved in the bathroom. The bloody bathroom. We suspected who they were. There was this family who were always in court when I was reporting. We suspected them. And then, the next time, Mum found them. She memorized the guy's face. Aldridge. So the third time, she knew it was him again.'

I frowned. I could see why a burglar would go through their entire house: there were artefacts in almost every dusty room: items from travelling; heirlooms; bows and arrows hung on the walls. I didn't say so, though; of course I didn't.

'Aldridge was like –' Jack mimed, his hand out over the sea, hovering just a foot above the water '– distinctive. Really little and wiry. We didn't just see them around – we *knew* them. Oban's small. We saw them along the high street. They used to laugh about it. Take the piss.'

I shook my head, confused. It was hard to follow his train of thought. I needed Audrey with me: she'd make him give us a straight timeline of events. Oh, how I wanted Audrey with me. I drew my coat around myself, around Wally, feeling utterly alone with this stranger – Jack? John? – on the boat. The air was getting colder.

He was rowing us in a circle as he spoke, idly twiddling with one of the oars. And he was taking me round in circles as he told me what had happened.

'We reported them. In 2008 and 2009. Twice in 2009. We didn't know who it was the first time, so we couldn't prosecute. The second time, Mum did know, and identified him at a line-up. I helped her. I showed her a photo from the newspaper. It was wrong but I did it, anyway. He – Lee Aldridge, but everyone just called him Aldridge – got charged but he got off because he had an alibi. Then later in 2009, after the third burglary, the day after they were arrested, they asked Mum in the street if she was missing any of her ornaments. But they used each other as alibis. There were loads of them, on this estate. They all said they were with each other. We'd even got CCTV ready for the third time. But they couldn't be sure beyond reasonable doubt. It was grainy, they said, and he had an alibi. They still got off. They always do. Not that I'm one to talk,' he said, the ghost of a rueful smile playing on his lips.

'What happened next?' I said, though what I actually wanted to ask was: *how did any of this result in you putting a gun to his head?* I didn't, though. It was funny – and would've been fascinating, if it wasn't happening to me – how we all had our own take on things. How the story, for Jack, began back in 2008, and for me it was just beginning then, on that little boat in the sea. Or rather, how it began with that email I saw in the night.

Jack paused before answering. 'Yeah. Everyone was away. Davey was asleep upstairs. He was up there, and he was terrified by it all. Kept checking the locks. We got the dogs. To guard the house. But they were soppy. Useless.'

It was starting to get dark. The man at the shore was waving to us to come back, but Jack ignored him, picking up both oars and rowing further out. The moon had come out, looking grubby and pockmarked in the clear sky.

'They bloody let themselves in, Rach. I knew who it was when I heard any noise at all. It was only ever them. The house was the only one for miles. Totally isolated, which they knew. Lee Aldridge – and Dominic Hull. He was just a teenager.'

The image brought goosebumps out over my shoulders. I couldn't imagine two men letting themselves into my house as if they were merely bringing home the shopping; how menacing that would be. How desperate I would feel if it was the fourth time it had happened; how hunted.

'And they were the same men?'

'Yes.'

The same men. The same men. Over and over. That would be . . . I couldn't bear to think of it. But I wouldn't do what Jack did. Never, never.

We were far from the shore in our little boat. The sea underneath us was iron grey, the lights of the shore getting smaller and fading.

And then I thought about what *I* had done. My brain was trying to draw a comparison, but I stopped it, snatched the pen away. No. No.

'I told them where to go. I yelled at them. They threw something at me. This statue of Mum's. From Thailand.'

He said it easily, as if one might always have statues lying around, but I didn't take the mickey. He didn't raise his eyebrows or smirk at me, either. His skin looked pale and his hair too dark. He looked tired.

'Was there a *struggle*?' I said, so unfamiliar with these situations that I started using words I had only ever heard on the news. *Struggle. Suspicious. Accused.*

'Yeah,' Jack said. He was staring down at the oars, then blinked, puffed air into his cheeks and glanced back up at me. 'Our gun was on the top of the bookcase in the study. Just an air rifle. I always put it there after practising. There's a tree in that garden with hundreds of holes in it from all that. The press got in and took a photo. Training, they called it.'

'God,' I said, but I was thinking that there was something strange about his tone. Everything sounded too practised. Rehearsed.

'I did it without thinking. That's how right it was.'

I didn't say what I was thinking: that I wasn't sure anything like that could ever feel right, that I didn't understand how an air rifle could do so much damage, that I was still reeling from the transformation my lovely boyfriend had undergone in front of me. The longer I stayed silent, the more questions I had. If Jack had such good aim, how did he accidentally hit the intruder in the head? How did he have the time to get the rifle from the top of the bookcase in a struggle? Jack was tall, but not overly so. The questions crowded into my mind like people arriving in A&E on a Saturday night.

'I . . . I don't know what to say,' I said instead. 'What . . . how did you come to . . . ?'

'To shoot him? I'll tell you,' he said. He didn't sound brash or annoyed. He sounded like a politician getting to the question they'd been wanting to answer all night. 'He was rooting through our stuff. Unplugging cables in the study. Bloody unplugging them. I grabbed him. His mate fled. He reached for me. He was still holding the statue. I reached for the gun and shot. Blindly.'

'Blindly?' I echoed. I let my mind spin over the facts, like digesting a patient's symptoms. 'I thought they threw it at you – the statue?'

'No.'

'You just said they threw it at you.'

'There were two.'

I looked at him for a long time after that.

'I just shot him. Dominic Hull,' he said after a while. 'Quickly. I didn't risk assess like the court said I should have. It was self-defence. The prosecution had to prove beyond all reasonable doubt that I intended to kill, or was wickedly reckless. But once I raised the defence of it being self-defence, there are cases that say the *prosecution* has to negate that claim. And if there's any doubt – any possibility of self-defence – the jury has to acquit.

It's the law.' He said it all so easily; the legal terms and proceedings so familiar to him.

'And it was unlikely. Low risk. I never thought an air rifle would kill anyone. But I just shot, before he did anything to me.'

'And then he . . .' I couldn't stop thinking about that phrase. *Wickedly reckless.* I couldn't stop thinking, too, about the target-practice tree. He'd called it *a mistake* after the Hoppings.

'People always ask that.'

'What?'

'What happened next? How did he die? How did I know?'

'What people?' I said, distracted from my original question.

More questions squeezed into the waiting room, barging past the others. Who knew? Was I the last? And the last question, the most irrelevant one, but the one that said so much: how come the whole family changed their name? Did I have to call him John now?

'The police. The lawyers. Mum. Dad. Others. Newspapers. No comment,' he said. 'I just said no comment.'

'Well, did you know?' I asked. 'Did you know you'd killed him?' I would have stepped more carefully had the anger not started simmering then, producing a gentle steam. Later, it would become boiling, roiling and angry, the water bubbles popping on the surface like lava, but it wasn't there, not yet.

'As I shot him in the temple,' he said, 'he reached for me.'

He wasn't answering my questions. He never did. I tried to steer him, but he wouldn't let me, whether consciously or unconsciously. It felt like being pulled out to sea against my will.

I couldn't help but think of the boy, and the look he had given me, when my hand was on the door. But it was different, it was different, it was different.

Jack continued. 'I called an ambulance. But I could tell. I took his pulse. Felt like I was in a film. It didn't hit me for ages – how huge it was, what I'd done. And I could tell, even though he was still moving. I could tell. There was a bit of blood, but that wasn't the problem. It went into his brain. That's how it killed him.'

It would, I found myself thinking. It would go right through the temporal lobe. It wouldn't have to pass through any bone. The softest bit of the skull. The deadliest part.

'They charged me. That night. With murder.'

He looked me directly in the eye then, for the first time since his confession. He was facing the last of the sun. A narrow slice lit up his brown eyes, so light they turned almost golden, like a watchful lion's.

We both understood; a coded message passing from his eyes to mine. I knew exactly what he meant. Even when the observations were all normal, and the blood results fine, death came with a presence of its own: somewhere between an absence of heat and pinkness and a distinctive pallor. Sometimes it marched in, taking life swiftly, but other times it stole in: quiet and slow, like a prowling cat.

The only difference was, of course, that I was trying to save lives and he had taken one. But the rest was just the same.

Jack asked me what I thought after five minutes of silence on our boat.

I said I thought nothing.

He told me the rest: that his real name was John Michael Douglas, that he'd of course lied about his friend with the assault, that the real atrocity was his act, that he was acquitted because a jury found he had used self-defence. That sometimes his acquittal caused irritation in the press and it reared its head again. That he was, in a way, infamous.

'It was of its time,' Jack had added, later, once it was so dark and cold we were both shivering and his lips had gone a reddish blue.

His tone said, somehow, that he'd been told this himself. By a friendly aunt or uncle, maybe. Or even by his lawyer.

'It was just at the time when they were clamping down on that sort of thing. Americans with guns had gone mental.'

'Right, right,' I said tonelessly.

'Loads of decisions to prosecute are about policy,' he prattled earnestly.

It was the most earnest he'd ever been; not in an explanation of his crime but in defence of it. I had expected contrition, and I didn't get it.

'It was the ultimate in bad luck,' he added. 'How

unlucky do you have to be to kill someone with an air rifle?' His tone wasn't as jaunty as his words: it was imbued with sadness, flat almost.

But I didn't exactly sense regret. I looked at him, fiddling with the oar, at his damp shoes, at his legs crossed at the ankles. I could see the socks I'd bought him a few weeks ago. They had ginger cats on. He never wore serious socks.

'Why would they prosecute you, though?' I said.

'To tick their boxes,' he said grimly.

'It sounds like – just bad luck?'

'I don't know. Policy, like I said.'

'But, Jack,' I said, using his name even though it wasn't really his name, 'how do I know you're not lying this time?'

His eyes darkened. He rubbed his forehead, looking down at the bottom of the boat. 'I don't know what I can say to you, to make you believe that this is it.' He looked up at me. His whole face seemed shadowed. He spread his hands wide, then left them resting on the oars. 'I don't know. I hope that you know I'm not. I hope you know that I love you.'

I went for a walk on my own as soon as we got back to the shore. It was dark, but I didn't care. I ended up sitting with my feet dangling down the cliff top and out into the Oban air. Thinking. And then I stopped thinking and I dialled Audrey's number.

'Jack shot a burglar,' I said. 'He was acquitted.'

Audrey paused, then said, 'Bloody hell.' She didn't

ask how I'd come to find out. She just said, 'Bloody hell,' again.

And then we lapsed into silence.

'Did you get the Clare's Law response?' she asked eventually. 'I guess it'll be clear. It was an acquittal.'

'Yes. But it was clear because he changed his name.'

'Did he kill him? The burglar?'

'Yes.'

'Murder? Or culpable homicide? That's the Scots' manslaughter.'

'Murder.'

We said nothing again.

'But he was acquitted. At least he didn't hit a woman. Or stalk someone. Or rape someone,' Audrey added. 'It's . . . I don't know. Who knows what you would do if someone came into your house uninvited.'

I loved Audrey's open-mindedness. And although my heart lifted with hope, and I said, 'Really?' I wasn't ready for all of that. There was something else bothering me. It wasn't just the crime itself. It was the other stuff: Jack's telling of it. His reaction to it. His reluctance. His lies. It was always that way. The problem was never the creature caught in the spider's web, but the web itself, the surrounding gossamer. That's where the anger came from.

'Really,' she said.

The clouds in my mind cleared momentarily. Maybe if my best friend – and a *lawyer* – could understand it, perhaps I could, too. But then, Audrey was very *into* grey areas herself, had slept with another man at university in the early days of her relationship with Amrit, which he still didn't know about. I had wanted to tell him during so many night shifts, but never had. Audrey viewed it totally differently to me. She would say they were hardly exclusive – and, anyway, nobody got hurt if they didn't find out about the past.

Then I thought again about the man lying lifelessly in Jack's parents' study, leaving in a body bag, and I thought I might never get over it, not even if I left him. Never. My baby would be tied to this man forever. Wally would have his genes. For the first time, then, Wally felt like *mine*, and not *ours*. I wanted to run away with my baby, and keep him safe.

More thoughts formed: what if Wally had been the burglar? A misguided youth? I cringed and touched my hand to my stomach. Slayed, *murdered*, because he broke into a house to steal a PlayStation. Was that fair? How could I ever say it was? In hospital, I'd treat a burglar. I'd treat a murderer. A terrorist. I'd help them.

I shook my head. 'There's something really odd about it,' I said a few seconds later. 'It's . . . I don't know. He's cagey about it.'

'Cagey? He lied to you. Shouldn't he be begging for forgiveness?'

I looked at the sky. He should be, I knew. I agreed with her. Maybe there was more to it. Maybe Davey did it? Maybe he did it for Davey? Maybe that was why Davey had said he was in trouble?

I wished I could know. I wished I knew.

*

'Rachel,' Jack's mum said to me later.

'Yes?' I replied.

I was standing in the kitchen, on my own. Everybody else was in the living room. I couldn't bring myself to make us all leave a day early. Not only because of the embarrassment it would cause, but because of Jack, and because of Wally. Those two people meant I let so many things slide. Because of how much I loved them. Because I wanted Wally to come home from school one day to both of his parents. And because of Jack. Just: because of Jack.

Jack's mum had a broom and had begun sweeping the orange-tiled kitchen floor. She was methodically making her way back and forth across the room.

'We don't like to dig at old skeletons, here,' she said quietly.

The mixed metaphor confused me, until I realized: she knew that I knew. He must have told her. I wondered if she went through this with every girlfriend Jack had. Maybe his girlfriends were blissfully happy for a while, and then they found out, and then they did things like this: stood in the kitchen angrily, keeping out of the way; stomped around, looking strange.

'No?' I said, standing up.

She took a step towards me, and I saw she wasn't being frightening: she looked kind.

'Jack did a terrible thing. But we want to move on. Look ahead. Not back.'

I frowned. 'Okay,' I said, too quickly, too compliant, before I really grasped her meaning: there were to be no more questions asked.

This enormous event was to sit silently at the centre of our relationship, looming so large that neither of us could see around it.

I was alone in the bedroom. There was another massive portrait of some past Ross – or Douglas – staring down at me as I lay on the bed.

'How are you doing?' Jack said quietly, sadly, walking softly into the room and shutting the door behind him. He'd let me be for almost an hour, and then he'd come up to find me. 'I've told everyone you're ill.'

'More lies. I know. I know you told them.'

'Yes. They know. But I've said you're not feeling well. They won't . . . they won't want to discuss it, anyway.'

'I should leave. You,' I said, flashing a look his way.

'I . . .' Jack spread his hands wide, helplessly. 'I don't want you to do that,' he said, sounding small and Scottish.

'What's his surname?' I said, gesturing up to the picture. I flung my arm out, wrenching my shoulder. My face felt hot. My voice was too loud.

'Douglas. We all changed it. Afterwards. When all the press got too much.'

'Wow.'

I couldn't look at him. I could barely speak. 'How many lies did you tell me?' I shouted, looking up at him.

He was sitting cross-legged on the bed, plucking at the duvet cover. It was oddly childlike.

'Well . . .'

'How many?'

'One, really,' he said. 'Just – a big one.'

'A whopper. You looked at me the other night in the armchair. And you promised.' My voice cracked.

That lie didn't matter more than all of the others. But every time I thought of that locked-gaze moment between us my stomach contracted.

He looked away at that, biting his lower lip, a shaking hand raking his hair back – like Davey was always doing. 'I know. I'm so sorry. That was self-preservation, and there's no excuse.'

It was a full and frank apology, unlike his criminal confession.

'It's not okay,' I said.

'Rach, you don't know. You don't know how it was. There were bloody reporters –' He gestured at the window, at the black Oban night. His Scottish 'r's rolled like thunder on *reporters*. 'They camped out. They're still there, sometimes. It comes up, again and again. We've moved. We've all adopted Mum's maiden name. It was a witch-hunt.'

'Did you think I'd never know?'

'No, I . . .' He stood to his full height, pulling a hand through his hair. 'I would have . . .'

'Wally and I – we deserved to know.'

'I know. It all got so serious so quickly . . .' He trailed off.

And even then, when we were arguing, I felt a dart of pleasure as I caught his gaze.

He smiled at me, tentatively. 'Not Wally,' he added. 'Just you. The way I felt about you. It was always serious. I feel like we're made for each other. We're just right, aren't we? Together?'

I looked away. 'You lied to me about your name. Your past. What you've gone through. You've had a lawyer. You've been to trial. Have you been to prison? I don't even know.'

'No. I promise, Rachel. This is all.'

'No?'

'Can you imagine me in prison? How would I survive?'

'That's true,' I said.

'I didn't plan it. A bad thing happened to me. And I just reacted to it. And my whole life changed in a moment. But I'm still me,' he said. And then, in a quieter voice, 'I am still yours.'

'*You* know that. But you know everything. Your history. What happened. But I don't,' I said. 'I know nothing.'

I looked at him. He stared back at me. It was true. This was our story, but it was more his than mine. It began for him years and years ago, and for me just recently. Where would it end? Would we go our separate ways today, tomorrow, next year? Would I become the only girlfriend he'd ever told, or the next one in a long list of people who couldn't come to terms with his past? Whose version was correct? Mine: *my boyfriend had a horrible past*? Or his: *my girlfriend wouldn't let the past be the past*?

We went downstairs together, after a while. Jack smilingly passed me a herbal tea as we watched a film, but our acting was wooden, like we were performing in a bad play.

And all the while, as the film flickered in front of us, lighting the living room blue and white, I was thinking: *it may have been a witch-hunt, but that doesn't mean you're not a witch.*

27

The main problem was that I couldn't stop investigating him. Not once I knew about the Wayback Machine, even though it hardly ever threw anything up.

Not once I knew the victim's name.

I did it at night, when I wasn't sleeping. That didn't help, the lack of sleep. Amrit had called me twice one night, quite late, but I couldn't face speaking to him, even though I was up. It was easier if I never saw anybody I had worked with ever again. It was better that way.

A few nights later, at gone ten o'clock, I opened my laptop and started reading.

I found two more screenshots of two more articles. One had a photo of Jack in it. That was it, after hours of trawling.

Soon, I came to know all the permutations of the small rotation of fragments of text I could find: the selection of grainy photographs they used. The photo of Dominic from Facebook taken in front of a giant Christmas tree, his hands raised to the sky. The one of Jack at target practice, grinning and holding a gun. Relics, hidden in the Internet. Preserved.

JOHN DOUGLAS: FRIEND OR FOE?

The Guardian
9 April 2010
TWENTY-FIVE-year-old John Douglas was in his Oban home that December night. He had no idea what would befall him. How could he? He heard, he says, the burglars entering for the fourth time in less than two years, and he acted.

WHO WAS DOMINIC HULL?

The Daily Mail
8 April 2010
THE HULLS live modestly, on a glum estate in east Oban. Dominic's mother showed me into their two-bedroom flat, past a threadbare brown carpet and a grey sofa and right into Dominic's room.

It is preserved, as if he never left. There are song lyrics everywhere. Rap, mostly. Hip hop. He's stencilled them carefully, framed them.

The rest is unremarkable. He played PlayStation games. He liked cars, has a few reviews of the latest models torn out and scattered around his room. But it is those words I can't forget. He wrote his own poems, his own raps, his mother said. He was buried with a notebook. That was who Dominic Hull was. And that's how he will be remembered.

http://thenewsinbrief.blogspot.com

Douglas: Live Blog

Day Four

8 April 2010

09.23: John Douglas just walked past me. He was nothing like I imagined. He was tall and muscular, yes, and had the concentrated stare seen in his byline photograph, his mugshot, on the way to his failed bail hearing. But as he pushed past me, a hand held up in defence, I glimpsed something else in his eyes: a quiet confidence.

Redacted

Every time I came across a story about him, it jolted me to read *John*. I don't know why that felt like the biggest aspect of it all, but it did.

It was so easy to do, googling him. Nobody would ever know.

Audrey and Kate took me swimming one evening that week. They were staging an intervention. I told them Jack and I hadn't broken up, but they just nodded. Audrey knew why. Kate didn't.

Kate was swimming, but Audrey and I were standing in the shallow end, up to our waists in water.

'She's really good,' Audrey said.

Kate was swimming length after length without pausing. Her body was svelte and muscular.

'She used to swim. For tennis training,' I said.

'Oh yeah. I remember that. Didn't she get up at five?'

'Yeah,' I said.

I loved that she knew everything about my life. Our shared history.

Something must have sparked a memory, because after a pause, she said, 'Do you miss Amrit? Working with him? You always had such . . . lols.'

'Yeah,' I said sadly, remembering all those shared Diet Cokes.

I even missed the parts of it that I had hated, the constant distorted tiredness from shift work. The inability to keep to firm plans, always being over an hour late to dinners. And the rest. The strange quirks of being a doctor. Sitting at a Hallowe'en party when half an hour previously I'd been stitching somebody's skin together. Listening to stories of office work when my job had involved the very extremes of human experience: being born and dying, and death-bed wishes, and seeing a patient's heart beating in the flesh right before me during an operation, and people who heard voices, and people who didn't want to be alive any more.

I looked across at Audrey. The air in the swimming pool was warm and sticky, and her veins were standing out, thick and fat against her skin. In the strangest way, I even missed cannulating, especially adults. The push and then the give as you found the vein. It would be like riding a bike, I knew it would. It would be so easy to go back. But I wouldn't.

Audrey changed the subject. 'I wanted to see how you were doing with Jack. I know it looks bad. I know you think I really liked Ben, but . . . I've never seen you with anyone how you are with Jack. It's like you're all lit up around him.'

'Ah,' I said, smiling. 'That's nice. That's really nice. You did like Ben.'

She walked a few paces, moving her arms through the water.

I remembered the night he finally left. It was awful, but not in the way I'd expected. It wasn't long after I'd left medicine, and the accusations that increased after I stopped practising had reached a height. He'd driven away, and I'd felt only shame. I'd opened the fridge and stared uselessly at a water bottle whose insides had misted over.

And then, the next day, the relief had started to creep in. That I didn't have to put up with somebody playing endless Xbox games, or tinkering with their car constantly. That I could stretch out in the bed by myself. That I could move. Get a flat. Get a pet. It wasn't love, I realized on the third night. It was as easy as that. Real life was complicated: I had driven him away with my paranoia, but it was actually for the best. We didn't love each other. Not properly.

'I think about him sometimes, you know,' Audrey said then. Her tone was strange. Tentative.

'Ben?' I said, confused.

'No. Chris. You know.'

I did know. The man she'd slept with. She hardly ever talked about him. Perhaps she was willing to now, to show me that nobody was perfect.

I nodded, remembering the precise moment she had emerged from his room, across from mine, at university. I'd only just introduced her to Amrit. They were smitten, I'd thought. They'd been on five dates.

I hadn't needed to say anything to her, just thrown her a questioning look across our halls of residence corridor.

'It was nothing,' she'd said, closing his door behind her. 'Amrit's away.'

We'd hardly said a word about it, since then. But it had made me view her differently – just slightly. I had thought about it on their wedding day, during my speech, and plenty of times after that, when I worked with Amrit.

'Do you regret it?' I asked now. Audrey stood very straight. She was tall, and usually stooped. She didn't look at all like a lawyer, I found myself thinking.

'Of course. I feel awful about it. Especially when I think about you and Jack. When you're the liar, it's sort of . . . justified.'

'Justified?' I said, bristling.

'No – not justified. But, like . . . I know how much I love Am. So I know how little it meant. I *know* that. If I told him, he wouldn't. He wouldn't know how truly meaningless it was.'

'Maybe it being meaningless makes it worse,' I suggested.

'Maybe.'

I looked across at her. She scooped up some water in her hands and let it trickle down her arms. There was a moment of silence, charged and heavy, and then Audrey looked up at me.

'What're you going to do about Jack, anyway?' she said.

'Stay. I love him. And the baby,' I said.

Wally was at the heart of it. Why I let things slide. Why I didn't scan and re-scan, when I was unsure, like I'd done at work. Why I blindly kept trying to patch things over, covering a wound so deep it really needed stitches instead.

28

One year ago

The boy's mum came over to me after I'd finished drawing the curtain around a girl with meningitis who was recovering well.

'Hi,' I said to her.

She looked expectant, like somebody about to open a million-pound negotiation. I raised my eyebrows and led her to a side room. It was a side room I'd slept in, often, on the sofa by the wall during night shifts.

'He's in for chemo,' she said. *'Palliative.'*

'Yes. I know.'

'But we saw the consultant on the ward round, yesterday.'

'Daniel Curtis?' I said.

'Yes. I think so. He gave us a pep talk – about how many advances have been made. About how, if they can keep the cancer stable, there's no reason why he won't live for years. Decades.'

'That's true,' I said. 'If we can keep the cancer stable.'

'Can't we? Can't *you*?'

'We'll do all we can.'

'I want to know specifically what you'll do for him. What you'll do to ensure it doesn't grow.'

I hesitated. 'Well ... his sarcoma didn't go into remission very easily. I need you to know that the typical survival rate in his category is twenty out of every one hundred. That's five-year survival.' I said it bluntly in order to be kind. It was better to know it all at once. So then she would be able to come to terms with it. To enjoy the time he had left.

'Twenty's not *none*.' She reached out and fingered the blinds, parting them slightly and peering out.

She wasn't looking at me, and I needed her to; to understand what I was saying. We wished it could be different, but it wasn't. The boy's prognosis was poor. It was poorer than other patients with his stage of disease. The best thing would be for his mum to understand this, so we could make him comfortable. So they could come to terms with death, before it arrived. To be at peace. That was what I wanted for them. That was all we could hope for.

'Yes, but there are some things specific to his case. He has a temperature. He's generally unwell. It was quite advanced when we caught it. It's ... I'm very sorry. But I want you to be aware. Of how long you've got together. Of how it's likely to be.'

She made a kind of gasping noise. It was awful, animalistic, as she realized the truth herself. 'So the chemo might do nothing?'

I nodded.

She seemed to think for a moment. 'It seems so easy. Just stop it growing.'

'It's not that simple,' I said. 'Though I wish it was.'

'He's been so upbeat since the consultant. I know he's going to ask you about it.' She pointed behind her, with her thumb. The nail was chewed.

'About his prognosis?'

'Yes.'

I fiddled with my stethoscope. I had a monkey clipped to it. It entertained the younger children during their obs. 'Okay,' I said. 'I'm happy to talk to him about it.' I would look him up again later, I decided. See how he was feeling. The social media window into his soul.

I looked out of the window, between the blinds. I could see the boy, sitting up in one of the chemotherapy chairs.

His mum was looking at me. She had an eighties perm, and her eyes were ringed with thick black eyeliner. She was silent again. And then she said, 'Who wins here?'

Her tone was imbued with the voice of somebody who'd had to advocate for her child for years. And he still was her child, in the eyes of the law and the medico-legal world. He was still a minor.

'What do you mean?'

'If you tell him.'

I met her eyes. There was a threat there, in their slight narrowing.

'Well, I would need your consent to discuss anything like this with him,' I said, mulling it over.

Whether or not he was competent to receive the news himself depended on lots of things: his age, his maturity, what he wanted to know, what his mum wanted him to know. But, ultimately, she held the trump card until he turned eighteen.

'I don't want him to know how long he's got. It's not good for him,' she said.

'I would like you to think carefully about that,' I replied slowly. 'If he's going to ask me, I don't want to have to lie. He'll ask others who are in chemo with him. He'll google it. If he really wants to know.'

Her eyes flickered in annoyance. 'Listen –' she said, reaching out to grip my arm.

Her hand was icy cold. I could feel it even through my white coat.

'– your instructions are not to say a word to him.'

'I think we should have a meeting. With the consultant. And the Trust's lawyer,' I said.

'Fine. But you won't be telling him. He's happier. He believes he's got years.'

I looked out at the boy. He was tapping away on his phone. I thought privately that he might not even have months.

It was awkward, uncomfortable, that Tuesday morning, that conversation. Later, in the debrief meeting, I had to repeat it all, in as much detail as I could. I stated what had happened, but couldn't capture the context. The stuff that wasn't verbal. The parking ticket she was holding between her forefinger and thumb. She kept flicking the edge of it. It was dog-eared by the end of our conversation. Nor did I detail her blackened tears as her eyeliner ran. Instead I just noted down the words, said it had been an emotional meeting. No context.

'I am not consenting to you telling him when he's going to die,' she said.

She couldn't have been clearer. No consent. No news.

I turned to the door.

It was classic denial. She didn't want to face it, and she wouldn't let him, either.

Newcastle Hospitals NHS Foundation Trust
NHS NUMBER: 0246503/6

PATIENT RECORD SUMMARY:

Note: Patient is <u>under no circumstances</u> to be told anything related to his prognosis.

29

Present day

I rang Audrey at five to ten in the evening, two nights later.

I'd lasted a day before checking the Internet again. It was all too easy, that sort of research. Mining for information. It felt distinct, somehow, from hiding in the bushes outside Jack's house, or driving past his place of work, though perhaps it was just the same.

'I was just thinking about you,' she said warmly. 'I'm at bloody *work*. Was going to send a Code Red text.'

'You're at work – why?' I said.

She seemed to regularly do longer shifts than I ever did, for no more pay. Audrey would often – back in my medicine days – describe herself as being *on nights* and *on long day shifts* all at the same time.

'Disclosure,' she said. 'For Adam.'

Adam was her boss, one of the other partners at the firm. He'd never spoken to me.

'No idea,' I said.

'I won't bore you with it. What's up with you? How's Jack?'

'I've been reading more articles,' I admitted.

'Why?' she said.

'Just trying to find out as much as I can about what went on. He's just so vague about it. Sometimes. It feels like he's not telling me everything.'

'That's not fair,' she said softly.

'No.'

'I've been meaning to ask – what did he get off on?'

'You sound like such a lawyer. He *got off* . . .' I said slowly, scrolling up through the articles to quote it to her. 'Self-defence, I think? I don't know, actually. I can't tell. They're only screenshots. I don't know where the articles are.'

'That'll help. Knowing that,' she said. 'If you can read the judgment you'll know why he was acquitted. Hang on . . .'

I heard the clunk of a door, a soft thud, then footsteps. Heels on marble. She was in the foyer – alone, I supposed. I hated that foyer. My stomach clenched every time I walked through it. It was so different to a hospital.

'Google this,' she said.

'What?'

'Type exactly what I say.'

'Okay.'

'H. M. Advocate v Douglas, 2010.'

'Okay,' I said, typing into my laptop. 'Nothing.'

'Okay, go to Scottish Law Reports. Google that. Then type that reference into the search box. Use my details to log in. We have access to all the law reports.' She lowered her voice and said, 'Audrey Kapur, password Amritsunshine1.'

'Got it,' I said.

It loaded. It was a thick block of text. Tiny font, no paragraphs.

'It will only have the headnote. Not the judgment. What does it say next to "verdict"?'

I read it off the screen. 'Not proven,' I said.

There was a pause. A loaded pause. A pause more pregnant than I was. It yawned on and on.

'Not proven?' Audrey repeated.

'Yes, that's what it says. Audrey, you're freaking me out. Say something. What's going on?'

'Do you know what a not proven verdict is?'

'Not really.'

'It is distinct from *not guilty*.'

'What do you mean?'

'It's the bastard's verdict, Rach,' she said softly.

My body went cold. 'The what?'

'It's . . . that is unusual,' she said. 'Did he say why? There's normally . . .'

'What?' I asked again.

'It's not a "not guilty", Rach. It exists only in Scotland. Type it into Google.'

I did as she said, my fingers shaking.

ITEM 11

Not proven is a **verdict** available only in Scottish trials. Such a trial may end in three verdicts: not guilty, which results in an acquittal; guilty, which results in a conviction; and not proven. Not proven technically results in an acquittal, though it is not to be confused with not guilty. It is usually reserved for times when the judge or jury is not sufficiently convinced of the defendant's innocence to return a not guilty verdict, but has inadequate evidence to convict him or her.

'What does it mean?' I said, a round of fear starting off like a huge ship's wheel turning in my stomach. 'I don't understand.'

'It's still an acquittal,' she reassured me quickly. 'Night, Sam. I'll send the power of attorney for signing once it's drafted,' she said to somebody else, then resumed. 'There are two ways to get off in Scotland. Not guilty and not proven. Not proven is . . . well. There will have been . . . some ambiguity.'

'He wasn't found not guilty?' I said, just realizing.

'No.'

'Wow.'

'I know. I'm sorry.'

The nuance between not guilty and not proven felt as wide as the Atlantic Ocean just then; important in ways I couldn't see, couldn't understand, like feeling my way around a room in the dark, making sense of the shapes but knowing instinctively where the walls were.

'The bastard's verdict,' I said dully. A hot flash came over me, heating my cheeks as if I had submerged myself in hot water. *The judge or jury is not sufficiently convinced of the defendant's innocence.*

I was trying to remember what exactly Jack had said

to me. Had he said he was found not guilty? No, I didn't think he had. He'd said acquitted, which was technically correct. But he wasn't getting off lying to me on technicalities.

I scrolled through the photos on my laptop. The latest photograph was a selfie, of him and Howard. They were in bed together, Howard sitting up in the crook of Jack's arm. He'd emailed it to me. The caption read 'squad goals'.

'I wish I didn't like him so much,' I murmured. 'He's so funny.'

'There is nothing so dangerous as a funny man,' Audrey said.

'True.' I sighed. 'He'll tell me it's in the past. If I ask.'

'Do you know why he was acquitted?'

'No. I don't really know any details. One of the articles said there was a question over whether he used reasonable force, but it's just vague. And he's vague, too. He talked about policy.'

'Do you know what we could do?' Audrey said.

I loved her for that *we*.

'No. What?'

I lay on my bed, moved the curtain slightly and peered out at the Newcastle night. The Wok Bar over the road had lit up my bedroom a reddish pink. I loved that city-centre flat.

'We could order the trial transcript,' she said. 'Anyone can. They're public documents.'

I looked out at the sky, bleached white from the city lights. He wasn't *not guilty*. And he hadn't told me.

More lies, even when he was telling the truth. Did he think I wouldn't find out?

'Do it,' I said.

ITEM 22

From Wikipedia: Because the 'not proven' verdict carries with it an implication of guilt, but no formal conviction, the accused is often seen as morally guilty . . . the one thing all not proven verdicts have in common is a central huge ambiguity; either as to the identity of the defendant or the evidence itself.

Adlamont Murder: Monson was working as a tutor when, on 10 August 1893, he took his charge, Hamborough, a young man, out for a day's shooting. A shot rang out across the estate in the afternoon and Monson was seen retreating with a gun. Later, Monson was seen cleaning the gun. Two weeks before his death, Hamborough had taken out two life insurance policies in the name of Monson's wife. Monson's account is that Hamborough shot himself by accident. Monson was found not proven at trial.

Madeleine Smith: Smith was, controversially at the time, dating a Frenchman her parents disapproved of during early 1855. The Frenchman, called L'Angelier, ended their relationship suddenly. Smith was seen ordering arsenic in a pharmacy, where she signed in as M. H. Smith. L'Angelier died on 23 March 1857 of arsenic poisoning. The jury at her murder trial returned the verdict of not proven. It could not be proven beyond reasonable doubt that Smith had met L'Angelier immediately prior to his death.

Google search: recent not proven verdicts

Dave Grimes: Grimes, at his trial for rape in March 2013, walked free following a not proven verdict. Catrina Evans, who accused him of rape, said: 'It's the cruellest, coldest act for a victim. It's a no-man's-land between innocence and guilt. It's cruel for everybody.'

I texted Audrey: *I can't find a single not proven crime where I don't think the defendant did it.*
Her reply came immediately.
I know, it said.

30

I slept early and dreamt of Dominic Hull. I got up in the night, fresh from a dream about him falling down a rickety set of stairs in a made-up house, and I typed his name into Facebook.

His profile was open. It was full of tributes. People writing *missing you* and *hope you're having fun up there, mate.* I scrolled to the bottom of them, back to 2010, when his own updates began. Just like that, from dead to alive with the scroll of a mouse.

I don't know what I had expected to see in his updates. Rants about people and drama, maybe. Gloating about robbing people. Or nothing. Facebook games or poorly written updates.

I didn't expect what I found: pithy, witty updates, all in rhyme.

> You see me in the Job Centre,
> Don't know I'm writing my journals.
> You didn't know I could rap like this,
> My Tupac rhyming internals.

I scrolled down. They were almost poetic in places.

> The evening pavement looked red tonight,
> Why didn't you come to hold me tight?

I moved on to his photos. He was posing, his biceps out, a cigarette in his mouth, in many. But he always had a notebook with him. A small one. Brown and battered. A biro clipped to its side. He was a writer, I guessed. And he might have been a burglar and a bully, but he was something else, too. His was a life filled with the things that were important to him. His family, his friends. His rhymes that scores of his Facebook friends liked.

I moved on to his parents next. Their profiles were open. They were campaigners, that much was clear. Not only for the removal of the defence of reasonable force, but also for the abolition of the not proven verdict itself, though they never seemed to mention Jack or the case specifically. They said the verdict increased uncertainty. They'd created petitions and Kickstarter projects for getting rid of it. I guessed that was why Jack's *atrocity* had reared its head again. They were lobbying the Scottish Parliament.

They tagged their deceased son in every update.

I was looking at their loss, their private tragedy, and yet I didn't shy away from doing it. It was all public, and that – somehow – seemed to make it alright.

There would have been a funeral. The coffin might have been white. He was a child, after all. Just like my patient; my boy.

Jack sent me a text while I was lying in bed trying to fall back to sleep. It was a selfie. It would have been sexy, the darkness around him, his shoulders tensed, were it not for the affected, self-aware pout, the ubiquitous peace sign favoured by Instagram users. I couldn't help but laugh at it, enjoyed seeing those dark eyes almost in real time.

He followed it up with a message: *any better than Facebook photos?* Then he rang me, straight after – once he'd seen I'd read it, I suppose.

'Hi,' he said. His voice was deep, somehow carrying with it the rounded, thick, silent Oban air. 'It's crap being like this.'

'Like what?'

'Together, but, you know. Awkward. Not mates. Not best friends.'

'We're still friends,' I said with a soft laugh. 'It's all just been a shock. That you'd been lying to me.'

And that was the only opportunity I gave him to tell me. I should have given him more, like setting rat traps. See if he told me. But I didn't.

'I've read more,' I said. 'You weren't found not guilty.'

Jack paused. It was infinitesimal, but it was there. And it was significant. Like the hesitation before pressing the brake when a pedestrian crosses in front of your car, or arriving on a platform just as the train doors are closing. Small but significant; life-changing.

'It was not proven,' I said. 'What does that mean?'

'Yeah.'

'What do you mean, "yeah"?'

My eyes had been closed, lying in my bed, and I opened them again. Everything was where it was, before all of this happened. My cotton curtains that

243

failed to block out the city lights. My neat bedspread. The Hippocratic Oath on my wall, engraved on a metal hanging. But everything had changed. Again.

'Well – there are three verdicts in Scotland.'

'*I know.*'

'It's not a big deal, Rach. They're both not guilty.'

'Really?'

Jack heaved a sigh; a sad sigh. A loaded sigh. I didn't mind, though: that part was real. 'It means nothing. I don't know – everything.'

'Hmm,' I said, wanting him to go on, praying he wasn't about to be notified that somebody had ordered the transcript of his trial.

'It means there was significant doubt about your innocence,' I said.

To my surprise, Jack laughed. 'Yeah, I'd say so,' he said. 'Hence the trial.'

The laughter was piercing in its inappropriateness.

'Why was it not proven?'

'I don't really know,' he said. His voice was musing. 'I wonder if it was policy.'

'How?'

'Well, I was scared. They said self-defence thresholds are lower when you're being . . . invaded. When you're scared.'

'Yes,' I murmured, and for the first time I felt a little glimmer of sympathy, like the first rays of sunlight in the morning, or a firework going off in the distance, its twinkles visible through spindly autumn trees. It would be scary to be repeatedly burgled.

244

I tried to imagine, lying there in my flat, how I would feel if I heard the door thud downstairs. Adrenaline would fill my system. Maybe I'd confront them. And then we would be rowing, fighting. Signs of a struggle. Who knew what I would do? Can anybody ever really say?

'They wanted to acquit me. But it's never right to kill someone. No matter how unlucky you were. Or how often they'd burgled you. So they thought, we'll get him off, but make him look culpable. To send a message to the public. I don't know. I don't know, Rach. Please don't . . . I love you. I promise I can make you happy. We'll be so happy together. Please don't . . .'

'Why didn't you tell me? You swore – you swore it was all.'

'Because . . . because I didn't want you to doubt me,' he said sadly.

'How do I know you're telling the truth now? You could be lying, still.'

He didn't say anything to that, except, 'I'm sorry.' Another sorry.

We talked for a while longer.

I looked out, down at the street, and saw a bald man with an earring wearing a Newcastle United football shirt – a Grade A Geordie, Jack would call him. In the Wok Bar, during a quiet moment, one of the chefs started sweeping up, wearing checked trousers and a pair of headphones.

'How's Wally?' Jack asked.

'Good.'

'I've been to the bloody walk-in centre and I feel like a twat,' he said.

'Which one?'

'Lorn. Don't laugh,' he said. 'It was actually really scary.' His voice was soft.

'What happened?'

'I had really sharp pains in my side. My *right* side.'

'Why didn't you ring me?'

'Because I knew you'd tell me not to go.'

'Where on your side?'

'Above my hip bone. In the soft bit.'

'So you had right iliac fossa pain and you thought you had appendicitis,' I said.

'Yes. I thought it had ruptured, actually.'

'Believe me, you would know if it had ruptured.' The words tripped off my tongue, and there was something lovely in how unconscious they were. Medicine was still there, inside me. 'Did it stop as you stood up?' I said.

'It got better, yeah.'

'I could have told you on that basis alone that it wasn't appendicitis. Its primary feature is that you can't stand up straight.'

I was still on the phone to him, but, in my head, we were in a consulting room. I could smell the tang of the bleach and see the computer with its Y and N keys rubbed clear of their lettering. He'd be lying on the bed, answering my questions, and I wouldn't be looking at the clock, or trying to stop myself checking the *Huffington Post* until lunchtime, or rewarding myself with biscuits for finishing a batch of typing. I'd be completely lost in it. In that juncture where the science, the examination, met the art – the patient's interpretation of their own symptoms. Their pain would be filtered through the lens of their experience. One person's ten out of ten was another person's four. I missed it so much, in that moment, that I closed my eyes and wished as hard as I had ever wished in my entire life that I could go back. Not to medicine, but through time.

'But – right-sided pain,' Jack said.

'Appendicitis can present on either side, you know. It's just slightly more common on the right.'

I was assaulted by memories of medicine as I said it. Of trying to help people. It occurred to me that fear wasn't a good enough excuse for what Jack had done. I'd been scared too: when young people wouldn't respond to CPR. When I saw elderly patients go white and thin and we'd have to move them to the hospice. When people receiving chemo got colds. I'd tried to help them, when I was scared. I hadn't done what he'd done.

'So what did they diagnose you with?' I said, trying to ignore my thoughts about him.

Jack went silent for a second. 'Trapped wind.'

I could hear the humiliation in his voice, and couldn't hide a smirk. 'Prescription for Imodium and a fart?' I said.

'Pretty much.'

We fell silent for a while. I could hear his breathing. It reminded me of lying next to him, in his arms, feeling his torso warm against my back, feeling so happy with him. So safe.

I thought of the boy, ever present in my mind. 'Do you dream of him – Dominic? I dream, sometimes . . . of patients I lost.'

It was the closest I'd ever come to discussing the boy with Jack. I'd been too convincing with my moaning about long hours, a failing NHS, the litigation culture we were forced to work in. He'd never once asked me straight out why I'd left. He trusted me.

'Dream?' he said. 'No.'

I frowned then, but I was drifting off to sleep, the phone warm against my ear, and couldn't analyse my emotions fully. 'No?' I said sleepily.

'No,' Jack said again.

We hung up a few minutes later.

31

One year ago

'It could be years, that's what he said,' the boy said happily. 'Years and years. Decades. He said it hardly changes anything. People could be hit by a bus, he said. Nobody knows how long they've got.'

I smiled politely as I walked across his room. He was running another fever, was being kept in overnight. It was dusky outside. His window was flung open, even though it was winter. His last, I was sure. I had looked at his Twitter account again. He had been upbeat. It had been nice to see, but bitter-sweet, too. Because he was wrong.

'But now,' he said, looking at me, 'I want to know what you think. Not some general oncology consultant who's never treated me.'

The words couldn't be clearer. We were alone. He knew the score.

'I'm not sure I'd want to know,' I lied, 'if I were in your shoes.'

'Yes, but you're not dying,' he said.

He blinked, swallowed, and I could see a sheen on his eyes. I'd never seen him cry. Not once. Until then.

'I can feel it, you know,' he said. He drew a hand to

his chest. 'I can bloody feel it. Cancer on my chest. It's heavy. I want to know when the end is.'

It was a stance I entirely agreed with. If I could, I would have to know.

'That's a huge question. Why don't you think about it?' I said. 'We'll chat to your mum and that consultant, and we'll all get together and discuss what's best for you.'

'How about you and I just discuss what's best for me – here and now?' he said. 'Let's not wait until I get to eighteen to discuss whether or not I'll see eighteen.'

He was so eloquent like that. He could have gone on to do anything. Maths, science, English. He could've been a writer, a doctor, a lawyer.

'You know that I can't say anything without your mum here – and without her consent,' I said. 'You're –'

'I know, I know. I'm a minor and you're a major. Right.'

'I could lose my job if I told you.'

'More than your job's worth.'

I didn't say anything to that. He was always good at getting to me; asking probing questions during chemotherapy. Treating me like a person and not a doctor.

His voice softened. 'Rach, I need to know when the ride's going to stop. I can't enjoy it, otherwise. I feel like I'm going mad. I'm living this.' He paused and swallowed hard. 'Even if it's not as positive as what the consultant said. I want to know. It's better for me to know.'

'I'm sorry,' I said.

'Please tell me.'

'You know I can't. Your mum's decision . . . it stands.'

'But . . . I won't tell her.' His tone was pleading. 'I just want to know the median prognosis. Just to plan my life. Relax a bit, if it's years. Get things in order, if it's months. Write some blogs, letters to people. Decide on my funeral music. I deserve to know. It's my body. It's me.' He laughed self-consciously. 'It's me, not you.'

He was staring at me, and finally I met his gaze. Outside, the air was dark but the sky was still light, illuminated.

'Why don't you sleep on it?' he said.

32

Present day

Dad met me and Kate at a cafe around the corner from him, for our Tuesday tradition that week, though he hated it there. He was obsessed with their staffing – *There are seven people here and only four of them are ever doing anything!* – and their pretension – *Why would you buy a lovely space and then hang forty mirrors on the wall?* – but we met there, anyway. It made us laugh.

'I must say,' Dad remarked, 'it's kind of nice now you're both less high-flying. Though your mum wouldn't approve.'

'Oh, thanks,' Kate said, but she was smiling. 'She really wouldn't.'

It felt good to laugh a bit about it. To be honest about it. How we felt. To not let death shroud our memories of her with loaded meanings.

Kate extended her leg out in front of her. She was still in her sports gear, but the coaching days were only as long as the daylight, so she was done by five o'clock at the moment. As for me, I was always done by five o'clock, now.

'We'd go months, sometimes,' Dad said. 'When you were both busier.'

'I know,' I said, and, for all I missed medicine, I was glad in that moment that he wasn't alone any more.

'Rach will go back,' Kate said.

Dad turned his owl-like eyes to me. 'Will you?' he said in surprise.

He knew more than most, about the boy. Less than Amrit and my colleagues, but more than most. More than Kate.

'No,' I said. 'I don't know. I can't see myself going back. No.'

And then I got a feeling I sometimes got when I remembered what had happened. Like putting on a cardigan of fear. Goosebumps across my back as I remembered the last time I saw the boy, and everything that followed afterwards. I shivered in the ambient cafe light.

'I'll order,' Kate said. 'At the bar. Sundaes?'

I nodded, unable to say anything.

'I thought it was all bound up with Mum,' Dad said. 'Seeing someone have cancer. Your first time bearing all the responsibility. Your first cure as a registrar.'

I was touched.

'All by yourself, I mean. And so soon after.'

'Mum?' I echoed.

'Sorry,' he said. 'I just thought that it must have been hard, treating someone with cancer by yourself. Spending loads of time with him. Watching him go through what Mum had. It was hard hearing it.'

'Yeah.'

'So I just thought maybe you should talk to somebody about it.'

'I don't need to,' I said.

A copper lamp was swaying above his head and he looked around him. 'This place is stupid,' he said. 'This lamp could bloody injure me.'

'But she wasn't . . . she wasn't quite Mum. Afterwards.'

We'd all had to rethink her, in those weeks that followed. I still didn't understand it. Sometimes I wished Dad hadn't told us. That he'd kept the affair to himself.

'Isn't that loss, too?' he said. He shrugged sadly, his shoulders inhaling and exhaling slowly. 'It's complicated,' he said. 'But with the boy so soon after, and then splitting up with Ben . . . it's been so much change for you.'

'I'm happier. Now. Medicine was such a nightmare. Incompatible with normal life.'

He nodded once, bringing a hand to touch his beard, which bristled. 'And Jack?'

'What about Jack?' I said.

'Well, clearly all is not well. In Oban you seemed so sad.'

'I am sad,' I said, my voice thick. I hadn't told him or Kate exactly what had happened. But it was clear they knew something had. 'You know, I thought Ben was cheating on me.'

The words were out and on the table in front of us.

Dad considered them carefully. 'And was he?'

'I don't know. I don't think so. But I ended us – by accusing him.'

Dad sat back, nodding thoughtfully. 'And then . . .'

'And then everything else. But now I'm doing it again. I'm accusing Jack of . . . things.'

'Ah. You mustn't, Rach. You mustn't think that he's – that he's her.'

'None of us had any idea,' I said. 'What Mum was doing.'

'No. People are complicated. But it doesn't eclipse how lovely she was.'

'Doesn't it? For you?' I said.

'No. Not completely. Partially.'

I couldn't look at him. Instead I looked at the checked tablecloth as my eyes pooled with tears. I could see Kate up at the bar, looking to all the world like a tennis player. I wondered what Dad thought of our stories now. Were we still successes, to him? Me, pregnant by my boyfriend of not even a year?

'Jack's fine,' I said bluntly. 'We're fine.'

I picked up a salt cellar and felt it, weighty, in my palm.

'Are you sure?'

'Yes, I am,' I said.

My voice sounded steady, not betraying the doubts I felt inside.

I arrived back at my flat and found myself back on the Internet again. I really should stop soon, I was thinking, as I clicked on a story about Jack Ross, the up-and-coming writer who'd won an award for his article in *Time For You Magazine*.

I frowned as I read it. Something didn't quite read correctly. I shook my head. I couldn't work out why. I traced a finger along the screen. He had been using the byline Jack Ross to write under since 2010. That made sense: he'd changed his name, after all. But there was something else. It was the name. The name of the magazine. *Time For You*. It sounded generic.

I put it into Google: *Time For You Magazine*.

Nothing. Nothing substantial, anyway. A magazine owned by a company called AIESEC UK popped up. It had a caption – 'It's high **time for you** to be enlightened' – but it wasn't *Time For You Magazine*.

I googled it with Jack's name, then googled his articles and the article given as the award-winning one: 'Michelin-starred Restaurants in the North'.

Nothing. Jack had written no such article.

I scrolled to the bottom of the article about his award and looked at the company name. *White Wash*, it said. I googled that, and there it was: the thing I sort of knew all along. *White Wash: Reputation Cleaners*.

He'd paid someone. He'd paid someone to write that article and bump it up Google. I thought of the other one, the charity run: the low-resolution photo that didn't look like him.

I dialled his number immediately. 'Did you pay somebody to write fake articles about you?'

'Yes,' Jack said, not wondering why I was asking such questions at ten o'clock at night. 'SEO, yes.'

'SEO?'

'Search Engine Optimization. You know, where you rank high on Google?'

'So you paid someone to write a fake article and bump it up the rankings – because you didn't want people to think you weren't who you said you were?'

In hindsight, he was trying to interject. I could hear it: not in any murmurings or interruptions, exactly, but in his bated breath; in his absolute silence.

'So that you wouldn't look like a start-up journalist, on your first article?' My tone sounded hopeful, sad even.

He paused then, for a second.

'Yes,' he said slowly, in the manner of a patient teacher. 'But also to push the others down. That was the main reason we paid them. Though I know how you found out,' he said with a laugh in his voice. 'Leaving a bloody advert for themselves on the bottom.'

I ignored that. 'The main reason?' I said.

'That article was a bonus, yeah. I wanted Jack Ross to look real. To have a photo, and stuff. To look like a rounded person.'

The running photo. The award-winning writer photo. Staged. Fake.

'But . . .'

'But the main thing I employed them to do was to push the other stuff down. To delete the court articles, if they could. To remove John Douglas. Or at least what he did.'

He. He called himself *he.*

'You know,' he continued, 'I still tried to write as John Douglas, for a while. I thought he could get rid of the crime. But he couldn't. Not entirely. You've seen, I guess. It's hard to delete someone – some*thing* – completely. Bits remain. Things get archived, though we tried to stop that as much as we could. But more things go up all the time. You ask someone to pull down an article but someone's taken a screenshot, and it's on Twitter before you know it. So I changed my name. It was a last resort.'

'How could they delete them?' I said, remembering the countless *404: not found* errors I'd received during my searching. 'Aren't they . . . isn't it just journalism?' My lip curled involuntarily at the hypocrisy, that Jack was a journalist who was trying to get other journalists censored, but I dampened it. Jack didn't write feature articles. He didn't invade people's privacy. He wrote about restaurants and the best views in Rome and what it was like to walk across the Agios Sostis bridge in Zakynthos. He wasn't *paparazzi*.

'If you've not been convicted, you can get some of them removed. Say it's libel. I don't know about the law and defamation and everything,' he said. 'But if you threaten it, they often do. So Dad hired someone to do that. And, you know. He's powerful. In Oban. In business.'

'Right,' I said.

'And if you can't get it taken down, you depress it.'

'Depress?'

'Pushing the articles down so they don't rank. So they don't come up on Google. White Wash knew all about Google's algorithms. Even now, I'm glad I did it. My journalism can live on. Without all that tainting it.'

He stopped speaking then. He knew he'd said enough. More sinister, somehow, than threatening newspapers was this manipulation of search engines: of the natural order. So people like me – innocent people who wanted to know what had happened – wouldn't find the articles; would find it hard and give up. Would get confused, and think it was someone else.

It was as though he thought that, in changing his name, somebody else had committed the crime. Maybe that was a necessary part of coming to terms with something so awful. But it seemed wrong to me. Manipulative. Cold.

The articles I'd eventually found didn't appear until deep into Google's search results. I'd just been persistent.

This wasn't only the murky legal world of a non-conviction: it was deliberate. Jack had set out to confuse, to misrepresent. And, again, that made everything just a little bit worse.

'Rach?' he said.

'Yeah. It just seems, I don't know,' I said. 'Mucky.'

I sounded like my father. *Mucky*. But it was mucky. There was no other word for it.

'I know,' Jack said softly, and his voice was contrite, quiet, empathetic. Embarrassed, maybe. 'You think you'd have the integrity to stand in a courtroom and tell the truth. You think you'd say *this is who I am: take it or leave it*. You think you'd want to let the newspaper articles stand, and use the same name. But some of them, the ones you can't see . . .'

I let him believe I hadn't seen as many as I had. How could I possibly tell him I'd used a bot that crawled the web, archiving it, unknown to the authors, to the subjects, of the articles? And the rest: that I'd done a Clare's Law search against him? That I'd had his trial transcript ordered? And yet – what if there *were* more? Worse articles?

'They decimated me. The press. I couldn't let it continue. I don't know. It was like I was constantly sweeping up. And then my lawyer's friend offered to help. And it seemed easier, rather than live with these fires blazing and never work again. Or try to put them out myself. Mum and Dad paid.'

I stared out of the window. It was during that stage of autumn where leaves were constantly drifting down like huge snowflakes, leaving smudges on the pavement like giant handprints. He'd bought himself a new identity. Privacy. *Innocence*. If that had happened to me, I wouldn't have been able to afford to do that.

'I need to go,' I said.

He sent me a long text after that.

Classic Jack, always preferring to communicate in writing, in verbose language. Instead of in person, by speaking.

I know this all looks mental and shit and shady. I promise I'm not a drugs baron or a member of the Mafia. Just your Jack who was unlucky a few years ago. I promise I will always be your Jack.

I replied immediately. I believed him. I wanted to believe him.

33

'What was all the target practice for?' I said. I did this sometimes. Homed in on small details as I processed everything.

It was a Sunday afternoon in mid-November. The trees were at their most glorious, wearing shaggy coats of autumn rust. The leaves would fall away in a few days. We were at a tourist attraction nearby that Jack was reviewing. It was a mock Victorian village, all fitted out with authentic penny farthings and an old mill and real shops staffed with actors in costume.

'What do you mean?' he said.

A spark of irritation crossed his features. It darkened them, drawing a line underneath his cheekbones. His lips folded in, but when he looked up at me he forced a smile.

'Were you just practising for nothing? When did you start?'

He swivelled towards me. His eyes looked amber in the sun.

A woman in Victorian petticoats emerged from a building in front of us. 'Good morning to you,' she said.

We ignored her. The sky was a bright, high autumn blue. The air was cold and crisp.

'Did you think I was practising so I could shoot people accurately?' he said.

He pushed his hair back. It had grown longer. He reached for my hand and we walked into the old school-house. It was empty, the classrooms protected by glass windows, so all we could do was peer in at the rows of old, dark desks, at the strange, preserved, closed-off classrooms. I shivered. It was cool and quiet. It smelt of wood and pencils and old stone. Nobody else was around.

'No,' I said.

Jack's hand was still around mine. You could have drawn a line vertically down my body, that day. One half would have been pleasure, looking at his wavy hair, his tight waist, listening to his funny comments, smelling his light, clean scent. And the other would have been pain; anger at his abruptness, as if I shouldn't be allowed to muse on his crime, as if I was being annoying.

'It was a hobby, Rach,' he said shortly.

I only hoped he didn't ask how I knew things. That he didn't ever discover my search history. It was insulting at best, alarming at worst. I could barely type a single letter into the search bar without Google suggesting things to do with John and not proven verdicts and Dominic.

We sat on a bench in the school changing rooms. Victorian satchels were hung up in front of us. A woman in costume drifted by and nodded at us.

'Y'alright,' Jack said to her. That was always his

greeting to everybody. The letters rolled together in a Scottish drawl.

'The yelling in the cafe. When Mez saw,' he volunteered.

I turned to him in surprise. He hardly ever offered up explanations.

'Yes,' I murmured.

'A journo recognized me. Wanted an exclusive.'

'Recognized you?' I said. 'It must have been so high profile. I never knew about it.'

'He was Scottish. It was a big thing in Scotland.'

'An exclusive on what?'

'*My side of it*,' he said. 'Bloody tabloids. I just lost it. They're like leaches. Feeding on our misery.'

I remembered a journalist outside the boy's inquest. I understood entirely.

We sat in silence for a few seconds.

'Tell me something,' I said to him. 'A Jack-thing.'

It sounded whimsical; the usual chit-chat of new lovers, but it wasn't. It was a desperate kind of searching. I wanted to get to know him. I was on that airport escalator again, trying to speed things up, to make the inorganic organic; like a company that had merged five times trying to mesh everyone together and pretend it had happened naturally.

'What do you want to know?' he said. 'How much I love you? Let me count the ways . . .'

'Something about you. What would your last meal be?' I said. 'Your death row meal?'

'Pak choi,' he said immediately. It had become

absorbed into our rotation of things we liked to say to each other and giggle about. 'Fillet steak? I don't know,' he said. 'What are the rules?'

'Three courses, anything you like.'

'But I'm about to die. I don't want anything.' He sneaked a look at me.

It was true; he was that way inclined. If at all anxious he simply wouldn't eat.

'Well, it's hypothetical,' I said. 'You can ignore that bit. Just pretend I'm asking you for your favourite foods.'

Jack paused for a while. Eventually, he said: 'Forty-eight McDonald's Chicken McNuggets, but I have to have a hangover.'

'You're going to have to explain that to me.'

'My best meal ever was the day after my eighteenth birthday. At school. In Fettes. The next day my mate who could drive took us to McDonald's when we surfaced at five o'clock in the afternoon. I was ravenous, suddenly. I ordered forty-eight. And I ate every single one.'

I couldn't help but laugh, and I did my best to ignore that he couldn't help reminding me where he had gone to school. That we both knew I didn't know. 'That's your best meal? Reconstituted chicken?'

'Yep. You?'

My phone beeped. It was Amrit. I called up the string of texts that I'd ignored, and Jack saw too.

'You never respond,' he said.

I shrugged, and he let it slide. It was too difficult. I couldn't explain just part of it. I'd have to tell him everything. The boy. My mistake.

'I don't think you can have much of a hangover on death row, anyway,' I said.

'Maybe not.'

'You hardly drink now.'

'No.'

'Is that because you drank that night?' I said.

To his credit, Jack understood immediately what I meant, and didn't try to pretend otherwise. He did, however, raise his eyes heavenwards. 'I hate talking about it.'

'I know. Your mum . . .'

'What?'

'Well, she doesn't want you to discuss it, does she?' I thought of her sweeping as she told me to leave the subject alone, of his dad's slick explanation at the loch. Not to mention the rest: footing the bill for reputation cleaning, lawyer's fees. 'No matter what your parents think. You can tell me. You don't have to obey them.'

It was a step too far.

'My parents?' he said, and he was properly indignant then. Moody.

'Sorry,' I said. 'But at the loch – he just stepped in.'

'Yeah, he did. That was Dominic's gran. As I'm sure you've worked out. Do you plan on cross-examining me on every day trip?'

'No.'

He was silent.

'Kind of,' he said eventually. 'I liked a drink. I'd had a beer that night. I *wasn't* drunk.'

'And?' I said, softly, not wanting to scare his confession away, like a stray cat I was luring out of a dark alleyway.

'It's the taste.'

'Of?'

'Anything,' he said. 'Beer, wine. They taste different, but it's the alcohol. That fizz. The feeling of unwinding.'

'What, the nice feeling?' I said.

I could hardly remember it. It was theoretical now. I wondered what my next drink would be. Prosecco? A toast to Wally?

'For me, the last time I felt like that, I ended up standing in front of a body,' he said. 'I don't know. I saw a woman about it. We did cognitive behavioural stuff. It was really wanky. She said she thought I'd stored the memories in a traumatic place. So now, even a mouthful of alcohol and I just panic. I don't drive, either. For the same reason. No, not the same reason. Because it's just a bit risky. What if I hit someone – didn't see them? I might end up in the same situation again. And I'd do anything to avoid that.'

I nodded. PTSD. Probably. It was a relief, in many ways. That he was traumatized. That the calm explanations were underscored by something else. Chaos, regret. I would be surprised if anybody went through what Jack had gone through without being traumatized. I saw it all the time in cancer patients. They reached remission and then their anxiety spiked. And they could never understand it; how come it seemed to only happen once the crisis was over.

'What was it like afterwards?' I said.

He responded immediately. 'Weird. Like everything was inverted.'

'Your life?'

'Well, yeah. Everything. It wasn't just the body. The law. It was everything. The media. People slamming me on Facebook. Our house looked different. Just – everything changed.'

He reached out and batted a vintage satchel. It swung. The hook it was hanging on creaked as it moved.

'You weren't on Facebook then,' I said automatically, even though it was showing a hand I didn't really want him to see.

He'd joined late. In 2010. I remember thinking how strange that was.

'I was, as John Douglas,' he said. 'Closed now.'

That didn't help. The literal closing of an entire life.

'Right,' I said.

'Then it was Christmas. Right after. And we were safe – you don't know how big a thing that was. And even though it came at a cost, we were safe. We weren't listening out for the locks being jimmied. We weren't pricing up the expense of turning the listed building into a double-glazed one and battling with the bloody councils over it. There was so much guff surrounding all those break-ins, and suddenly it was gone.'

I shivered in the school cloakroom. Those words. Those words. Relief. He was relieved that he had killed someone. A vigilante. He was glad, on some level. It was *convenient*. Could this really be true? What if he'd planned it all along? Intended to kill?

I thought of Wally inside me. Connected to me. Made of Jack and me. I thought of the way Jack made me feel. Treasured, in the way he savoured my Rachel-things. The way he flung an arm across me in his sleep and scooted me closer to him.

I had to accept it. I had to move on. For Wally. It was a horrible situation, to be burgled repeatedly. There was a struggle. It was an accident. It was an unusual situation. Mitigating circumstances. He wasn't a sinister person. *We* had to move on. I consciously turned my gaze to him.

'How was Christmas?' I said.

'Uneventful. Flat. It drizzled. We went for a walk. We didn't talk. All the legal stuff was kicking off, but we didn't want a break from it. We just wanted to know. Davey was struggling. Though he got a Rubik's Cube, which he loved.' Jack squeezed my hand. He paused, then said, 'Happy?'

'Yes,' I said, and that seemed to relax him.

His left hand drifted down to the front of my coat. He undid the button, and his hand crept in. It was cold, but I liked it, anyway.

'How is he?' he said. 'We won't find out the sex, next week, will we? I want a surprise.'

My stomach was taut underneath his hands. The bump was almost there. Soon, it would round out, and I'd look pregnant.

'I can read the scans.'

'Can you?'

'Yeah. It looks either like a turtle or a hamburger,' I said.

'Which one's the boy?'

'The turtle.' I grinned.

'Oh,' he said. His face transformed, from sullen to happy, dimples creasing either side of his mouth. That smile. The straight teeth. The pointy incisors.

'What will Wally's surname be?' I said quietly.

Jack paused. His smile disappeared. It was like the sun going in. 'I . . .'

'Exactly,' I said. I looked down at my hands. The nails were bitten.

'Wally Ross-Douglas-Anderson?' Jack said eventually.

'Maybe we could amalgamate them all. Dougrosson.'

'I like that. Another new name,' he said.

And it was his laugh that annoyed me then. Like the first little crack of an eggshell. It wasn't funny. Not at all. Would we tell our child their father had killed someone – and changed his name to hide from it? Or would we keep it from him? I didn't know which was worse.

'It's not fucking funny,' I said.

My words sliced through the air between us, and Jack immediately shifted away from me. From us.

'I am well aware of that,' he said.

I wasn't being fair, I know I wasn't. I was making jokes about it on my own terms, then snapping at him if he did the same.

'What's going on?' he asked.

'Nothing. Nothing. I just sometimes feel –' I stopped, looking at him.

A year ago I had never met him. On this day last year

he was living his life in Oban and I was living mine in Newcastle and he was nothing to me. It sometimes felt as though my life had been one novel that had been swapped for another. I was a doctor with a boyfriend called Ben. And then I was a pregnant secretary with a boyfriend whose name I had to think twice about. We needed time. If only we could have bought ourselves time, I thought, looking at the wooden coat pegs lined up in front of me. A few seasons would have been all we needed. To settle in.

'I sometimes feel like I don't know you at all,' I said.

'You do know me.' He shifted closer to me. His thigh was warm against my tights. 'What do you want to know?'

I almost asked him then: more questions I had waiting, about the lawyer's texts. But I didn't. I couldn't put pressure on it – our new, tentative normal – so soon after he'd entrusted me with his confession, as if it was an egg that I might crush in my palm.

I tilted my head back. What did you need to know in order to know somebody? There was nothing I could say.

'Your favourite book,' I said, eventually.

It didn't mean anything, not really. It was a pithy question, like someone's *Desert Island Discs* or their favourite colour. It wouldn't tell me what I needed to know: was he good? Was he a good person? What went on inside his head? How would he react if I angered him? How easily did he forgive? What would he do if faced with a situation where it was harder to do the right thing? These were the important questions, but I couldn't ask them. And if I did, he would tell me what I wanted to hear, like a poor job interview candidate whose only weakness was their perfectionism.

'Hmm,' he said. 'Can I be unpretentious?'

'Please do,' I said.

I felt a positive rush then, like opening a bottle of fizzy lemonade. I loved him. That was what mattered. Not the past. I wouldn't read that bloody trial transcript. Why would I?

'*Bridget Jones*,' he said.

'*No*. You managed to finish *Wolf Hall*. Surely not,' I said.

He held his hands up. 'I know, I know. But I can't remember such an enjoyable weekend as reading that. I laughed my tits off.'

I giggled, shifting closer to him. 'Mine's *Harry Potter*,' I said.

'Pair of literary fools,' he said. 'I'm glad you didn't say Shakespeare or something. Another thing I like about you. You're unpretentious.'

So then I knew his favourite book. Not the one he'd talk about at dinner parties, but his real, uncool favourite. I thought it mattered, that we had climbed a rung on the ladder of fully knowing each other.

But we hadn't, of course. Up against everything, knowing his favourite book didn't matter at all.

34

It was the morning of our twenty-week scan and I was in the bath. My entire body was underneath the water. The only things exposed to the chilled November air were my knees and my face. Jack's house was still cold. He just didn't feel it. I kind of liked the contrasts, though. The warm bed, our cold noses. The cold air, and my hot limbs underneath the steaming water.

'Hello,' Jack said, arriving in the bathroom to brush his teeth. 'Wow,' he said.

'What?'

He was wearing a grey long-sleeved T-shirt. He was laughing. 'I've just never seen anyone lie in the bath like that. With just your face out. Like a hippo.'

'Oh, a hippo, thanks,' I said, but I was laughing, too.

'Are you looking forward to seeing Wally again?' Jack said. 'He just bloody licked the bottom of my tea-cup,' he said, pointing at Howard, who was, as ever, one pace behind Jack.

'Licking your pheromones,' I said. 'Your juices.' I raised my eyebrows.

Jack laughed, that low, sardonic chuckle I loved so much.

'You've embarrassed him now. Look,' Jack said. He pointed to Howard. 'He's limping.'

I looked at him. He was, ever so slightly. I leant over the side of the bath and picked Howard up. I palpated his sides, his abdomen. And it was as though it was a patient's soft body underneath my fingertips. I was brisk, efficient, as I did it, my body remembering the motions. Time seemed to slow down as my fingers worked their way down his leg.

Howard didn't react at all, just sat purring in my arms. I held his back left foot in my hand. 'If it's the same as with humans,' I said, 'he's fine. No tender spots on his metatarsal bones or phalanges.' I pressed on his heel. 'No break in his heel. Tibia and fibula fine. They probably have different names, though,' I muttered, letting Howard go.

'You know all that?' Jack said.

'Yeah. I would've been a pretty bad doctor if I didn't know tibias and fibulas,' I said.

Jack was still looking at me, a strange, sad expression on his face.

I dressed carefully, like I was going on a first date. I unwound the bath towel and put my bra on, looking at myself in the mirror. As if in a nod to the upcoming scan, my belly was, for the first time, big in the morning.

'Look,' I said.

'I know.'

'I look like I've swallowed a bowl,' I muttered.

'You look lovely.'

'Pregnancy is a magical time,' I said, grabbing a

handful of underwear from the drawer. 'But lots of your pants don't fit.'

Jack held up a finger. 'I can't believe I forgot this,' he said.

He started rooting around in his backpack. He took it everywhere when he was writing. His MacBook Air. His reusable Starbucks cup. A notepad. He was a cliché; a lovely cliché. I heard a rustling and he pulled out a Topshop bag.

'A present for the mother of my child,' he smiled. He passed it to me.

I reached a hand inside, felt the stick of a coat hanger and a crinkly present. 'You've wrapped it,' I said.

'Yes, with one caveat,' he said. 'You didn't have any Sellotape. I was going to give it to you at yours, after we went to Oban. So I used this weird stuff.'

I looked at the present. It was small, and neatly wrapped. I ran my finger over the edges. It was wrapped with what I always used, what I always had to hand: Transpore dressing tape. 'It's medical tape,' I said with a smile. 'Transpore.'

'Oh. Sorry.'

'No, no,' I said, a memory assaulting me.

Getting Kate's Christmas presents on Christmas Eve, during a run of night shifts, and wrapping them in medical blue tissue roll and Transpore dressing tape. 'Oh, thanks,' she'd said sarcastically, but everybody had smiled. They knew to expect it, with me. In return, she'd bought me five tennis balls, the next year.

I unwrapped two pairs of pants. I unfolded them.

One said *Beefcake* on it. The other said *PUGLYF* with a pug on the bum.

'Wow,' I laughed.

'They didn't have maternity so I got you big ones,' he said.

'Beefcake.'

'I just want you to be comfortable.' He reached for the Beefcake pants and turned them over. On the bum – the massive butt – was a cartoon hamburger.

'I think I need to wear them to the scan,' I said, giggling as I pulled them up my legs.

Jack took the tag off, gently, behind me, his hands cool against my hips.

'They'll think we're hooligans. They'll call social services,' he said.

I turned around and caught sight of myself in the mirror. A rounded stomach. An old bra. And enormous Beefcake pants.

'You look like a person who's got their life in order,' Jack said, covering a cheeky smile with his hand.

'No joke, these are seriously comfortable,' I said.

I pulled some jeans on. He slipped a top over my head, and we left.

There was a letter for me on the passenger seat. I'd left it in my car. I was supposed to open it on the way to work, but I'd forgotten. Jack passed it to me, wordlessly.

I didn't know it then, but the distinctive teal-coloured logo was hiding inside. I opened it in the car, before starting the ignition. It was from the GMC. It had been nearly a year. My qualification as a doctor was to lapse if I did nothing by the spring.

My whole body went cold. My teeth started chattering. I'd thought that wouldn't happen. I'd been paying my licence fees. I thought I had longer before the whole thing lapsed. There it was. In blue and white. It would all be over soon. Everything I'd worked for. All those bloody OSCE exams. All those skills I had. The ability to take a history. To palpate an abdomen and find the point of pain easily. To cannulate even the most destroyed vein; I was the person everybody asked to cannulate. It was my thing. They'd all lapse, those skills. They'd fall away, like animals dying by the side of the road.

'Lapse?' Jack said, reading over my shoulder.

'Yeah, if you don't do professional development. And pay a licence fee.'

'You'd lose it all?'

'Yeah.' I couldn't look at him.

My feelings were written all over my face, as though I'd been asked to throw out my most sentimental possession, or ship Howard off to a new owner.

'Jeez, Rach. Are you sure?'

'Very,' I said, folding up the envelope, reaching across him and putting it in the glove box. Away. I couldn't talk about it. Not then.

'Would you have to go back to med school? Do it all again?'

'No,' I said.

'Oh, good.'

'Because I don't want to be a doctor.'

'But you would have to – if you did?'

'I don't even know, to be honest. I don't know what the procedure is.' I turned the key in the ignition.

I wanted to change the subject, to distract Jack. To distract my own thoughts so I wouldn't have to face the prospect of thirty more years typing attendance notes for lawyers.

'Look,' I said, pointing to the utility-room window.

The back door was painted green. It had a watering can next to it. And in the window of the room was Howard, his large eyes looking forlorn.

'Jesus, he's fat,' Jack said with a laugh. Howard's neck did look enormous.

'It's a bad angle for him,' I said.

'I feel weird about that letter,' Jack said, buttoning up his coat. It was a parka, dark green.

That was the first day I'd seen him in a winter coat, having met him in the spring. He looked nice. Cool. A bit posh. Like a hipster. Irresistible.

'Don't,' I said. 'Trust me – nobody wants to be a doctor in the NHS at the moment.'

He paused, was silent for a long time. I thought he wasn't going to answer me, but then he did.

'Fair enough,' he said.

But I kept looking at the glove box. I kept seeing the letter inside it. And, when we got to the hospital, I opened it, just a fraction, while Jack was at the parking payment machine. I pulled the letter out through the slot, and put it in my pocket. Maybe I could do some professional development. Some locum work. Maybe.

I knew the way to the sonographer's room. Thankfully, it was in a different block. I didn't have to see any of my work colleagues, or my old Block B1, or the third room from the left where it happened.

'Jesus, five quid for two hours,' Jack said, feeding coin after coin into the metre.

'Blame the government,' I said.

'I *do*,' he said, raising an eyebrow and looking at me.

The atmosphere between us was strange since that letter. I felt more than a little guilty. The guilt had started to trade places with the anger. He didn't know my story. Hardly anybody did. But it was different, I kept telling myself. It was nuanced. Definitely not the same as what he'd done.

The sonographer was called Sandra. I think I had seen her in the hospital canteen. She had dark hair and lots of freckles.

The room was dimly lit. It had the same blinds as the rooms I saw the boy in. There was a distinctive smell about my hospital, the Royal Victoria Infirmary. I stopped being able to smell it, when I was there so much it felt like home. But I could smell it again, going for that scan. The lemon, bleach and antiseptic of all hospitals; and other smells, too. The Costa from the main thoroughfare. The smell of the carpet in the side rooms that I slept in after they had been hoovered. The hot, musty smell the old computers pumped out into the offices.

The sonographer was faffing with the computer. It had frozen. She was moving the mouse back and forth, giving me a rueful smile. It unfroze.

'Ah. Rachel Anderson,' she said. 'I thought I recognized you.' She turned and smiled at me.

Jack raised his eyebrows.

'That would explain why I haven't seen you,' she said.

I merely nodded, instead of correcting her. Lots of doctors went on maternity leave early. It was too physical a job to do pregnant, for some. The aches and pains after a fifteen-hour night shift were enough on their own. And then there was the sickness. You had to have a strong stomach for medicine.

And so I let her believe what she probably believed: that I was married, that I was ready, that I hadn't quit my job mere months before getting pregnant, thus ensuring I was eligible for precisely no maternity pay. Not that it mattered – except it did. It mattered a lot to me.

I looked at Jack. He was looking at the screen. This would never happen to him, I found myself thinking. People would never say, oh, Jack Ross. Because he had changed his name. Changed his identity. Did he now naturally answer to Jack and not John? I wondered.

'Sorry about this,' Sandra said as the computer froze again. 'We just have to wait. It's so slow at the moment.'

'I remember it well,' I said. 'Nothing's changed then?'

'God, no. You were a paediatric reg, weren't you?'

'Yes,' I said.

And, despite myself, I felt a flush of pride. Despite how it ended, despite the fact that it was over, I had still been there. I had still been Rachel Anderson, MB ChB, BMedSc, MRCPCH.

Sandra wiggled the mouse again, but nothing happened. She reached forward and stretched her fingers, opening the flimsy metal blinds.

'It's set to snow,' she said, indicating the spindly November trees, the branches bare like they had been caught just out of the shower. Already, then, my mind was cartwheeling over what she'd said, scanning for something, though I didn't know it.

I looked at the sky. It was white and heavy, had that reddish-orange quality. It had been mild, though, this morning.

'Doubt it,' Jack said. 'It's not cold enough, is it?'

'Just what I was thinking,' I said to him.

'Remember the last time it properly snowed?' Sandra said. 'People are only just ready for more again, aren't they? A few years back now. 2009? Yes – it was 2009, because Julia was just born . . .'

The computer beeped.

'We're up and running,' Sandra said.

I lay back on the bed and unbuttoned the top of my jeans. The gel was cold and wet against the denim, which stuck to my stomach.

'I'm looking forward to seeing Wally,' Jack said to me. He was sitting at the end of the bed, leaning forward, looking expectant.

I was still looking out at the slices of sky just beyond the blinds. The gaps between each slat were so small, I could barely see anything. Snow. Set to snow. And then, after the winter, Wally would be here. Our baby.

Sandra put the ultrasound sensor on my stomach and the room was filled with a muffled kind of white noise. And then. We heard it. A heartbeat, racing along like a train.

Jack leapt up, his hands going to his head. 'Look,' he cried.

And I wanted to stand, too, and hold him, and look at the amazing baby we had made. 'Wow,' I said.

I hadn't expected to be moved – had seen more ultrasound scans than I could count – but I was. There was Wally. Half me, half Jack. It felt like our future was unfurling in front of us. We would show him Oban. His accent might be ever-so-slightly Scottish, his hair dark like Jack's. I'd teach him basic anatomy and Jack would do spellings. And then, when Wally was in bed, Jack and I would sit alone downstairs, right next to each other, and marvel at him. I was so happy, so looking forward to the future, it filled me up like helium.

Evidently, Jack was feeling the same, because he looked over at me, and said, with tears in his eyes, 'Having a baby with you is pretty much the best thing ever.'

'I know,' I said, torn between wanting the scan to be over so I could go and feel his arms around me and wanting it never to end, to stare and stare at Wally forever with Jack.

'I hope he's just like you,' he added.

And Sandra smiled, and I was proud. Of Wally. Of Jack. Of us. Of our life together.

'Come,' I said to Jack.

Sandra shifted out of the way and Jack walked over and stood by my head and held my hand.

'I can't wait twenty weeks,' he murmured, smiling excitedly.

'They'll fly by,' I said, looking up at him.

Wally's heart was still racing. We stared at the screen, looking at his arms and legs, how he lay on his back. Was that a thumb in his mouth? We looked at his spine and his tiny feet. At the shape of his nose. Neither of us wanted it to end, and after a while Sandra raised her eyebrows and told us she had another appointment waiting.

Jack and I giggled, and kissed too extravagantly in the lift on the way out, our bodies touching. The gel that had soaked my top got on his, and we laughed and said it looked like he'd had a scan, too.

35

'Do you remember that snow?' I said conversationally once we were on the A-road home. 'Did Scotland get it?'

'No, I don't think so,' Jack said.

'Surely, it must have?' I said. 'It was awful here.'

It was in 2009, didn't Sandra say? That made sense. There had been feet and feet of it. Roads closed. It was on the news every night. The whole of the north changed. We didn't know where the pavements were, and it didn't matter because there were no cars, anyway. Argos sold out of sledges. Dad and I used baking trays on the mounds on the Town Moor. Mum had hated that. We couldn't open the garage door because of the height of it. It went right through to the second week of January. People started stockpiling canned goods. And then it all melted, and everybody was relieved. Even now, people seemed to want it to snow less than they did before; nobody had forgotten how the snow that Christmas affected the north. It hadn't snowed as heavily since.

'Maybe? That was right after,' Jack said.

'Ah,' I said. 'But you said . . . that your Christmas had been drizzly?' I looked across at him.

He'd paled.

Hadn't he said that? Drizzly, and uneventful. That they'd taken a walk. Nobody had done any walking. There had been relentless blizzards. How could he have forgotten? How could he not know? How could Scotland not have been affected? I was sure it was the whole of the UK. A white-out.

Haiti. And then Haiti happened. And he didn't know about that, either.

'Oh, I . . .' Jack shifted uncomfortably, getting his phone out.

'Where were you?' I said.

And the look on his face told me everything I needed to know.

He *had* been in prison. The thought hit me like an avalanche. He hadn't got bail. And then a fresh surge of anger came over me, like an overflowing bath. It dripped at first, slowly, but then built up until great waves were slopping over the side. I had believed lie after lie after lie. Drizzly. Too much detail. I should've spotted it. Who would tell you what the weather was like, anyway, when you asked them how Christmas was?

God. He had lied. He had lied to me again. He may not have done it explicitly, but wasn't that worse? It was evasive. Insidious. Like smoke that got thicker and thicker without you realizing it, until you couldn't breathe.

The scan was ruined. That perfect moment of feeling like our future was right there waiting for us. We couldn't even get through a day – a scan – without a lie surfacing. Where would it end?

That was the worst of it. The lying. I had thought we were finally being honest. That I knew everything. That we were, I suppose, on the same side. But I wasn't somebody he was confiding in. I was somebody he was hiding things from. There was a barrier between us, and it was him.

But there was something else, too. It was almost intangible. Perhaps it was easier to accept that he had made a terrible mistake one night in December a few years ago than it was to appreciate that he had been in prison. I might not have understood the events of that one night, but, once I knew he'd been in prison, I realized I did not understand an entire period of his life. Where was he? Which prison? For how long? What was it like?

He'd been detained. A convict. He was put there by the state. They felt that was the best thing to do with him. And then I remembered it. A line from one of the available articles I'd unwittingly committed to memory from too much scrutiny. *On the way to his failed bail hearing.* God, it had been right there in front of me.

I said nothing for a while. I was thinking. My top was sticky with the gel and I wanted to get inside, change it, and not speak to Jack.

I drove us to my flat. Jack didn't say anything.

'I need a change of clothes,' I said woodenly. 'This gel's gross.'

'I bet,' he said.

Once again, I found myself wondering how things might have been if we hadn't been in this situation. If

285

he really was Jack, and he hadn't murdered somebody years ago. If we had waited a few years. Got engaged. Got married. Got pregnant on a honeymoon in the Maldives. Maybe we'd be pulling up to a house in suburbia we owned jointly. The nursery would already be decorated. Neutral colours. A wooden cot. A nursing chair with a fluffy white throw on it. Jack would want an outrageous name for the baby. I'd want something more traditional. He'd suggest *Maldive* for where the baby was conceived and I would swat him with a Sophie the Giraffe that lay waiting in the Moses basket by our bed.

We wouldn't be here. It wouldn't be like this. I wouldn't wish this on anybody.

36

He followed me inside. I was too annoyed to stop him, and I didn't want to row outside, pregnant, in the street.

I closed the door behind us. Jack was leaning against the counter. He was wearing jeans he'd turned up at the bottoms and a white long-sleeved T-shirt. He looked gorgeous, standing there with his parka folded over his arms, in front of him, awkwardly.

'Were you in prison?' I said.

He looked at me. His head was tilted down ever so slightly, but his eyes were on me. His facial expression wasn't changing at all, but I could see, behind those eyes, that his thoughts were racing.

He looked at me closely. And then he said, 'The snow gave it away, didn't it?' and that was the moment.

The only sound was my boiler firing up. 'Your reaction to my question did.'

'Yes. I have been . . . I went to prison.'

'You said you didn't. When I asked.' I thought back to that lie: *No. I promise, Rachel.* I winced.

Where was the line? When did I decide this had gone too far? I had thought it was that I didn't know his name. And then I had thought my deal-breaker was that locked-gaze lie. And there I was, having shifted my boundaries again. It stopped here. Lava-like fury ran just underneath the surface of my skin.

'I'm sorry.'

I couldn't imagine it. That man in front of me with his expensive coat and the cat that he loved. His freelance, middle-class lifestyle, the elderflower cordial he liked to drink.

And the other stuff, too. The stuff that was solely Jack. The way he kept Howard's flea medicine with his own, right there in the bathroom medicine cabinet. The way he retweeted Emma Watson's feminist speech. That he always said how much smarter I was than him.

That man – my boyfriend – had been in prison. We'd been lied to again and again, Wally and I. We didn't deserve it.

'It was the shame of it,' he said, still looking at me. 'The photos. I got them taken down – I was cuffed in them. It was like being a second-class citizen. People were afraid of me. And people were afraid to be seen with me. It was a thing that happened to other people. You know? Wrongdoers. And then it was me. I thought about moving far away, but Davey . . .'

'I can't imagine,' I said.

And I couldn't. But I also couldn't imagine not telling him. There he was, in my kitchen, fully in my world, his baby inside me. And I had no access to his life at all. I knew nothing. He had deliberately locked me out, even though he knew it would hurt me.

'It's where the hypochondria comes from. Nobody

had my back, there. I got these nosebleeds and nobody gave a shit, even when they went on for hours. It was probably stress, but unless you were dying, nobody cared. You were on your own.'

I nodded. I could understand that. Health anxiety almost always sprang from a traumatic life event; a moment when everything felt at stake and you were alone with it.

'Everyone watched loads of television. I watched clocks. I still dream about it sometimes. When I was out it would sometimes occur to me that, even months later, I was living by the prison menu. Mash on Tuesdays. That I could actually choose whatever I wanted to eat for dinner, and buy it. Or that I could leave my room before nine in the morning. So many things.'

He looked at me sadly. I think he knew.

'You should have told me. When I asked,' I said.

'I know.'

'Is *this* all?'

'Oh yes, this is it. All of it,' Jack said.

But it was hollow. The lava erupted then.

'You've said that so many times,' I said. I was sobbing suddenly, like I'd skipped the start of a cry and gone straight to the middle. 'And I've never left. I've never left you. Not when I found out I didn't know your name, or when I found out what you'd done and that you'd lied, again and again, about the verdict, and I . . .'

Jack came over to me, tried to put his arms around me and the bump, but I shook him off.

'I can't, I can't, I can't,' I said. 'I love you. I loved you. But I can't . . .' It felt like my chest was cracking open with the pain of it.

'No, Rach. No,' he said.

'What is it?' I shouted, his arms still partially around me. I leant back and looked at his red-rimmed eyes. 'What *is* it that's so bad about that night that you lie and lie – over and over?'

Jack dropped his eyes at that, avoiding mine.

I waited for an answer, but I didn't get one.

What I did get was clarity. I didn't regret sleeping with him, kissing him, discovering Scotland with him. I didn't regret getting pregnant by him. None of it, on its own. No. I regretted ever meeting him at all. If I could have politely told that Scottish stranger where the Monument was, and moved on, I would have.

And, with that thought, I asked him to leave.

He pulled the door closed behind him, the bristles on the underneath of it brushing the carpet softly.

PART 3
Why?

37

I knocked on Mez's door. I was ghost walking, again, unable to stay in my claustrophobic flat, needing company, wanting distracting chat.

I heard his voice echo from within. Kate would be at the tennis club. It was a Sunday night – club night, and there was always a juniors' match on.

'Mushrooms,' he called to me.

That made me smile. I let myself in the front door, walked down the wooden-floored hallway, and into the garage via the side door. It was in darkness again, the mushrooms bigger, their whiteness like creatures' eyes in the gloom.

'Alright,' he said. It had been two days since the break-up. I'd spent the first day throwing up, thinking of the time lost; our lovely spring/summer, the stupid things I did. I wished, the day after we'd broken up, that I'd never seen the email in the first place. That I didn't know. That, if only I'd been practising investigative medicine, I wouldn't have been so obsessed with investigating him. Or maybe I should have been wishing that Mum hadn't died. That I hadn't somehow learnt the message that people aren't always who they say they are. Maybe then I'd still be with Ben, unknowingly unhappy.

I thought about the things Jack had lost, too. How he might have avoided all of this by sitting me down outside the Monument and telling me all about it. I could have made up my own mind then. Or maybe sometime after that; the first time I asked, or even the second.

But then, if we're wishing things, he might have truly avoided it all by moving house. Being firmer with the police. Not happening to be in on that night. Not owning an air rifle. Anything, really.

I missed so many things about Jack. The way he covered his mouth when he was laughing, as if he was doing something naughty. His silly selfies. Howard.

And I was mourning the future, too. That Wally wouldn't spend Christmas Eves with both of his parents, dressed up like a Santa or a Christmas pudding, overindulged in the morning. That he'd never cringe at his parents kissing in the playground. That birthdays would be spent shuffled between the two of us, or awkwardly with both of us present at his party. That he would have to tell every anecdote, everything that happened to him at school, twice, and that it would be diluted for either one of us in the retelling. That he would feel independent much earlier than his little friends; aware of one parent's fragile emotional state around the other. That he would never sit and feel small and looked-after next to both of us. I thought of the things that I would miss, too. Half of his life, if we were to split his custody. Half. A first step? First laugh?

My eyes spilt over with tears and I gasped. It was

doubly painful. I loved him. And Wally loved him. That was the worst.

'Y'alright?' Mez said, poking his head around one of the mushroom beds.

And his northern lilt, the *y'alright*, was so like Jack's that I sobbed properly, loudly, then.

Mez wrapped his arms around me. He smelt like family. Of Kate's washing powder and their familiar house smell; the Air Wick in their hall, the candle in their bathroom. He was wearing a long-sleeved T-shirt. The arms were too short for him. They always were.

'Jack and I are no more,' I said.

'I know,' he said. 'I know.'

I cried even harder at that. He knew. Everybody knew, of course. We were doomed from the start.

'He did something and we couldn't get past it. In the end.'

'I'm sorry,' Mez murmured.

'I've ruined Wally's life,' I sobbed.

'No, you haven't. It's a spectrum, isn't it? Jack might've been a bad boyfriend – I'm guessing – but he's not a bad person.'

'Hmm?' I said.

'Oh, you know. You trust your dad to love you and want the best for you, but you also trust that he's a pedantic idiot at times,' Mez said. He took a step back from me, his hand connecting with my shoulder in a sort of friendly punch, then picked up his watering can again. 'But don't worry, because you can still trust Jack. Not in the way you trust a boyfriend – to not lie to you, or to be faithful – but just as the father of your child. To do right by Wally. Can't you?' he said, turning his gaze on me. 'It's a spectrum, isn't it? Trust.'

'No,' I said, not really fully understanding what he meant. 'It's all wrong. It all feels wrong.'

'Kate and I aren't perfect right now,' Mez said to me. He put the can down noisily and started fiddling around with plant food in slippery sachets.

'I know,' I said.

'I crossed a line. She hasn't forgiven me. It's been – I guess it's been hard since your mum.'

'I know. It's . . . it's so complicated. The way we feel about it. Death makes everything complicated.'

'Yep.'

'Which line did you cross?'

'She says I abused her,' he said.

I could see the scepticism on his face. Ah. That was why she hadn't forgiven him.

'And *did you*?' I said.

'No. We were just, you know, rowing. About schools. Politics. It was stupid. I got self-righteous, maybe.'

'What did you do?'

'I don't know. Shouted a lot.'

'Hmm,' I said.

I treated a woman once, in A&E, who had been hit by her partner. She looked at me, one eye ringed with a bruise in its inception, and said, 'Men don't understand what it's like to be around people they're constantly afraid of.'

'Shouting can be abusive,' I said. 'Especially if it's just one of you. If you're not listening.'

296

Mez shrugged.

I couldn't live with that, either, I thought. Maybe I was stupid. Stuck up. My standards too high.

'We're married,' he said shortly.

It was weird to slowly learn that my brother-in-law was flawed. He had a quick temper, didn't listen, didn't see that shouting at a woman was wrong. And Kate was flawed, too. She baited him. Caused arguments. I saw her do it. They weren't the perfect partnership. There were cracks. Who knew if they would last, either? Could any of us communicate successfully? I didn't think so. I shivered in the garage, smelling the peat of the mushrooms. Everybody was so messed up.

'Give her a break,' I said. 'She's just left her whole career behind.'

'She did so well. She should be pleased she did so well.'

I just looked at him.

After a second, we heard the squeak of the door handle. It was Kate. She was early. She was in sports gear, a sweaty headband wrapped around her forehead. It was how she was; how she would always be, to me. She looked strange in day clothes with her hair down. Like an off-duty ballet dancer.

'You win?' I said to her.

She was looking more toned again. Coaching seemed to suit her.

'Yep,' she said. 'My girls did.' She brushed past Mez, not saying anything, and stood next to me. She reached out and fingered a mushroom. 'We're harvesting soon,' she said to me. 'You should help. It's super freaky. Their roots look like jellyfish.'

'No thanks,' I said.

She smiled at me. 'What're you up to?' she asked.

'Moaning,' I said. 'I miss Jack.'

'I know.' Her neon-pink headband was glowing in the darkness. She didn't say anything for a few moments. 'It's failure, isn't it? In all its forms, it's the same.'

'No. Not for me,' I said. 'It's heartbreak.'

'That, too,' Kate said softly. 'It's the worst.' She swallowed hard, darting a glance at Mez.

And I saw, then, that even though they were angry at each other, there was a foundation beneath them. Mez knew, better than anyone, how Kate felt about failing at tennis, even if he viewed it positively and she negatively. Jack and I didn't have that. We had never had that. He knew nothing of the boy, of my biggest failing. We didn't know each other.

And how must it have been for her, to admit defeat and come home? She simply wasn't good enough. She had to do something else. To pass the baton, and coach others in how to play instead of playing herself. That had to be hard, slicing through her self-worth like a guillotine.

'But my coach had a lot to say about it – failure,' Kate said.

Have the baby. Go back to medicine. I don't know. Keep going.'

I looked at Mez watering the plants and thought

back to when Jack left. 'Wally will be from a broken home,' I said.

It was so silent in the garage I could hear the water slowly trickling through each layer of soil, getting quieter and quieter until it faded away.

'What's a broken home?' Mez said. 'One where his parents argue all the time but are together? Or one where Mummy and Daddy never really lived together but are both happy, maybe with other people? What's broken about that?'

Maybe he was right. Maybe Wally would be okay.

But I didn't think I would. Not ever. Not ever again.

When I arrived home I went straight to bed, even though it was still early. It was like a pain; a weight on my chest, missing him. I checked my phone. There was nothing. I missed my mum, right then. Just for a second.

I texted Dad. *Everything's shit*, I wrote, while crying.

Think of me, he wrote back immediately, *balancing my chequebook even though it's the twenty-first century.*

I smiled faintly at that, and fell asleep, Wally turning somersaults inside me. My only comfort: I wasn't alone.

38

One year ago

I slept on it, and that made it worse. If it had happened spontaneously, if I hadn't been able to help myself, maybe it would have mattered less.

'Rachel,' he said as I walked into his room the next morning. He looked brighter, but I knew it was to be short-lived, like an artificial flower blooming unknowingly in a greenhouse. Snow was drifting down outside, the flakes fat and Christmassy. The first snowfall of the year. It only lasted a few minutes, that day, and then it stopped.

'Hi,' I said.

'Have you thought about it?'

I met his eyes. His hair had never really grown back, and his head was bald with a slight fuzz around the temples. His eyes still looked like his own – cat-like and elongated – but he was otherwise unrecognizable as the boy who'd come in for his first appointment.

'Why do you want to know?' I said.

'I have to know.'

'You can never un-know it. Once it's there in front of you, you'll know it forever. It will change everything you do.'

'Rach, I'm begging you. Life's not worth living right now. I don't care what it is. I don't care if it's different to what the consultant said. You know more about my cancer than anyone. I want to know what you think. Please tell me. Please just tell me. I feel like I'm going insane.'

I hesitated, waiting.

'Rach?' he said.

He was already sickening. He just didn't know it yet. I could see the evidence. He was an iPhone addict, and he wasn't checking it as much. He downed Coke, incessantly, despite the health warnings the well-meaning nurses issued to him, but there was a half-full bottle languishing on his bedside table. He'd missed *Match of the Day* last Saturday night because he was sleeping.

A chilly breeze came in through the open window. It was almost the shortest day of the year. Outside, it was like a winter postcard, frost on the ground. It was a strange night. He was in a room with two beds, one of them empty. It was dark save for his reading light.

I could barely look at him; another reason why I was not a very good doctor. Death had stolen in, was practically sitting in his lap. At the very least, it was in the visiting chair next to him.

'Come on, Rach. You know I've got *capacity*, or whatever bullshit term you use.'

I shrugged, raising my shoulders helplessly. 'It's not actually up to me,' I said.

'So in all of this,' the boy said, waving a slender arm around. His elbow was sticking out like one of Kate's tennis balls, his hands pink. He'd lost weight. 'There's the bureaucracy of the hospital paperwork and who has to decide for me – the law, the courts, the doctors, the nurses, my mum – and then . . .' He leant out of the bed, lowering his red hand as near to the floor as he could. The effort cost him, I could see. 'There's me. Right down here. On prognoses concerning me.'

I said nothing. I didn't know what to say.

'Is that right?' he asked.

'Yes,' I said. I couldn't fault his logic, nor his eloquence.

The truth was, I thought he deserved to know. That humans deserved to know, if they wanted to, that their time was limited. It wasn't the right thing to do to lie to him. He deserved to know when things were his *last things*; his last time seeing his best friend, his last time seeing a band live. His last game of Scrabble. He should know.

But I also thought he could handle it. My instincts told me he could. That his mother was being over-protective. And I trusted those instincts.

He pinched his lips together. They blanched white, with anaemia or fury, I wasn't sure.

'Please, Rachel,' he said. 'I have to know.'

'Months,' I said. 'Months.'

He looked at me. He seemed calm. 'How many?'

'It's in your lungs and your bone marrow. I'd say it's

in your blood. You should . . . you should be getting your affairs in order.'

'And will it . . . what will kill me?' he said, looking at me, his eyes wide.

'We don't need to go there,' I said.

'But I want to know. I need to know what I'm up against. How many months will be good?'

'A few. Two. Three. Then you'll have fluid on your lungs.'

'That'll be what kills me?'

'And the tumours. On your lungs. I would guess.'

'So I'll . . . I'll drown?' he was staring hard at me. 'Rachel – I need to know. I want to know the warning signs. So I can say my goodbyes.'

'Yes,' I said.

'Shit,' he said. 'Months. Until I drown. *Months*.' His jaw slackened. He looked aghast, struggling to sit up.

I couldn't stop looking at him. He was completely shocked. I'd done that. A feeling of dread washed over me like a cold shower. I couldn't take it back.

He stared at his hands then, and I closed my eyes tightly, wishing, for the first time in my career, that I really could step back in time. Just a few minutes. Just a few seconds. And undo it.

I could barely speak. It was uncharted territory. I'd gone against the GMC's guidelines. I'd done something a consultant wouldn't do. All because it felt like the right thing. Looking at the boy in front of me – just a child, and not a man – I couldn't understand myself.

Couldn't understand how I could have told him. How would I explain it to anybody else?

My crash beep went off. I looked down at it. An arrest down the hall. 'You alright?' I said to the boy.

'Thank you,' he said, bringing his hands together, as if in prayer. His cannulas trailed behind them. 'Thank you for risking your job. For telling me. I can get on with planning now. Thank you, Rach.'

39

Present day

Somehow, broken up from Jack, my obsession with finding answers intensified.

I would be in the bath, or lying in bed, or eating cereal in the morning, and I would remember a place I hadn't looked.

Had I looked properly for John Douglas's cached Facebook account on the Wayback Machine? I would suddenly think as I was filling the kettle.

Or, what about googling his Twitter username and seeing if he used other sites with it?

It was funny, really. Things with Jack had been difficult more than they had been fun for almost the entire relationship. He'd killed someone. He'd lied about it. But the other things were the things that I thought about most. The way he entwined his legs with mine in bed, his cold feet on my calves. His beautiful prose. The time I mistook his hot chocolate for a Bovril and Jack said he was flattered I viewed him as a Bovril-drinking alpha male. The way he always let himself into my flat, didn't knock. Because he knew he was special. Because he knew that he had unlimited access to my life. That I would never shut him out. That I would never *need* to shut him out.

And I think that was why I didn't stop googling. Not because the mystery wasn't solved, but because of how much I loved him. We were broken up, but I still loved him. And I wanted to be near him. So I carried on.

I should have been doing something else. Talking to friends. Crying. Even going through his old text messages in a heartbroken way instead of a stalking way. And I did feel like that. I felt like half a person, going about my pointless life without him; food didn't taste of anything at all.

It was called ghosting, apparently. When you break up without closure. Or, rather, when you break up without saying goodbye, but it still felt applicable to me. I'd been ghosted. He hadn't explained anything to me, not properly. I felt half there, transparent, as though automatic doors wouldn't open for me and I might fall through my very sofa as I lay down. I'm sure others saw me as a woman who left on her own terms because she'd been lied to, but that wasn't true. It was nothing like when Ben and I broke up. I'd walked home slowly from work one night a week after Ben had left. I'd dawdled, taking photographs of the winter skyline, and I'd felt a curiously new sensation of freedom. It was tentative, and a bit frightened, but emerging all the same. Without Jack, I felt nothing. I couldn't even remember what I enjoyed doing. I felt like half a person. Less than.

My closure was the Internet. I was looking at Jack's Facebook timeline. We were still friends – he would never do something as hostile as delete me – and I'd scrolled down to the first ever posts. I'd done this before, but this time I'd clicked *all posts* not *highlights*, and there were loads more.

A wall post from a Duncan James caught my eye. *Hi*, it said. *I know you from SOS forum. How's things?* Jack hadn't responded.

I googled SOS forum. There were no relevant results, but another forum said: *SOS Forum was forced to go underground after a prosecution based on its posts in 2008. Those in the know will know how to find it ;-).*

And that's when I started thinking, remembering what Kate had said. About the dark web. What was the browser called?

Tor. That was it. I was grateful for my good memory, the memory that had got me through med school and saved lives.

I could just have a look. Nobody would ever know.

I went to Tor's website. *Anonymity online* was its strapline.

I downloaded Tor – it referred to itself as *second-generation onion routing*; the internet was so baffling – searched for the forum, and the rest was easy.

I received a prompt to join the forum. Without thinking, I pressed 'register', then realized that I couldn't join with my current email address. I went to Gmail and set one up – findingout1986 – and then registered using a password whose numbers matched my bank card.

I signed in and was directed straight back. I searched for *air rifle*, found a post by a user called Sprat9, and started reading.

Sprat9: Me too, Roller. I still think about him every single day – every day without fail. At the time of year that it happened I think of the days leading up to it and after it. The anniversary is the worst. Same as his birthday. To think, I never knew him, never celebrated it. In the other seasons I think of how things might have been for him now. And in the times in between it hits me randomly; when seemingly happy in a restaurant, about to place an order, I will think of when his eyes widened right before it happened. Disbelief. It was disbelief. Just before turning out the light sometimes I think of how his parents were informed – that late-night phone call, identifying his body, the ragged wound the **air rifle** left – and I have to keep the light on a little while longer. So I don't have any answers, I'm afraid, but there's somebody here all the way across the ocean who entirely understands.

Next to his username, it said: *posts: 120*. A hundred and twenty posts on a forum?

Jack had never mentioned anything like that, was derisive at times of people on forums. 'The way they get all cliquey and flounce off, eventually,' he had once said to me as our starters arrived in a restaurant. 'It's so weird. Like a crazy subculture.'

I'd never really wondered how he knew.

Now I kept reading.

Sprat9: I've been tormenting myself with my victim's old posts online this week. I think I've found him. He was a poet.

JonnyJ19: How do you know it's him?

Sprat9: I just know.

JonnyJ19: Can you show us a post of his?

Sprat9: There was one, talking about his plans for the Christmas break. He wanted to write a song. A rap.

JonnyJ19: You can't live your life looking at stuff like this, mate. You've got to move on. There's a cause and effect between your actions and his life, but it doesn't mean you're responsible for his life. It doesn't.

Sprat9: Doesn't it?

JonnyJ19: I remember the circumstances of your situation and I think I know who you are. I know how hard that must be for you. My friend was in the car with me when I crashed and that's how he died. Yours is far more complex. Maybe you should see someone?

It wasn't really the things he was saying. It was the way he said them; his tone. It was imbued with a sadness, a regret he'd never expressed with me. Right there, in the safe confines of the dark web, he was being real.

40

My neighbour emerged from her flat just I arrived home from Kate's on a chilly Saturday. We'd spent some of the afternoon discussing Mum. The things we liked about her. The things that hadn't changed in death, after discovering her infidelity. The way she collected fridge magnets, obsessively, from holiday destinations. The fridge was covered, encrusted with them like limpets. We liked the way she'd always been honest with us about motherhood. I wondered what she'd say to me now, what advice she'd give. The way she called at 6 p.m. precisely, every Monday. On the dot. As though she was demonstrating her reliability, her love, in her behaviour, if not her words.

'Rachel, I signed for something for you,' my neighbour said.

She was a nervous character, overly concerned with the goings-on of the building, and it was almost impossible to end a conversation with her within a reasonable amount of time. She liked to summarize and recap and discuss the reasons why the maintenance of the building had changed from once a year to twice.

'Thanks,' I said.

I reached out and took the parcel from her. It had a silver Royal Mail Special Delivery sticker slicked across its front. I turned it over, looking curiously at it, and that's when I saw it, and realized what it was. A blue court stamp. Glasgow something.

It was the trial transcript. I dropped it into my handbag. It was thick and weighty.

I went into my flat, wordlessly. I heard my neighbour calling out after me, but I ignored her.

I tried not to read it. I knew it was a terrible thing to do, to invade Jack's privacy like that. And I didn't need to know now. He'd gone. It was over. But the thing I'd learnt most about myself over that long, cold, depressing autumn was that I didn't have any willpower. Where decisions needed to be made, over and over, I would always fail, like a smoker forced to sit next to a brand-new packet of cigarettes with a lighter right beside them. It felt impossible, to me, to resist. To resist again and again.

But then, could anybody coexist in one room with a transcript of their ex-boyfriend's murder trial and not read it? I couldn't.

I made a cup of tea and ran a bath and played two goes on Words with Friends against Kate. And then, trying to distract myself, I sent Audrey a screenshot of a BBC news headline about a man who collected all the meerkats from the annoying adverts, entitling it: 'Weird Richard II'. But, despite all of this faff, it was inevitable that I would open the parcel and read every word.

The bubble wrap on the inside of the jiffy bag stretched and strained, and eventually I ripped into it with my teeth. The transcript was too big for staples so it was divided up with elastic bands.

One bundle was labelled *procurator fiscal/prosecution*, one *defence* and one *judgment*. I spread them out in front of me on the living-room floor amongst a couple of old mugs and a pair of socks I'd removed while watching television one night.

I stared at the letter.

Dear Ms Anderson,

I enclose the transcript of H. M. Advocate v John Michael Douglas which took place on 5 to 9 April 2010. The charge for this is £312. Please pay by cheque within 14 days, made payable to Scottish Courts and Tribunals Service.

If you have any queries please do not hesitate to contact me.

Yours sincerely . . .

There was a phone number at the bottom, and the website address, but nothing else.

I began to read.

ITEM 14

CASE
in the cause
H. M. ADVOCATE

against

JOHN MICHAEL DOUGLAS
HIGH JUSTICIARY COURT

5–9 April 2010

Prosecuting barrister: Nina Smith QC

Defence barrister: Michael Fitzpatrick QC

Before: The Honourable Lord Orwell

Extracts from Procurator Fiscal – Prosecution

Detective Inspector Burr, Examination

Nina Smith: Can you please confirm your name and address for the record?

Charlotte Burr: Detective Inspector Charlotte Elizabeth Burr, collar number 9630 for Strathclyde Police, stationed at Oban Police Office, Albany Street, Oban, Scotland.

NS: What has your role been throughout investigating the defendant, John Douglas?

CB: I reviewed all of the evidence that came in for the defendant's case.

NS: And what did that include?

CB: Listening to the defendant's 999 call, his no comment interview, the evidence surrounding the reports from that night.

NS: Tell us about the call first. What was the defendant's demeanour like during the call?

CB: Calm. He was very calm.

NS: The prosecution will now play a recording of the call.

Recording – exhibit CB1

JD: Police and ambulance, please. I . . . There's been an incident. With an intruder. There's been an accident. He's bleeding. A bit.

999 Operator: Slow down. Please confirm your address.

JD: The Highlands, Oban. The big house on the hill.

999O: Ambulance and police are on their way. What is the situation?

JD: Dominic Hull. He's . . . he's been shot.

999O: Where?

JD: In the head. In the head.

999O: Is there bleeding?

JD: Yes. Not lots.

999O: You need to lie him in the recovery position. Which side is the bullet wound on?

JD: The right.

999O: Please lie him on his left-hand side. Recovery position. Do you have a piece of material to wrap around the wound? Apply as much pressure as you can.

Anna Wiley, Cross-examination

Nina Smith: And can you confirm your relationship with the defendant?

Anna Wiley: I am the psychiatrist for the defence.

NS: And was the defendant prone to anger? Outbursts? A temper?

AW: I wouldn't say prone.

NS: But you might say . . . he has had outbursts?

AW: Well, he clearly lost control during a very stressful situation at his house in Oban but –

NS: Yes or no.

AW: Yes.

NS: So it could be inferred that the defendant is prone to outbursts? That he has a temper?

Michael Fitzpatrick: Objection. My learned friend appears to be giving her own evidence.

NS: I'll rephrase. In your opinion, what does the evidence tell you about the defendant's temper?

AW: I suppose it can be inferred that he has one. But don't we all?

NS: No further questions.

Lee Aldridge, Examination

Nina Smith: Can you confirm you were present at the Douglases' house on the night Dominic Hull was killed?

Lee Aldridge: Yes, I was there, for a while.

NS: And had Dominic Hull ever burgled the Douglases before?

LA: No, not to my knowledge.

NS: And had he ever been in their house before?

LA: No. Some of us had. But he hadn't. Not ever. He was only young.

NS: Can you walk us through what happened?

LA: We walked into the Douglases' house.

[Long pause]

NA: It's fine, Mr Aldridge. Charges have been dropped. How did you get in?

LA: The door was wide open. Not just unlocked. Opened.

NS: As our other witness, who lived in the nearest house, corroborated.

LA: Yes.

NS: Did you believe the house was empty?

LA: No. We didn't know. We just saw the open door. We were looking up at the house, anyway. Scouting it.

NS: How did you see it?

LA: It was the back door, to the conservatory, which was at the top of the big hill. You could see it for miles. It was about midnight.

NS: So what did you do?

LA: We saw it was open, so we went. We didn't really think about it. We took Dominic, for his first go. An easy one.

NS: And then what happened?

LA: We walked in the back door. It was dark in there. We thought Mr Douglas was somewhere else. But then the light flicked on. And it seems. Well.

NS: Yes?

LA: It seemed . . .

NS: Can you finish your sentence, please?

LA: Mr Douglas was waiting for us.

Michael Fitzpatrick: Objection. The witness cannot know the defendant's state of mind or intentions.

The Honourable Lord Orwell: Sustained.

LA: What shall I do?

The Honourable Lord Orwell: The jury should disregard that question and the answer given by the witness and should place no weight on them at all in their consideration of this case.

NS: What was the defendant doing – Mr Douglas?

LA: He put lights on somewhere else in the house. To lure us in. So we'd think he was somewhere else. He opened the door. And he waited. He fucking waited for us in the dark. Ready.

NS: And then what?

LA: He flicked the light on. And there he was. He was sitting in a chair, holding an air rifle. Ready to shoot.

NS: And then what happened?

LA: Dominic – he was overexcited. He went in, ran through the house, to the study, I think. I was frozen to the spot, staring at John, in the corridor.

NS: And did Mr Douglas say anything to you?

LA: Yes.

NS: What?

LA: He said . . . he said we shouldn't go any further.

NS: What happened next?

LA: I ran. I ran off. I was shitting myself, miss.

NS: And what did you hear?

LA: The air rifle. As I was running down the banks, slipping on the wet grass, I heard the shot ring out. But I didn't go back. I was too scared to.

NS: And would you say, in your opinion, that there was a struggle?

MF: Objection – how could the witness know?

JO: Overruled. Answer the question, please, Mr Aldridge.

LA: [A pause] No.

NS: If you had to estimate, how long would you say elapsed between you leaving, and the shot being fired?

LA: Fifteen seconds.

NS: Fifteen seconds?

LA: About that. Yes.

John Douglas, Cross-examination

John Douglas: I swear that the evidence that I shall give shall be the truth, the whole truth and nothing – and nothing but the truth, so help me God.

Nina Smith: Good morning, Mr Douglas.

JD: [Silence]

NS: Was the door unlocked, Mr Douglas?

JD: [Silence]

NS: Mr Douglas? Were you trying to lure them there?

JD: Yes, the door was unlocked. Yes, it was open.

NS: Were you trying to lure them there?

JD: Yes.

NS: Were you waiting for them?

JD: Yes.

NS: Were you holding a gun?

JD: Yes.

NS: In the dark?

JD: Yes.

NS: Did you turn the light on and point the gun at them?

JD: Yes.

NS: Did you intend to kill them?

JD: No. No.

NS: Why did you pull that trigger, Mr Douglas? Please tell us in your own words.

JD: I . . .

[Brief adjournment]

John Douglas, Cross-examination: resumed after adjournment for Mr Douglas's comfort

John Douglas: Sorry, I . . . I'm screwed, aren't I? There was a struggle. There was. He grabbed for me with – a statue. I thought he was going to club me. So I shot. It was self-defence. Self-defence. They were in my house. They shouldn't have been in my house. Even though I did lure them there. Even though it all went wrong.

Extract from judgment

The Honourable Lord Orwell: As the jury has, unanimously, returned a result of not proven, John Douglas, you are free to go. Unfortunately you have already spent four months of your time in prison. However, it's important that such serious cases are investigated and that justice is seen to be done.

41

I felt the truth right in my stomach, as if it was a real physical thing, like a stone being dropped down into the well of my gut, the ripples reverberating outwards.

He'd planned it.

I sat still for a long time after reading the transcript. There were stacks of it. Five days. Eight hours a day. All transcribed, word for word. I read every bit.

I wasn't aware how much time had passed. I really wasn't. The sun set across the room, moving right to left. And then the moonlight skated across, chasing it. The air had darkened from blue to grey to black around me. I reluctantly put the lights on, too late, when my eyes were strained from reading in the dimness.

I was not existing. I was not Rachel. I didn't eat. I didn't drink. I sat in the centre of the living room, the pages spread around me like a clock, and I slowly rotated, like the hour hand, moving in a circle as time slipped away. I was those pages and those pages were me. Soon, they became well thumbed, like old books, the witnesses like ghostly friends as I reread their moments on the stand.

My hips were aching. My eyes were stinging. I hadn't felt like that since night shifts. Maybe even since medical school. Even my bump was aching. And of course it was: I hadn't fed Wally. Hadn't slept enough.

'Right,' I said to myself, looking around the room at the evidence. The literal evidence. It was strewn around me. Like I was a conspiracy theorist heading towards a breakdown. God. It looked like a nest. A wild animal's pit.

Stiff from sitting cross-legged, too warm from sitting on the section of the floor where the central-heating pipes crossed underneath it, I stood up. The patch of carpet where I'd been rose and regained its form.

He'd planned it.

I thought back to what Davey had said. *What Jack planned.* They all knew. All of them.

He'd opened the door and sat there, in the dark, holding a gun.

My shoulders became covered in goosebumps. I'd been alone with him. I'd been in a remote house in Oban with him. That man, that man who'd planned to kill that boy.

Never mind the rest. Everything he'd told me, from the moment he met me, had been a lie. His name. The verdict. The nature of the crime. That he'd never been to prison. That they'd repeatedly burgled him, when actually Dominic had *never* burgled him. That he hadn't planned it. All lies.

What really happened was this: he'd lured them in to teach them a lesson. And then he'd killed someone.

42

You'd think I'd have stopped after that. That should have been the end. The bombshell of his planned *murder* that had me winded, reeling.

But I didn't. I wanted more. Like an alcoholic on a binge, I wanted to unravel it all, to find it all out, to be sure I knew the worst of what my baby's father had done, like a criminal investigations department finding a body and ransacking the entire house to check there wasn't another. I was desperate to check there wasn't anything worse.

But I was also thirsty for the other stuff. The trial revelation had been so shocking, so awful, that I needed to see something else. Something of him. Some atonement. I wanted more of the regret I'd seen on the forums. It was intoxicating, I'd wanted it for so long.

I bounded over that line. That line that nobody crosses. The line that is quite possibly illegal.

It was surprisingly easy to log in to his email. It began with an email, and it ended with one, too.

Forgotten your password? Answer two of these three security questions:
  What is your place of birth?
  What is your mother's maiden name?
  What is the name of your secondary school?

I almost laughed. It was that easy. Maybe I did know him, after all, I thought with an ironic smile.

I typed them in.

What is your place of birth?
What is your mother's maiden name? **Ross**
What is the name of your secondary school? **Fettes**

Thank you, it said. *Now please change your password.*

I typed something in, utter nonsense. It didn't matter. He'd have to change it back, anyway; would think he'd been hacked. I started reading.

I was rushing, even though there was no need to. I started at the top. Emails between him and editors – ones he'd chased three times, all laid out neatly in rows. I looked at a few more – more work – and a round robin about the rugby club, wanting to arrange a curry the next Thursday.

I typed in the search bar: *Dominic*, and pressed enter. He'd changed his email address. Not set up a new account. Everything was there. Ported over. Historic stuff.

ITEM 15

It wasn't how people said it was. Of course it wasn't.

My younger, learning-disabled brother, Davey, was upstairs. Some of the press didn't realize that, because he lacked the capacity to be called as a witness. But he was there. I wanted to protect him. Partially. But that's not the whole story.

But maybe the events start two years earlier. A new

323

family moved to Oban. It was the sort of place where you knew of a new family. It was small like that. Insular, I guess. They were the Hulls. I don't know how many of them there were. Eight or nine. I still don't know now. The public gallery blurred into one. My lawyer advised me not to look at them.

During the first break-in they stole our keys which sat – naively – just inside the front door. They smashed the glass in our door, reached around and turned the key, and then just walked in, like a courier delivering a parcel, or a friendly neighbour. They grabbed three bunches of keys and drove off in the cars.

We claimed on the insurance, of course. Of course we did. The cars were replaced. The window was fixed.

But things were never the same after that. The night after it happened, the window was boarded up. We couldn't get someone to fix the kind of glass it needed to be for weeks. The wind rushed around the board and it rattled and squeaked in the night. Davey, my brother, kept coming down to check it.

And then, a few months later, when we wanted a new computer, things felt different. How could we buy anything – an Apple Mac, a big-screen television – when we knew it would attract these people? But, still. We were advised to live our lives, so we did.

The second time reoriented things again. They came in the back. Another smashed window. A different one this time. There were forty more windows. Davey counted. Would there be forty more break-ins? This time, they took the new computer and an iPad. The council wouldn't let us put double-glazed windows in. It was a listed building, they said, and they wouldn't give us consent for double-glazing. It would keep happening, we were sure.

The press thought we should move. But it's not that simple, is it? It never is. Things had been adapted for Davey, and, besides, there was a defiance about us. We thought: *why should we?* And, in the context of a couple of break-ins, you'd have thought the same, too. We couldn't know everything that would come after. How could we?

The third time, Mum surprised them. She recognized Aldridge.

It was the fourth break-in that went wrong. For everybody. For Dominic.

I can't underestimate the kind of anger that sits beneath the surface after things like that. I carried it everywhere with me. Not only in the amount of time that dealing with the burglaries took up – the endless insurance requests for documents, the window replacements, the police reports – but the other stuff, too. It's true, what people say, that it's like a violation. Home was an extension of us, and we had been violated.

We couldn't see a way to stop it. Even if we moved, they'd find us. We were the richest family in Oban, and everybody knew it. You should see the email trails, the calls, the reports we gave to the police. But none of it got us anywhere. 'What are we supposed to do?' Mum said to me, bewildered, after the night it happened again.

And, of course, we weren't supposed to do that. But there was a problem, and it wasn't being sorted.

Then December the 1st rolled around.

Dear Mr and Mrs Hull,

I never thought I would have to write something like this. That's a clichéd way to begin, isn't it? But it's true. Clichés often are.

I am sure I am the last person you want to hear from, but I wanted to write to you. I am not going to explain – you would surely never understand, and nor should you – but I wanted to tell you that Dominic didn't suffer. He didn't die afraid and he did die quickly. He didn't say much, I'm sorry to report. He didn't say much during his death. The bullet

I was glad that email was unfinished. I wondered what these drafts were the result of. Some sort of therapy, maybe?

I tried another set of key words: *break in.*

There were over a hundred hits.

ITEM 16

casey.jones@scotland.police.uk
Sorry to hear of your second **break-in** . . . This is looking like a problematic family. I will try and get intelligence on them from their old address. We will come by for finger printing but I have to tell you that I am not sure much can be done if the families on that estate use each other as alibis.

orders@CCTV4U.co.uk
Thank you for your enquiry about CCTV and security lights and we are very sorry to hear of your **break-in**. They most

certainly are motion sensitive. Would you like to proceed with the order?

j.douglas@gmail.com
I need a locksmith following a **break-in**. Do you have any availability urgently?

info@oban.scotland.gov.uk
I am sorry to inform you that your request for consent to double-glazed windows has been denied despite your **break-in**. The appearance of listed buildings in Oban must be uniform in order to preserve the character of the building. If you wish to appeal against this decision . . .

They went on and on. The emails with the police especially. There was an email trail about the failed identity parade, the first time, but it got worse after the second break-in. The tone of the police emails – *What do you expect us to do?* – coupled with the desperation and volume of the Douglases' emails made me start. They ordered CCTV. Security lights. Sensors. They changed their locks. They replaced and replaced and replaced their windows, only for them to be smashed again. They weren't allowed to get double glazing. It would be incompatible with the old frames.

I had sympathy for them. Just a twinge.

You have been logged out, Google displayed at the top of his email account.

I didn't realize why.

43

I pushed the laptop away and drew my knees to my chest, amongst the detritus of my stalking. The trial transcript was still strewn around my living room like there'd been a great gust of wind that had disturbed a neat stack of papers and blown them around. The laptop was still open on his logged-out email. It looked like the flat of a mad woman.

I stared at it, thinking nothing except how that lovely relationship – the way we laughed at Howard sprinting around the house in the middle of the night, holding hands underneath the duvet – had become this.

My door opened ten minutes later. I hadn't locked it. And there he was.

I jumped.

That man who'd deliberately lured those boys in. Like a killer. Like a psychopath.

Jack knew the code for my building. I was not allowed into his world without breaking in, but he was allowed into mine, I saw.

He leant against the kitchen counter, lit up by the spot-lights, balancing his weight on the tips of his fingers.

'What –?' I began.

'What's going on?' he interrupted.

He looked bigger than before, imposing, in my kitchen. I imagined another news headline about him.

Pregnant woman found ... I shook my head. No. He wouldn't ever hurt me. But how could I be sure?

'What do you want?' I said. I looked around me, in spite of myself.

He'd arrived too quickly for me to tidy up.

At first I thought he wouldn't notice. It didn't look that bad. It was just a few papers.

But then I saw it through his eyes, and it was frightening. Pages everywhere. His email inbox on my screen. Oh God, his email inbox.

'Rach?' he said.

He took a few steps into my living room, then knelt down on my carpet, like an archaeologist about to uncover something historically significant. His body language covered up the real anger within, and I was taken in by it.

He looked up. His eyes met mine. 'Have you been in my emails?' he said. And, as he said it, his eyes landed on a page of the trial transcript. He reached out, his fingers stretching for the loose, well-thumbed pages. 'What is this? Is this like . . . a *dossier* on me?'

I saw his eyes rove over the sheets. Pages and pages of his trial. The worst week of his life. Oh God, oh God.

He stood bolt upright, then looked straight at me. 'What's this?' he repeated.

Seeing the pages again, in his hands, ignited my anger. That he'd looked at me, time and time again, and lied. That he'd planned the whole thing. That he didn't see fit to tell me that; to be honest.

'You fucking lured those burglars in,' I said. 'You trapped them.'

Jack's eyes went very round.

'You wouldn't tell me,' I said, heading, ill-advisedly, for the immediate defensive path. 'You wouldn't explain anything.'

'So you . . . is this my trial?' He glanced at it again.

Of course he hadn't realized straight away. It was just pages and pages of incomprehensible witness cross-examination. He'd probably never seen the entire trial written down.

'Yes,' I said. I was no longer scared of him. I was bolstered by my anger.

'Where did you . . . ?'

To my surprise, Jack was bewildered. That I'd got my hands on it, ordered it behind his back. And rightly so.

And now I had to live with the fact that I didn't know what I was capable of. Which was similar to how Jack lived, too. It was strange and horrible how things worked out. I blinked. Was it really only a few moments ago that I had justified hacking into my boyfriend's email? I didn't recognize myself. How awful I had become.

'I ordered it. Tell me what happened with those boys, Jack.'

'Did you log in to my emails? Google said . . . I saw the IP address for a new login. It had your service provider on it. BT. Central Newcastle. Was it you? That's why I'm here. I want to know.'

'Did you plan to lure Dominic in and kill him? Were you really waiting? If so, how the fuck did you get off?' I said nastily. 'You must have had a brilliant lawyer. A snake.'

Jack's expression darkened at that. He looked down at the floor, sucked in his breath, then looked at me again. 'You tell me. Looks like you've made a fucking Freedom of Information Request instead of asking me.'

'Instead of asking you?' I thundered.

'I do not need to defend myself to you about something of which I was acquitted,' Jack retorted.

'You were not acquitted. You are not *not guilty*.'

His mouth tightened around its edges. If I just focused on that mouth, and not his arms, rigid by his sides, or his legs, spread wide, aggressive, I could pretend we were happy, and he was just moistening his lips ready to kiss me. I stared and stared at that mouth.

'I was acquitted, Rachel. And if you don't agree with that then I don't think we've got too much more to say to each other, have we? You're ordering things about me. You're reading my personal emails.'

'Yes,' I said. 'I . . . yes.' My eyes felt moist.

'You're not who I thought you were,' he said sadly. His eyes were in the shadow of his brow.

'Neither are you,' I said.

His mouth turned down. He brought a hand to his forehead and rubbed it. 'God, I loved you,' he said.

That sentence broke my heart more than all the others. More than all the lies put together. 'What about Wally?' I said.

'I'm not saying . . . I'm not saying I'll never see you again,' Jack said with a snort that sounded almost derisive. It was cruel, that little laugh of his. So different to the low chuckle that I had loved so much.

'But what?'

'I don't know, Rach. Co-parenting? Split fifty-fifty? I don't know. Let's not.' He took a deep breath, then blew slowly out of his mouth, like a smoker. 'I need to decide where we're at. Then the other stuff.'

'Fine.'

'The reporters did what you did,' he said. 'They do bloody hack your voicemail. My pin's 6865, if you want to join them.'

I blushed. It was the same as the security code to unlock his phone, and I knew it. I didn't tell him.

'Or maybe you want my bank pin?' he continued.

He was berating me. I'm sad to say he seemed to square up to me, like a puffed-up tomcat. I felt a dart of fear then. At what he might do. At what he had done. Maybe one day I would let myself into his house and he'd raise that gun to me, I found myself thinking. He'd lied about everything else so far. Why not that, too? Maybe he *was* capable of harming us.

'You killed somebody,' I said softly to him. 'And I am in the wrong for trying to find out more about it? You were a closed book.'

'You don't bloody know me,' he roared, in full-on Scottish mode.

I took a step back at that. My hand went to my stomach, instinctively.

'You don't know me,' he said, more softly this time. He glanced down at my belly, then met my eyes again.

'Why should I believe you're good when you murdered somebody?' I said. 'I spent my career saving lives. You

332

killed someone. And you planned it. You bloody planned it. Davey as much as told me, and you said he was mad. I went and asked him, and you stopped me again. It was premeditated. Malice aforethought,' I shouted, the words springing to mind from the transcript. 'Malice.'

He stared at me then, so hard I wondered if he would say anything more to me ever again. 'I don't have to listen to this,' he said.

'Don't then,' I yelled. 'Go!'

But although I was angry, something significant was waking up inside me. I'd been in his emails. Was there really ever an excuse for that?

'Did you find what you were looking for?' he said to me, turning as he walked towards the door.

His eyes were cold stones. Maybe it was because of the emails, but I suspected it was also because I admitted that I'd asked Davey again. His expression had changed when I'd said that.

'Not really,' I replied.

Though the sad thing was: I had. Those emails, with their sad tone, the repeated enquiries of the police: they had almost been enough for me. I had started to feel the things I should have felt towards my boyfriend: understanding, sympathy, love.

'Well, if you want to know anything further, I refer you to my court case,' Jack said. 'You think I'm a fucking murderer?' The swear words were biting in his soft Scottish accent. 'Fuck you then.'

He crossed the room, opened the door, and left.

And that was that.

333

44

One year ago

I called in on the boy again, the next night. I wanted to see him, to check on him, even though it would annoy him.

'Alright?' he said.

He was sitting up, reading a book. I looked at the cover: *We Were Liars*.

'Contemporary young-adult,' I said, gesturing to the book. I was trying to make conversation, to make sure he was okay. I wanted him to talk to me about Freud and Marx and all the things he liked to sound off about.

'Yep.'

He put the book down, splayed on the bed, and looked at me.

'You alright?' he said with a smile, and I knew then that he was okay.

'Just weathering the night shifts.' I smiled, hovering in his doorway.

The window was still open, letting in the chilly air.

'I bet,' he said. He reached for the remote control. 'Nothing on at this hour.'

'I doubt it. Aren't you tired? Or cold?' I looked at the window.

'Always was a night owl,' he said. He glanced over, then back at the television, then over to me again. 'Would you mind adjusting that?' He pointed to the bracket that supported the television. It was sort of a long, sturdy arm, with a forty-five-degree angle in the middle.

'Okay,' I said. 'Though this is definitely outside my job description.'

'You're good like that,' he said softly.

'How are you feeling about what we . . . about our chat?'

His eyes met mine. 'Good. Thank you,' he said. 'Thank you for telling me. I will never forget it.' He nodded, once, looking away moodily in a teenagerish way, his eyes clearly misting over, even though he tried to hide it.

'How's that?' I said, wrenching the arm.

He appraised it. 'A bit higher,' he said. 'I want to recline and watch it lying down. I'm tired.'

He was worsening, I thought. I was adjusting his room for him, to make him more comfortable as the cancer raced ahead. The television stand was now more than six feet from the ground, and he seemed satisfied with that. He could watch it while he lay down. While he dozed. While he slept more and more.

He threw me a grateful look as I left. My hand lingered on the doorframe for a split second longer than usual.

45

Present day

There were a few things that made me do it. Jack leaving. The discovery that he'd planned the whole thing. My mind was reeling.

I wanted to inspect myself, as if under a magnifying glass. Jack hadn't been perfect. Mez and Kate weren't perfect. My parents' relationship hadn't been perfect. My mother had led a secret life.

And I wasn't perfect, either. I wanted to retrace my steps. I wanted to go back and meet myself, to go home. Like studying an advert for a missing person, I went back to the place where I had lost my way. Rachel Anderson. Age: 29. Short. Average weight. Last seen outside the RVI.

I suppose it was going back there that made me recall it properly. I'd not set foot inside that part of the hospital since the day it happened. I had since kept my feet outside the linoleum floors of Block B1 where I had worked. Ward G. I'd never forget it.

It was late, and I drove straight there. My body remembered the drive — left at the roundabout, indicate right immediately and turn off the road. I felt the thrill of driving a route I knew well; the swing of taking a corner at just the right pace, the fluid motion of the steering wheel like a silk scarf underneath my fingertips. I knew nobody would be there; they were always so chronically understaffed.

I drove to the back of my block. All of my favourite car parking spaces were empty. The one in the shade of the big tree. The wide one on the corner. I parked underneath the tree, spindly without its leaves, and sat back in the driver's seat, staring at the door of the hospital.

I never went in the main entrance. Hardly any doctors did. We all had our favourite doors near our wards, performed actions that only existed in muscle memory. I would put the code in – C2578Y – and swing the door open, push the next one, squirt the alcohol gel on to my hands and push the final door open. Sometimes, after long shifts, at busy times, I would go to press a non-existent alcohol gel dispenser in my own house, the base of my palm pushing the wall before I realized where I was. That sort of thing happened all the time, back then. I found those times stressful, but remembered them fondly now. Isn't that always the way?

One of the only times my role crossed with Amrit's was when a baby called Adam was born at twenty-four weeks' gestation. We practically lived in the hospital. The rota was abandoned. At the end of it, when he was taken off the High Dependency Unit and transferred to the ward, I took a cup of tea outside to celebrate. I kept remembering the worst of it – resuscitating him over and over, the drugs that didn't work, his heart defect that wouldn't close over. I hadn't been to the toilet without my crash bleep for a month. I had no idea what the weather was doing. I had brought more and more underwear and socks to the hospital and been home less and less. But, sipping that cup of tea, I started to remember the good things, too. The joys of being a doctor that I didn't know were joys until I did it. A shared cheer, delighted, with Adam's parents in the HDU when he took his first breath.

And then, much, much later, I would know yet more joys. A curry out with everyone where we toasted him. Seeing him a year later, walking steadily, obsessed with *The Gruffalo* book. Realizing it was worth it: all those professionals. All those months. All that input, to save a life. It would all be worth it to see him seriously proffer me a baked bean over his birthday lunch.

I finished that tea, tasting its rich tannin, and fell asleep on the grass. It was the best nap I'd ever had. I fell asleep on my front, on the lawn, underneath a balcony, and a nurse called the crash team. They thought I'd jumped. We all had a laugh about that as I rubbed the sleep from my eyes.

I eyed the door now, outside the hospital in late November, alone. Nobody was coming or going, but it was close to nine in the evening. And then I saw him: Amrit. He often stood outside after a birth, collecting himself. He was emotional like that. And he was so good at his job that nobody minded his occasional disappearances.

The moon was slung low in the sky, lying on her back. And then I had a rush of thoughts, all at once, so significant, so anxiety-inducing, that I would have bent double if I could have; if Wally hadn't been so big by then.

If it had been a few weeks ago, when I was still unsure of the details of Jack's crime, of the victim's injuries, I might have – if the timing had been right, in the gap between finding the Google results and finding out what Jack had done, maybe, maybe – gone inside, used my old NHS password, and looked up the victim. It would have been easy. I could have read about the trajectory of the bullet and exactly which lobe it had entered and with how much force. I could have read the autopsy report and understood it. And, if it had been a few weeks earlier, I might have done that.

How awful I would have felt. I could feel my mind trying to justify it now. He'd kept it from me. I deserved to know. But nothing could excuse it. I didn't have any boundaries. I thought about how I'd continued to check up on the boy's Twitter. It wasn't just Jack I'd done it with. It was inexcusable.

I was nosy. Investigative, to put it kindly.

It all seemed to happen at once. One moment it was quiet – the moonlight illuminating the steam coming out of one of the vents next to the hospital canteen, the windows along a corridor illuminated sodium yellow – and the next Amrit was glancing over at me.

Before I really knew what I was doing, I was getting out of my car and walking over to him, raising a hand in a self-conscious wave. He was wearing his scrubs. Scrubs always made the best pyjamas. There was something about them that I liked. The medicinal smell. The threadbare softness. The loose fit. But I'd thrown all of mine away.

He looked over at me. 'Welcome back,' he said simply. 'I knew you'd come.'

46

One year ago

I wasn't called to his room. There was no crash call or loud buzzer. No warning sign at all. I just went to see him, later that night, for no reason other than to look in, to spend time with him, to make sure he was okay. To check, maybe, that he'd managed to get some sleep.

I could say I knew as I approached his room, but I didn't. The truth is, I had no idea.

I was walking at full pace when I opened his door. I was prepared with a one-liner about how he should be reading *War and Peace*, not YA books, to improve his vocabulary to beat me in Scrabble.

I opened the door, and stopped dead.

He'd used a Newcastle United scarf, the one he always had with him.

He was hanging. There from the television frame, a puddle of urine beneath him.

The circus had begun around me. The consultant was called in. He'd been sleeping, was puffy-eyed as he arrived. The nurses stood around, shivering, as the consultant examined him. And, of course, the boy's mum was called in.

'There'll be an inquest, won't there?' one of the nurses said to me.

I was standing, separated from them all, alone in a corner, in the darkest part of the room, looking at the aftermath. The scarf. The television arm that I'd adjusted. The floor being mopped. I wasn't looking at his body, which had been placed back on the bed as if he was still alive.

I could hear the boy's mum in the corridor. I turned away, towards the wall, folding my arms in on myself. It was the worst moment of my entire life.

'What's happened, what's happening?' she was saying. 'Let me in there,' she shouted.

Daniel, the consultant, stopped examining the boy, gave me a curt look, and went to the door. I was supposed to go with him. Oh, how could I go, how could I face her and tell her what I'd done?

'There was a note,' the consultant said to me in a low voice.

'Was there?' Instinctively, I reached my hand out.

But he looked at me. 'For her,' he said, a quizzical look crossing his features.

She was out in the corridor, standing alone, a handbag clasped between her fingers, swaying slightly as she held it, the bag almost touching the floor. I closed my eyes, a slow blink, and braced myself.

'We need to have a word in a room,' Daniel said.

'What's happening? Where is he? Is he alright? He was running a fever, but he was *fine*, we played Minesweeper.'

'Let's step in here,' Daniel said.

I had to admire his composure. Next to him, I was shaking violently.

She looked at us, expectantly, her eyes glassy, and I saw then that she knew already. Only she was trying not to know. She daren't know.

'I'm very, very sorry –' Daniel began.

Her features collapsed in on themselves before he could finish.

I bit a fingernail, looking away. I couldn't handle it.

'No,' she said. 'How? How?'

I held my body tight, as though that could stem her emotions, as Daniel dealt the blow.

'I'm very sorry to say he took his own life. Last night. In the night,' Daniel said. 'I'm so very, very sorry.'

At first she said nothing. Her face remained the same. And then she coughed, making a kind of choking noise. And then she covered her face with her hands and screamed, just like he had, in my office.

My mind arced back over it. His tattoo. Throwing that paperweight. Quoting Marx at me like he was an adult. But really, he was pretending. He didn't have capacity. He was immature. Volatile. Not ready. I should have kept him in denial. Been less brutal in my honesty. My gut instincts had been wrong. Totally incorrect. Catastrophically incorrect. I had killed him. My hands may have been clean, free of blood, but I had killed that boy. It had been me.

My face became hot as I stood, then sat back down again. Daniel looked at me, irritated.

The mother turned to me, blinking in disbelief. And then she said it. Putting together her child's death and my reaction to it. 'You told him,' she said. Her voice was quiet, but her gaze was locked on to mine.

I couldn't do anything but tell the truth. 'Yes,' I said. I wanted to add that I was sorry, that I had been wrong, but I couldn't.

She looked away from me. 'Why?' she said, still looking at the window. 'I told you . . . I told you not to.'

'Told him what?' Daniel said.

'His prognosis.'

His brow creased. 'How did you know his prognosis?'

'I told him what I knew.'

'But those would be guesses. Cancer is so unpredictable.'

The boy's mum's wails got louder, at that.

Daniel's face closed down. 'We need to speak alone,' he said to me, raising his eyebrows. He was dismissing me, I saw.

I got up to leave, hovering at the door, waiting for closure, but the boy's mum wouldn't look at me.

'I did everything I could for him,' I said, my voice thick. 'Everything for his cancer. Everything in his . . . what I thought were his best interests.'

'Well, you were wrong. Look what he did . . .' She paused. 'How?'

Daniel understood immediately. He was far better than me at subtext, at understanding people. 'He hanged himself. I'm very sorry.'

I left then. It wasn't right to, but it wouldn't have been right to stay, either.

And it wasn't right to tell the boy, but I'm not sure it would have been right to keep lying to him. Nothing worked in those situations. Nothing was right.

Shortly after the boy's mum went in to see him, Daniel suspended me. I didn't see him until the inquest, where I was examined and cross-examined by a snobby barrister.

My last words to Daniel, as I left, as I was wrenched away from my patients, were, 'Make sure Maisie in bed three sees the monkey on your stethoscope when you're doing her obs. She likes it. It helps her.'

47

Present day

We sat on the tarmac of the car park in the cold November night.

'What're you going to do?' Amrit said. He had new trainers on; they were a bright white.

'What? Nothing,' I said.

'Well, you can't go on creeping around hospital car parks,' he said.

I turned to him. He was leaning back on his hands, looking up at the sky.

'I just missed it.' I thought about Jack as Amrit sat silently next to me. I was just like Jack. A vigilante, thinking the laws of medical ethics didn't apply to me. But were either of us *bad*? I wasn't. I had meant well. But I'd messed up.

And had I been honest with him about my past, either? I hadn't, of course. And Jack wasn't digging around in my emails.

I winced at the thought. It was never okay to invade somebody's privacy like that. I had, somehow, discounted that in my desperation to find out the truth. But it was wrong. Totally wrong. My cheeks burned with the shame of it.

I kept looking at the little window opposite, where it had happened, almost expecting to see the boy rise up against it. Or Dominic Hull. Reaching a hand up to knock, notebook in the other hand.

They could have been the same boy. They were around the same age. They even looked alike: a shock of dark hair, that goofy way of standing slightly slouched over.

I picked up a small stone from the surface of the car park and rolled it around before letting it fall through my fingers. Everything was such a tangled mess. Who knew what was right or wrong any more?

I turned to Amrit. 'Jack and I have split up. I just felt like I wanted to be here. Home.'

'Medicine isn't a choice,' Amrit said. 'It's a calling, isn't it? And it's trying to get a response out of you. It's not going to take no for an answer.'

'But what should I do?' I said, turning to him, one of the only people who knew. 'I can't come back.'

'Why not?' he said softly. 'You made a mistake. Jesus, we all do it. Remember when I loaded up that woman's driver with three times the lethal dose of morphine?'

'That's poor maths,' I said. 'This was wilful. Besides, we double-checked yours. Just in time.' I picked up the stone again from the surface of the car park, scoured a shape on the ground with it. My belly was stretched against my top, like a giant orb sitting right in front of me. 'I basically killed him.'

'It wasn't wilful,' he said. 'People understand . . . yes, you intended, in the moment, to do something, but it

346

can still be a mistake. Nobody thinks badly of you, Rach. You resigned before they could even tell you that.'

I dropped the little stone again. It rolled a few inches away from me, just out of reach. I thought of Jack, holding that gun. Could that have been a mistake, too? And could I understand it, even though my entire career had been spent fixing bodies, not injuring them?

I didn't know. But I could learn how to forgive. Starting with myself.

'The inquest – the lawyers' questioning. That conclusion. The coroner read out exactly what happened. What I did. What the boy did. The Trust's lawyers said the CPS might do something.'

'But they didn't. Nor did the GMC. You shouldn't do it again – don't get me wrong,' he said. 'Not like that. Not in such an impulsive way. But you're needed. Good doctors always are.'

'I don't know if I could do it again,' I said. 'If I could come back and not freeze.'

And that's when I started to cry, big, fat tears. I'd hardly cried as an adult. Medicine had dried my tears up for me. It was hard to cry about normal things when you'd seen the things we had.

'I loved that boy,' I said softly through my tears.

Amrit put his arm around my shoulders, scooting closer to me. He smelt of disinfectant, the tang of alcohol gel just evaporated off his skin.

'My first death was hell,' he said. 'Do you remember after it? He was a baby. Called Sam. He was miniature.

But perfect. Totally perfect. There was no reason for it. He wasn't really very premature. Placental abruption. He came out – he slithered out – white. Not moving. I knew then. We worked on him, with him, for forty-five minutes, and the entire time his mother was screaming and screaming. I went outside afterwards. Headbutted a lamp post. I had a huge bruise. It's thankless, this job. Never in any other job do you see how unfair the world is – how meaningless, and how meaningful, all at once.'

'I remember Sam,' I said. I remembered all the deaths, but especially the babies. 'His parents had another baby the next year, didn't they?'

'Yeah, they did,' Amrit said.

'How can I go back?' I said.

Amrit didn't look surprised that I was asking. Instead, he said, 'How can you not?'

'But if I did want to be a doctor again . . .'

'Be? You never stopped.'

'No?' I said.

'No. It's not something you *do*. It's something you *are*.'

I couldn't help but smile at that.

'You care too much,' Amrit added.

I half smiled. Ben had said the same. It was true.

That was another way of looking at it. Maybe I wasn't nosy. Maybe I was misguided. Maybe I cared too much about people. About healing them. Solving them. The boy. Jack. Even Ben. Atoning for the boy with my own child. Atoning for Mum with the boy. Mum's affair had made me paranoid that Ben would cheat on me, but there was something about me, native me, underneath all that. Maybe it was caring too much. Maybe it was being too inquisitive. Sleuthing too much. Overanalysing. Not respecting boundaries. Not being able to impose them on myself. Maybe that investigative quality had made me a better doctor, and a worse one, all at once. What did it matter? I had learnt my lesson now. No more. No more privacy invasions.

'Audrey cheated on me,' Amrit said after a few minutes.

I looked sideways at him.

'At uni,' he added. 'Early on.'

I didn't say anything. One of the worst things about finding out something awful was finding out everybody else either knew or suspected.

'I wish it hadn't happened. It's a blight on everything. But what can you do? You just have to keep buggering on,' he said with a soft laugh.

'Did she tell you?' I said.

He shook his head. 'He did. Bastard.'

'Hmm.'

'But it's weird when the most perfect thing in your life has such a stain on it. I get it,' he said, looking at me. 'But it doesn't mean you run away. You keep on. You go back.'

'Maybe I will,' I said softly.

'You know the note they discussed at the inquest, though. You know what it said.'

'Yes,' I said, remembering.

Don't blame anyone but the cancer. I'm just taking back control, like Hume once said: the power of acting or of not acting; the determination of the will.

I'll always love you all.

'His mum came in again. Later. Much later. After the inquest. She mentioned you. I've been trying to tell you,' Amrit said.

I thought back to his texts and calls. 'Oh.'

'She seems philosophical now. She knows you meant no malice.'

'She hates me.'

'Maybe. You did her out of a goodbye. But she knows. She knows now that he would have died, anyway. That he – evidently – preferred to go this way.'

'Hanging would have been a horrible death,' I said, trying not to cry. 'I bet he regretted it. That's why he wet himself. The fear. He couldn't take it back once he'd kicked the visitor's chair away. He regretted it. He acted on impulse. Like a child.'

'No, Rach, no,' Amrit murmured, but then he stopped speaking, and just sat next to me and looked at the sky.

And that, somehow, was enough.

But then, I had changed my perspective – from adamant I was doing the right thing to certainty that I hadn't, and the knowledge that, with hindsight, of course I wouldn't do it again – and so maybe she had, too. We all rewrite our own narratives constantly. How we see things. Tragedies and successes. They change, like shifting sands, when viewed from different points in our lives. Look at Jack. Look at Kate. Look at me.

Jack had stepped in for Davey, being overprotective of him in the face of the burglaries. And so had the mother for her boy. And so had I for the boy, in a different way. We were all partly acting for other people, and maybe we were all wrong.

'How many tragedies do we all cause in a lifetime?' Amrit said, as though reading my mind.

'I don't know,' I said.

'Loads. Some are just more obvious than others.' He'd always been so wise, Amrit. When he wasn't wise-cracking about labour and drinking fizzy drinks. I had forgotten how much I liked him.

I thought of Jack, churned up by the legal system, and then I thought of myself. We were both at fault, for sure. Both the main causative force in our victim's death. Both equally sinister. A doctor going against a child's parent's wishes. A man lying in wait for a burglar. I shivered.

The truth was, I realized with a start, it wasn't Jack I didn't trust. It was myself. After everything. Mum. Ben. The boy. And now Jack. And, when you don't trust yourself, you can't trust anybody else, either.

48

I liked to talk to Mez about the break-up. Kate gave me space, quietly disappearing whenever I went over there. Mez and I went on a walk, one wintery Sunday afternoon in December, to Jesmond Dene Park. It smelt heady, of mouldering leaves and peat and the earth being replenished.

Mez bought me a latte, in an older brother sort of way, declining the gingerbread syrup. 'Apparently, it's Christmas,' he said, handing it to me.

'Seems so,' I said, and my stomach lurched at that. Soon it would be the next year, and Wally would be almost here.

I was quietly ready. I had a Moses basket next to my bed. I kept reminding myself that I would just take it one day at a time, that it would be fine, but I didn't need the reminders, not really.

But it was the other stuff that was weighing me down, the businesslike texts I received from Jack about plans for the birth and upcoming scans. They were the worst. Where previously I'd had a whole raft of Jack-ness to enjoy – his humour, his kisses, even his cat – I now had only a few polite, sparsely worded text messages. Instead of looking at his body language, his facial expressions, I inspected the double spaces after his full stops – a grammar rule he would defend to his death.

His texts said things like *hope you're feeling well* and *let me know if anything changes.*

I was like a spectre in my own flat, wandering around, unable to settle to anything. I still imagined him kissing me late at night, when I was in the bath.

'How is Mr Ross?' Mez said.

'I don't know. Seems fine. Back in Oban a bit more,' I said. 'But he's still under contract for *City Lights.*'

'What about Wally?' Mez kicked up a leaf with his Converse trainer.

I brushed my stomach with my hand. It was tight, like a fully blown-up balloon. It was strange to think of a baby nestled in amongst my organs. I couldn't quite imagine it.

'I don't know . . .' I said. 'We need to talk about it.'

But, of course, we couldn't communicate enough to have a relationship. How could we surmount the most difficult of communication tasks: post-break-up civility? Co-parenting a child? It wasn't as if we didn't have the back story, the emotions, the love, either. Late at night, I still cried as I remembered the best bits – the day we met, our first date – and all the moments surrounding those, like firework clusters.

I had so many memories for such a short relationship. Not the usual stuff that I'd had with Ben: shirts hanging in wardrobes, a pair of snow boots in the loft, a joint bank account. Jack and I had other things. More poignant things, I thought. The way the light looked on the Tyne Bridge the night we first kissed, our mouths tasting of garlic and pasta. The Howard-shaped hole at the foot of my bed. The gap in my morning routine as I would usually log on to read his latest tweets. The places where his body belonged: his fingers around mine in bed, the absence of his firm chest against my back as I slept. How he never seemed to ask anything of me. How he never got worried about Wally and how we'd cope. How he never asked me about leaving medicine. How he never expected me to have a better job. I couldn't even go near the Monument; I would avoid that route, even if it meant walking much further.

'You should sort it,' Mez said. 'Even Kate and I would struggle with that. But you have to sort it.'

'Even you and Kate,' I said, but I was smiling. 'All good again?'

'Yes. I apologized. Shame Jack can't.'

'He has apologized.'

'Oh.'

'It's not that. I trust him not to be a dick. He'll make it easy. I know he will.'

I trusted him to be reasonable. To be nice. To be kind. Of course I did. Every action of his was imbued with those qualities. The way he prepared my dinner sometimes and brought my plate first, complete with a drink. The way he had been careful with his reaction to the positive pregnancy test, because he knew I would remember it forever. The way he wrote about feminism and pitched the articles to the *Independent*, even though they never took them. The way he never missed a vaccination for Howard. That he wanted the best for Wally. He was good in so many, many ways.

Hadn't I thought, outside the hospital, that neither of us was bad? We'd been in extreme situations, that was all. And though the Hippocratic Oath hung on my wall, did it always apply? Couldn't people make mistakes? And yes, sometimes those mistakes would be catastrophic. Like mine, like Jack's. But what if I'd been so intent on understanding what Jack had done, trying to excuse it, that I had missed the obvious thing? That I had to simply accept it, and then forgive it. For the sake of Wally. For our future parenting.

'You trust him to be a good co-parent?'

'Yes,' I said. 'Not just that. I trust him – completely. To be good.'

The words were out of my mouth before I realized what I was saying. But I did trust him, I realized. I knew him to be good. He regretted what he had done. He would never, ever have committed a crime if he hadn't been pushed into that situation. It was a one-off. That much was obvious. Or maybe, the truth was that I had decided to trust Jack.

'You trust Jack?' Mez said, lowering his coffee slowly from his mouth.

His eyes were on me. His hair was rumpled, shining blue-black in the weak winter sun.

'Yes,' I said.

It wasn't a state of mind. It wasn't something that *was* or *wasn't*: it was a decision. We should have worked on it. It wasn't something to be solved by me hacking into his emails, but something that could have happened with time, and with experience.

'If you trust Jack,' Mez said, echoing my thoughts, 'then what are you doing here without him?'

'I don't know,' I said to Mez. 'I have no idea at all.'

I went to Mum's grave that night. I recognized her headstone as I would have recognized her across a crowded room: immediately.

I told her everything, sitting in the cold and talking until my voice was hoarse. I told her about her own death. How I'd seen her wither and crumple until she seemed to disappear against the pillows. I told her about the days afterwards. I told her it used to hurt my feelings when she mocked me.

And I thought she understood. Apologized, even.

I told her how nice it was when she rang me regularly. That she cared.

I thought she understood that, too.

I told her about Ben. About the things I'd accused him of. Incorrectly, probably, though I would never know for sure. And then I told her about the boy. About the mistake I'd made.

I could almost see her. Her eyes so like mine, her body language tense and coiled as it had always been, listening intently.

'Don't worry about Ben,' she would say. 'You would've broken up, anyway.'

Before I left, I closed my eyes and imagined how it would be if I saw Ben again now. I'd apologize. I'd try and explain that it hadn't been personal. That it was about Mum's death. That it was about the boy. I'd become paranoid from too much bad news and from my world – my parents, my career – shifting under my feet like quicksand.

He'd get it, I thought. He'd always been logical. He'd empathize once he understood.

I didn't know what Mum would have said about the rest. It felt too tangled to unravel. But, as I left, I felt better about Ben. And solving one thing was better than nothing.

49

It took two forms, and one week, and there I was. I was more junior, here. Of course I was. The *mistake*, the time off, the switching of specialities: they'd all had repercussions. I was an F2 again and not a registrar. But I didn't care. The NHS had taken me back like a loving mother, no questions asked, even though I was due to give birth in three months' time.

Dad had texted me this morning: *good luck*, he'd said. *Mum would be proud*. I'd blinked back tears. She would've been. I knew she would.

The hospice had a different smell to hospitals. Drifts of roast dinners, of perfume, of the outside world. Less disinfectant, less *medicine*. I looked down at my scrubs; even the largest size they had was tight across my stomach. I fingered my stethoscope. The metal was cool against my throat.

'Hi, James,' I said to the lad in bed seven.

He was lying down, looking out over the hospice's gardens, which were full of topiary and fountains. I could hear the trickle of the water sometimes, when things were quiet, at night, or in the mid-afternoon slump. There were things hospitals didn't have: bird feeders hanging up outside, a tuck box for the nurses. Unhygienic things, too, like cushions, and animals coming in to provide therapy. Everybody at the hospice knew the score; they'd come there to die. It wasn't as depressing as I thought it might be. It was more peaceful than dying in a hospital. The drugs were for comfort, not brutal necessity.

'That makes me need the bloody toilet,' James said, indicating the water feature outside.

He had cystic fibrosis. He'd always known his life might be short but, he hoped, meaningful. He was about other things, too, though. He liked M&M's so much he went to M&M's World in London. He was colour-blind. He liked playing hockey and the banjo.

He was wearing faded jeans and a white T-shirt. I could see some chest hair appearing over the top of it. He'd only moved in yesterday. An iPad lay discarded on the bed.

'I never thought it would be like this,' he said.

He was sitting cross-legged on the bed. He looked a little tired, slightly pale, but perfectly healthy. We'd run out of treatment, though. It wouldn't be long.

'Like what?' I said with a smile.

I looked at the clipboard hanging on the wall – not on the end of his bed. It wasn't a hospital bed. It was wooden. It made all the difference.

'Like, this reminds me of being at *uni*. There's a pool table. It doesn't smell of . . . the hospital smelt of death.'

'No,' I said. 'Palliative doesn't mean end-of-life immediately. It means nice things.'

I felt a pang again. Mum hadn't had enough nice things. It had taken her too quickly.

I'd never have wanted to work in a hospice a few years ago. But it was the juncture where painkillers met making people laugh, making them comfortable. Being there in their last moments, being at ultimate peace. Deciding when to treat and when to leave things. Being completely honest. Letting the patients be in control.

But most of the time it wasn't at all medical. It was a game of chess with a teenager who laughed so hard he doubled up. It was a walk in the grounds, talking about the latest episode of *Homeland*. It was bringing someone bacon and eggs because they fancied it and they'd been getting a bit thin.

James pressed the home button on his iPad. It sprang to life. An email was waiting, previewed on the screen. Like that email I saw so many, many months ago. He looked up, and saw me staring.

'What?' he said with an amused smile.

'Nothing,' I said.

James looked at me, his brow wrinkling, a strange smile on his face. 'What . . . ?' he said.

'Never mind,' I said. 'You just reminded me of somebody I used to know. Of something that happened. Ages ago.'

I handed him a cup with two pills in, and he necked them. I squirmed under his intense gaze.

'Seems like somebody important,' he said. 'Tell me your secrets – I'm dying.'

I laughed, a small laugh. 'Don't say that,' I said.

I had none of the ethical dilemmas I'd wrestled

360

with when acting for a Trust, underneath a consultant. I could form all the relationships I wanted, here. It was encouraged.

'Was he important?'

'He was,' I said.

'Well, then. Got to do what you got to do,' he said.

'We were a bit too different in the end. Or maybe too similar. And, you know, timing,' I said.

And it was true. Our relationship couldn't handle the experience of putting it on a conveyor belt moving too quickly. Not many relationships could. Our luggage had weighed us down on that baggage carousel, but it was the movement that threw us off.

'It's over,' I said, raising my head to look at him.

'You get one life, though. You know?'

I took James's blood pressure and stared out at the grounds of the hospice. The trees were moving slightly in the breeze.

I'd had a hand in a patient's suicide. Jack had shot a burglar he absolutely shouldn't have. Our lives would have been easier if we'd done the other thing, at those junctures. Our actions had brought about catastrophic consequences.

But what did we deserve? A distressing trial? A total career break?

We'd made mistakes. We were human. What of the people who hadn't been burgled repeatedly, or who hadn't had to lie to a dying boy too many times already? We had been in the wrong place at the wrong time, Jack and I. We were all culpable. But only some of us were unlucky. If Jack hadn't been burgled, he may never have hurt a fly. He wasn't reckless, dangerous. I didn't think so, anyway.

They took one moment, those lawyers, the coroner who ran the inquest into the boy's death, and built a whole picture around it, taking only the relevant – only the damning – parts of our lives, our stories, which fitted. They discarded the rest, like ripping out, blacking out, the edges of a painting.

And they didn't even know. They weren't even there. They could only try to reconstruct what had happened. At best, it was a replica. A poor facsimile of the truth. They could call in experts on bullet trajectories and suicide notes and forced entry into a house and on advanced Ewing's sarcoma. But they didn't know. They weren't there. They weren't there when I made the decision to be honest with the boy, and they weren't there when Jack made the split-second decision to shoot.

Jack wasn't there when I did it. And I wasn't there when he did it.

And all we could ever try to do was understand, and move forward, and forgive.

He'd lured them there. But couldn't I understand that? He'd intended to frighten them, to make it stop. What led up to it was desperation. He didn't intend for it to all go wrong. He lost his temper. But not after a split second. After months of intrusion. Both of our acts had been premeditated. I'd slept on mine, after all.

And besides, couldn't I understand the qualities that Jack's action represented? Anxiety, protectiveness?

And even if I couldn't understand those qualities, couldn't I forgive them? Maybe. Maybe, if I really loved the person, maybe I could.

'One life,' I said to James.

'Mine's over. But yours ain't, Rach,' he said.

'Rach, I like that,' I said.

The boy had been the only other patient who had ever called me that.

James smiled at me, winked, and I left his room, moving on to my next patient.

Trust. It was just trust. And forgiveness. I had realized too late, but at least I finally knew.

50

Two months later

He didn't ring the doorbell. He never did.

I heard the noise in the hallway and was halfway across my cluttered lounge – filled with breast pumps, top-and-tail wash bowls and others things I did not even understand – when he opened the door himself.

Jack's bottom lip was wobbling like a child's, and he raked his hair back with a shaking hand. It had grown long, his hair, and was curly at the ends, little ringlets. The back was tufty, sticking up, in that way that it always did.

'I should have been convicted,' he said. He sounded more Scottish than I remembered, his words almost indecipherable. 'I am guilty. That's what I'm hiding.' He was holding a blue plastic box, and he gestured to it.

'What?' I said.

And then his lip-trembling became more violent, and tears appeared in his eyes. I stepped back, alarmed, and trod on a pile of muslin cloths which littered the floor.

'What do you mean?' I said. Jack wiped a tear from his cheek with the heel of his hand.

I turned off the medical podcast I was listening to. It

was about the effects of caffeine on heart rate, and I didn't want to worry Jack.

I was trying to enjoy the rest of my alone time, reading books, watching seminal films I had somehow missed. But I wasn't enjoying it at all. I was lonely. That was the problem. I couldn't even grab an acquaintance and go and sit in a bar. The depressing judgemental looks were too much; I shouldn't even be drinking lemonade in Lloyds Bar on Saturday nights. I should be enjoying cosy evenings with my husband, reading from the baby book, jokingly eating hot curries and pineapple and drinking raspberry-bloody-leaf tea.

Audrey had been over a lot. She texted every day; almost hourly, sometimes. She told me about her new colleague. *I suspect him of being a kidult*, she wrote. *He brings multipack Petits Filous in and puts them in the work fridge (???).*

She was forever making me laugh, but, like an ice block, my loneliness took hours to thaw, and I froze again as soon as the contact ceased.

It wasn't even the aloneness, exactly. I could cope with that. I'd been single before. No, it was the other stuff. That alongside my current predicament was another life where Jack and I had stayed together. Where we were the excited couple in John Lewis, the ones counting down nauseatingly on Facebook to the arrival of their due date. The ones who lost sleep, late at night, worrying as their lives were about to change forever.

It was the comparison between me – alone, like a

whale, in the bath on Monday night, Tuesday night, Wednesday night – and how it should have been, laughing as Jack massaged my belly gently. That's what upset me the most. I would never again be a woman pregnant with her firstborn. We'd robbed each other of the pure enjoyment of it – like Lee Aldridge and his mates, breaking in and stealing whatever they wished.

Jack waved a hand, frustrated. 'I lied in court. It's worse than what you read.' He thumped the box down on the carpet. Then, like a man who'd reached right inside himself and pulled a demon out, he leant forward, his elbows on his knees, and sobbed. 'I so wanted it to be over,' he said.

I stood over him, not knowing what to say. It was just getting dark outside. Five minutes ago I hadn't seen him for three months. And then, suddenly, he was there, in my living room. He stood up straight, then sat down unthinkingly on the birthing ball.

'Why don't you start from the beginning?' I said gently, like he was a thick-file patient with a huge history.

And it was just us in my dimly lit flat with the hum of the fridge across the room in my tiny kitchenette. A space in which to talk, no pressure, just the two of us. Nearly three.

'It was a December night in Oban . . .' he said.

And there began his story. Not my own take on the press's slant on it. Not cobbled together from his emails. But from him.

'Davey was upstairs. I wanted to . . . I don't know. I felt like his parent, some days. The break-ins upset him so much. I felt like I should act for him. To get rid of them. Like a lioness chasing off predators.'

My throat felt tight. It didn't matter, it didn't matter, I kept telling myself. We were broken up. Doomed, anyway. But it did matter. More than almost anything. And it would matter to Wally, too.

'I saw them. Not Dominic. The others. Aldridge. And his mum, Pauline. Earlier in the day. Just on the promenade, in the harbour.' He waved behind him, as if we were standing right there in Oban. 'Right by the boats, actually, you know where we . . . ?'

'I know.'

'And he said something to me, about Davey.'

'What?' I said. I sat down on the floor, right in front of Jack, as if I was praying to him.

Absent-mindedly, I thought, he reached out and touched my shoulder, just briefly. His index finger lingered there, for just a second.

I looked up at Jack. My eyes ran over his dark red lips, his brown eyes, his messy, curly hair. He had a full beard again. I wondered if he was up against a writing deadline, or just sad, like I was.

'Aldridge said he reckoned that, next time – he said it factually, like there definitely would be a next time – he thought he could get Davey to just pass him stuff. Because he's . . .'

He didn't finish his sentence, and he didn't need to. The sad thing was, Aldridge was probably right. Davey

367

might have been persuaded to hand over his worldly possessions. And maybe that wouldn't even have been a crime, I didn't know. It was awful, that sentiment.

'He said then we wouldn't have an insurance claim. Because Davey would've given them away. Like gifts.' Jack was crying again now, tears dripping on to his legs and on to the blue birthing ball he was sitting on. 'I can't bloody sit on this thing,' he said, slithering down on to the floor next to me.

And, just like that, his right hand drifted down and settled on my knee. Tickling, pleasurable: that's how it felt. Like my whole knee was happy, radiating right around my body.

We sat, both of us cross-legged, looking at each other.

Jack continued. 'I remember the Christmas lights were up, and Aldridge was standing right in front of a really bright sign, and I couldn't see his eyes. I didn't say anything. And, in the end, I never told anyone. And neither did Aldridge, obviously.'

'Why not? Isn't that provocation? The police might have understood.'

'What – that I shot someone because they'd intimated something about my younger brother? If anything, that would've made things worse. You don't know how it was. The police, they really didn't care at all. Provocation wouldn't have been a full defence. And they would've denied it . . . it was just – it was impossible. The whole family used each other as alibis, so nobody ever got convicted of anything. They had it all sewn up and if it ever got to a trial, the juries believed them. So much so that they could say stuff like that to us, in the street.'

'So then what?'

'So then I made a plan. That night I'd leave the door open. Not just ajar. Fully open. Mum and Dad went away that day. Davey was upstairs, otherwise engaged. I'd leave it open that night, I thought, and sort them out. Threaten them.'

I waited, but Jack didn't say anything for a few minutes. I could hear his breathing. It was deep and even. He'd stopped crying, though his hands were still shaking.

'I'm sorry,' he said. 'It's hard for me to . . . to relive it. It was the day my life changed forever. Was made worse – forever.'

'Not forever,' I said softly. 'It doesn't have to be.'

We stared at each other for a few seconds. His eyes were on mine, but they were calm. Not flitting around. Not lying, maybe.

We moved to the sofa.

'I *wasn't* afraid of them,' Jack said, settling back.

He took his shoes off, slipping them off at the heel with the other foot. It was nice, that. He felt at home. He was wearing the ginger cat socks.

'I never thought they'd hurt me. What I was afraid of was that it would carry on that way forever. Always being robbed – over and over. Our home not really being our own. Davey being afraid of them and, I don't know, abused. That was the fear.'

'So.'

'So I opened the door. The most obvious door. I'll show you one day, if you like. It was high up on a hill.'

'I've seen a photo.'

'Of course you have,' he said, but he said it with a tiny smile. 'Well, it was obvious that the door was open. I sat . . .' He stopped, thinking. 'Fuck it,' he said, looking at me. 'This is what I did: that day, after I saw them – it was dark at four o'clock up there – I turned the far room light on. We called it the snug. Put the TV on. I went outside, down the bottom of the hill, and I checked. You could see it. You could see the light. From outside.'

I frowned, not following.

He misinterpreted me, reaching for me. 'I never thought it would happen. You make a stupid plan. You just step outside. The very first step of the plan. The first point along the way. But then, when I was out there, looking, I saw them. They wore these . . . like headtorch lamps. Like people wear to bloody car boots. At first I thought I was imagining it, it was just a flash in the dark. But then I saw it again. It was getting closer. And then it was happening, my plan.'

'Your plan?'

He inhaled, then breathed out again, pausing. 'I trapped them,' he said. His voice broke. 'I went from a normal bloke in a shit situation to . . . I don't know. A monster. A bloody monster.'

My hands had gone cold. 'You trapped them?'

'Not like that. But I made it so they would definitely

370

walk past me. And I could frighten them. There was a corridor. From the conservatory, where the door was open, all along the house, to the stairs. I knew they'd go that way. They'd think I was in the snug, right at the very back. So I waited. In the dark. In that corridor that I knew they'd come along. I waited. Holding the gun.'

'Go on.'

'They arrived. After less than five minutes. I remember thinking to myself: *I can't believe this is bloody happening.* It was just a stupid plan. But it worked. Well – not in the end, obviously. They crept past me. Dominic was running, excited. I turned the light on – there was a lamp, by the chair, in the corridor – and I said, "If you take another step, I'll shoot."'

'You said that?' I felt frozen. Started shivering.

'Oh no, no,' he said, seeing my expression change. 'I didn't – I never intended. Jesus. I just wanted to scare them.' He looked at me again, then rolled his eyes. 'I know how that sounds. But I was bloody desperate, Rach. It sounds mad,' he said, sitting forward, becoming more animated, 'but I didn't even consider the danger of it. How it might end. I was in charge, and I wasn't going to shoot anyone. I didn't even know that it was already a crime to threaten someone in that way. I just thought I'd wait for them and hold the gun and I'd scare them off. They were only young – young lads. We all were. I so wanted to sort it, before my parents came back. Tell them it was over.'

'I knew,' I said. 'You told the story wrong. You said

371

they threw something at you and then you said they were still holding it.'

'I know. I was telling you lies. I didn't want you to know I'd lured them in. I slipped up.'

'But what went wrong? With your plan?'

'They were like, recruiting him. Training him. He was sixteen. Aldridge had said this was his first burglary. They chose me, that night, because it was easy, even when the door was locked. That's what Aldridge said. They were angry when they realized I'd been lying in wait. The energy was just so confrontational. And I couldn't stop thinking about what Aldridge had said about Davey. They stopped. Stock-still. Dominic called me crazy. That was – that was the last thing he said. His last word . . . they turned around, back down the corridor. They got to the conservatory. They were almost out. Aldridge sprinted off. So Dominic was on his own.'

I closed my eyes. Please, don't have shot him when he was leaving, please no.

'Part of the problem was that I was already nervous. Holding the bloody gun. Pointing at them. It was trained on them as they were leaving. I'd never held a gun and pointed it at someone. Never. I didn't know how I'd got there. And then. Well. That's when it happened.'

'What?' my voice was hoarse.

'Dominic – he . . . he turned. Twitched, towards me. Just a tiny bit. And the expression on his face was demonic. Mocking.'

'Did you lose it? Get angry?'

'I thought he was going to lunge for me,' he said, looking at me imploringly, his eyebrows raised. 'But it's true that there was no struggle,' he said, visibly deflating in front of me, like a pool of hot wax on my sofa.

'Did you intend to kill him?' I said.

'I remember thinking it was all lost, that it would be this way forever, that Davey would be scared forever and not want to take the bins out – remember how he loves that? And then I just shot. That's the truth of it. The months of agony and intrusion all mounted up, and suddenly I could see a way out. And then I just pulled the trigger. There was no struggle. No statue,' he said sadly. 'That was my story in court. And, later, for you. But I placed the statue in his hand after I'd killed him, when I realized there was no evidence he was going to go for me. So his fingerprints were on it. And I'd been aiming for his temple. I wish I hadn't been. But I was.'

51

I stared into my lap. Desperate. He was desperate. Just like the boy had been. Looking for a way out in all the wrong places.

'Do you regret it?' I said.

Jack's head snapped up. 'Every. Single. Day.'

I nodded. That was enough for me. No matter what our morals, our views, our vocations – we all made mistakes.

'I thought you were going to tell me that Davey had done it. That you'd taken the blame for him.'

Jack shook his head again. 'No. No, that's not what happened,' he said. 'But . . . what was traumatic – other than literally ending someone's life, of course,' he said, and then he gulped and started crying again, 'was that I didn't know myself. Every night after it, when I went to bed, it was like there was a stranger with me. I didn't know my morals. What I was capable of.'

'I know,' I said. 'I've been there.'

He looked up at me. 'Have you?'

'I didn't leave medicine because of Jeremy Hunt or the NHS or the hours or the pay,' I said. 'I left because I made a massive, massive mistake.'

'What?' he said.

His eyes were wary. I could see why. All that time I'd

been on his case, reading about him, so obsessed with his crime, as though I was perfect myself. And here I was, months on, finally telling him that I wasn't.

'I told a teenage patient of mine his prognosis, against his mum's wishes. I knew him very well, but it wasn't the right call, because he was a minor and volatile. I told him he actually had months, not years. And I told him how he'd die. And then he hanged himself. After our conversation.'

Jack paused, looking at me. 'I see,' he said. 'The boy.'

'Yes. The boy.'

'You talk about him in your sleep sometimes. Elijah. I didn't want to ask . . .'

That made me cry, right then. He hadn't pressed me about my crime. Because he was good.

'Yes. Elijah.'

'Well, who am I to talk?' he said. 'It's hardly the same as what I did.'

'Sometimes it feels as though it is,' I said.

And I could feel every muscle in my body relaxing. My deltoids. My rectus abdominis. My glutes. I was right to have trusted him. He was reasonable. Level-headed. He wasn't using the boy as an excuse to storm out, to claim I hadn't been straight with him, when he could have. He was a decent person. With me.

'I'm so sorry for all of the . . . the hacking,' I said. 'That's not me. At all. I was just, I don't know. Desperate to *know* you. The things I did . . .'

'Don't tell me,' he said. 'I don't want to know. That's why I left, though,' he added. 'Because I didn't know

375

you. I just didn't know you. I hadn't known you long enough. So you were invading my privacy and making me tell you stuff and I didn't know if that was you being you or you acting out of character. I didn't have any context for you. I needed to have a million moments with you before I knew you were . . . good.'

'Likewise,' I said. 'I was trying to have those moments by reading about you. I should have just – God. Just got to know you. Slowly. I was rushing because Wally was on his way and everything felt so urgent. But I should have just calmed down. Trusted you. No, not trusted you. Trusted that you would tell me.'

'You never said anything at all,' he said. 'About Elijah.'

'I know. I'm sorry. I just . . .'

And that was as far as we got. My sentence trailed off. We were quiet for a while.

'So,' Jack said.

'So.'

I finally knew. He'd told me everything, I was sure of it. It was obvious. In his shaking hands, his tears, his openness. His admission that he'd been wrong. He was finally being honest. I could see that.

The worst had been revealed.

The prosecution had been correct. Jack had lured the lads there. And he had intended to shoot. There had been no struggle; no defence in law. He'd aimed. He should have been found guilty, not 'not proven'. He was a murderer, in those very specific circumstances, and he'd lied about it. Invented a struggle. But was he *bad*? He would never do anything like that again, of that I was certain. Not only because he wouldn't be forced into those horrible circumstances again, but because he had learnt his lesson. Should he have been sent to prison for life? He'd taken one, so maybe. But who would it have benefitted?

And even though the worst had happened, that seemed almost beside the point. He had told me the truth, and I trusted him. And that mattered more than the past, the crime, the intention.

'You know now,' he'd said. 'Mum, Dad and, I suppose, Davey know. We agreed I would lie in court. But other than us – nobody else knows.'

I liked that 'us'.

Later, I told him about the aftermath of the boy, his funeral, how I had left things with work. He told me that Hull's parents had tried to challenge the law of double jeopardy, which was when his lawyer Gavin texted him. They'd failed; their final appeal.

He told me that he was relearning to drive, that he'd managed to have a beer recently. We talked about whether he had ever considered not calling 999, hiding Dominic's body. He said no; was appalled by that.

He showed me what was in the blue box. It was full of articles. He proffered them to me. He said I could read them, but I didn't need to. They were his.

Private.

'You can look whenever you like,' he told me.

'I don't need to,' I said, though I was happy he had offered; that he had let me in. 'Where was it?'

'I brought it down with me from Scotland. I don't know why. I can't get rid of them. It's funny, isn't it? We've paid thousands of pounds to get rid of everything on the Internet. We've changed our names. But I can't bear to part with this little box. It's like I will have learnt nothing if I throw it out. I need it.'

'Where was it, though?'

'In my wardrobe. I thought you'd find it – that day I made you take me to that cafe. What a dickhead,' he said, shaking his head. 'I was just so scared, if you were in my house on your own, you'd find things. On my computer. In my house. I knew you had doubts. I thought you'd look.'

I shrugged. 'I might have,' I said.

'So when I woke up and remembered the meeting, I pretended I was late – so that you'd drive me. I actually sat there for forty minutes on my own, after you'd dropped me off, feeling like a tosser. You looked so tired and pale in the car. Who makes their pregnant girlfriend do that?'

'A twat,' I said, but I grinned.

And then he turned to me on the sofa, so close to me, just looking at me. Then he reached over and, so gently, removed a strand of hair from my face.

And neither of us was scared any more.

52

We were in bed with Howard on a Saturday morning when it began. A dull backache.

I took a paracetamol, turned to Jack, and said, 'Pregnancy takes your waist, your slim ankles and, finally, your back.'

'It's weird, it's coming and going,' I said, later, to him. We were both reading. Howard was lying between us on his back.

'This might be our last quiet Saturday,' Jack said, turning to me and putting *White Teeth* down on the bed.

I was a week overdue.

'No way – next week, Wally will be just there,' I said, indicating the middle of the bed. 'Next to Howard. And we'll have to tell Howard what it means to be a big brother. But it'll still be quiet.'

Jack smiled, his eyes widening, lightening. He reached to touch Howard's belly. Slowly. Howard never liked that, was minded to clamp all four paws around any intruding hand.

'You're going to have a baby brother or sister,' Jack said to Howard. 'But Mummy and Daddy love you just the same.'

'You're supposed to get the older sibling a symbolic present,' I said.

'What do you think he'd like – a ceremonial Waitrose meal?'

'Definitely,' I said, stretching and wincing as my back seized up again. 'Meat and jelly are his true loves.'

'Coming and going, did you say?' Jack said.

'Oh no, I've alerted the hypochondriac,' I said, waving a hand and shifting myself up to a sitting position. 'Ignore me.'

'Coming and going like in waves?' he said. 'Like, maybe, a contraction?'

'I . . . I . . . oh,' I said.

'I thought *you* were the doctor,' he said.

'I totally am,' I said, flashing him a smile.

Another contraction gripped me, radiating around from my back and sides and to my stomach.

'Wally's imminent,' I said.

'Shit,' Jack said. 'Are we having a baby?'

'We very much are,' I said.

I grabbed his arm, happier than I'd ever felt in my entire life, even mid-contraction.

'I wonder if they can give me some Valium?' Jack said as we sat up in bed together.

I swatted his arm, laughing, unable to stop myself.

'Not yet,' I said. 'We've got ages.'

Jack turned to me, his eyebrows raised. 'Don't we need to dash out now?' he said.

'Nah. Wait. Wait until they're a few minutes apart. They'll only send me away.'

'Really?' Jack said. His eyes were wide. 'But you're – you know. *In labour.* It's dangerous.'

I laughed softly. 'I'm going for a bath,' I said, walking naked across the hallway and starting it running.

My steps felt heavier. I was unused to this new, stretched circumference of mine, how easily I bumped into doorframes and how often my own elbows brushed my protruding stomach. I couldn't reach down to get things in the shower. I could bend a few inches, and then I'd get stuck. It was strange, that time, that weird body.

I'd moved into Jack's Newcastle house. He'd gone permanent with *City Lights*. He'd stopped freelancing, got up at 7.30 a.m. every morning. We'd put curtains up, finally. I'd taken control of the thermostat.

'Howie missed you,' Jack said, bringing him into the bathroom.

Howard looked disgruntled, his orange brow furred.

'He missed his night-time routine.'

'And I missed Howie,' I said.

My voice had changed. It was high-pitched again. Happy. I was back with Jack, and a doctor again; a combination I'd never before experienced. Jack would text me during my shifts: funny memes he wanted me to read, interesting articles about medical ethics, anxious medical questions. I read them all and smilingly answered over a cup of tea and a KitKat on my break. He'd be cooking when I got home, Howard brushing around his legs.

Howard reached and batted my face with his paw.

'Hey!' I said.

And Jack laughed. 'He's upset with you, for reading my emails,' he said.

There was an edge to that comment. Perhaps there always would be.

He would often mention this, ask questions about my hacking. I would blush as I answered them. It was sad, the way he looked at me sometimes. As though I, too, had violated him, stealing in on him in the middle of the night.

But, then, I looked at him sadly, too, sometimes. Thinking that he was a murderer. He was. Wondering at all those lies he'd told. Thousands of them.

'He's upset with *you* for taking six months to tell me the truth,' I said.

We looked at each other. Neither of us spoke.

Jack cleared his throat self-consciously, then kissed me softly.

Things weren't perfect, but they were ours.

53

Walter Douglas was born on 2 April. The spring leaves were beginning to sprout out of the end of the twigs, as if the trees were just beginning to take their winter gloves off. And, as I felt the peculiarly warm slithering sensation after the last, sweaty push, a manoeuvre I had coached many a woman through, the world reoriented. Like a spotlight went on, focused on Wally, and the rest of the lights in my world dimmed. It was just Wally, Jack and I, lit up brightly in the centre of the stage.

And everything I'd thought about motherhood had been incorrect. Of course I could be trusted. It was the most natural thing in the world. Instinct completely took over. It wasn't like the boy. Wally was – truly – mine. I wish Mum had been there to see it. To see how I turned out. Because of, and despite, her.

None of the clichéd events happened. I could hardly remember his weight: we were almost drunk with tiredness. There was no photograph of Wally on my chest, skin on skin, with Jack posing in the background. We didn't announce it on Facebook.

Instead, parenthood became a different kind of bliss, and it was totally unexpected to me. It was calm and warm. Snuggling in freshly washed pyjamas on Jack's sofa. All of us snoozing intermittently. Wally on Jack's chest; a sight worth a million labours. Wally smelt delicious, of warm milk and lavender and hot baths. I was fascinated by him: the tiny fingernails, his brow – he had Jack's heavy brow – and his slightly longer second toe. He got that from Kate and Mum.

We didn't see anyone for ages. It was just us. Nice lunches. Lying on the sofa. Looking at Wally. That was all we did.

'We're so sad,' I said as we were studying Wally's feet. 'This is literally all we do.'

My laptop bleeped then.

Mission request from Davey.

'You're very privileged,' Jack said. 'He hardly ever plays with anyone else.'

I thought about the moment Davey and I had shared in the living room together. Without him, I might never have found everything out. I was grateful to him, and I hoped he knew that. Neither of his parents had apologized, but that was okay. I didn't need them to.

Jack leant over me. Wally was sleeping, scrunching his face up as he dreamt, moving his legs like a little caterpillar. Jack smoothed the dark hair from his forehead, releasing more delicious baby scents.

'He's not made that face before,' Jack said.

Howard leapt from the floor and on to the sofa, settling down on Jack's lap.

'You're very important, too,' Jack said to Howard.

We both laughed, and Wally yawned.

Audrey texted me: *Well done on becoming a real-life Big*

Boy! she wrote. *May he not grow up to be Weird or Kidult, just perfect xxx.*

I cried at that text, because I was mad and hormonal, and Jack made me a cup of real, caffeinated tea.

'I'm going to venture into the outside world,' I said later, standing up.

Wally stirred but stayed asleep. My body was starting to feel like my own again, even though my stomach still felt like somebody else's; jiggly, doughy, strange. But the rest was coming.

'Really?' Jack said.

'Just the garden,' I said.

I couldn't quite articulate the reason why I wanted to go. It felt as though the world had become filled with firsts again, experienced through Wally. The first time we went into the garden. The first time he had his hair washed. His first sneeze. Life was beginning again for me in the springtime.

I took him to the back door to walk in the early spring air. I was holding him with both hands, and shifted him so my right one was free. I turned the key but the door still wouldn't open.

I looked around. 'Coming for Wally's first garden walk?' I said.

Jack was reclining on the sofa, looking at his phone. It was no longer angled towards him, now that I knew everything. I could see Words with Friends lit up, blue and yellow, on the screen. He'd been playing with Kate, though I suspected Mez was taking her turns for her.

'Course,' Jack said, springing upright. His socked

feet slipped on the wooden floors. They had pandas on, those socks, which made me smile. 'Oh, hang on,' he said. 'I know it's against *fire safety*, but I put loads of locks in, when Mum and Dad bought it.'

He stopped speaking, then looked at me. And it was the same look he had given me countless times before. A loaded one I'd come to recognize as evidence he was thinking of Dominic and the burglaries and everything that had happened.

And that's when I realized.

He was rifling about in the big wooden chest in the living room. He emerged with four keys, then drew back a bolt lock, too.

'You're free,' he said with a laugh.

'I don't think I've ever really been in your garden,' I said, sidestepping what I'd just seen, looking at Wally instead.

He was opening his eyes and squinting. They were a deep, navy blue.

My feet were getting soaked in my ballet flats in the spring puddles, and I was looking at the sun setting over the garden.

I drew my coat more tightly around me and looked at the orange sky to the west.

Those locks. They'd done it for me.

All my digging, all my sleuthing, stalking, ruminating, and it had been a cluster of locks on Jack's back door that had done it. He didn't want to be burgled again. That much was obvious. And, strangely, those little rusty keys he was holding safely in his hands while he was smiling at Wally and me was enough. For us. He would do anything for his parents, he had said, as he laid those rat traps. He would do anything for Davey, to keep him safe. And he would do anything for us; for Wally and me. It was his biggest failing, but also his biggest strength.

I was culpable. Jack was culpable. In the end we all were. We're all guilty of something. We all cause some pain. Some strife.

We went back inside after a few minutes. We were cold.

'In for the night?' Jack said.

I nodded, still not saying anything.

He turned the keys in the locks one by one. He drew the bolt across the door with a scrape, and that was that.

We were locked in, with him. Despite everything we knew about him. Despite all his flaws.

The world was locked out, and he'd let us inside, all together.

Safe.

Acknowledgements

Gosh, haven't we all dreamt of writing an acknowledgements section? And now here I am, my mind blank.

Let's start at the beginning: Clare Wallace. Thank you. For picking me out of the slush pile. For nurturing my novel. For the edits. For the shared avocado on toast while we discussed horrendous crimes and plot points. For late-night WhatsApp messages, endless games of Words with Friends and, of course, for getting me a book deal. It's true to say I couldn't have done it without you. But it's truer to say I never thought I'd make a friend along the way, too. To Naomi Perry, for stepping in, for your concerted efforts and always super-fast email responses. To the brilliant Darley Anderson rights team for their boundless enthusiasm and brilliant 'We've sold your Russian rights!' emails.

To the whole team at Michael Joseph: to Kim, for acquiring *Everything but the Truth* and making a chilly day in February one of the very best of my life. For your thoughtful edits and incisive tracked changes (never once have I rejected a change – I think you might actually be the better writer of the two of us). To Maxine – thank you for the edits, for having me and for sharing your wisdom with me. I'm so unbelievably lucky and excited to be working with you. To my brilliant copyeditor who actually googled the Valencia Open, Shân Morley Jones. To the sales, marketing and publicity team at Michael Joseph for your continued hard work and enthusiasm.

Everything but the Truth wouldn't be the book it is without some very special people. To Darin Millar for reading an entire draft alongside the Archbold textbook and advising me on criminal law (Scots law, no less; I'm sure I am your most difficult case). I don't know how I can ever thank you. To Sami Saba-Davies, for reading an early draft and for being so nice about my many medical errors, and for taking such an interest since. Thank you for always answering immediately my extremely obscure and often quite worrying questions. To Chris Priddle, for talking to me for hours at a barbecue about your tennis career. I'm sorry I put the entire thing in a book.

To the Espresso Mushroom Company, for letting me ask absurd questions about mushrooms (so many, you sent me some in the post to grow myself).

There are a whole host of other people who answered questions about criminal law, police procedure, air rifles, medical tests, and so on – too many to thank, but you know who you are.

And now to the personal acknowledgements. To my mum and my dad, for being the first two people I called the day I became an author who was to be published. I can't think of a finer accolade than that.

To my sister, Suzanne, and her endless patience with

my 'What would happen if . . . ?' messages. I'm extremely glad you became a doctor!

To Dad, again, for the endless, endless cups of tea and walks. Thank you for saying, 'But what is this character *like*?' and, 'No, that wouldn't happen.' Really, your name should be on the front with mine.

To my friends and family who took my downbeat and excitable calls during the years of ups and downs before I got my deal.

And to the Doomsday Writers, of course, for all the hand-holding, amusement and drama as we navigate the publishing terrain together.

To my beta readers, Valerie and Tom. Thank you for your early praise and tactful suggested changes.

To the authors who took the time to read an early proof and comment: it never fails to amaze me how supportive and lovely the writing community is, especially for debut authors. Thank you.

And lastly, and most importantly, to David. I couldn't write about love without knowing you.

Reading Group Questions

1. Throughout the novel Rachel struggles with the possibility that she does not truly know the father of her child. To what extent can you ever truly know somebody? Is there a specific point when you have to decide to trust them implicitly?

2. How does the novel explore the split between our public persona and our innermost thoughts? How important a role do technology and social media (like Facebook or Twitter) play in our relationships with others?

3. The novel is split into three distinct sections: 'Who?' 'What?' and 'Why?' Why do you think the author chose to structure the novel in this way?

4. Beginning with an ending, and ending with a beginning, the novel is split between the past and the present. What does it take for Rachel to finally forgive both herself and Jack? Can we ever really 'move on,' or do we simply learn to live with our past?

5. Consider the title *Everything but the Truth*. Why is honesty so important to Rachel? Do we always have a responsibility to tell the truth, or does the truth sometimes do more harm than good?

6. Rachel and Jack come from very different class backgrounds. How does the novel address the theme of class conflict? Do you think it impacts upon the characters' behaviour or beliefs, and if so, to what extent?

7. This novel presents us with a series of moral dilemmas, with its characters responding in different ways. What conclusions could we draw about moral behaviour? Is it more important to be right, or to be good? Is it possible to be both?

8. At the end of the novel, Rachel returns to medicine to work in palliative care. Why do you think she made this decision and was it the right one?

9. There are many different types of relationships explored in this novel, all with varying degrees of love, respect, trust and compromise. Do you think that Jack and Rachel have similar priorities when it comes to their relationship with each other, and how do these affect their relationship?

10. Both Rachel and Jack are put under pressure in different situations – Jack, in his personal life where his family is threatened, and Rachel, in her professional life. How are Jack and Rachel's responses similar and how are they different?

11. Discuss the theme of motherhood. How does Rachel feel about becoming a mother, and how is she affected by her own family relationships? Jack's family relationships?

12. 'Do no harm' is the first rule of the Hippocratic Oath. Is it possible to live by this rule, or do we sometimes have to be cruel to be kind?

13. What do you think of Rachel and Jack's actions? Should either of them have behaved differently? Do you feel that either Jack or Rachel crossed a line, and at what point?

Turn the page
to read the first chapter of

ANYTHING
YOU DO SAY

the new novel by
Gillian McAllister

Coming early 2018

I

It starts with a selfie. He is a random; we are not even sure of his name. We are always meeting them whenever we go out. Laura says it's because I look friendly. I think it's because I am always daydreaming, making up lives for people as I look at them, and they think I'm inviting them over to chat.

In the frame of his phone screen – camera facing forwards, to us – his teeth are white and slightly crooked, his nose hooked.

Laura leans over to press the button on the phone. Her long, slender arm is captured at the edge of the display. It's covered in bangles and bits of thread and a homemade bracelet. She's a hippie at heart.

She takes the photo, and now we are frozen on his screen. I wonder if he'll keep it, that photograph of us that now belongs to him.

'No filter,' he says to us.

'What?' Laura says. She doesn't use Instagram. She feels no need to check in to places or share her moments with anybody. She is nowhere on the internet, and I'm sure her life is better for it.

We break apart from our tableau at the bar, but he stays standing next to me. He rocks up and down on the balls of his feet. He's all in black, except his red trainers.

I turn to Laura. She's had her hair cut. It's a pixie, again; messed up, the fringe sitting in her eyes. She looks androgynous, slightly goofy. I could never pull off that haircut. People would mistake me for a child. She never wears any make-up, but doesn't need to, with straight, white teeth, naturally red cheeks and dark lashes. Her eyes crinkle at the corners even when she is not smiling. What she wants more than anything is to be an artist – she creates hyperreal paintings that look like photographs – and she doesn't want to live her life like other people's. She's obsessed with it. She will sometimes say things like, 'What's the correlation between wearing a suit and doing a good job?' or 'Why do you need a house in the suburbs and a mortgage like everybody else?' I would never say such things. What do I know about real jobs, real houses, I will think quietly, while, it seems to me, the rest of the world holds forth.

'Great shoes,' she says now, dipping her head down underneath the bar. They're new. Cream silk, with ribbons that tie at my ankles. Laura lives in flats, the sides of her feet dry and hard from never wearing shoes at home. They live on a barge, Laura and Jonty. They moor it wherever they like. I sometimes want to do the same, bored of our tiny basement flat, but Reuben tells me I'd hate it; that I am a fantasist.

'Thanks,' I say. I bought them on a credit card, at almost midnight, the other night. I'd forgotten until they had arrived, experiencing a common sense of wonderment, and then recognition, as I tore in to the parcel.

'Are they Reuben-approved?' Laura says. Reuben is one of the only people she consistently misreads. She converts his shyness into something else. Disapproval, maybe. She may be right. He had raised his eyebrows as I unpacked the shoes, but said nothing. I shrug, now. 'What's his is ours,' I say, though I'm embarrassed by the notion. Reuben works far harder than I do. Everybody does.

Laura's bony shoulders are out even though it's December. Her top is simple, a plain white vest that's too big for her. It's the kind of material that doesn't need pressing. I don't iron anything. If I ever try to, our iron deposits a brown, sticky substance everywhere, and I have given up. In my head, I call it my Joanna-ineptitude; situations in which I fail where most others succeed.

'Looks like you've got a friend for life,' she says.

I turn. The man is still standing next to me. I can feel the entire length of his leg against mine as he shifts his weight, trying to get the bartender's attention. 'Two more for these ladies?' he says.

We say yes to the drinks, and maybe we shouldn't. We are becoming giggly. They arrive, placed on black napkins which dampen with condensation from the glasses. Laura sidles slowly along the bar.

I follow, but so does he.

'Your work or mine?' Laura says, her head bent towards me so that he can't hear. This is how our long chats begin. We once joked we should have an agenda, and now we kind of do: work, relationships, family. Then everything else. Whatever comes up.

I let out a sigh, but it does nothing to dispel the knots that have appeared as soon as she mentions work. 'I did a sudoku puzzle on my lunch that was more stimulating than my entire day yesterday.'

'Mmm.' She sucks her bottom lip in, looking thoughtfully across the bar. We hate our jobs in completely different ways. I have no idea what I would like to do. Laura knows exactly what she wants to do, and can't do it.

'You need a thing. I need not to have a thing,' she says.

'Yep. That's about it.' Nobody else could say something like that to me, except maybe Reuben. 'I'm one dimensional,' I say to her.

'You're too smart for your own good,' she says back.

'No. I'm the thick Murphy.' My brother, Wilf, went to Cambridge, and now owns a whole host of London properties, and none of us can ever forget it.

'You're a very bright *Oliva*,' she says. Reuben's surname.

I look down at my drink, stirring it with the black straw whose end I've chewed. Reuben says I should just forget it. Stop torturing myself. Nobody truly has a thing. But . . .

'Er,' Laura says, looking at a spot just above my head, as though she's seen a spider on the wall. I turn, and the man is leaning over me, a protective arm right behind my shoulders. Now I know he's there, I can feel every molecule of him. His arm lands across my back like a heavy rucksack, and I wince. I try to shrug it off, but he claps it down on me. It's weighty, unpleasant. My body is against his, unwittingly, and his armpit is warm and sweaty against my shoulder. He smells beery, of that sweet alcoholic scent usually reserved for the morning after the night before. A kick of mint behind that. I see after a second that he's chewing gum.

'Haven't even introduced myself,' he says, interrupting my thoughts. 'I'm Sadiq.' His dark eyes appraise us. He holds a hand out to me, then to Laura. She ignores it, but I take it, not wanting to offend.

'Thanks for the selfie, but we're good now,' Laura says. 'Just catching up. Alone.'

Even this does not put him off. 'Baby, don't be cold,' Sadiq says. I can't help but look sideways at him. His nose is aquiline. I can't place his lilting accent.

'We're not cold. We want to speak to each other, not you,' Laura says. It's typical of her. All through university, people would underestimate her. She was softly spoken, small-boned, would sit, almost huddled, with her arms folded right across her middle, so people thought she was meek. But she wasn't, not at all.

She wordlessly picks up her drink and we walk across the makeshift dance floor, squeezing against bodies that jolt unpredictably. The only place available is right next to the speaker which is pumping out a dance hit Reuben hates. It's thrumming in my ear, the bass reverberating in my sternum. Opposite me, I can see a couple standing close to each other. The woman has an afro, a slim waist slightly exposed between a black top and trousers. His hand is on the wall behind her. He's talking softly in her ear. I wonder what their evenings look like. I bet they listen to indie music on the radio while cooking from scratch. Or maybe they paint together, every Sunday; a weekend ritual. Abstract art. It would get all over their clothes, their walls, but they wouldn't care. Yes.

She catches me looking, and for the millionth time in my life, I am pleased that nobody can read my mind. She draws a hand up to her hair, embarrassed. I look away, but not before noticing that her nails are painted a jewel-toned plum; glossy and perfectly even. Ah. She is one of those. A Proper Person, I call them in my head. Proper People have well-fitting clothes and neat hair and glowing skin and you can break it all down into its component parts, but the thing is – they just look ... groomed. They are doing something right. Something intangible. I wonder if they've all been told, like some rite of passage, and I haven't.

'What?' Laura says, following my gaze.

'Oh, look,' I say, as the couple embrace again.

'Oh to be young and in love,' she says, and I look curiously at her. I no longer see Jonty kiss her. Their relationship seems pally, somehow; more about team-work than romance. No doubt she thinks the same of Reuben and me. Reuben seems reserved, closed off, dismissive. Until the door closes behind us, that is.

'He was a weird one,' Laura shouts, pointing with her drink over to the bar. 'Sadiq.'

'I know.'

'Pushy.'

'Oh, he'll leave us alone now.'

Laura raises her eyebrows but says nothing.

'Jonty is acting strangely,' she says after a moment.

I look up in surprise. 'Really?'

'He said he didn't like my latest project. He's never said that. He's never cared.'

'No?'

She rakes her fringe back. It snarls, sticking up slightly before drifting down and puffs air into her cheeks. Lovely Jonty; he's been sacked from every office job he's ever had, because of lateness. He often forgets he's going on holiday and has to be ushered to the airport in surprise. Posh and affable and a bit hopeless: what *he* wants more than anything is a quiet life, a G&T on the pavement at his feet. I like to consider what everybody I meet truly wants. I started doing it when I was a teenager, and I haven't been able to stop.

'What's going on with him?' I say, frowning. He has been temping, painting perfume bottles with glitter for the Christmas season. He says it's quite meditative.

'I have no idea. Do you?' I am often asked for advice about people. Nothing else, of course. Nothing highbrow. I am never asked for my opinion on medicine or law or planning permission or transfer deadline day or the war in Syria. Just people, and the things that they do.

'What's he saying to you?'

'Nothing. Just – talking about the future more, maybe.' She shrugs. She doesn't want to discuss it any further, I can see. 'How's that masters?' she adds.

'What masters?' I say absent-mindedly, lost in thought about Jonty. Talking of the future is so out of character for him. What could he possibly . . .?

'The cultural theory one.'

I frown. Did I apply for that? It does ring a bell. 'Oh, still pending,' I say vaguely.

I am forever applying for masters courses and grants and pitching articles to the *Guardian* and thinking maybe I would like to be a coffee-shop owner. All sorts. *Maybe I will farm cocoa beans in South America?* I will Whats-App Laura. *You burn too easily though,* she will send back. *Maybe wheat in England instead?* And even though it's endless, my career pondering, and must be tedious, she takes each and every whim as seriously as the first.

'Good luck,' she says with a smile. She looks like she's going to add something else, but then her gaze drifts to just behind me, and she never starts her sentence. Or rather, she starts a different one. 'Okay, leaving time,' she says.

I look behind me, and there's Sadiq.

I shrug, irritable, and move away a few feet, but he moves after me, an arm reaching out.

'Leave us alone,' Laura says.

'You don't want to be talking to me like that,' he says, and my head turns, and the song stops, leaving a beat before a new one starts, during which time I can hear blood pulsing in my ears.

And suddenly, it's not funny anymore. It's scary. A frisson of fear moves through me. Images pop into my mind. Images of women, followed down alleyways, coaxed into passenger seats, dismembered in car boots. I move further away from him, towards the wall, away from Laura. I think of the couple I saw earlier, and how happy they looked, and wish Reuben were here. He wouldn't say anything; he wouldn't have to. He has a presence like that. People seem to behave for him, like naughty children.

Sadiq follows me, blocking me in. Behind him, Laura's eyes are narrowing so they are almost entirely closed and now he is squaring up to me, right in front of me. I walk away from him, dodging around him, but he grabs me, pulls me back, and grinds into the back of me, his hands either side of my hips – either side of my bum – like we are in a sex scene. I stand completely still for a second or two. Shock, is it? Whatever it is, it's two seconds during which I can not only feel his hands, his breath on the back of my neck, but his erection, too. Hard against the back of my thigh. I can't help but imagine how it looks. The thought intrudes in my mind like an unwanted internet pop-up, and I wince. I haven't felt another man's penis in over seven years. Until now. What would Reuben say? He'd call him a fucking dickhead, that's what he'd say. The thought comforts me.

I move slowly away from him, smiling awkwardly because I don't know what else to do, the shock of being touched against my will like jumping off a pier and in to the sea. I can still feel him. The warmth and hardness of him. My teeth start chattering. I don't say anything. I should, but I don't. I just want to be gone.

Laura is taking the drink out of my hand and trying

to find a surface to put it on. In the end, she places it on the top of the speaker – she can only just reach – and she grabs my coat, and my arm, and we turn to leave.

He grabs for me again. A cat-like swipe. He catches just my finger, as I'm leaving. I try to pull it away from him, but he's stronger than me. I could shout, but what would I say? A man grabbing a woman's hand in a bar hardly feels like a crime, though maybe it is. Instead, I am complicit, almost holding his hand. Nobody knows it is against my will. Nobody knows what's going on in my head. His hand is momentarily like a manacle around mine.

He squeezes it, hard, enclosing it in the whole of his palm. He releases, and squeezes again; a kind of sexual threat, and then he lets go of me entirely.

Outside, the winter air puffing out of my mouth like chalk dust, I can still feel his body against mine. I am imagining it, but my thigh feels wet. I reach a hand down to check. It isn't.

Laura hands me my coat. 'Jesus,' she says. 'I've not had to leave a bar because of a nutter for a while. Are we twenty again?'

She's making light of it, and I'm thankful for that, but I don't say anything. I can still feel him between my legs, that pressure, the feeling of fullness. Was that a sexual assault? I guess it was, but maybe I am somehow to blame. I shudder, wrapping my coat around me.

'You all right?' Laura says.

I nod, once, not lifting my head again, looking at my

406

cream-ribboned shoes. I don't want to discuss it. Like the congestion zone charge I ignored until it was too late, and we had to pay double, and Reuben got cross, I sweep it away into a back room in my mind.

'Yeah,' I say. 'I'm grand. It's not a Friday night without a nutter.'

'Okay,' she says, still looking warily at me. 'I had a bad feeling about tonight.'

It's a very *Laura* thing to say, and it's another reason she and Reuben don't get on; her mysticism, his vehement logic.

She gets a scarf out that's wrapped around the handle of her bag and puts it on. Over the road, two restaurants have their Christmas lights out. Champagne-coloured fairy lights wound around potted trees. 'So that's Little Venice,' I say. We like to explore the hidden parts of London. We always go somewhere new. Our rent is too high to endlessly go to the same places: it feels like we are making our money back, somehow.

'Maybe we won't do it again,' I say.

I check my watch. It's too late to go on anywhere else. I'm enticed by the thought of Reuben at home in our living room. He'll be wearing soft clothes. He'll have the lights dimmed. The television on low. A glass of red on the arm of the sofa, the stem held in his elegant fingers. He likes wine; will even drink it alone. I drink Ribena when I am alone, but we are different like this.

'Which way you going?' Laura says to me. She points

with a thumb behind her. She lives north of me, all the way in Holloway.

'Warwick Avenue,' I say. 'That's the easiest.' I see a dark figure dart behind her, in the awning of the bar we've just left, but it disappears before I can properly look at it. Maybe it's the couple, moving as one, off home, I think. It's gone now, whatever it was. Nevertheless, a small acorn of worry nestles in my stomach.

Laura smells of cologne as she reaches to hug me. She's wearing a maxi skirt and biker boots. 'WhatsApp me when you're back,' she says.

I nod. WhatsApp is our medium. Tens of messages a day. Newspaper articles. Tiny snapshots of her art. Beers consumed in the middle of the day with Jonty. Screenshots of funny memes. Selfies from me, bored at work. We love it.

I set off towards the canal, crossing the bridge. It's wrought iron, blue. It reminds me of the playground at school. My fingers trail over the bars. And that's when I hear it. Them. The footsteps. Surely I'm imagining it? I stop. But no. There they are. A heavy tread.

I could turn around. Go back to the bar. But is the bar safe?

What do you do, I find myself thinking, when you think somebody is following you down a deserted strip of canal? When you could become a statistic, a news piece, a tragedy? Nothing. That's the answer. You carry on. You hope.

I never thought something like this would happen to me. I suppose that's what makes me behave as though

I'm in a film: I have no idea what else to do. I stop, for a moment, testing him, and his footsteps stop too.

I start again, this time faster, and I hear him begin too. My imagination fires up like a sprinter off the starting blocks and soon I can't tell what's real. Is he right behind me – I can't look – and about to reach for me? The pounding of his footsteps is consistent, slapping against the wet concrete, but I can't tell any more than that.

I will call somebody, I decide.

I turn left down a side alley I would never usually turn down. Just to see what he does. I walk past white houses with balconies. Millionaires' houses. The occasional bay window is lit up, little orange squares in the night, tasteful Christmas trees glowing amber like fireflies. I would usually peer in, invent lives for them, backstories, but not tonight.

He has followed me. Five more steps. His thunder along behind me. I can't look over my shoulder. I am frozen.

I start to plan. I could call Laura. Could she get over here quickly? No. I break into a little run.

I could knock on a door. But . . . am I definitely being followed? They'd think me mad. It is strange how much I think of people's opinions, their perceptions of me, right now, just like I did in the bar when I didn't cry out when he grabbed my hand. I want these people, these strangers, this collective unconscious, to like me.

I turn right, off the side street, back to a main road and cross it. I get out my phone, ready to dial – 999? No, it seems too extreme. I call Reuben instead. He takes an age to answer, which is not uncommon – he hates the telephone – but then his deep *hello* echoes through me.

'You all right?' he says. I can picture him, now. It's a comfort. He'll be reclining back against the sofa. His hair will look auburn, not ginger, in our dimly-lit living room. He will be frowning, his eyes a dark, foresty green.

'Reuben,' I say.

'What?' he says. He would be sitting forwards now.

'I'm being followed,' I say in a low voice. I don't know why I don't shout it out.

His eyebrows would draw together. 'By who?'

'This bloke. From the bar.'

'Where?'

'Can you just – stay with me? Walk me to the tube – virtually?' I say to Reuben.

'Of course,' he murmurs.

'Okay,' I say.

'Okay,' he echoes, but his voice is crackly. I pull the phone away from my ear and look at it, the light from it illuminating the clouds of my hot breath.

There's a set of stairs in front of me, leading down to a bridge. I dart into the corner where the stairs begin, to see if he follows. I put one foot on the first step, frozen, not able to look behind me.

And now he is behind me, too. And now, it's not my imagination. I know. He is right behind me. His body ready to hold on to my hips again. To push himself into me, against my will. There is his red trainer. Oh God. He is here.

'Hello?' I say desperately into the phone.

Reuben crackles back, and then, the three beeps. *Call failed.*

I sprint down the stairs, and I'm a few steps down them when it happens, as I knew it would. His gloved hand behind me. It lands on the railings like a bird of prey. The gloves are exactly the sort he would wear, I find myself thinking. Designer. Sporty. He looked lithe.

I hear an intake of breath, and know he is about to speak, to threaten me. Perhaps his mouth is right next to my ear, his body poised to grab mine, to thrust again, and so I reach my hand out to grab the railings. They're cold and wet; they soak my gloves. It must have been raining heavily earlier.

And then I am acting before I know it. He comes down by my right-hand side, ready to overtake me on the wide stairs. I turn. His hood's up, but I can tell it's him from his gait. I am remembering his body against mine again, and imagining yet more horrors – his sweet breath into my mouth, his penis up under my underwear, against my jeans, a full, damp, painful wetness – I bring my hand down on his, briefly, hard. He lets out a surprised cry. And with my right – my dominant hand – I push his body, firmly, squarely, the hardest I've ever pushed anything in my life. I release his hand as he falls – I'm surprised he falls; he's at least six feet – and he tumbles like a stunt man down the concrete stairs to the tow path. He stops, on his stomach, at a strange angle. I am breathing hard, and I stand there, watching him, astonished. That I have done this. That

I am safe. That he is lying there, not moving, and I am here, almost at the top.

I am still looking down at him. I have done this. I have done this to him.

I start to feel a weird, panicky hotness. I reach to undo my coat, wanting to feel the sharp winter air on my sweat-covered chest. My glove is sopping wet as it touches my skin. My forehead is slick with moisture, from perspiration or the fine mist descending from the sky around me, I don't know. My bowels want to open, and right in the pit of my stomach I feel a hornet's nest of fear beginning to buzz. I bring my gloved hand to my forehead and wipe it uselessly. Oh God. What have I done?

One minute ago I was scared for my life and now I am scared for his.

My mind scans over the time in the bar. Feckless Joanna. I should have ignored him, told him to piss off, like Laura did. I never do the correct thing. I end up in messes. I avoid things and then they get much worse.

I close my eyes. Oh, please let me go back to Before. Before we met Sadiq. Before we left. Before he followed me. Before I pushed him.

But we can't. I can't. And now . . . It is After. I look down at Sadiq. His left arm is underneath him, twisted strangely. He's fallen only seven steps, but they're concrete, and wet. His right arm must have reached out in front of him. It's landed just to the side of his face. He hasn't moved at all. I should go to help him. Call an ambulance. Confess. Or I should run away, in case he's about to get up again. Sprint home. Pretend I never did it. Go back to Before, even though I know I can't.

The streetlights are too bright, illuminated once by themselves and a hundred times in each drop of misty rain. I can see moisture on the concrete steps like thousands of beads of sweat. I can feel the cold air seeping in to my coat and Sadiq is lying still but breathing in and out in and out and I look down at him and then around me and think: I could run or I could stay and call him an ambulance and . . . and now it is decision time.

2

Truth

I stand and stare at Sadiq. I could walk away. Avoid it, like I've done for my entire life.

I turn around, my back to him, and take three steps away. And then I stop, looking over my shoulder, sure that he will have risen up behind me like a villain in a fable. But he hasn't. He's still there. Still lying down. Still not moving.

It starts raining more heavily, the drops fat, striking my nose and leaving a trail of smaller drops as though they've been shattered apart.

I am still looking over my shoulder as I think it: I could leave. I look around me. Little Venice is deserted. I look up and down the length of the canal. Nobody.

And that's when the sweating gets worse. I puff air in to my cheeks and raise my eyes heavenwards and try to think, but all I'm doing is panicking. It's as though all of the world's dread and fear and madness have been set free inside my abdomen. My mind is racing, but saying nothing – empty chatter – and my hands are flexing and making fists, alternating clenched and open, like starfish, and my legs are wobbling.

I look down at Sadiq. Are those headphones? One

earbud has fallen out of his ear, the cord white against the concrete like a worm.

I wonder what Reuben would do. Perhaps I can call him back, and ask him. No. I am certain of what he would say. He always does the right thing. His favourite poem is *If*. His favourite TV show is *The West Wing*. He is a social worker for Islamic Relief. My mind throws up these headline points in support of its application to make me leave, now, and never tell him, and it won't stop. Reuben stacks chairs up at the end of the working day even though it is the cleaners' job. He was adopted, thirty-two years ago, and has never once held a grudge. I scraped another car's door, once – so lightly as to be almost imperceptible – and reached to rub at the scratch with a tissue, and Reuben was on his feet and writing a detailed note, leaving our details, before I could even protest. He chooses, again and again, *the right thing*, even though it is hardly ever the easy thing.

For God's sake, ring 999, he would say, panicked, astonished I was even asking the question. Perhaps it would forever change how he looked at me; that I had to even ask. He would – finally – see me as I truly am; flawed, selfish, pathetic.

No. I can't be like that. I venture down two steps. I can hear something. A voice. I stop again, sombre for a moment, saying a mournful goodbye to my life as I know it. Am I sure? If I call now, there'll be a procedure. An ambulance, dispatched immediately. I'll be in a system. Not Joanna anymore, but . . . somebody else. A number.

It's been over a minute. Maybe two. One hundred and twenty seconds of staring.

Where is that noise coming from? I am sure it is a woman's voice. I creep two steps closer, and realise: the headphones.

And even though I have decided what to do, I am procrastinating. Trying to stall the moment when I have to make that phone call, even though I know that makes things harder, not easier. I've been procrastinating my entire life, and I'm not stopping now.

One more minute passes. The rain gets heavier.

I don't know what spurs me in to action. Perhaps I needed those three minutes to come to terms with how things will be; to move in to the After. Perhaps it was to make sure he wasn't about to reach for me, grab me. I don't know, but I pull out my phone, standing almost at the bottom of the stairs, and dial 999. I have never dialled these numbers in my life, though it feels as though I have, from BBC dramas and books and films.

It doesn't ring. There's a strange noise, then an operator answers immediately. I descend gingerly down the remaining stairs as I hear a Scottish voice, as if I can only get close to him now I have her protection.

'What's your emergency?' the woman says.

'I . . . there's a man who's been injured,' I say.

As I stop, above his body, I can hear the noise again. It *is* a voice. *Take a deep breath in for five counts*, it is saying. Some sort of hypnotherapy. Meditation, maybe.

'Okay, my love, how badly injured is he?' she says.

'I . . . don't know.'

'All right – what's your name?'

'Joanna Oliva,' I say, though I wonder after uttering it whether I should have used a false one.

'Okay, Joanna. We're going to send a first responder,' she says. Her tone is neutral. She doesn't provide reassurance. She doesn't explain what a first responder is. I wonder what her hopes and dreams are. Maybe she had an emergency, once, and now she wants to help others. I close my eyes, imagining I am somewhere else, and on the phone to a friend. Perhaps I am by the sea, somewhere, on holiday, and calling a friend because I am bored. Or maybe I am idly calling Reuben on the way home to him, which he hates me doing.

I give her the address. Well, an address of sorts. One of the side bridges. The centre of Little Venice. The canal. I can hear her typing.

'And now I'd like you to assess the man, is that going to be all right?' she lilts. I wonder if she was hired because of the soothing quality of her voice. Maybe she does television adverts in her spare time. I cannot stop the thoughts. It strikes me as strange that I am still me; still overly imaginative Joanna, even when thrown into these most extraordinary of circumstances.

I lean down and tentatively touch his shoulder, his black jacket. It's softer than I thought it would be, almost fleecy. Wait – were those his trousers? He's in tight black trousers, almost leggings. I was sure he wasn't wearing those, that he was in jeans, in the bar. But there are the red trainers. Just the same.

'He's face down,' I say. 'On some concrete – he

fell . . . he fell down some steps. Seven,' I add uselessly, because my guilt has made me count them.

'Okay and is he breathing? I don't want you to move his neck. Okay? Okay Joanna?'

Her tone frightens me. Everything frightens me. It's like the world's been filtered, black, and I can feel the hot, sweaty nausea again. I say nothing.

'Okay?'

'Yes,' I say. There's a man lying injured beneath my fingertips and I did it. I can hardly dare think about it. It's like looking at the sun.

I can't turn him over. I can't do it.

The voice from the headphones is still speaking, about imagining a beach scene, waves rolling in and out, and I listen to that instead.

'Can you look, listen, and feel for whether he's breathing? Do you know his name?'

She enunciates these words like a primary school teacher. Look, listen, and feel. I do not know what these words mean. I look over my shoulder, at the illuminated street, slick with rain, and along the canal, to the bridges stacking behind us, almost all aligning, tessellating, like my vision has gone blurred.

Look.

Listen.

Feel.

I stare down at him, face-down on the pavement.

I run my fingers underneath his shoulder and crouch down to look at him. 'Oh, oh,' I say to her, involuntarily. His face is sopping. At first I think it's blood, when

419

my fingers touch the wetness, but it's cold and thin-feeling.

And then I realise. My eyes see it as they adjust to the dark. It grows in front of me: a puddle at the bottom of the steps. Caused by a tree a few feet away. Its roots pulling up the pavement, cracking it, making it uneven, creating great craters.

One of which is filled with water.

He's totally submerged, in dark water, on the dark ground – I didn't realise.

'He's face down, in a puddle,' I say. Surely she will help? She is on my side; she must be. She is a good person, working in the 999 call centre.

'Roll him on to his side, quick as you can, out of the water,' she says. 'Does he have a head or neck injury?'

'I . . . I don't know. I pushed him. And he fell, down the stairs,' I say. Nobody can blame anybody for being honest. Nobody can prosecute for an innocent mistake.

'Quick as you can,' she repeats. I roll him over.

His black hood is still drawn partially over his face. The rest is in shadow.

'Now I need you to check he's breathing. Look, listen and feel, remember? Can you repeat that back?'

'Look, listen and feel,' I say woodenly.

'Look for his chest rising. Listen with your ear at his airways. Feel for his breath.'

I stare at his chest. I lean my head down. I can hear everything, suddenly. The roar of distant traffic. The trickle of water into the canal. The sound of the rain-drops splattering on the concrete. But nothing from him.

I take my glove off and rest my hand against his nose. There is nothing against my fingers. It is unnatural, like looking at somebody with a vital detail missing, like eyelashes or fingernails. My knees hit the concrete, and the contents of my handbag scatters over the ground. Lipsticks I never wear because they make me self-conscious roll all over the place. It's a state. 'He's not breathing,' I say. Panic rushes in again.

'And now it's very important to get him breathing. Is he definitely not?' she says. 'Put your cheek to his mouth. I want you to tell me whether you can feel his breath against your face.'

I wince. I don't want to lean down, expose my vulnerable cheek, my neck, to his mouth., as though he might be a predator playing dead. But I have to.

There's nothing against my cheek. No movement. No warmth. No rustling of the strands of my hair by a breath. Nothing.

'He's definitely not breathing,' I say.

Her voice is crisp, patient, sympathetic. 'We're going to do five rescue breaths first,' she says. 'Because he's been drowning.'

Drowning. Drowning.

'Okay.'

'Open his mouth. Lie him on his back. Tilt his chin back. Being careful of his neck. Chin lifted high, all right, Joanna? Tilt his head back. Are you ready?'

I move him onto slightly flatter ground, and onto his back, and as I do so, his hood falls away and I see his face.

It's not Sadiq.

His eyes are widely spaced, but that's where the similarities end. His features are delicate. There's no heavy brow. He's got hollows underneath his cheekbones. It's not Sadiq. It's not Sadiq. It's not Sadiq.

'I . . .' I don't say any more, though maybe I should. 'Shit. I'm – I'll do it now,' I say, but inside, my thoughts are rushing like water through a burst pipe. It's not him. It's not him. I have pushed – I have injured – a stranger. This man wasn't harassing me. He didn't follow me. I look at his trainers again. They're the same. The same stupid trainers.

But of course: he was out running. Trainers. Headphones. All black. How could I have made such a catastrophic error? How could I not have checked? How could I have presumed there was a pursuit where there was nothing? Merely a man – another man, a different man. It is hard to re-orientate my thoughts, away from having been pursued to . . . something else. That didn't happen. Like a dream, it wasn't real.

The voice keeps coming out of the headphones, getting louder and quieter as I move.

I could hang up the phone. I could run away. Get a flight somewhere before I'm stopped. Would I be stopped? All of my knowledge has come from the television. I can't remember the last time I cracked open a newspaper. I know nothing about the real world, I think bitterly. Reuben would know what to do. He is a Proper Person who knows about global politics and can point to Iran on a map and knows what sautéing is. But of course, Reuben would never be in this situation. Good Reuben.

My body feels strange. My eyes are dry and heavy. The

world shifts as I look at it, like I'm in a kaleidoscope. Perhaps I am drunk. I have had four drinks. Maybe I *am* drunk and soon I will wake up, blinking, in Laura's bed with the crazy seventies-printed orange duvet cover, and Jonty will bring me a cup of coffee he's made with slightly curdled milk, and we'll wonder at how I could've got so drunk. I'll explain it was because I'd had no dinner. And we'll laugh. Jonty will be painting his perfume bottles – he'll be behind, and doing them sloppily. Or maybe I'll wake up and Laura will say, over Cocopops, *No, we didn't even go to Little Venice . . .*

I lean over and breath into his mouth. It's strangely intimate. My lips have only touched Reuben's, for seven years, and now here I am, touching another man's lips.

Five breaths. Nothing happens.

She tells me to start chest compressions. There are *no signs of life*, she says.

I lean down and lace my fingers as she tells me to, the phone on speaker on a step. His chest yields under them, surprisingly so, and I compress a few inches easily.

It happens suddenly, after five chest compresses. He reacts to me, his lips tightening. He sucks in a breath, his slim chest expanding and his body jerking as though the ground's moved beneath him.

'He's . . . something's happening,' I shout. And then he's coughing. Hacking, productive coughs. I look away, not wanting to be privy to these moments. Maybe he'll open his eyes. Maybe he'll stand and walk away, disgruntled and inconvenienced, but fine, like we are motorists who've damaged the other's bumpers. Maybe. Maybe. I close my eyes and wish for it.

'He's coughing,' I say. My voice is wooden. I can't tell her I got the wrong man. I can't tell her anything.

'Okay, good. The ambulance is nearly with you,' she says. Sadiq – no, not Sadiq – is still lying there. His eyes closed. Chest rising steadily. 'Can you put him in the recovery position?' she says. Another surge of fear rushes through me like the tide's coming in and I try to ignore it, biting my lip. It is no longer fear of Sadiq. It is fear for what will happen to me, now.

'Okay,' I say. 'Okay.' I heave him over. There is no sign he's conscious. His eyelids don't flutter like Reuben's do just before he wakes on Sunday mornings – the only morning of the whole week that we always spend together; the one where he is not with his charges or helping his MP or leading protests. This man's arms don't hold their own weight like Reuben's do when he rolls over and beckons to me, wanting to hold me, even in his sleep; instead, they flop on to the ground like they're weighed down unnaturally, curling like an ape's.

And then, when he's in the recovery position, one knee bent up as the woman tells me to, I see the ambulance. The lights are flashing in the glass-fronted shop windows along the street above us. I see the ambulance's light mirrored in the windows across the street, a few seconds behind itself, reflected and refracted across each display. No. No. I am wrong. I see that it's not an ambulance. Not at all. I see – I see now – that it's the police. There's a police car, just behind the ambulance.

The ambulance is for him, but the police car is for me.